SHADOWS
of
ANGELS

D0451138

A Novel by
MARILYN BROWN

Covenant Communications, Inc.
American Fork, Utah

Printed in the United States of America
First Printing: March 1993
93 94 95 96 97   10 9 8 7 6 5 4 3 2

Shadows of Angels
ISBN 1-55503-521-3
Library of Congress Catalog Card Number: 92-75977

Covenant
Communications, Inc.

For Bill

Foreword

Long ago, Marilyn McMeen Brown dreamed of completing a literary work about the Mormons. She says, "The stories about our magnificent Mormon culture have only begun to be told."

Marilyn, who has spent nearly half a century engrossed in becoming a writer, received the first Mayhew prize at Brigham Young University in 1962. She is also the recipient of the 1982 novel award given by the Association for Mormon Letters. The author of more than a dozen novels, she won an award in the 1983 LDS Novel Contest for *Goodbye, Hello*, published by Randall Book, and she received first prize in the novel division in the Utah Fine Arts Literature Competition in 1991 for *Road to Covered Bridge*. Her hymn, "Thy Servants Are Prepared," appears in the current LDS hymnbook.

After graduating in 1964 with a master's degree in English literature from BYU, marrying, serving in various Church positions, and helping to raise a family of six children and six grandchildren, she returned to the University of Utah for a Master of Fine Arts, which she completed in June of 1992. "As a Mormon woman, I hoped to accomplish raising a family as well as learning to write. I knew it might take a long time."

Tired of the spiritual decay of much modern entertainment, Marilyn is excited to see the increased interest in Mormon fiction and believes that "One of the best ways to share the everyday good we work hard to perform in our lives is through fiction."

Marilyn admires Mormon readers who search for material that will increase their faith. "I love this people and their courage to do right in a world rampant with moral weakness. They can understand their pioneer ancestors and appreciate their problems, their sacrifices for future generations, and their willingness to submit to God's will. We have so much to give. I want to broadcast these gifts to the world."

Shadows of Angels, the sequel to *Thorns of the Sun,* completes Covenant Communications' newly revised and edited publication of Marilyn Brown's classic pioneer saga, *The Earthkeepers,* which was released in its original form in 1980. The story will continue in Marilyn Brown's next work, *Royal House Hotel,* which features the Eastman family at the close of World War I.

Synopsis of
Thorns of the Sun

Thorns of the Sun *leaves Mara waiting for her missionary Bret and vowing to care for the deceased Blueflower's little Indian baby Sobe with the help of her Indian friend Rain. Rain had come to the Eastman household because the Mormons took care of the widows and children after the militia destroyed their men for stealing cattle. Through many trials and events demanding courage and strength, the Eastmans have lovingly cared for their Indian friends and survived the Indian wars and the deaths of their daughter Sophia, her husband John, and their baby Martha. Though more Indian wars threaten the residents of Utah Valley at this time, the Eastmans are looking forward to some growing years of prosperity due to the windfall inheritance they received from a deceased aunt in the East whose grandaughter Caroline came to live with them. Though Mara is happy caring for Sobe, she feels some pressure from her friends Nancy and Sully to enter into their family in plural marriage.*

Chapter One

A STARTLING VOICE OUTSIDE THE WINDOW WOKE MARA FROM A deep sleep. Waking in the shadows, she leaned toward the light from the window. The house seemed unreal, the room unreal. What seemed real to her in that moment between sleeping and waking was her dream. Years had passed and still she dreamed . . . about Bret.

"Hup ho!" a voice cried out.

She rubbed her eyes awake and listened. She had heard rumors that Bret had returned. In her dream he was riding toward her on a huge black horse. She ran to him, but the sun was suddenly covered by a cloud and he was lost in a mist.

"Eastman!" Someone was calling.

Above the voice, she thought she could hear the sound of trowels as the first shift of volunteers, up before dawn, built the city wall. The crew was getting closer to the Eastman house now. A part of the gloomy structure approached the west rim of the city park that lay north across their street. It was an ugly wall—being built because the settlers had killed Kickingboot and buried him improperly— although there had never been enough of the wall to protect the city from the Indians these last years. Listening carefully, she could hear the whoosh of the grout and the clack of the tools jarring the adobe bricks into place. But this morning she could hear more than just the sound of the wall. She could hear horses. And that startling voice.

Through the poplars that now just reached the sills of the windows, someone was calling up to Papa. "Ho, Eastman!" she heard again. Then she heard other voices as the volunteers dropped their work. Papa's bed creaked as he rolled over. His room was next to the bedroom she shared with their adopted Indians, Rain and Sobe—they pronounced his name "So-be"—their little Indian boy.

"Snake Indians!" A man's voice swore. "Pack of Snakes! They just started a fire in Salem!" Mara heard one of the riders call to Papa. She listened, not breathing. She heard her father's legs hit the floor like a load of potatoes. The floor moved under him, and she could feel his weight on it. She could hear him lumber to the window and throw up the sash.

"Bee feathers," she heard him say under his breath through the open window, through the leaves of the poplars that shimmered in the light. "Indians again!" When he called down, his voice was just a rasp in his throat. "I'll be right down."

Mara froze at the sound of her father loading his gun, then at the sound of his boots on the stairs. The fear never faded. Attack after attack, the fear stuck in her throat.

The sun streamed into the room through the leaves and outlined Rain's body under the covers against the far wall. Little Sobe had crawled in with her. He was lying against her back, all of the covers pushed away from his toddler legs and arms. The light played on his face. Rain was a lump under the quilt. Mara could see her high cheek bones. Rain and Sobe, the only two Indians left to them now, were curled up asleep inside these walls. Perhaps they were the only friendly Indians they would ever know. Now the new wall would shut the others out. It had been almost three years since they had killed and buried Rain's husband and Squash's brother, Kickingboot. And there were no friendly feelings anymore.

Mara got up quietly so she would not disturb Rain and Sobe.

Below her, Papa shut the door so hard the house shook. Mara felt it in every bone.

"Aagh," Rain cried out. She too must have felt the house shake. Or she cried out in her dreams, believing she was still an Indian slave, or she dreamed of the deaths of her Indian husband, Kickingboot, and her mother, Spirit of Earth.

Mara went to the cot and covered Sobe. Rain tossed and cried out again as she had hundreds of times in her sleep. The terror of the attacks had kept fear alive in all of them.

Mara heard her mother rush down the stairs. She followed Papa out into the yard with a chunk of bread. Ashel, a tall twelve-year-old now, scrambled away from his seven-year-old cousin Caroline, and begged his father to let him go too. But Papa had already mounted his horse, and the horse was lumbering down the road by the time they ran after him in their night clothes.

Sobe began to wake up and rub his eyes. Mara picked him up off the cot and took him to her bed so that Rain would go back to sleep, but Rain opened her eyes.

"You were dreaming," Mara said, pulling the covers up.

"Soldiers," Rain said.

"Go back to sleep, Rain."

But Rain shook her head and sat up. In her broken English she said, "I dreamed of soldiers. Coming here. Here," she said, pointing her finger to the floor.

They never knew when the militia would be coming through to stay on their way to or from Salt Lake City. If they were successful at stopping the attacks in Salem, they would pass through Provo. No one knew. But sometimes Rain had uncanny dreams about both the soldiers and her people. Once she told Mara that her mother had come to her in the night and told her to read the Book of Mormon to the robber Indian Squash. But when she had tried, Squash had leaned over and slammed the pages shut.

Mara dressed quickly and went downstairs. In the sunny yard she looked up, and saw Ashel and Caroline waving to her from their perch in the poplar trees. They sat in the tops like giant birds. She stood in their shadows to get out of the piercing light of the morning sun and looked toward the road. She saw Nancy approaching them. Mara could see that Nancy was breathing hard.

She finally realized that Nancy was running to her. Mara felt her heart sink. Nancy, in her condition, should not have been running. Mara hurried to meet her friend and put her arms around her. Nancy had been crying.

Oh Nancy, she thought. Nancy, who had miscarried so many times that she was feeling desperate. Sometimes Mara didn't want to talk to her because Nancy continued to beg her to marry her husband Sully—to be the second wife. Nancy wanted and needed someone in her family to have children. Together, Sully and Nancy had taken Mara with them in their new carriage and shown her a spot on the hillside where they would build a house for her if she became Sully's second wife. She had almost consented, but she had never loved Sully; she loved Bret. For a long time Mara thought she would have shared anything with Nancy, except Sully.

"Nancy, oh Nancy," Mara whispered.

"It's gone," Nancy said into Mara's hair. "I've lost the baby."

"Oh Nancy, you deserve more . . ." Mara said, as if she were also saying it to herself. For a few moments, they stood holding each other.

Nancy drew back and dried her tears with the back of her hand. "But I have something to tell you."

"For me?"

"Yes. You will like it, though I don't."

Puzzled, Mara could not guess. "Then tell me," she said.

"Bret's home."

Mara searched Nancy's face. All the light in the yard pressed on her. The children in the poplars began to rock the limbs back and forth, back and forth. The shadows flickered, then fell away from her face. In the distance, she saw her Papa riding back toward the house in the company of two Indians. Her heart beat fast.

"Sully got a letter from Ella."

Mara drew back and tried to find a message in Nancy's eyes.

"I brought it," Nancy said.

Bret had come home. Mara had always known this would happen someday. How did she feel? She didn't know. Shock went through her. "Let me see it," she said.

Nancy fumbled with the envelope she had tucked into her bodice. Mara restrained herself from tearing it out of Nancy's hands.

To the Tuttle family, May 12, 1851

My dear adopted boy Sully,
Thank you for your letter. You have always been like one of my own. I was so glad to hear that Nancy is pregnant again. You will have many children someday. That I know.

Captain Scott sends his love, as I do. He is taking the militia down Tuesday. Bret has finally come home, though he was very ill. As soon as he could raise his head off the bed, he joined up with the militia. You may see him when he follows the expedition to Fort Utah. Perhaps they may stay with you, for they will surely need a warm and dry place.

The children are well. We send our love. Ella.

Mara watched her father over the top of the letter. He and the two Indians were coming closer to the house.

"Don't think that . . . just because I wanted you to marry into our family, don't think that I'm not happy Bret is home," Nancy said.

Mara studied the letter again. She folded it slowly and placed it back in Nancy's hand.

"You don't seem very happy," Nancy said.

Mara held Nancy's hand. "I'm . . . I don't know how to feel. But in the meantime, we're in trouble."

Nancy turned as Papa rode up with Angatewats and Squash.

"How much flour do we have, Mara?" Papa asked.

Not that again. "We gave them a bag a week ago," Mara gritted her teeth. She wanted to scream, "Get out of here, Squash—all you ever do is take from us." She wanted to say, "Papa, the militia is here. We just received word from Ella. They're coming this way. You don't have to give everything we have to them!" She wanted to shout "Bret's here!" She wanted to claw Squash from his horse. She recognized one of their own blankets under his saddle. His threats to take a white man's life for Kickingboot's improper burial won him anything he asked for from Papa—even their own bedding! She wanted to scream, run to the Indian and tear him up, but she stood without moving.

"I'll get the flour!" Ashel called from the tree. He scrambled down out of the leaves and tore through the yard to the cellar.

Papa sat on his horse uneasily. Ashel, strong for a twelve-year-old, carried the bag of flour on his shoulder. Mara helped him lift it to the back of Squash's horse. Without a word, the two Indians turned toward the hills.

Papa looked down at the two girls and smiled. "The militia is coming," he said.

On the following Tuesday, Mara stood at the south window of the children's bedroom and watched the militia march into Provo in ragged rows. Mara saw her father walking with Sully and Bret. Though she had been unable to recall his face, she could have recognized Bret Hunt from a hundred miles away. Still, he was taller than she remembered him—and broader. His body had filled out into a man's body, but he was the same Bret—the heavy light brows under the thick sandy hair.

The ranks began to set up camp in the park on the north side of the street. Mara did not follow the others out of the house, but crossed the hall to her own bedroom and stood watching at the window.

Bret was talking to Papa. "Let him come to me. Let him wonder where I am. He must have wondered all this time where I was, how I was doing. He must never know I am thinking about him now," Mara thought.

She watched him, her head reeling. At first the relief that he had returned safely overwhelmed her. But then came a growing sense of fear. Fear that he wasn't there, that he was still just a dream, a vision appearing before her. He was as graceful, as strong-looking as she had remembered him. She was afraid she had forgotten his face. But she had remembered him correctly. Who was he now? After all these years of wanting him, of longing for him, there he was. But who was he? He seemed to be someone she didn't really know. Someone who would have to be introduced.

As she had hoped he would, Papa brought some of the men with him to the house. Sully and Joshua Hunt, and yes, Bret. Scott Hunt had stayed in Payson with another group and had sent his two oldest sons to Provo.

Clutching her hands to the curtains until her knuckles were white, Mara stayed at the window. The militia, exhausted from quelling the Snakes, dispersed to several homes to spend a few nights before returning to Salt Lake City. Papa walked toward the house with Bret. Joshua and Sully followed them.

Mara held her breath, pinched her cheeks in the mirror, smoothed her shiny dark hair. She knew she was more beautiful than when he had seen her last. She parted her lips slightly. She could hear the men open the door and enter the foyer.

"If we didn't hold them with that last one, we'll stay until we do."

She hadn't heard that voice for almost four years, but she remembered it now. It was Bret's voice.

"We've got plenty of provisions to take care of you as long as you stay with us." That was Papa's voice.

Mara knew that wasn't true. No one in the valley had that much. When they were feeding the Indians as well as each other, there just wasn't enough to go around.

"I'm sure the Indians will learn to leave us alone."

Bret Hunt. She had imagined what this moment of seeing him again would be like. She had imagined running into his arms. She had imagined him sweeping her off her feet. But now her limbs felt like water. She stiffened, scolding herself for her lack of confidence. She felt a pounding in her head, in her breast—a pounding in her whole body until there was almost pain.

"It's good to see you again, Sister Eastman," Bret was saying.

"How nice you can be here to visit us. We haven't heard anything about you for such a long time," Martha Eastman said in her flat voice. "We're glad to have all of you for supper. We hope you can stay longer."

Mara knew she ought to be downstairs now helping her mother and Rain with the meal. She could smell the hot bread that had just come out of the oven. She walked to the stairs, touched the banister as though it might hurt her, stood poised for a moment, then descended. As she had hoped, Bret had been waiting for her. His eyes searched the stairs. He smiled at her. She felt weak. Bret. You'll never know how long I've waited for this moment, she thought to herself. She smiled. She forced herself to be cheerful, to hide the breathless fear.

"Bret. Bret Hunt! It's good to see you!"

"Mara Eastman! Hello!" There was anxiety in his face. He was excited, too. He was as glad to see her as she was to see him.

He was afraid, too. "Have you been well?" For a moment something in his tone alerted her. It reminded her of something. For a moment she thought it could almost be Scott Hunt talking. She had thought she wanted to belong to Bret's father as his fifth wife. And it might have happened, except that Scott's youngest and newest wife, Kate Wright Hunt, had made sure it would never be. She shook off her uneasiness and glided down the last steps toward him, conscious of the effect of her entrance. She felt Sully's eyes on her. The others gathering in the foyer looked up, a sudden quiet coming over them. Then they continued to stamp on the hall rug as they walked toward the dining room.

She must speak, say something casual to break the tension. "We didn't hear from you while you were in England. How was your mission? We have a great deal to catch up on." She tried to sound poised, cheerfully interested, but she feared the tremor in her voice gave away the desire pounding inside her.

Bret smiled, but his eyes looked dim and far away. He answered smoothly. "We do need to catch up, Mara. How have things been going for you?"

"Mara hasn't seen any of her Salt Lake friends for a long time." Papa came up behind Bret, gazing with obvious pride at Mara. She was grateful for his help. "She really has had little news from the City." Mara looked at Papa's face as he came to take her arm. Bret looked away from her now, looked down at his feet. Something was wrong. As she turned with Papa to go into the dining room, she caught Sully's gaze. His brows knit and he turned away. What was wrong? Sully was defeated now, once and for all; that was it, she thought. He had never given up, even after two happy years with Nancy. He had let Mara know that both he and Nancy wanted very much for her to join their family. How foolish he was, thinking she would have him now when she had refused him before. Poor Sully. Perhaps he would always care for her. Didn't he want her to be happy? He always said he did. But then why did he look away in such discomfort now?

"Did you convince a lot of people of the truth of the gospel?" Mara spoke to Bret again as she walked between him and Papa into the dining room.

"We did," Bret said. Mara could not guess what caused the hesitation in his voice, the confusion in his eyes. They shouldn't have seen each other this way first. They should have been alone. The more they conversed, the more Mara grew afraid at his closed, careful answers. Something was in the way, and she began to feel that Sully and Papa were aware of it, too. Perhaps someone had told him that she once might have married his father. But no, Scott Hunt would have made all that clear to him. She would have to wait until she could talk with him. But if the militia stayed tonight, there would be time.

Mama and Rain had prepared a feast. Mara helped pour the water and set the last few things on the sideboard.

"This is wonderful of you, Sister Eastman," Bret said. There were the breads, some puddings Mara and Rain had made yesterday, cuts of cold meat, buttermilk, and cheese. The dinner passed with good-natured conversation about their success with the Walker war. At times during the meal, Mara watched Rain's eyes, wondering how she must feel about their talk of fighting her people. Though Rain delighted in holding Sobe in her lap and in feeding him, there was still pain there. Mara kept thinking how much more beautiful and happy Rain was now than she would ever have been staying with her own people. The Eastmans were her own people now. She was wearing a white basque that Mara had given her and a full-sleeved blouse, which opened at her dark throat. She ate like a lady with a spoon, dabbing her mouth with a napkin. She is beautiful, Mara thought. I do like what we have created in Rain.

Bret ate with perfect manners. There was something proper and British about him after his years in England. The impetuousness of his boyhood seemed to have vanished. Beside him, Joshua ate quickly, silently, his eyes riveted to his plate. The center of attention, Bret talked. "We took that one group at Salem without one man so much as grazed with an arrow."

"They have more guns than arrows now," Papa said.

"They don't know how to shoot," Bret laughed. "They're clumsy as monkeys, I really believe they are."

Mara looked at Rain. Bret didn't notice the blank expression in Rain's wide eyes.

Sully, sitting near Rain, spoke. "I've seen some that can shoot good. They're not all clumsy." He looked at Rain with concern.

Then Bret saw. "Oh well, yes. Some of them can shoot quite well, I'm sure."

There was heavy silence until Papa said, "Anybody going to help on the town wall tonight? It's our favorite pastime around here, next to eating, eh, Mama?"

Anxiously, Mara watched Bret pick up his napkin, dab his mouth, and get ready to leave. "I'll help." It wasn't going to be easy. Her heart sank. She would have to follow them.

9

"Mama, can I go with them?" Ashel said. "I can help them."

I guess so," Mama said. Caroline squealed and clapped her hands. "That is if Mara and Rain will help with the dishes and put Sobe to bed."

Mara nodded. Wide-eyed, Rain accepted, too.

The August evening seemed to stay bright longer than usual. Mara took Sobe to the bedroom by herself. She could see the wall from the south upstairs window as she sang the little boy to sleep. She stared at the sky growing violet, the fields green in the distance, the men at work like tiny insects building the stone wall.

Sobe, sleep, my sun and rain,
My stars and all I see.
Your angel mother sings to you
Of her eternity.

The violet sky darkened. What was wrong with Bret? If only she could see him tonight she could tell him everything. She would know. If it was her relationship with Scott Hunt, so long ago, for such a short time, she would explain. She was embarrassed at his unwillingness to arrange time alone with her. It must be plain to the others how she had hoped that something might happen between them. Had she been too obvious?

Mara slipped from the house without telling Rain or her mother where she was going. The deepening dusk would bring the men from the wall now. Walking down Second South, she thought she heard men's voices, though she could not see the wall beyond the rows of homes. The gray air still seemed dense with the day's heat.

Suddenly out of nowhere came a terrifying scream. She looked up to see a fat Indian on a horse riding down the street in her direction. It was Squash on his mare, and he was dragging behind him two saddled horses.

"Stop him!" Ivie Richards screamed as he ran several yards behind the horses, his gun cocked. Someone fired a shot, but it missed. Squash bent his fat body low over the horse's neck. Mara leaped out of his way. Then she saw that one of the ponies was Pawface! Sully had been using him to haul stone. Quicker than she had time to think, she leaped to the horse and reached for his saddle. She clung to the horn, half running, half dragging as the horse reared back, feeling her weight. "Stop, Pawface!" she yelled. The horse bucked and tugged back, slowing Squash. The other horse belonged to Richards.

"The savage! Thief!" Richards shot again. This time the bullet wounded the Indian's horse, and the animal buckled and fell. Squash rolled over the horse's body and fell to the ground, still holding the two ropes in his hands.

"I've got you now," Richards growled, approaching Mara and Pawface, his big shaggy mare not worse for the ride. Mara turned away from him and brushed the loose hair from her face as she stood by Pawface trying to calm her. Breathless, she did not say a word. Richards was saying it all.

"I'm going to kill him. Dirty Indian! He takes everything!" Richards swore a string of thunderous invectives. He reached the Indian lying hurt on the ground. Though he must have been in pain, Squash tried to stumble free of Richards' grasp. His leg may have been broken or his ankle sprained, Mara couldn't tell. He lurched forward trying to shake free when Richards grabbed him.

"I'm going to kill you! You dirty thief! Stealing my cattle every day, and it was you who slaughtered the calf. Don't lie out of it. It was you!" Standing over him, he grabbed the Indian's neck and wrenched it, enraged.

The fat old Indian, wide-eyed and silent, shook his head madly. "No. No. No kill calf."

By now the other men had arrived. Standing near Pawface, Mara watched Richards with sick fear in the pit of her stomach. Squash and his people had also been robbed. Everything Richards now owned had once belonged to Squash and his people. But no one seemed to think of that. Like the others, she stood by word-lessly. In the dusk she searched in the crowd for Bret.

Richards' hands tightened on the Indian's throat. Sully came forward and Papa lunged toward Richards. "Stop it!" he cried out, but Richards threw Papa back with his large arm. Sully was on him. But Richards threw him back also. "I'm going to kill him," he said between his teeth.

Sully lunged for Richards again. Richards turned, and with one foot on Squash's ankle, grasped his rifle from the ground and with the butt end of it hit Sully in the side. Sully lurched back.

Richards swung round and held the rifle across in front of his body with one hand on each end. "Don't stop me!" He turned, growling like an animal. Then he held the rifle out, cocked it, and stood facing all of them, gun ready. Squash moved. Richards reached back with his left hand and grabbed Squash's clothes. "I'm going to kill him," Richards said. "And you can all watch. I hate the dirty Indians. I'll never know why you're willing to buy him off—why you are trying to save him. He ain't done nothin' but take everything we have."

Squash jerked away from Richards. With one hand still on the Indian, Richards leaned back and swung the rifle against the side of the man's head.

Mara gasped. Squash hated all of them because they had buried his brother without ceremony. But Richards was cruel. She remembered her own fear of this cruel man.

For a tense moment, the men watched while Richards hit Squash again. Squash leaned stunned and Richards hit him again. No one moved. The men watched uneasily while Richards held the gun toward all of them.

"Anybody who tries to stop me—one move and you're dead," Richards said. "And it don't count for you, Squash," he added. "You're dead anyway."

"Hold it." Mara turned, surprised. It was Bret. He stepped forward. "Don't you have a system of dispensing justice down here? We do in Salt Lake City." The words carried a challenge in them.

Mara watched Bret. On his mission to England, he had become a man.

"Who's your deputy? Don't you have a prison for thieves?"

Mara looked at Squash. His face was full of fear now, with Richards' gun at his back.

"Put him in prison," Bret said. No one else had thought of it. Sully nodded.

Papa came forward now. "I think the young man's right, Richards. The war's over. Maybe it's time we stop killing and start dealing out justice like civilized people." Richards' eyes flashed. Mara was afraid he would not agree, but would kill Squash on the spot. "Maybe if we were less like them. . . ." Papa spoke again. "They take from us, but we are also guilty of taking from them." Papa spoke softly. All the men crowded around Richards. Richards moved back. Papa slipped the gun out of Richards' hands. Mara stared at the Indian who lay in a heap on the dusty ground.

"We do have a jail," Sully said.

By now, more of the townspeople had gathered. On Papa's order, Ashel ran to fetch Eames to open the jail.

It was almost dark. Papa and George Allen lifted Squash to his feet and half carried him as he stumbled forward, his feet dragging. Once or twice he tried to wrench out of their grasp, but they held him. Richards picked up his gun at the side of Squash's dead horse and dusted it off. Mara watched him. He looked up and caught her stare with a dark look.

"I saw you stop Sully's horse," Bret had come up behind her. This was the moment she had imagined. He was tall, and she could feel his breath in her hair. "You were fast. And that horse must have known you well."

As she turned to him, she saw the cloud in Sully's eyes, and the darkness in Richards' face—Richards who had wanted Mara as he had wanted Kate Wright. She heard Richards mount his horse as she turned. She heard the thunder of the hooves as he rode away. She was always glad when Ivie Richards rode away.

"Mara, for the longest time I been thinking." It was Sully, coming beside her as she stood facing Bret. "You ought to have Pawface."

"Pawface!" Mara was still holding the bridle, petting the horse's neck in her nervousness. If there were any horse she had dreamed of owning. . . . She turned to Sully, amazed. "Sully, I . . ."

"No, you really ought to have Pawface. I would have given her to you long ago, but you know I've kept hoping you'd join the family." Sully smiled. "She would have been yours then, anyway."

Sully's openness in front of Bret, his kind admission of defeat touched Mara. Sully had given her his favorite horse, with no hope of reward for himself. Mara was amazed.

"Oh, Sully, thank you. But I . . ."

"No 'buts.' She's yours."

"Thank you so much."

Then Sully turned and was gone.

Her head still whirling, Mara leaned toward the horse, holding its face in her hands. She felt Bret close beside her. Would it be possible that now everything was hers? Pawface . . . and Bret?

"Oh, I have always loved this horse," she whispered.

"She's a beautiful mare," Bret said. Then he touched her waist. She turned toward him. His eyes were watching the crowd follow Squash to the small new jail in the city building. She watched them too, for a moment. Then they were alone in the street, just the two of them.

"I've thought about you a thousand times," she whispered. "It was you I cared about most, Bret. Always. I could never really think about anyone else. It was always you." It seemed to her that she could enclose them with her voice in a private world where not a soul could hear.

"Mara." He took her in his arms and she moved toward him, feeling him against her, the warmth in his embrace.

"Oh Bret, Bret. All these years." She lifted her face to his and closed her eyes. She waited for his lips, but he did not kiss her. He held her face with his hands.

"Mara, you are beautiful, just as I remembered."

When he did not kiss her, she opened her eyes. She saw his eyes, but she saw pain in them. She saw his mouth open just a little.

"Does this remind you of that night long ago when we stood in the street outside my father's house?" she asked.

"Mara, there is something I must tell you."

Stung, Mara drew back in his arms. Something was wrong. She felt exposed, as though she had given herself away and suddenly discovered that she was refused. No, that couldn't be. What was it?

"Mara, I have wanted to talk to you. . . . I just haven't known how."

What? Tell me what for heaven's sake. But the panic in Mara did not find her voice. "What is it, Bret?" she said. "What is it?"

"I heard you were betrothed to John Smith as his second wife before he was killed."

"Yes." She had thought of marriage to John a long time ago, but why did that mean anything to Bret? What was he talking about? That was a long time ago!

"Mara, you are not unwilling to enter into plural marriage, then?"

Mara's nerves tightened. Of course she was not unwilling. It was the way of the Church now. She had seen how well it could work, how happy it could be, in Bret's own family—except when a person like Kate Wright was involved. Perhaps Bret just wanted to be sure she would accept other wives before he asked her to marry him. She knew it was important for a man's kingdom on earth and in heaven. "Yes," she said simply, feeling somehow broken, disappointed. "If in the future you . . . if my husband . . . were to want . . . I . . ."

"It isn't the future I'm thinking of, Mara," Bret broke in. "I . . . Oh, Mara." He took both her hands and looked at her sadly. "When I returned from my mission, I had been ill." She had read about his illness in Ella's letter. "Hannah Wright came to visit Kate. She took such a kind interest in me. She told me you were going to marry Sully." Hannah! "And Mother and Father spoke of you often and always said how much Sully had always loved you, how they didn't think he had given up—even after his marriage—even after all these years. . . . You and Hannah are such friends. I thought she must have heard something no one else knew. She said you had finally agreed and that it was all settled upon. There must have been some mistake. She said that you had always been fond of Sully, but that Nancy . . . and that you and Nancy had always been so close and that since Nancy had been unable to have children. . . ."

The pain lashed Mara's heart. "Hannah told you. . . ?" She could barely speak for the anger that burned her.

Hannah!

"Mara, don't be angry with Hannah. There was some mistake." Bret's voice sounded strained. He squeezed her hands so that she could not draw them away. "You can understand my position. Sully is like a brother to me. I could never have thought of you until I found out, until I came here and heard from Sully's own lips that you would never . . . He said there would be no hope for you and him. Mara . . . is it true?"

"Yes, yes, it's true," Mara said, pulling her hands away from Bret and turning from him. She could not force from her mind the image of Bret, ill, in the care of Hannah Wright, known even as far as Provo as the most beautiful woman in Salt Lake City. Hannah! Cold, evil Hannah. How could he have believed her? How could Mara forgive him now, accept him now after this?

"Mara." His hands were on her shoulders, his voice in her hair once more. "Now that I know . . . Mara, you are just as beautiful as I remember." She turned to him in spite of herself. She could forgive him, if she never had to see Hannah again.

"Mara, I know we could be happy together, all of us. Once

15

Hannah knows the truth, I know she would accept you . . . you are such good friends . . . it would be perfect. . . ."

There was a sound in Mara's head. It was an explosion, as though her dreams had been blown apart and scattered in the air. Her hatred for Hannah Wright—and for Hannah's lies—filled the space where the dreams had been. Bret kept talking, holding her in his arms, but she didn't feel him anymore.

"The wedding is set for next month. If you would, you could come then and you could both be sealed to me at once. Or if you prefer your own wedding, we could wait a while. I'm sure Hannah . . ."

Hannah! Mara thought that if she heard Hannah's name on Bret's lips one more time she would scream. She put her hands on Bret's chest and pushed herself out of his arms.

"Mara, I know this is sudden, but you must know that I have been fond of you, and I know Hannah would accept you. She told me about the Indian baby. Of course you could keep the boy."

No! How could he be saying these things! How could he imagine! Hannah Wright . . . accept Mara Eastman! Oh no! She hadn't waited all these years, longing, dreaming, only to share a man with Hannah Wright. She felt naked, torn apart. Hannah Wright who couldn't even bear to live in Provo, who said she hated ugly Fort Utah and the wild beasts who walked like humans. How could Bret, who had told Mara we should be kind to the Indians, even *think* of Hannah? Hannah Wright, as evil and manipulating as her sister. They said Scott Hunt was just being kind to Kate when he rescued her from Ivie Richards. But Bret was plain stupid. Scott Hunt and his stupid son could just rot with Kate and Hannah. If they were no better than that, if they could be fooled so easily by selfish, cold women who lied their way into men's arms, they could rot with Kate and Hannah. Mara laughed inside herself as she thought of Kate Hunt, of Hannah. It wasn't even men's arms they were after. It was money, importance, a good name. Well, neither father nor son would ever know now what it could have been like to be married to Mara Eastman, a woman who could love. Oh yes, she could love. Mara gritted her teeth. And she could hate.

"Mara." Bret's voice was so kind Mara thought she could kill him. "Mara, won't you say something? Won't you tell me what you are feeling?"

Tell him? How could she tell him that she had waited for him, loved him, longed for him? How could she tell him that she had also loved his father and might have married him but for Kate Wright? How could she tell him that Hannah Wright was the last woman on earth with whom she could ever share a man? How could she tell him that her dreams had just flown out of her in pieces?

"Mara." He reached for her again. She backed away from him, falling against Pawface.

"Mara, you're trembling. Are you cold? Let me take you in." He touched her arm.

How could she tell him how she hated him for making a fool of her? He had believed Hannah!

The air seemed heavy, cold. Yet it was August, a hot night. Bret took her arm in silence. She held Pawface's reins as they walked back to the house.

"We'll be leaving in the morning," Bret said as they climbed the stairs to the front door. "I'd be happy if you would go with me. I'm sure Hannah would be glad. . . ."

Hannah. "No." She was proud that she kept her voice steady, even. "No, Bret. No, thank you. I don't think so. I don't think so." She opened the door without waiting for him to open it for her, dropping Pawface's reins on the stoop.

"Later, then? I could come back down for you after the wedding."

She forced herself to turn to him and look him full in the face, smiling. "No, Bret. I really don't think so. No, thank you." She turned and went through the doorway.

"I'll take Pawface to the stable for you."

"Please don't. Sully will do it."

"Good night then, Mara. I'll see you in the morning."

But in the morning, she did not come down when Sobe and Rain came down. She covered her head from the harsh light with her pillow until she thought she would suffocate. When Mama called, she didn't answer. When Papa came to look in on her, she feigned sleep. She listened until there was quiet. When she went downstairs, Bret was gone.

For the next few days, unable to think or even see clearly, Mara clung to Sobe as though he alone could understand. She didn't want to see other people, except for her own family. She knew she could be with the ladies of the Relief Society who were socializing and quilting. But the only time she left the house was to take Sobe to the outhouse or to go with Rain to take meals to Squash in the jail.

The August heat gripped the city. The corn dried. By the first of September, all that was unharvested withered on the hot desert floor. Mara watched the grass fade from green to brown, the tips burning before they broke. Her heart seared with them. Not even her father could cheer her, though he tried. Only her attentions to Sobe and visits to the jail with Rain told her she was alive.

On Friday, three days after the capture of Squash, Arrapene, shouting like an angry banshee, led a group to the jail and shot into the window. The Eames boy was on guard. Arrapene shouted curses at him. Carl Eames shot back but only into the sky.

On Sunday, Squash tried to break out of prison. He had been thrown a knife, and he used it on Carl Eames, hacking at his back. Ellis Eames took his injured son's place guarding the jail.

On Monday morning, Eames lay asleep on the front cot when Rain and Mara brought food. Even the hot morning air was full of something different, heavy, dark.

"Let's not wake him," Mara said quietly, tiptoeing ahead of Rain into the gray block cell. "If Squash is asleep, we'll put the biscuits outside of his door."

But Eames woke as the girls walked toward the cell. His eyes were still heavy. "Who . . . what?"

The cell was quiet. Mara could not see Squash through the bars. She turned quickly when she heard Eames' voice.

"Who is it?" He blinked at them. "Oh, just you. Go ahead. The key is in the drawer. He's tamed down—won't hurt you."

Mara reached for the key. Something was wrong. The cell was quiet. Rain held the basket of biscuits while Mara moved toward the door to open it. As she reached it, she peered into the darkness. At first she could not see Squash, and then she made out a dark shape back up against the wall to the left. She cried out in sudden fear. The limp gray body hung like a bag of rocks against the corner from a rope tied to the topmost bar in the cell door.

"He's hanged himself!" Mara cried out. Rain moved into the room and stood dumbly with the basket still hanging on her arm.

Eames came now, lumbering to the cell. He squinted into the darkness half awake, his eyes blank. He gasped. Finally he said apologetically, "I didn't see him do it." The body was cold.

Weary and stunned, knowing that civil justice had failed, that nothing ever seemed to go right with the Indians, Mara did not leave the house again for a long time. Her mother tried to encourage her to go to Relief Society, to be with people, but she stayed home and clung to Sobe. Finally, Mama wanted to spend the day with a sick neighbor and begged Mara to go to Relief Society in her place. "They're drying fruit at the church kitchen and I said I'd be there. Please, honey, help me out just today."

It was a hot late September day. Still clinging to Sobe, Mara walked to the church, holding him against her shoulder as she stood at the open windows, not wanting to go in. She still held him as she overheard voices speak her name. Her heart froze. She could not identify separate speakers. The voices seemed to blend into a terrible recrimination. She held Sobe quietly against her cheeks while she heard everything.

It was Mara Eastman who found him hanging in the cell. She pays more attention to those Indians . . . .

When you laid out your racks, they should have been cleaned before you (slice after slice) put down the peaches (one after another), the pears, the apples. Small apples, and so few, but a harvest all the same. And you should never slice too thin. Or there is nothing left. Too many cuts make nothing.

No one understands why Snake . . . what was it? Squash? Killed himself. Or did he? Eames was sleeping so late. Do you think he rigged . . . no, that's not possible. Was it Indians? Cherries are very good. There are so few now. But you should pit them, or you don't necessarily need to pit them, but cherries dry better pitted, opened up like peaches. Cherries stain awful. They do stain.

It was Mara Eastman found him. And then she feels so sick about his death—or about something or other—she doesn't come out to nothing much anymore. She puts far too much of herself into keeping them Indians alive. And it is promised they will die. They will die, all of them but a handful. Yes, there is a handful that should be left . . . what was it for? To save us? Was that what the verses said? That they should save us one day? Doesn't sound likely. What do they know? And we will take off someday in our spirits and leave this earth behind us. It hangs on us like burrs, holding us by its thorns, then whipping us with the hot sun, lashing us with dry wind.

If you want the best cherries, stir them, grind them, roll them out on leather to dry and peel them up from the sun. Save every one of them. Don't let a one fall.

Look, there are at least two buckets of them cherries off that tree. I would like to know who cut this long branch off here and took too much. It's raw. The edge is raw as an old arm broke right off, the bones showing.

I think Mara Eastman was broke up about more than that Indian. I thought it was pretty plain Mara Eastman was broke up about that young fellow . . . what was his name? Scott Hunt's boy. It wasn't Caleb. Joshua? No, he's the younger one. I don't remember. But he came back from his mission and got engaged to the Wright girl. No accounting for any man's taste, if you ask me.

You can't tell me those pears is fine. All I'm going to have when I'm done is jam. The sun will rot 'em. That's what it will do . . . rot 'em like syrup. And I think you ought to leave them other pears to ripe up whole before you do any cuttin' at all. Only eighty pears on the whole tree!

When old Walker died, I said to myself that's the end of the Walker wars, though they was sure hanging around after that Snake died . . . that Squash . . . Squash? Did you notice that? I saw they were hanging around here the last few weeks.

The pears is tough as apples, but they'll dry. That's true. I've seen these green pears hard as wood dry up just fine and taste mighty good come a hard winter, which this winter is likely to be.

And though she takes care of Rain and that pretty baby Sobe, Mara Eastman should have accepted Sully Tuttle's offer long ago. A girl turned twenty-one and unmarried yet! There's no question but that there's still a chance for her to have Sully's babies seeing as how Nancy can't. I don't say having babies is all there is to this life, but most of life has to do with either bringing people into the world or else giving them comfort and happiness while they're here.

The gray color comes on the prunes faster. . . . Did we have prunes? I'm sure we'll have a lot of black tacky pieces as hard as stones. *It's good for hunger in the hard winter, and I'm sure we're just beginning with hard winters. There's more of everything, you can expect it. Perhaps someday even more of blessed sunshine and rain.*

Seems like some people just don't see clearly. Take Mara Eastman . . . always had a cloud in her eyes when it come to Sully Tuttle, and him even willing to raise that Indian baby . . . though what man wants to raise an Indian or any baby not his own unless he's got real compassion, which Sully Tuttle does, still loving that girl. . . . Now, whoever made that baby really ought to take it, but most likely the father is Richards and he turned and ran before he could tell whether or not the baby might be a half-breed. He always was a shameful coward.

Do you really think that Indian baby is his? I mean Richards'. That's what they say, but you know Mara Eastman always swears it was some Indian husband his mother had who was killed in that cattle business, back at the start of all this Indian trouble. Well, it could be, but another rumor I been hearing is that the baby belongs to Scott Hunt! I know he wouldn't have done a thing like that, but he was down to get them Indians and bring them back about the time that baby must have been conceived.

I say take the pits out. I don't need pits when I'm chewing so hard. They break my teeth. I'm taking my pits out. There's plenty other things with the pits in.

That baby could be Hunt's, and nobody be the wiser, for it's a handsome baby. Though its hair is as black as any Indian's, it's got a bright face and fine features, with the body and build and brain I might say of a white child. But maybe that's just Mara making him into her own, spending the kind of time with him she should be spending with children of her own.   .

I don't suppose we'll ever know. No, I don't suppose. There is some things better left unknown, though whatever man might be the father of that baby could well deserve to be proud of it now. It's a handsome child and the Eastmans raising him and that little orphan Caroline to be strong members in the Church.

I want a few apples. Just a few. I know that's all there is. I'll take mostly pears because they taste sweeter. Peaches get sticky and there weren't many. Just give me a few of them apples and I think my family will be set. We did manage several barrels of wheat. Two hogs cut and dried, and I had flour left over from last year. You know, if you pray always, like we was promised, the food goes farther. No, I'm serious. Try it. I done it this last spring before the radishes and chard come up. And my chard just sprang out of the same roots as last year.

If we could just get rid of those Indians, things would be look- ing pretty good here. Town's growing, people doing well. The bank, the Eastmans' hotel. Oh I know I'm sounding unchristian. Martha Eastman tells me I do when I talk against the Indians. She's still grieving over her Spirit of Earth, but if I never saw another Indian I would feel just fine. We wouldn't never have to finish that wall.

There was a long moment of quiet. Unnoticed, but heartsick, Mara turned with Sobe in her arms and walked home.

Chapter Two

IN THE AUTUMN OF 1855, ARRAPENE SENT A MESSAGE TO BRIGHAM Young. He had seen his brother Walkara in a dream. "Fight no more with white man," Walkara had told Arrapene. There was something in his dream he didn't understand about the Indians being all washed up on the shore.

Sully heard about Arrapene's dream and rejoiced. He had never wanted to fight the Indians. He had suffered nightmares since the day Tony Richards had shot Old Bishop five years before. Five years. They had weighted Old Bishop down with stones and dropped him in the river. How naive they had all been to think they could be rid of the trouble just like that. Sully had suffered deeply remembering how he had cut the heads from the bodies on the ice. How could he have done such a thing, even though it had been at the surveyor's request? Over the years he had also grown sick to remember how they had killed Kickingboot and buried him improperly. It had taken years of praying for forgiveness and giving the Indians everything they wanted to heal his guilt.

To celebrate the new truce, the people of Provo held a party for all the Indians—all that were left, anyway—in the park across from the Eastmans'. The men killed two head of beef and roasted them in pits. The women baked corn bread and biscuits in big dutch ovens. Sister Eastman made the butter. The old Indians sat around for two or three days, smoking and eating. "As if they owned the country," Sully heard one of the good sisters say. "As if they owned it. . . ." Some people would never understand. There were some people who just would never see beyond the noses on their own faces.

Of course, the Indians still lapsed occasionally into violence. Angry over the hanging of a couple of their young men up in Salt Lake Valley, they made raids. There wasn't any way to get an Indian to understand the white man's justice. But Sully didn't blame them. Justice was a hard thing to understand. Sometimes Sully thought there was no such thing as justice. So much depended on one's point of view as to how things really were. At times it appeared that God was not always in his heaven and all was not right with the world.

When the grasshoppers came in 1855, Sully had routed the canal around the field and beat and drowned those he could. But it hadn't done any good. When they came back in such hordes in the summer of 1856, Sully called Nancy to the window. They stood with their arms around each other watching the scourge spread like a black cloth over the young corn. They saw the leaves ripple and fall, the green fields change color, become stubble, die—all in one morning. Sully didn't say anything. He just held Nancy tightly and waited until the grasshoppers passed. Then he went back out onto the gummy earth and planted again.

At night in the dark of their small bedroom, Sully came to Nancy. Tired after her own hard work, leaning against pillows, against chintz spreads, calico and homemade lace, Nancy cried. Sully came into the bedroom, stained with sweat, his hands black with dirt. From the bed, she waited for him while he washed at the basin and dried his rough face. She curved against the pillows and watched him, her eyes sunken above her sunburned cheeks. She spoke with her eyes, though she did not breathe a word. Her eyes asked the same old questions and received the same answers, all in silence. "Will we have any food at all this winter?"

"I don't know."

"Why are they sending more people into the valley when we have nothing to feed them?"

"They must come."

Sully shed his clothing. He moved to the bed feeling ripples of weariness in his muscles, his blood beating in his limbs, dropping through his veins. He saw Nancy's eyes, and he saw the deep color, the weariness in them. Nancy, he said without his voice, but with motion. Nancy, Nancy.

Her touch was warm, a healing balm. She drew the soft tips of her fingers along the roughness of his arm. There were other questions in her eyes that were never spoken. "Will you still want me though I have never given you a child?" Words hurt too much for both of them. "How can God leave us without children for so long, forever?" No words, yet.

Nancy. Nancy.

Once, after Mara had said no again to Nancy and Sully's plea, Nancy had told Sully to take someone else as a wife.

"No. No. We have each other and I love you. It doesn't matter."

But he knew it did. It mattered to her. It had been four years. The house was still empty as a tomb. So they clung to each other alone, fiercely, prayerfully, urgently. At times, their only means of support was the sale of a few colts to the Eastmans and to townspeople who, although they had little of their own, would give a peck of flour to own a fine young horse. They waited out the grasshoppers, the slim harvest, and the bleak famine. They gathered the saccharin that fell on the leaves that autumn. To the common greeting "Have you got your breadstuffs?" they could usually answer "yes," but once when she brought Sully's bread and bacon to the field, Nancy was so hungry she could not help but eat the bread on the way. She fell in his arms crying when he asked her where it was. How long, oh Lord? Why, why, why?

In the autumn of 1856, the Church declared a reformation and all the members recommitted themselves with a new baptism. It had been a mild October, but while the priests said their prayers over the heads of the people standing knee deep in the water, snow began to fall on the river, spreading the ceremonies with a cold blanket of white. The silent snow fell in great drifts around Sully and Nancy's door, so deep they could barely get away to go into Provo for church.

A hush fell over the meetinghouse that first snowy Sunday of October when Ephraim K. Hanks from Salt Lake City presented himself at the podium and asked George Albert Smith for twenty volunteers to ride with him as far as Fort Bridger or farther to rescue a handcart company marooned by the storms.

Nancy clung to Sully's sleeve. He held his palm over her hand. "I really ought to go." Nancy didn't say a word. "As able-bodied as

I am . . . and you with your family close." She leaned her head against his arm in silence.

Sully left early Monday morning and did not arrive home until late November, his fingertips frozen, a few of the tips of his toes scarred with black useless flesh. He brought with him the family of William Jones, whose wife had died from exposure on the journey west. The father and his two young children moved into Sully and Nancy's home with a few of their meager belongings, their illnesses, and their insatiable appetites. Brother Jones lay ill while the two young children played around Nancy's feet during the day. She adored them: a girl four years old and a boy two. Nothing was too good for them. And she filled her days scraping meals from the little they had, stretching soups, creating new dishes from roots, old apples, and the scrabbly dried prunes. Sully was only too happy to share what they had in order to see Nancy so contented.

As he mended, William Jones, a smooth-featured man with dark curly hair, talked with Sully about buying a carding machine and establishing the wool business, which he knew from his work in Scotland. Sully took him immediately to see Hart Eastman, who suggested they set up the business under the guise of the Deseret Manufacturing Company to be operated under a corporative agreement until such a time as Jones might go on his own. Jones pitched himself into the carding business with so much force that the two children were left almost always in Nancy's care, and she became more and more attached to them as the winter months wore into the spring of 1857. There was always the danger, Sully warned her, that William Jones would remarry and take the children, and he knew Nancy braced herself for that day, though Sully feared it would crush her heart.

The long famine wore on until the first spears of chard broke the dark soil, and then there was suddenly a new threat, more terrifyingly dark even than hunger . . . the threat of war.

It was not Indians this time, but the equipped military forces of the United States of America with their combat knowledge, gunpowder, money, and supplies. The unbelievable truth came through a messenger to Sully in the fields. The boy bearing the news was a breathless child on a worn horse. "Brigham Young is no longer governor" was his message. Sully stopped his plow and ran to the house.

"It's happened, Nancy. It's happened," he said, still hardly believing it. There had been rumors. Now it was fact. In order to separate church and state, the Congress of the United States had now proclaimed their own governor for the territory of Utah and would bring him here accompanied by enough militia to install him by force if necessary.

Riding in from his business in town, Jones had already got wind of the news. He sat and spread his hands flat on the table. "There's some men going to stop them in Wyoming. News is they should reach Fort Bridger about September. If we can have enough men make scattered attacks, Indian fashion, we can ambush them," he said.

Sully was grateful for Jones' determination and strength. He somehow felt safer with such a friend. "Do you think they'll do it? Come here . . . and force us to take a man as governor we've never even seen or know a thing about?"

"They're on the way," Jones said, "and if Nancy will keep my children, I for one will be there to stop them."

Sully went with Jones to join the ambush forces in September as news of the troops bearing down on them reached the frightened settlers in valleys from north of Ogden to as far south as Manti.

The presence of the militia only a hundred miles away spoiled for Sully his joy at the blessings of the bounteous harvest of 1857. It was the end of the famine. But Sully was at war. And with Jones and two or three hundred other volunteers from valley communities, he set fire to U.S. camps, destroyed supply trains, set up barricades that took time for the troops to break through. They helped stop the U.S. militia at Camp Scott, where thousands of U.S. soldiers set up winter quarters, unable to enter the Salt Lake Valley.

The winter of 1857-1858 was a long and torturous season crowded with suspense. Everyone worked, danced, and worshiped the same as always, but there was an uneasiness, a fear, a sense of uncertainty about what would happen, and when, and how much.

Then in March and April of 1858 came the news that after four months of camp, the winter-weary but fortified United States army was on its way.

Sully felt the panic. It struck the people of Deseret from the most influential leaders to the least farmer and merchant. Would the Saints be driven again?

"We do not want to fight the United States," Brigham Young said. "But if they drive us to it, we shall do the best we can, and I will tell you, as the Lord lives, we shall come off conquerors."

On a warm misty April morning Sully was working in his field high on the east bench. As he stretched from his labor and looked out through the mist across the valley he thought he saw movement. He strained his eyes as the rising sun drove out the night. People. They were moving in a great caravan through the greening fields, dragging their cattle and their belongings with them toward Provo. Sully watched, amazed. He made out a figure on horseback riding toward him. He didn't move. This was no militia. These were families—men, women and children in wagons! The rider was near. It was Joseph Hunt, Aunt Chloe's younger son!

"We've come, Sully!" he shouted. "The whole city!"

Taking Joseph with him, Sully went to the cabin to tell Nancy that the people of Salt Lake City were moving into Utah Valley.

"And we've left our houses stacked with straw ready to be burned," Joseph said.

Nancy's face turned white. She was mending a tear in a calico apron. The apron fell from her hands and her fingers shook as she reached to pick it up again.

"Then they will come here. And we'll all be killed together."

Sully came to her and pulled her close to him. "There can be no fighting if we do not return fire."

"Where shall we go?" she asked, her head on his shoulder.

"South. Perhaps south. Perhaps Mexico."

Sully and William Jones rode with Joseph out to meet the caravan moving slowly down the arroyos and the marshlands, skirting the lake. It was a giant lumbering swarm of wagons, teams, cows on ropes, bleating sheep, and sore-footed cattle. "It's like Moses and the children of Israel," Jones said. Old men on canes hobbled to keep up, children ran, played games among the wagons. Many of the wagons were piled high with furniture tied hastily under flapping old patchwork quilts.

They found Captain Hunt at once, his great family gathered about him, the young children laughing at the good fun.

Captain Hunt and his wives were not laughing. "If they burn us out we may have to stay with you," Captain Hunt said, and Sully saw that he was not joking.

"I'd be glad if I could repay one small bit of the hospitality you showed me in the past," Sully said. He introduced Captain Hunt to William Jones.

"They tell us we'll be setting up camp in the city square for the time being, though I'm not sure how all of us will manage without draining your meager resources."

Sully felt the weight of Captain Hunt's words, but he shrugged them off, knowing in the deep weariness of his bones that most of them would survive no matter what happened. They must, and they would.

Inside the city, the caravan filled the streets. The park filled rapidly with tents, the clusters of wagons parked in circles. Cattle polluted sidewalks and lawns, women built supper fires on small pads of soil, the young children waded in the cold water of the canal.

"This is it, then, driven like cattle," Sully said more to himself than to anyone around him. But Jones heard him. "They can't possibly stay here more than a few nights," he said.

But it proved to be almost two months. Two months of increasing disorder, crowded quarters, scurvy, the blight. Several times in May Sully and Jones brought Nancy and the children to visit the Eastmans and the Hunts. Hart Eastman had brought the younger Hunt children and Ella, who was not well, into his house. "It's the least I can do after all your help to my family while I was away," he said. Like Sully, the Eastmans and the Hunts began to rely on Will Jones' strength and knowledge as he worked along with them during these difficult times. By mid-June the heat had dried up the water supply, and it was Will who organized a movement to help the Salt Lake Saints dig holes for ground water. The park reeked of sour odors and swarmed with flies.

"It's hard to watch our brothers suffer in our own front yard," Hart Eastman exclaimed to Sully one hot day. He had taken all the sick children into his home, but there was only so much he and his small family could do no matter how great his financial resources—all the money in the world could not buy food that was not available or more medical services than there were to be had. He put up a couple of Brigham Young's families in his East House Hotel while Brigham Young stayed in Salt Lake City to negotiate with the advancing army. When Kate Hunt's oldest girl Stella became ill, Brother Eastman insisted Kate's whole family move into the hotel as well. Aunt Chloe and Aunt Polly were well and were helping at the camp in the park. Captain Hunt stayed there with them.

Sully worried about Kate being in the hotel. Mara had just begun working there, and he knew that any mention of Kate or Hannah Wright hurt Mara—even now. But she didn't seem to notice that Kate was there. Sully brought Nancy often to help Rain and Sister Eastman care for all the sick children. When the little ones were finally tucked into bed, Nancy and Sully often drove to the hotel to fetch Mara.

On these evenings, Sully watched Mara carefully, worried. He always felt hollow inside when he looked at Mara, but there was no hurt anymore. It was hard to remember the terrible longing he had suffered for the girl who had now become this pale, thin, woman. But she was still beautiful, and he still cared for her, worried over her. After Bret Hunt married Hannah Wright, it seemed Mara was not the same anymore. She had many suitors, married and unmarried, many offers. But it was as though she looked at them without seeing them. She seemed to be in another world. To Sully and Nancy she was kind, but even Nancy said Mara was different, withdrawn.

"She's hurting herself more than anyone else," Sully told Nancy. "I am worried about her."

One evening Sully and Nancy fetched William Jones from the carding shop after they picked up Mara, and the four of them stopped for a cold lemonade in the hotel. William Jones seemed taken by Mara, as most men were at first, and he tried to begin a conversation about her work and about his trek across the plains. Mara admired Mr. Jones for his expertise as he had helped Sully and the families from Salt Lake City. She was polite to him, as she was to everyone. But she was still distant. "It is as though her heart has closed over a bitter wound," William Jones said on the way home.

Sully watched her avoid the Hunt family. All of Aunt Ella's boys and their wives stayed with Aunt Chloe and Aunt Polly's families in the square. Once when Sully and Nancy had come to see Mara at the hotel, Hannah and Bret came into the hotel to buy a newspaper, holding their little girl by the hand. Mara vanished into the back room when they walked through the door, and she did not come back until they were gone.

Not until June 30 did news come that Brigham Young had conceded his governorship to Governor Cumming, who had been appointed by the U.S. Congress. Although Utah people were promised amnesty and informers said that troops were just walking through rather than preparing to fight, the return of the Salt Lake City people was cautious and slow. When the U.S. troops set up Camp Floyd only about twenty miles northwest of Provo in a spot on the other side of the lake, Provo people felt uneasy. On the first night in July, Sully and Nancy came to the hotel to visit Mara. They were sitting on the bench near the front when four men from the army came into town and found the place open for business. Mara was at the desk.

"Do they serve liquor in this town?" a tall one who led the group asked her. Sully saw Mara draw back. The others in the room fell silent. Chatwin's distillery served drinks, though Brigham Young had spoken hard against it. The man inquiring was very tall and thin.

"Cat got your tongue?"

Mara did not respond, as though she were collecting her thoughts. Sully's heart began to pound.

"Well, a little Mormon girl. So many of 'em around they can't get a word in edgewise. I suppose they don't learn to talk when they're young." Behind the leaders, a stocky, dark-haired older man moved up toward the counter, his uniform open at his throat showing knotted gray fuzz on his chest. As he moved closer, he placed his thick leathery hands on the counter top.

"Just how many women do you compete with to get into bed, girlie?"

"Or are you married?" the tall one joined him, his mouth curved in a grin.

Mara stared spitefully. She did not look afraid.

31

"Enough men's around now to give all you fillies all you need ever' night."

"Look at the pretty little thing get her dander up."

Mara was the only hotel employee in the room. The manager, Mr. Dawes, had left for a few moments. Sully looked around him. There were only a few others in the room: two old ladies bent over teacups at a table and the broom boy cleaning up in the vestibule.

Sully sat on the edge of the bench and grasped Nancy's hand.

"We don't serve drinks here," Mara's voice sounded forced, far away, tight.

"No drinks here! What kind of a hotel is this, anyway?" The tall one turned to the others who were close now. "No drinks here! Now look, girlie." He drew closer, looming over the counter. "You're wondering what we're doing here. We didn't come to chat with you seldom-kissed Mormon girls." He leered now. "Although it might not be such a bad idea fillin' in where your scarce husbands leave off. If you'd like to come out, I'll show you a good time."

Mara's eyes smoldered now. One of the soldiers laughed.

"She looks green."

"Are you green, girl?"

"She's not even broke I'll wager you."

The hair rose on Sully's neck. The tall man's arms were easily three-and-a-half feet long. In a flash his hand was on her dress, groping toward her collar. Sully was up on his feet, moving toward the men on legs weak as water. "Leave her alone." He heard Nancy gasp behind him.

Mara's hand flew to her collar and she tried to break away. The large dark fingers clutched at her lace.

"Come on, pretty," Sully heard the heavy voice snarl.

One of the men turned and stood in front of Sully. Sully tried to push him away. The fourth man tripped him, and he lurched forward. The soldiers laughed. Sully swung his fist, hit the fourth man in the ribs.

"Oh," the man turned on Sully, a hiss in his teeth. Slowly, the other two turned on Sully while Mara struggled with the tall soldier who had leaped over the counter and was holding her tightly from behind. Sully kicked one of them in the shins, but he grabbed Sully's hair while the other soldier gave him a blow on the jaw. In a moment Sully lay on the floor, his mouth bleeding. He felt Nancy lift his head.

It was then that the officer appeared at the door. Flanked by two others, there would never have been any mistaking this man's authority. The man who was holding Mara let her go immediately as the officer entered the hotel. The others scrambled to their feet. Sully leaned on Nancy and sat up, his head spinning.

"What's going on?" the officer's voice boomed. Sully's head hurt.

"You swine, Anderson." The officer strode forward. In only a few steps he was with them. "I can't trust you and Carradine for five minutes."

The officer was surprisingly young and also tall. Sully saw that his coat was pressed smooth, his shirt white. Across his shoulders were epaulets and stripes and insignia. He was a lieutenant. He had dark hair and an imposing face. He looked strong and power- ful enough. His eyes had an almost fearsome flash in them. But he was so clean and neat. Even his hands were clean. He was not like the soldiers Sully knew. He was not a man who got his hands into the earth. But the men obeyed him. Sully was almost afraid as the officer walked toward him.

"You cut this man's mouth, Carradine? Can't you leave these people alone? Can't you get it through your stupid skulls that we're on the edge of war with these people? And in case you don't know it, war wouldn't be much fun . . . for them or for you." He knelt on the floor beside Sully and Nancy. He reached toward Mara and she handed him a towel.

"Any more of this kind of brawl and the Mormons will send their wives after us with rolling pins."

Sully didn't know whether this man was serious or joking. No one in the room moved. He put the towel on the side of Sully's face and it immediately colored with bright red blood. Sully lifted his hand to his shirt; it was also sticky with blood.

"Are you his wife?" the officer asked Nancy.

"Yes," Nancy said, her voice trembling.

"Lieutenant Phillip Hurst. Happy to meet you, ma'am. I'm sorry for the rude behavior of my men."

"Oh, sir, I'm so grateful for your help."

"He'll be all right when the blood stops. Do you have a carriage?"

"Yes . . . yes. It's just outside." Sully could barely speak. His head whirled and his stomach was sick. He closed his eyes.

"He'll be all right, but he ought to get to bed. One of my men can drive you safely home."

Sully heard Mara's voice. "It's all right. I know where they live. I'll take them."

"I still need you, Miss Eastman." It was Dawes, the manager, who had returned at last. The men with the lieutenant lifted Sully to his feet.

"I'm sorry," the lieutenant said to the manager. "Is there anything I can do to right things . . . mister . . . mister. . . ."

"Dawes. It's all right," Dawes said, rubbing his palms together and then smoothing down his hair, "Miss Eastman's father will be grateful for what you did."

"Miss Eastman. . . ." Sully saw the lieutenant look at Mara. "I'm pleased to make your acquaintance, Miss Eastman. I'm only sorry I was not here sooner."

"Her father owns this hotel, and he don't like brawls, if you know what I mean," Dawes mumbled. "We appreciate your help."

"Yes, we do appreciate it," Mara said as the soldiers helped Sully through the front door.

Alone in her room at last, Mara could not push Phillip Hurst from her mind. She undressed slowly, letting her apron, her dress, her petticoats fall to the floor, leaving them where they lay. She sat on the bed, pulling off her stockings. She put out the light and crawled into bed. She saw him still, as one sees a burst of light, and then, shutting one's eyes, sees the blaze etched on the eyelids. He had looked into her eyes. "I'm pleased to make your acquaintance, Miss Eastman," he had said, bowing from the waist. "I'm only sorry I was not here sooner."

But it would not do to think of Phillip Hurst, Lieutenant, United States Army, the enemy from Camp Floyd, an outsider. He had made light of Mormon women. He no doubt held in contempt all that was sacred in her life. It would not do to think of him. But she thought of him from the first moment she saw him and she could not stop thinking of him.

She remembered each word, each movement. "I believe my men were looking for the distillery." Mr. Dawes had told him that Chatwin's was down the street. Brigham Young didn't like it one bit, but it was there, he said, it's a free country. "I'm very sorry my men should have stumbled into your fine hotel instead, sir." It wasn't his hotel, Mr. Dawes said. It was Miss Eastman's father's hotel. "I hope you will accept my sincere apologies, Miss Eastman, and extend the same to your father. Perhaps I may have the opportunity to tell him myself. . . . You were not hurt?" She said she was not, and he reached for her hand. She feared for a moment he would kiss it, but he only held it, lifted it, let it go. "Good-bye, then, Miss Eastman. I am truly very sorry." And then he was gone. That was a real gentleman, someone said.

Mara heard the voices downstairs. Sully and Nancy would be telling the story one more time to Mama and Papa and Rain. Another voice. It would be William Jones. They would tell it all over again now to him. But they did not know. They had not seen. They could not understand. "I'm pleased to make your acquaintance, Miss Eastman. I'm only sorry I was not here sooner." They could not know what it meant.

She was not a fool. It did not do to imagine it had happened if it had not. But Phillip Hurst *was* pleased to make her acquaintance, and she was certain she would see him again. She was frightened at how much she wanted something to come of this meeting.

She began to imagine that one day he would lead her out the hotel door into the night and stand with her in the light from the moon. As though it were real she saw him touching her shoulders, holding her face in his hands. She felt him kissing her face, her eyes, softly. Kissing her cheek with a breath, kissing her neck, pulling his arms around her, twining his fingers in her hair and down her back. She thought she could imagine his hands holding her face, lifting her mouth to his. . . .

Her fantasies flew, spinning a future for which there was no present. She was terrified of the risks that would come when time would bring the future to her. But she felt as helpless to stop herself as if she were falling from the sky.

And then she imagined the dancing. . . . She imagined him twirling her into his arms and beginning a waltz . . . around and around the room. He was gazing into her eyes, whispering "I need you, Mara, my darling." She was tossing her head back to tease and then melting into him as if she could pass through him. They were dancing around and around. The faces . . . watching. Papa, Mama, Sully, Nancy, and their friend Will Jones. Scott Hunt and Kate. Ivie Richards. All were staring with wonderful awe. Bret, with narrow eyes, was watching as she whirled around the room, beautiful in the arms of the handsome lieutenant. Hannah was pulling Bret's arm to make him turn away. Bret was walking away from Hannah toward her. Phillip Hurst was whirling her away, permitting no one else to touch her. . . . The faces were vanishing. She and Phillip Hurst were suddenly alone in the room—in the universe.

She did not sleep. More quickly than she could believe, she had passed from thinking of Phillip Hurst to yearning for him. Through the night, she let the yearning wash through her and flood the scars in her heart, until the terror of a future that could not be and the pain of a past that could not have been flowed out of her. When the sun rose, Mara was alive for the first time in three years. For the first time in a thousand mornings, the light did not hurt her eyes.

They would think she was ill from the fright of the night before, and they would leave her be until she wanted to come down. It was never hard to get them to believe she was ill. Sobe would look in, but if she pretended to sleep, even he would go away. She was afraid of hearing a voice. If someone spoke, it would not be the same.

It was late in the morning when she at last began to dress. She must dress with care. She looked at herself long in her glass. She touched her face, not as soft, not as full as before. Was it not as pretty? Something seemed dark around her eyes. She pinched her cheeks, patted her neck. It was a long time before she was ready. She came down to the silent kitchen and ate a very little bread and milk to make her legs feel stronger. They were all out in the garden, and Papa had gone to the investment office he built on Center Street which he was trying to develop into a small bank. She was glad to be alone. No one could know what it was like to be Mara Eastman. Even when she chose to be with people, she felt alone in their presence. Perhaps it sometimes seemed too painful to reach out, or she didn't know how.

She left for the hotel at eleven o'clock. She was to work early today. She remembered that there was something with Sully and

Nancy and William Jones for this evening, but she did not want to be part of it. It was in another future. The one from before Phillip Hurst. "I'm sorry I was not here sooner," he had said.

She walked to the hotel quickly, barely nodded at people she passed. There were always people, living their lives, changing. But she was always alone, not changing with them, living in no time, only her face growing older to tell her she was of them. She did not want anyone to see that she was alive again. If they saw her, spoke to her, they might know. It would be harder then when she would have to die again. On the street, among the people, she could only keep Phillip Hurst in her mind with effort. She had to try to remember why she was alive today.

The hotel lobby was cold. No one was at the lunch tables. Mrs. Dawes was still upstairs making the beds. The dark wood in the hotel lobby oppressed Mara. She set the tables quickly, not looking around her. She did not want to see anyone. The tables done, she fled to her small desk behind the counter in the lobby. If she looked intent on her bookkeeping, perhaps no one would speak to her. She could finish the columns before noon if she worked fast. Mr. Dawes would be in from the fields by noon. She could smell the bread baking in the kitchen, but Mrs. Dawes did not come out. No one came for tea. She worked furiously to add the columns, her head bent, her back to the counter.

The sound of the bell on the counter startled her, but she did not turn around. She knew without looking. It was him.

"Do you spend your life in this hotel?"

The sound of his voice so filled Mara with happiness that there was no room in her for fear. She turned to him with delight and smiled back into his smile. "I'm my father's right-hand man," she said.

"No. That you are not." Mara felt the blood rise to her face. She glowed with pleasure. He looked only into her eyes, yet it seemed to her that he saw her all at once, every part of her, and she was not afraid.

"It was quite a fright my men must have given you last night," he said, still smiling at her with his dark eyes. "But you are none the worse for it."

"I'm quite well," she said.

37

"Yes, you are. Quite." He looked at her, smiling, leaning over the counter, reaching to the side nearest her and grasping the edge with his right hand. "Quite well indeed." Then he stood back laughing. "I wish I could say the same for my horse."

"Your horse?" Mara laughed, too, standing from her chair and coming to the counter.

"My mare. She's lame. Is there . . . is there a good blacksmith in town? Someone who has a way with shoes? I'm very partial to this mare."

Mara knew of Hurly, east on First North and across the street. The East House Hotel was on First North and Main. Just two blocks east of the hotel, inside the block, was Hurly, the blacksmith.

"I doubt I can find it myself. But if you would be so kind as to show me. . . ."

The excitement pounded in her, but she was not afraid. "You can find it," she said. "Here." She came around the desk and walked across the lobby to the First North street door. He followed her. She smiled inside, knowing he watched her. "There." She pushed open the door and pointed east. He stood just behind her now. She could feel the buttons on his jacket cross her back as he leaned to hold the door for her.

"Two blocks, you said?" His voice was in her ear.

"East. Then in the middle of the block north. Take the second entrance into the driveway. . . ."

He drew his arm across her waist as he moved around her to hold the door with his back and stand facing her. "Why don't you just come with me?"

She wanted to lean forward. She would have been able to rest her cheek on his chest. "There's no one at the desk," she said, stepping back into the lobby.

"And no one coming in." He turned toward the kitchen. "Ask your cook to keep watch."

It had been a very slow morning. Mr. Dawes was due back in a quarter of an hour. She walked to the kitchen door. "Mrs. Dawes," she called. "A gentleman has asked me to show him the way to the smithy. I'll be back very soon."

"Go on, dear," Mrs. Dawes called. "Nobody's coming. Henry will be here any minute."

He still stood holding the door. She crossed the lobby to him and walked out into the sunshine. He closed the door behind her. "She's a very good mare," he said. "I need somebody better than the military iron man to see to her." He came to his horse, stooped, lifted her foot from the dust. "This edge gets worn too quickly, and the nail falls loose. If it's not far, we'll walk her."

"She's a handsome horse," Mara said, feeling the sunshine hot on her hair.

"Yes, she's beautiful," he said. "And she's been a good animal."

"Except for the coloring, she reminds me of my wild mare." Mara touched the mare's neck. "Yes, she's like Pawface."

"Wild?" He stood up close behind her.

"Yes. We've been able to tame quite a few wild horses here. We usually get them from the Indians. Pawface came in our gate with a raid the Utes made on the fort."

"I've seen the wild ones. Sometimes they are more beautiful than the finest cultivated. . . ." She heard his voice stop. He reached for the bridle.

He walked a long stride. Mara found herself almost skipping to keep up with him.

"I'm sorry. I'm going too fast," he laughed.

The smithy was back in the shed behind Hurly's place, toward the center of the block, hidden by trees. Hurly was busy, and the lieutenant asked if Mara would wait with him. They sat on the grass in the shade and talked. He told her where he came from and what he did in the army and she told him how long she had been in Provo and how many were in her family. He asked where she had been before Provo and she told him of Salt Lake City and Nauvoo.

He listened to her talk of the death of their prophet, Joseph Smith, and their leaving Nauvoo—the bad time in Winter Quarters and the walk to the West. He shook his head. "I hadn't heard about Mormons until I was assigned to come with Governor Cumming. You've gone through a lot for a religion. It's hard to understand. I've never had much to do with religion. I can't say I see why you do it."

Mara tried to explain that life's troubles were temporary. "It's the kingdom of God that matters, and our happiness through all eternity.

We must do God's will on earth if we would dwell with him in happiness forevermore." She knew she sounded like a sermon.

He shook his head again. "Well, it seems a waste of a good life to me, to spend it in misery when you don't have to. Unless you're mighty sure about this kingdom of God." He laughed. "And you tell me. How can you be sure about that, eh?" Mara felt uneasy at his laugh. She wasn't used to trying to explain her religion to anybody. It had always been the part of her life that didn't need explaining. Even if some people didn't always live up to their beliefs, almost everyone she had ever known had at least understood what they were.

"I can tell you, Miss Eastman," he was saying. "It wasn't a pleasant winter. We weren't feeling exactly friendly toward the parties that burned our wagons, whether they were men seeking to protect their eternal happiness or not."

"We were afraid. There is so much to lose. . . ."

"You should have been afraid. They talk of you people as though you are some kind of insects to be exterminated. They say you are human devils." He laughed. "Well, your men may be a little greedy about women, but I haven't seen any horns in this town."

"We are people. Just people." Mara's head was light. This wasn't it. This wasn't what should have happened. She would have to excuse herself, leave. She might cry if she stayed.

But Phillip Hurst leaned toward her. His voice was soft, kind. "I see that. I see that you are people." He put his hand over her two hands. "I mean no harm."

Hurly found a small sharp stone inside the horse's hoof. The smithy was dark except for the white heat of the anvil and the flames of sunshine that shot through the slats in the shed. Hurly was big and heavy. Sweat poured from him. "And don't you run her hard lessin' you want to get her foot sore as a tinker's burn," he said, puffing.

Phillip Hurst smoothed the horse's mane and led her out into the sunshine. "Do you want to try her, Miss Eastman? She can take both of us . . . strong as an ox, swift as a deer," he laughed. He seemed to laugh more than anyone she had ever known.

He mounted with a single leap and reached for Mara. He took her arm and lifted her to the horse's back behind his small English leather saddle.

The horse walked strong under them, her neck high and her mane bristling.

"She's beautiful," Mara said.

"She trots better than any animal I've ever owned and pulls a pony trap like no one else's horse in New England. Took to the mountains and the bad weather like a heroine. I wouldn't go anywhere without her."

The sun was hot in Mara's hair. But she felt the breeze in her face as Maggie stepped into her trot.

"You'd best hold on tight," he said. "Go, Maggie." He touched the mare ever so lightly with his heel and she cantered out so smoothly that Mara barely felt the change, but so quickly that she had to hold to the lieutenant's waist to keep from falling.

He headed the mare north toward the river. Mara tasted the wind, did not speak. As she clung to him, she felt the hard ribs of his body beneath her hands.

He did not stop at the river. He urged Maggie into the water, and the water swirled around the horse's legs.

"Where are we going?"

"You'll see." Out of the water on the opposite shore, he held Maggie to a walk and stopped her in a dense grove of cottonwoods a few yards up from the bank. He dismounted and reached up to Mara. "I wanted to come here with you," he said.

Still, Mara was not afraid. But a haunting uneasiness fell around her now. She pushed her hands against his chest as he drew her from the horse. Why had he brought her *here*? What did Phillip Hurst know of this place? He let go of her waist and turned toward James Bean's cabin, not twenty yards away. Mara had been here on Pawface, many times, with Ashel and Rain and Sully and Nancy. It was the place where John had been shot.

"The old cabin was inhabited by Indians."

"Yes, I know." Mara almost whispered.

"They must have left it long ago."

"Yes, after the war."

"War?"

She cleared her throat and tried to make her voice sound sensible. "Our militia forced the Indians back into the hills. They had been raiding . . . they attacked. . . ." She turned away from him and looked out of the grove away from Bean's cabin. "We never seemed to be able to make a go of it with the Indians."

He stepped close behind her, touching her shoulder. He turned her around and pulled her in front of him. "How about soldiers?" he said. "Do you think you can make a go of it with soldiers?"

Mara's heart seemed to stop. She looked up. "I don't know," she said, feeling a little frightened—of herself, most of all.

He stood with her for a moment and then pulled her into his arms. Without stopping herself, she leaned against him and closed her eyes. "I . . . don't know."

"You don't know . . ." He spoke into her hair. "Well, I don't know if Mormon girls are allowed to be kissed by strangers. . . ." He brought his hands up her arms and held her face. "Miss Eastman . . . Mara . . . you are so beautiful." He drew a finger down her cheek. "Such beauty should not be left . . ." He kissed her. Gently once. Again. Again. She lifted her arms and put her hands in his hair. He caressed her back, still kissing her mouth, her eyes, her brow. He stroked her hair and kissed it. He covered her with kissing. She fell toward him, giving herself to his touching, his mouth.

"Oh lady, lady, you are marvelous," he whispered. "I knew it. I knew it." He breathed as though he had run a long distance. He held her back from him and looked down into her eyes. "Come with me," he said. "Come with me."

He led her to the cabin and pushed her into the tall grass by the west wall, gently holding her as she fell. He fell into the grass beside her and held her to him, his mouth on hers. He rolled away from her, took a breath like a swimmer rising for air. She throbbed with emptiness, waiting for him to return. He turned on his side, looking into her eyes. "I want you, my beautiful one," he said. His hand trembled. He reached for her.

She stiffened. No. Not this. Not so much. She thought only . . . she did not know what she had thought. She wanted him. His urgency was for *her*. She shouldn't have led him so. And now that he needed . . . she had no right . . . it wasn't fair to him . . . but she felt sick in the deepest hollow inside her. She closed her eyes and covered his hand on her blouse. "Oh, Phillip. . . ." she said. "No . . . I can't."

She turned from him. His hand fell away. "You are a virgin," he said.

She did not reply.

"My God."

Mara watched the clouds gathering over the low western hills. Not your God, Phillip, she thought. Not yours. The sun shone hot through the scant shade of the tall grass. She sat up and drew her knees up under her chin.

"I suspected it," he said softly, rolling onto his back in the grass. "I should have known." He lay silent in the grass drawing deep breaths, turned to his stomach, lay with his face on his hands. At last he lifted his head, resting on his elbows. "I thought you would be like any other woman attracted to a man. No matter what you say about . . . eternal happiness." There was anger in his voice.

"Phillip, please. I am . . . I need. . . ."

"You need marriage first. I know. To some pious fellow who would give you a houseful of babies and several dozen other women to share the burdens."

She could not speak for the pain in her heart.

"I thought the Mormon men had just made up a religion that would give themselves an excuse for being like the rest of us. I never could see what was in it for the women." He paused. "They have you convinced, haven't they? For some sick reason, you want that miserable life, you believe in that glorious heavenly kingdom."

Mara was angry now. "What I want, Phillip, is love. And a chance to love back with all I have in me. Not just in a dream, and not just for one moment in the grass by James Bean's cabin." She had said it. He had made her say what she had not even let herself think for a long time. "I want love, Phillip. Forever. Yes. Forever and forever."

He sat up in the grass. He gently stroked her back. The thrill went through her again. "My poor proud beauty," he said softly. "Is there no one? No one for such a fine proud beauty?"

"No," she said. "No one."

"So beautiful. And not one of them has won you yet. It's a miracle." She looked at his face, but there was no trace of mocking in it. "A man could go mad from wanting you," he said. "If only I could take you with me." She looked away from him quickly, afraid her eyes betrayed her disappointment. "I'm leaving for

Camp Scott in the morning," he said. "I didn't want to leave without . . . without you, to remember."

She felt her heart shrink away inside her. It was too late. He
was going.

He stood now and brought her to her feet. "But I'll be back. In a
few weeks." Her head wheeled with too much feeling. He would be
back! She did not know she cried, but her face was wet. He took her
face in his hands and kissed her tears. "Thank God I was enough of
a gentleman not to force you against your will. I don't need that to
remember." He held her gently to him. "I had a religious girl once.
Lord, how I loved her!" He stepped back and looked into Mara's
face once more. "There is something about the religious ones. It's
the light in their eyes, I suspect. There's a light in you, Miss
Eastman, though I think when I found you it was near to going out."

She leaned against him and he held her so close it hurt. "Tell
me," he whispered. "Would you ever see me again?"

She pulled back from him and looked into his face. "Yes,
Phillip," she said.

"I'm not a Mormon. I don't think like a Mormon. I doubt I can
even understand how a Mormon feels. Will you see me again?"

"Yes," she said.

"I will be in Camp Scott for three weeks. Then I'll be back."

"I will be here."

"I'll take you to the hotel now. Your man Dawes will wonder."

"Yes, Dawes," she said. She had not even thought of Dawes.
What would Dawes say? What would he tell her father? She had
grass in her hair. Her dress was crumpled.

"Take me back to the smithy."

He paused. "Yes. Yes, I suppose so." He sighed. "Your
Mormon mother and daddy wouldn't like it if they knew their
daughter had been kissing a soldier."

"No, they would not."

"You knew that when you came here with me."

"We both knew it."

"But you came."

"I came. I am not a child."

"Oh no," he said, throwing his head back and laughing, looking
at her and laughing again. "No child!"

"Phillip. You mock me."

"No, my darling. I'm not mocking you. But you are a puzzling creature."

There was nothing to say then. No way to end it. The wild joy, the passion, the disappointment, the sudden emptiness, the new hope. There were no feelings left but a strange uneasiness. She felt less fear if she kept her eyes closed.

He looked into the distance. "Yes, puzzling. I don't understand. And I think that you understand even less of me."

Mara was silent. There was no more to say.

"I'll take you to the smithy," he said at last, quickly, as though his mind had turned to something else. He leaped into the saddle and brought Mara up after him. At the smithy, he looked at her once more.

"Good-bye, Mara."

"Good-bye, Phillip." Her heart pounded in emptiness. "You will come back again?" He had said he would. She should not have asked. But she could not help it.

"Yes, I will," he said, and he turned on his horse and was gone.

Chapter Three

IN THE SUMMER OF 1858 THE ALLENS RAISED A BUMPER CROP OF peas. Sully had never seen a crop like it. George Allen, hungry for peas, had almost overdone it. There were two half-acre plots separated by the canal, which was full of water almost all summer long. And it was not just the peas that did well. Everything grew. There were potatoes this year, radishes, carrots, turnips, parsley, squash, as well as corn and wheat and chard. Mother Allen teased her husband, saying he had enough peas to feed an army. Her teasing gave the intrepid Will Jones an idea. On the evening of the brawl, Sully had sat in the Eastman parlor, his jaw swollen and aching, his head throbbing as Nancy told Will Jones about the fight in the hotel and the handsome soldier who had rescued Mara. After making sure Mara hadn't been hurt, Will Jones began to talk about peas. Sully and Nancy and the children could pick the peas. Sully would go with Will Jones to Camp Floyd where they could sell the peas.

Brother Eastman was skeptical. "Dangerous," he said.

Will Jones shook his head. "There's little danger. George Allen's got too many peas. Peas will get money. A pea merchant will be a welcome sight in the desert. Everyone will get paid."

All that was left was to ask George Allen. Nancy said she would ask. Father Allen agreed happily, and the next morning Sully rubbed his sore jaw and picked peas with Nancy and the children.

With his load of peas, on his way to pick up Will at the shop, Sully dropped into the hotel to see how Mara was, but she wasn't there. He rounded the counter into the kitchen and found Mr. Dawes helping Mrs. Dawes with the ham.

"My wife says she went off with a soldier man at about quarter to twelve to show him the smithy," Dawes said.

Sully pulled out his pocket watch. "It's been an hour or so now and we're somewhat concerned," Mrs. Dawes said.

"I don't care if she is the hotel owner's daughter," Mr. Dawes sounded angry. "She's got a job and she ought to be here when she's supposed to be here."

Lying on the floor last night with the blood running down his face, Sully had known that he would be worrying about Mara and the U.S. Army. He turned his cart north along Main and stopped at the carding machine shop to pick up Jones. Jones left his hired boy at the carding machine and climbed into the wagon with a hello and his broad grin.

"We'll make money, all right," he assured Sully, glancing at the crop of pea pods safely picked and in baskets. In his lap he smoothed out a dozen bags that had once carried wool. "We can use my wool bags if we need to."

"Have you seen Mara Eastman by chance?" Sully asked him. "One of the soldiers has got her."

"You don't say."

"I do say. And if it's my guess, she's in danger and I say we ought to look for her at the smithy before we go up to the fort."

"You think that independent woman needs anybody's help?" Will Jones exclaimed. Yet in spite of the negative tone in his voice, he seemed quite willing to go with Sully to find her.

She wasn't at the smithy. Hurly had seen her riding off with what he called the "smart dressed lieutenant." He said they both climbed on his lame horse.

Sully struck the cart back toward Main street, frowning. He was as worried as he had been last night when the big one had fisted him to the floor.

"You really care about her, don't you?" Jones said. "I'd like to believe otherwise, but I think she is . . . cold . . . a little snooty. . . ."

"It's her sister's death that done it. And since her mother killed the Indian, the whole family hasn't been the same."

"The Indian?"

"Rain's mother, Spirit of Earth. There is something awful about the murder by your own hand of somebody who lives right with you. If she done it. And believin' she done it is the same as if she was the one."

Jones was quiet for a moment. "That has spoiled Mara?"

"No, that's not all of it. She lost her fiancé killed by Indians, her sister's husband. Then her sister and her niece died, too. Lost her whole family-to-be you might say. . . ."

"So, there are plenty others who would have her. Maybe even a fellow like me could be talked into it. Yet she doesn't want to give anybody the time of day."

"Well, there was somebody else she . . . counted on. He let her down."

Jones was quiet a moment. "You never let her down. . . ."

"Not that I know." For a few miles Sully didn't say anything more. He felt more sadness than he had known in a long time. He looked into the hills. Toward the western ridge near the north shore of the lake, he saw a lone horse against the sky, led by a figure in blue.

"A soldier boy," Jones exclaimed, pointing.

"Walking," Sully said. "His horse as lame as a three-legged ox."

As they drew closer, they saw the beautiful mare limping.

"She's a high class beast," Jones said. "And lame, all right."

At that moment, the soldier in front of them turned and when he saw them come up behind him, he waved. Jones returned the greeting. Sully sat still, remembering too well the men in the hotel last night. Suddenly he felt small hope for their mission as merchants of peas.

"What if they don't like peas?" he said.

"They'll like peas," Jones said with confidence, sounding in good spirits.

"What if they don't allow locals to make sales to the military?" The young soldier looked to be a high ranking officer by his fancy uniform.

"Well, we'll soon find out," Jones said, jumping off the cart.

Sully recognized the soldier now. It was the lieutenant who had broken up the brawl. Sully felt a chill go through him. What was he doing out here with dust on his polished boots and a lame horse?

"Phillip Hurst," he said to William Jones, holding out his hand.

"William Jones. Glad to make your acquaintance. Sully Tuttle," he nodded Sully's way.

"I remember Mr. Tuttle."

Sully shook the hand from his seat in the wagon. "I need to thank you. I'm afraid I didn't do it proper last night."

"That's all right. I regret that my men should have caused you such trouble. I'm glad I could help."

"This is the man that saved you and Mara in the hotel?" Jones said with interest.

"He's the man," Sully answered, narrowing his eyes at Hurst and his lame horse. He had been with Mara. His uniform was wrinkled and dusty. Sully wanted to get down from the cart and knock Phillip Hurst into the ground.

"I think you're just the man we want to see," Jones was saying as though he'd known him for a hundred years.

"Oh?" Hurst turned away to stroke the neck of his lame mare.

"How are you doing in the federal quarters for vegetables? We want to show your men some of our produce. They might enjoy a relief from sourdough and beans."

Sully watched the men talk. Jones had no fear. Sully admired his dauntless friend; he himself could not have done the talking to anyone. Least of all to Phillip Hurst. What had he done with Mara? If he had done her harm, Sully vowed he would never rest till he had done Phillip Hurst his due.

"So we propose to see if anyone wants our peas," Jones was coming back to the cart with Hurst. "We'll give you a ride the rest of the way and we can tie your horse to the back."

"Much obliged." Hurst leaped into the cart. He was very tall, yet slim and graceful, the tight curls of his black hair flat against the sweat on his neck. A man like that could turn a woman's head. He reminded Sully of Bret Hunt. Sully's heart twisted inside him. He was worried Mara wouldn't see this man for what he truly was, worse than Bret Hunt, a snake in the grass. "We'll see if we can't use a few of your peas," Hurst said. Sully felt sick.

"If you like the idea, there is more we could provide you. We spend our lives producing food. We'd be glad to let you share the benefits of our work."

Sully was amazed at how Jones could make taking someone's money sound like a favor to the other fellow.

The camp sat in the wide valley behind the ridge that rose across from the lake. Sully drove north and then west along the lake's north shore. They crossed the lowest foothills by trail, reaching main quarters at about supper time, coming to the neat camp with stars and stripes waving over it from a very tall pole. The tents were staked out in rows, one after another, as exact as a checkerboard. General Johnston's tent stood in the southeast, its doors facing the mountain, a set of smaller supply tents and cook tents surrounding it.

"We haven't had many visitors, not even Indians," Phillip Hurst said. "Though we've had a few."

Four stanchions of hastily cut wood in each corner of the camp stood from an attempt to build small forts supplied with guns set up on stilts, gunner nests, gun holes, and a lookout. "Indians don't come here much," Hurst laughed. "They sense they'd never get past their own noses so to speak."

The great brown plains stretched beyond the fort, and in the bleak distance, they fell upward to the blue-topped hills and the hazy sky. "Out there somewhere are hundreds of Indians wondering whatever will become of this land," Phillip Hurst said. "There's plenty of it out there but I have a feeling they won't take this piece of it again."

On the road into camp they were met by stares, hoots, wolf calls, threats, foul language. Sully suspected it was nothing to what would have happened if Phillip Hurst had not been riding in the cart with them.

"Well, what do we have here!" A gray-haired man stood in front of Johnston's tent, his hat crooked and his uniform unbuttoned to the waist. Sully thought he looked like one of the rioters in the hotel last night, but this soldier wore a patch over his eye. He didn't remember anyone wearing a patch over his eye.

"Beware the natives!"

"No, watch out for Mormons now!"

"What do we have here?" His voice was gruff. His big strawberry nose was surrounded by the furrows in his cheeks.

"Captain Cradlebaugh, sir!" Hurst smiled at him and saluted as he leaped down from the cart.

Cradlebaugh swore. "Where'd you pick 'em up, Hurst?"

A crowd gathered. Sully watched Jones' face. He seemed unafraid. Jones was walking into hell as though he were going to enjoy it.

"Gentlemen, beings as how we're domestically rather than militarily oriented. . . ." Sully listened to Jones' voice wishing he himself could be a thousand miles away from here. Jones kept talking cheerfully and fast. "We've been growing produce the likes of which you have not seen in this part of the desert." Jones stretched his hand out to indicate the rocky hill under the camp. "And from the lush green agriculture of our valley which you see below us . . ." Jones was standing on the cart, talking like a preacher to a crowd of hecklers. Sully wanted to disappear into the earth. Jones swept his arm toward Provo. "We've been raising more food in Provo than we can use, gentlemen, and for a small price we're willing to sell you some of our most delicious peas." He pointed to the produce in the cart. The soldiers began to shout back and forth amongst themselves.

"Hah! Take off his hat! Where's his horns!"

"You want to see his horns?"

"I don't see 'em! Show me!"

A big soldier suddenly leaped up and knocked Jones' hat from his head. He rubbed his hands in Jones' hair. "He got no horns at all," the soldier said, pretending surprise.

"You mean he's a regular man?" another soldier shouted.

"I don't believe it! See if he's a man!"

"I'll find out in a hurry!"

Another leaped to the cart and dived for Jones' pants. Sully slapped at the soldier with the ends of the reins he held in his fists. The horse started forward with a sudden jerk.

"Much obliged for the ride!" Phillip Hurst yelled, leaning back his curly black head to laugh and waving his hand as the cart moved.

"Get him, Emery," another voice hollered. The men jerked the horse back and flooded to the cart. Five or six climbed in before the side of the cart began to break. They grabbed the baskets of peas and flung their hands into them with glee, tossing the small green pods into the air, flinging them out onto the ground. Jones sailed out with his fists, hitting, hollering: "Damn you, damn you all! You'll pay for this!" Sully gathered as many of the baskets into his arms as he could and bent over them, protecting his father-in-law's hard-won crop with his body. Several blows from soldiers fell on his back and shoulders.

"Mormon peas! Who wants Mormon peas!" the soldiers began to chant.

"All right. All right now," the gray-headed Cradlebaugh moved over to the broken cart. "Come on, men. Leave the Mormon pea pickers alone."

But no one heeded him. Jones was still throwing his fists into the air hitting but knocking no one down. A big man grabbed Jones' neck. Jones hit him in the head. Angry, the soldier grunted and closed his fingers on Jones' throat. Jones made a strangled sound.

"That's enough now," Cradlebaugh came forward. "You'll rouse the general and he's in a good slumber." Cradlebaugh pulled at the trouser leg of the big soldier who finally loosened his hands and pushed Jones away. Jones steadied himself and nursed his throat with both hands. Sully's back ached.

"All right you two. Now get on out of here."

Jones glared at Cradlebaugh. His voice was level and firm. "We'll go when we have been paid for our peas."

A breathless silence fell over the group now. The big man clambered away from the wagon, brushing off his sleeves. Sully's heart beat faster. He would have turned the cart and vanished. Will Jones stood still on the lip of the broken wagon.

"We brought produce with the intention of selling it, not giving it away for your amusement. You've taken it. You owe us fifty cents."

Cradlebaugh's one eye blinked, glared into Jones' steady gaze.

"Owe you fifty cents!" The big soldier laughed.

"We have government supplies enough for our needs," Cradlebaugh said.

"You also have fresh peas. They are lying on the ground," Jones said. "They are yours now, and you owe us fifty cents. In the American way. . . ."

"Americans! This Mormon wildcat calls himself an American! You're as American as my Chinese mother-in-law." The camp broke out into loud laughter. "Fifty cents for dirt!"

It was getting noisy again. Old Cradlebaugh threw up his hand. He was stocky, with long arms that reached to his knees. "Hold it!" he hollered. "Hold it!"

"Give them fifty cents," Hurst said when there was quiet again. "They were worth the fun. Eh, boys?"

A chorus rose behind Hurst. Sully could not see for the hatred of Phillip Hurst that clouded his eyes.

Jones stood without flinching. "As soon as we get our fifty cents we'll be gone," he said.

Cradlebaugh looked at Jones for a long time. Sully didn't care about the peas anymore. All he thought of was Phillip Hurst, laughing at the two Mormon pea sellers. He wondered what Mara had had to do with him. Phillip Hurst moved through the crowd of soldiers, laughing, slapping them on their backs. Sully could not hear what he said.

"All right, Mormons," Cradlebaugh said. "Take your fifty cents and be gone with you." He reached into his pocket and brought out the money."

"And for another fifty cents, we'll give you the rest of the load," Jones said. Cradlebaugh looked at Jones, looked at the money. Sully had protected three pecks of peas. Only two had been spilled. "A real bargain," Jones said. "Half again as many for the same price and in baskets that haven't been spilled." He split a pod and held the peas out to Cradlebaugh.

With his one dark eye peering from beneath a bushy gray brow, Cradlebaugh stared at the peas, then reached for them and threw them into his mouth.

"Not bad," he said as he chewed. "Not bad at all!" It was supper time. "You better try some of these," he said to the man next to him.

Two soldiers bent down and scooped a handful of pods from the dust. They split the pods and rolled the peas into their mouths. "Could be worse," one of them said, bending down again to scoop a handful and throw them over his head into the crowd. The men began to whoop and holler and shell peas as fast as they could go, tossing the pods by handfuls to one another like candy on the fourth of July.

"Aw, go on with you," the one-eyed Captain cried to William Jones. He reached in his pocket. "I've got a a dollar, if you'll be gone with it." Jones leaped from the wagon and began unloading the peas. Sully, eager to get out of the place, leaped down, too.

"Get them empty flour bags," Jones said, taking the baskets from the broken boards. "We'll empty the peas into them bags. They cost hardly nothing. Save our peck baskets."

Sully worked watching Cradlebaugh standing in the dust eyeing them with his one beady eye, his fists on his hips. Phillip Hurst leaned on his lame mare, laughing at the men eating their dusty peas.

"Bloody Mormon peas!" The men were laughing, too. "Bloody Mormon peas."

When the peas were in bags and the baskets back in the cart, Jones turned to Cradlebaugh. He pointed to the peas. Then he held out his hand.

"Do you think he deserves it, Cradlebaugh?" one of the men hollered.

"Kick him out of camp."

"Fifty cents will buy a whole bottle of hard whiskey!" another shouted.

But Sully could see Cradlebaugh was done with the fooling. "You're a hard man, Mormon," he said to Will Jones, and he gave him the coins. "We aren't here to cheat you, but we want to see justice done." Sully heard a hint of something unsaid in Cradlebaugh's words: "We want to see justice done." Sully looked at Cradlebaugh. He was cool and very strong. Phillip Hurst had disappeared into a tent.

Sully wanted nothing to do with selling more peas or squash, or lettuce or carrots, or produce of any kind, even when Jones presented him twenty-five cents for his crew's labor to pick the crop. Jones gave the Allens forty cents and kept thirty-five in his own pocket.

"That's fair. Forty percent for sales," Jones said. "There wouldn't be any money at all if I hadn't stood up on the wagon for it." Sully had to agree that was true. He had to admit that the success of their sales, if it could be called a success, was entirely because of Jones. But Sully had thought the peas worth more. Jones agreed that the next load must fetch a correct price.

"They'll think they got a terrific bargain. They'll enjoy their dinner. And they'll welcome us when we come again."

But Sully didn't go with Jones on the following day. He told Jones he would go back to his north fields and try to raise something Jones could sell, but no, he wouldn't do any selling himself.

But Ashel wanted to go. Ashel was big for seventeen and as game as ever for excitement. Sully knew Ashel did a good man's work at the Eastman place, cultivating the fields, milking the cows, tending to the calving, and building sheds and fences, while his father worked at the investment office, stimulating business for his small bank. Ashel said he would go with Jones to the Army post. Sister Eastman was not pleased.

"I don't think you and your ideas for commerce are going to do anyone good, Brother Jones," she said. "Ashel, you stay home here."

"Please, Mother. Mr. Jones picked up some money."

"In a brawl."

"Let him go, Sister Eastman," Jones said. "No harm will come to him. There won't be a brawl today." Jones had packed squash, cucumbers, and beets in his peck baskets.

"I need you in the fields, son," Brother Eastman said gruffly.

"Please, Papa. My gosh, let me go do something I want to for once. If we raise the stuff and can't use it all, we've got to sell some of it. Work ourselves into a market."

"We'll do all right," Jones said. Sully wished he could be so sure.

Mara was not there to put in a word for her brother because she had gone early this morning to the hotel. In the back of the yard, Caroline and Rain came out of the henhouse with eggs gathered in their aprons. Caroline hurried to Ashel. Rain followed.

"I'm going, Papa," Ashel said.

Brother Eastman stood very tall, his hands in his pockets. His eyes narrowed. Sister Eastman came to his side. Ashel stood facing them, his lanky frame as tall as his father's but not yet filled out. Sully looked at Ashel. He had become a handsome young man, with his light brown hair and bright blue eyes. There was strength in his shoulders and his brown arms.

No one spoke for a long time. Though he admired his stout-hearted friend Will Jones, Sully wished Will would just give it up.

"I guess let him go," Sister Eastman said, trying to stop trouble between Brother Eastman and Ashel.

Brother Eastman's eyes seemed far away as he answered. "Well, if he gets killed, send us his body."

Sully thought he sounded half serious. Jones laughed. But then the laughter seemed to make everyone uneasy.

When Ashel turned to leap onto the cart, Caroline ran toward him again, the eggs rocking in her apron. "Can I go?" she begged Ashel.

"No," Ashel said. "You can't."

There were good-byes, good lucks. Sully stood quietly, glad to be going home. Nancy came to the door with Jones' two children clutching at her skirts. She gave Jones some bread and cheese for a noon meal. Sully helped Nancy and the children into the wagon hitched behind George Washington and old Mrs. Artemus Blake.

"My stars, girl, get back." Ashel was trying to get Caroline to leave him. He turned away from her. "You can't go, and that's that."

"Oh, please. Please, Ashel. Mama, I want to go too."

"No, girl. Don't think of it," Sister Eastman said.

"Caroline, get back," Brother Eastman said. "They need to move the cart."

Caroline had a stubbornness like none Sully had ever seen in a child. And she tagged Ashel every minute. Suddenly the cart began to move forward. Caroline tucked her apron in one hand, holding the eggs like a sack of marbles, and ran alongside the cart, hanging on to it with her other hand.

"Get off there, Caroline!"

"Ashel, you meanie!" she screamed. "I want to go."

Ashel looked down at her with a grin. As she ran, she lost hold on the cart, and to get a better grip, she let go of her apron. As her hand flew up, the apron fell, and the eggs spilled onto the ground and broke in a big sticky mess in the grass.

"Caroline! Now look what you've done!" Sister Eastman cried.

"Get out of the mess, Sobe," Rain said in her patient voice. Then she tried to pick up one or two of the eggs. But they were all smashed.

Now Caroline lost hold on the cart completely, and she stood in the road alone, her hands on her apron as Jones and Ashel drove off waving and laughing. Sully watched her turn angrily and walk toward them. He hadn't really noticed Caroline for a long time. She was beautiful, almost a young woman. She would be thirteen years old before long. Her anger reddened her cheeks, put a light into her eyes. Her hair was the color of corn silk.

She didn't say anything, but she began to storm off behind the house, Rain following her.

"Clean up them eggs, girl. You spilled them," Brother Eastman said.

She stormed back, picked up her apron, and without hesitation grabbed the sticky eggs with her bare hands and plopped them into the clean cloth, wiping her hands on her skirt. Sister Eastman, exasperated, shook her head.

Rain knew Caroline never left Ashel's side. And she thought she knew just how far Caroline would go to be with him.

Rain followed Caroline to the pump, and Caroline told Rain she was taking Tarboy out to the hills for a short ride. She would look for some berries for supper. She would be back soon. She would finish her chores before she went.

"Just tell the others I've gone for a little while," Caroline said.

"I'll go with you," Rain said quietly.

Caroline stopped. She looked a little nervous. Rain did not speak. She could never speak much. She had always been filled with quiet. She was almost twice as old as Caroline. And she should watch over her.

"I will go with you," she said again.

"No, I'll go by myself. It's all right."

"I need the ride anyway," Rain said firmly, feeling responsible. "I can go with you at least a short way."

Caroline's deep green flashing eyes looked stern.

"We're going to see if we can find some berries," Rain said to Mama, who herded Sobe into the house after Sully and Nancy left. Mama seemed anxious and worried for Ashel. "All right," she said. Rain knew Mama trusted her. "But chores first, girls."

Rain hurried through her chores. When she finished, she looked for Caroline in the house, but she did not find her. She ran to the barn, and there was Caroline just climbing onto Tarboy's back. Rain did not take the time to saddle Pawface. The mare nuzzled Rain's hand as she placed the bridle into her mouth. Rain was at least a hundred yards behind Tarboy when she followed Caroline out into the road. Caroline would not wait for her. Tarboy would not have waited, anyway. Rain knew Caroline could handle him, but he was the most excitable horse she had ever known.

Tarboy was the product of Sully's wild mare, Tar, probably studded by George Washington, although there had been other horses in the field that summer and it was hard to tell. Tarboy was lean and sleek. His coat was the same shiny black as his mother's, but his temperament was less predictable. Sully had sold two other colts as well as Tarboy to the Eastmans the year of the famine, but Tarboy had been the children's favorite. They had not been able to ride him for two-and-a-half years until Ashel finally broke him and let Caroline learn to handle his reins. Caroline loved challenges and Tarboy was difficult.

Rain could hardly get old Pawface to catch up with Tarboy. Pawface almost lumbered now, as she had begun to age. Rain stayed a short way behind, once or twice galloping to catch sight of Caroline as she turned a corner or turned into the fields off of North Main.

After about two miles, Rain knew, as she suspected, that Caroline was not going for berries. For she was headed northwest through the valley and around the north shore of the lake on the way to Camp Floyd, to follow Ashel.

Rain suddenly felt angry, and she dug her bare feet into Pawface's flanks. Pawface responded, leaped unexpectedly, and with sudden speed, was close behind Tarboy in an instant. Tarboy began to run. Surprised, Caroline screamed. She lost control. Rain followed as closely as she could on Pawface, but Tarboy sprang into the distance on his young eager legs, beating the ground.

Rain was afraid. Caroline was standing in the saddle now, bending over Tarboy's neck, holding on fiercely. But Tarboy began to buck and try to shake her off. They were at least four miles north of town now, west of the river. Rain thought Sully or Jones and Ashel might still be on the road, but there was no one in sight. Caroline screamed once more and the horse veered into a gulch and jumped an arroyo with a great easy stride. But the jump loosened Caroline's feet from the stirrups and she flew headlong into the dry grass. Rain closed her eyes, seeing the pinafore sail through the air, Caroline's arms like small sticks between her body and the ground. Tarboy did not stop, but sped into the distance, free of his burden.

"Oh," Rain breathed, hurting with a terrible weight of guilt. She should never have started up behind Tarboy. But it was too late to undo it now. She could not ride the horse backwards, her old mother would have told her.

Then, suddenly, Tarboy stopped in a faraway field of young grass, and the hot silence bore down on Rain's heart.

Caroline did not move. Frightened, Rain went to her, knelt by her and turned her head from the dust crowding into her mouth. The hot sun beat on her head with fury. Rain shaded her from the sun.

"Caroline!" Rain whispered. "Oh Great Father of Heaven! Caroline!" Breathless, Rain gently nudged Caroline's shoulders, pushed aside the golden hair. Still Caroline did not move. Rain sat back on her heels and looked out at the bleak brown earth that spread about her for endless miles. The lake shimmered in the west beyond a few straggling trees, and behind the lake lay the brown hills which shielded them from the military camp. "Caroline!" She thought about Caroline. She thought about what she would do.

For a few moments, she sat letting the sun beat on her head. She feared the hot morning. She feared Caroline's unconsciousness was close to death. She made a small tent of Caroline's pinafore to cut out the hot July sun on her arms and neck, and held the pinafore with a steady hand. The girl lay in the dust like a limp rag, both arms broken. Rain saw that one of the bones came out from the flesh.

"Oh, Great Father," Rain whispered again several times, praying to her old Ute god Tovats, or the Mormon God, the Heavenly Father of the Eastmans she had learned about in their Sunday School. She prayed to whoever would listen. There must be help.

As the crow flies, Sully's farm was a mile east of where Caroline lay. Rain thought about Sully. He had been at the Eastman house when they left, but he would be on his way home now. If only she could bring Sully with her heart.

In the days of her grandfather, the Ute medicine man sent dreams, received messages, sometimes over two hundred miles. She remembered sitting at her grandfather's feet hearing him tell stories of his own father's hunting journeys, of the time he spoke to his grandfather in a dream, telling him where he was when he lay wounded in the hills.

"How do you send messages, Grandfather?" she once asked him.

"You sit very still," Grandfather said. "You are quiet, still. Do not think of other things. And never get angry. That is bad. Be always steady-hearted."

It was the nature of Sipapu. She had also been as quiet inwardly as her father, as passive. She had often waited for messages "from the great father." "No one tells me your grandfather is dead," Sipapu had said to Rain. "But I know he is dead." A week later, the Utes found him murdered, face down in a creek. "Grandfather sent me a message in a dream."

Now Rain sat still, remembering what it had been like to be an Indian, a human being, as they called themselves. Often she felt she was no longer an Indian. She remembered those moments of her early childhood when she lived close to her grandfather, when she and her mother spent hours in her grandfather's house, weaving or grinding herbs for his poultices. Then she remembered her grandfather's death and then her mother's death. She heard the sighing wind, the breath of her mother's voice in her ear. The only one who could possibly hear the beating of her heart might be Sully, if he would listen, for she could not leave Caroline. She touched Caroline's hair, lying in golden curls in the dust. Someone must come.

She bent her face in her hands and sat very still, angry with herself for allowing her heart to respond to Caroline's disobedience as a white mother would respond to her white child. "A child does wrong, it is for him to worry. If you become angry, that is for you." Many times Sipapu had spoken to Rain about children. She had wanted so much for Rain to give her a child with Kickingboot. Rain's mind passed over those moments in Kickingboot's tent. She had almost forgotten. She had put from her mind all that had happened before she had decided to live forever with the Eastmans. She had decided not only to forget about her life with the people she had known as a young child, but to find protection from them with the help of the Eastman family and Sully, the Allens, Brother Jones, and the others.

Now the memories of Kickingboot seemed to crowd toward her with dark fury. She tried to still the small and great fears that began humming in her breast. She opened her eyes. Caroline still did not move.

Now, if Rain followed the white man's ways, she would run frantically toward Camp Floyd, or Sully's ranch, for help. But though she scolded herself for the anger that had caused her pain, she could not move now. With all the human being left in her rising to quiet her, she sat still. Her body filled with heat, with tension, with singing nerves. But her heart was stilled by a longing, a reach. Of all the white men she knew, surely Sully could hear her. He was the kindest of them.

"Sully," she thought. She reached for his blue eyes, outlined his face in her mind.

It was not sleep, yet something like sleep . . . deep falling away into shadows, away from the sun that beat on her head, a whirling into emptiness, a melting into the ground where she sat. She felt the air closing in on her brain, and she saw Sully's face as clearly as if he were before her at this moment.

She was not sure how long she squatted on the ground, her elbows on her knees, her head in her hands, the darkness floating in her brain. But she started when she heard a low moan. She lifted open her heavy eyes, and the brilliant light blinded her. Caroline was moving. Caroline! Rain stooped over to her and placed a hand on her back.

"Oh." Caroline's cry was guttural.

"Don't move."

"I can't move."

"Stay. Just stay. Quiet. Your arms are broken."

In a few moments, Rain, who had lived with anxious people for a long time now, rose to her feet and found her limbs trembling. Her legs were hot and wet. As she rose, she felt a breeze in her hair. She stood for a moment, searching the horizon. Over the small hills to the west of the lake would be the camp of the soldiers still almost twelve or fifteen miles away. Sully was closer. She measured the hills, the mountains she knew well. In the distance, against the eastern hills, she thought she could see a figure on a horse. She stared for a long time. A silhouette against the sun rose

like a phantom out of the windblown brown earth. It was Sully.
She waited for him.

Sully recognized Rain from a great distance as she stood alone in
the empty land. She looked tall, her hair very black and blowing in a
soft breeze away from her face. When he saw her, he spurred the
horse forward. He saw that beside Rain on the ground lay a heap of
someone, someone in trouble. Rain was silent when he came to her.
She had not been crying, but trouble had taken the brightness from
her eyes.

"Caroline!" Sully dismounted and knelt beside the broken body.

"She's still alive," Rain whispered. But she had again lost consciousness.

Sully touched her. She must not be moved. Then he caught
Rain's gaze as she stared at the empty horizon.

"We'll build a stretcher," he said. "I'll fetch wood."

"Wood?"

"There are some trees near the lake. Stay here." He leaped to
George Washington's back and rode west as fast as he could go.
He found two saplings, chopped them, and tied them to his saddle.
His heart pounded in fear for Caroline.

Rain was waiting for him, watching Caroline. He wrapped the
strong poles into both ends of the wool saddle blanket and made a
tight, narrow stretcher. While he tied the twigs close together, he
talked to Rain.

"I had a feeling that you were here," he said softly. "I was there
at the Eastmans' when you left. Then the strangest feeling came
over me that you needed me, and how I knew you were here, I'll
never know, but I just came."

Rain did not speak. She lowered her eyes. Her hair fell over the
high bones on her cheeks. Sully had never noticed how beautiful
Rain's hair was.

"It looks like Caroline's back is hurt. We shouldn't move her,
but we can tie her to these poles and cradle her alongside the horse
or maybe tie her between two horses and yoke them. Do you think
it will work?" He looked at Rain, but she did not look up.

"How did it happen?" Sully said. But then he knew. He knew
Caroline and Rain. And he knew Pawface and Tarboy. "Pawface
sometimes frightens Tarboy," he said.

Now the pain came into Rain's eyes. It spread on her face. Sully felt it. He felt her pain. He felt a quickness in her breath that frightened him for a moment. He knelt to Caroline's side and gently, carefully moved the stretcher under her and tied her body to the trees with a hemp rope, her arms securely to her sides.

"She is broken. So broken. It is so. . . ." He couldn't find a word. "To see her like this . . . she was so lovely." Sully stood up and looked at Rain. Her eyes were dark with fear. "Oh Rain, please. I can't . . . it was an accident. She never should have disobeyed. She should never have taken Tarboy. But it is is done. Don't blame yourself. I'm not blaming you." He reached out to her and put his hand on her shoulder. Suddenly Rain's eyes filled with tears. She leaned away from him and crossed her arms in front of her as though a sharp pain ripped through her. Then she fell forward to the ground and began to sob. Sully knelt to her. He had never before seen an Indian cry.

Ashel was full of satisfaction as he rode back into town in the cart with Will Jones, the five dollars heavy in his pocket. He could see a prosperous future before him, a good life as a merchant-farmer. His mother and father would be sorry they were so doubtful of him. Wouldn't that pile of coins on the table make Caroline's green eyes shine?

Pulling the cart up in front of the house, Ashel didn't even wait for Will Jones to climb down. He jumped to the front porch, ran to the parlor, and dumped the pile of coins on the table shouting, "Look at this!" His voice echoed in the silence. Mama sat in her big chair, her face white, Papa grim beside her holding her hand. Sully and Nancy were there, and the children, all of them pale as ghosts. Rain sat facing the hearth, her back bent, her head in her hands. Ashel's blood froze inside him. Where was Caroline? No one spoke. He whispered it. "Caroline."

Papa rose from Mama's side and came to put a hand on Ashel's shoulder. "She's been hurt, son. Doctor says. . . ." Papa cleared his throat. "Doctor says she will never walk again."

Ashel spent the evening riding, away from the house. He could not even go in to see her. Caroline. He tried to escape his last vision of her running along holding to the cart, pleading to go with him, looking up into his eyes.

She had always been there, tagging along behind him since she was the little cousin from the Boston side of Mama's almost otherwise extinct family. She was cute and easy to tease. She would get mad and pout and stamp her foot. He liked to make her stamp her foot like that. As he got older, she annoyed him sometimes. He had tried for a while to avoid her, to sneak away. But he found he missed her. Finally, he accepted her constant presence. He had come to need her. He hadn't wanted her to come to Camp Floyd, though. He didn't want her there, around all those soldiers. And besides, it was time he went off to do his man's work without her. She should stay home.

For the first weeks after the accident, Ashel carried his heavy guilt without relief. Guilt that he had been the cause of her accident, and guilt at the odd sense of freedom he felt at being able to move around for the first time in many years without Caroline behind him. The guilt grew, pressing down on him. It all pressed down. Caroline's lifelessness, the grim quiet that surrounded her and filled the house, the large hard casts on her body, her dull sad eyes. Ashel wanted to push it all off, to scream, to shout at the heavens to let them all out of it, out of the guilt and the grief. He heard his mother's prayers and wished he felt he too could be heard by God. Nothing seemed to do any good.

Once or twice he thought of getting drunk. Ashel hadn't seen many drunks before the army came. Now Chatwin's distillery and the brewery, both businesses instituted against the wishes of Brigham Young, began to flourish as no other ventures in town. Even the East House Hotel business picked up. The ride to Camp Floyd was nearly four hours, and often the soldiers were too drunk and tired after their evenings in town to ride all that way in the dark, so they would bring their liquor with them and spend their nights in the hotel.

Ashel knew all the good Mormon mothers and fathers watched their boys with fear. For some of the boys, the crowds of rowdy, gambling soldiers were a great attraction, as Ashel well knew. But for himself, they were just a bunch of loud brawling sots, little more than worthless scum. Ashel liked to work. He had no time for wasting. Until the accident.

Now time seemed to hang on him. The moments of guilt and anguish stretched into long weeks of waiting and watching. The darkness of the shorter days began to fold over the valley like sleep. Only Papa dared to say anything funny, like "Bee feathers! We're glad she's alive!" For a while, no one else said much anymore. Caroline lay so still. Even Ashel could not make her smile. Sobe sat beside her practicing his reading. Rain and Mama made hot packs for her swelling and cool cloths for her face. The doctor came every day.

But there was no noticeable change. Mama watched Caroline closely. She watched Ashel, too. He could often feel her eyes on him. What did she want? What was she afraid of? Why did she watch so?

Ashel went to the hotel on a hot night in August. The young lieutenant who often sat in the dining room with Mara was there. Hurst. The one who had saved Sully when he got knocked down trying to rescue Mara from the soldiers their first day in town. Hurst had a bottle on the table before him, as usual. Tonight it was dark red. The lieutenant called to him as he had before. "Have a drink, Ashel?" Tonight for the first time, Ashel wanted to say yes, all right, he would.

But Mara would see. The same as his mother, Mara would watch him. She may laugh and flirt with the lieutenant and with the others. But if ever she caught Ashel's eye, she always looked at him with that same dark watchful stare.

Yet, being at the hotel, being near Mara, was the only thing that seemed to relieve him a little from the heaviness of Caroline's tragedy—even without getting drunk. He knew Mara had resented his being there at first. He wondered if she thought he had come to spy on her, watch over her and the lieutenant. Ashel knew that Sully hated Phillip Hurst, though he would never come right out and say why. Sully never did say much about what concerned Mara. It was Will Jones who told Ashel about meeting Hurst on the way to Camp Floyd with his lame horse. It was Will Jones who had reported what the blacksmith said.

But Mara seemed almost glad for Ashel to come into the hotel now. She thanked him for being there to take her home on the evenings when Sully and Nancy could not come. The Tuttles stayed more often on the north farm as harvest drew close. Sully had cultivated a hundred new acres in the fields on the bench and planted a couple of orchards. It seemed that the only time he came into town now was when he wanted to talk with Papa and Will Jones about their Deseret Manufacturing Company and their dream of building a giant woolen mill someday. Will, with his unfaltering energy, seemed to believe a woolen mill would be a smart economic move.

As Mara cleaned up the kitchen with Mr. and Mrs. Dawes, Ashel would sit at a side table and watch Hurst and the other soldiers raise their glasses to "General Johnston's army," the "Captain's trench," the "mess table," the "Captain's dog," and "the suspenders on Cradlebaugh's socks." Tonight he heard a toast he hadn't heard before: "A toast for Mara Eastman, the prettiest wench in Provo." He looked up. Mara had come out of the kitchen with a tray of clean glasses. She did not see Ashel. She went to the table where Phillip Hurst sat with three other men. The men reached out for her, but she twirled away from them, until she came near Hurst. He grabbed her by the wrist, then held her close. Mara pulled away from him, pretending to be angry and offended, her dark eyes flashing. Hurst and the others laughed loud. Hurst leaned back in his chair and roared with laughter. Mara smiled and tossed her curls like a common saloon girl, her face bright.

As she turned away from the men, Ashel saw that she noticed him sitting at his side table. The smile disappeared and her face turned red from her neck to her hair. She went into the kitchen.

Ashel left without waiting to take Mara home. When he saw her the next day, Mara didn't say anything about it and neither did Ashel, though he thought he should. He wondered if this went on all the time when he wasn't there. He hadn't seen it before. He wondered that Mr. and Mrs. Dawes didn't notice, didn't tell Papa. He thought he should tell Mara what she looked like in there with those men. But she was old enough to know what she was doing, he guessed. And as the day wore on, he had to admit that he hadn't been as shocked as he had pretended to himself to be. He had to admit that it was good seeing some life in Mara again, after years of her quiet retreat. It was good seeing her, seeing anyone in the family, alive—even like this.

Ashel went back to the hotel again that night. Hurst was there. He looked slightly drunk. He saw Ashel, and he picked up his bottle of liquor and came to Ashel's table and leaned over him. His breath smelled of strong alcohol. "May I sit down?" he asked, his voice a little thick.

"Yes, fine. Help yourself," Ashel said. He didn't see Mara anywhere.

"You know, this place reminds me of a pub," Hurst said, pouring himself another drink and spilling some.

"A pub?"

"A pub, son. A public house. A friendly British proper virgin . . . *version* . . . of a saloon." Hurst threw his whiskey down his throat with one swallow. He looked straight at Ashel. "I know what you think," he said. "*You* think your sister doesn't deserve to work in a place like this. Don't you?" His voice was blurred. His throat sounded full of gravel.

"I don't . . . I don't know. I don't know what you mean."

"You think she's better than the rabble that frequents this place." He waved his glass at the soldiers at the other tables. "Well, she thinks so, too. She sticks her nose in the air all hoity-toity. She's the owner's daughter, you know. Of course you know. She thinks she's better than the best of us." He stopped for a moment. Ashel didn't like it. He thought Lieutenant Hurst liked Mara. He didn't like him to talk this way. He was drunk. "But she isn't," Hurst started talking again. "She isn't one bit better than any of us, not her. She's no nun. She'd as soon climb in bed as the next 'un if it weren't for her religion tightenin' her up tighter than bee lips."

Ashel stared. His eyes felt stung open. Hurst looked up, into Ashel's eyes. He sat back and rubbed his head. "Don't get me wrong, son. I don't mean any offense. You got a ready sister, that's all. You got a ready sister. And one of these days she won't keep the lid on it all."

Hurst left then, and Ashel sat still, feeling sick in his stomach. He didn't understand what Hurst could be saying. Mara had always been a little spirited. At least until Bret Hunt married Hannah Wright. But what could Hurst mean? What did he know of what Mara really was?

That night on the way home Ashel could hardly make himself speak. Mara climbed on Pawface behind him. She smelled of perfume. "You sure you're ready to go?" he said. He knew he sounded mean. He couldn't help it. He hoped Mara wouldn't notice. But she did.

"What did he say to you?" she asked, almost in a whisper.

Ashel stiffened in the saddle. He took a deep breath. "Mara, are you in some kind of trouble?"

"Ashel, what did he say to you?"

He would have to say something now. He would have to. He was her brother. "Mara, you've been seeing that army lieutenant, haven't you?" The sound of Pawface's hooves on the dirt sounded like thunder in the silence. He felt Mara's hands tremble where she held onto his waist, but her voice when she finally spoke was calm.

"Yes, Ashel, I have."

Ashel's head pounded.

"But you know it would kill Mother and Father if they knew," she continued. "So you mustn't tell them."

Ashel didn't say anything.

"Please, Ashel. You mustn't tell. Not ever."

"When do you see him, Mara? When?"

Mara reached around him and pulled back at the reins to turn Pawface toward the park.

"Ashel, if I tell you, you must never breathe a word of it to Mama and Papa. I will take you into my confidence, but you must promise never to tell."

Ashel's voice stuck in his throat. He couldn't speak. But he knew she would tell him anyway.

"Not here," she said. "Let's walk." They climbed down from Pawface, and under the bright September moon began leading her down Center Street and into the park. The air held a hint of a fresh autumn breeze.

"I told Mr. Dawes that I would not be coming in now until two o'clock because of Caroline. I still leave at eleven, and I go to meet Phillip at the river."

"My gosh, Mara. How do you expect to get away with that? Surely Mr. Dawes will say something to Papa. . . ."

"Mr. Dawes is afraid of Papa, Ashel. He never says anything to him. Nor does Mrs. Dawes."

"But Lieutenant Hurst is not even a Mormon! He's a gentile!"

"Oh Ashel, you've got to hear me," Mara said, her eyes wide. "Ashel, maybe you wouldn't understand yet, although I believe you could." Her voice rose now. He was afraid for her. "Oh, Ashel, please. I would never have told you if I didn't believe you could understand."

In Mara's voice was a kind of sadness he had never heard before. Her eyes seemed to burn from a fire inside her. He hadn't seen that kind of fire in the girls he knew.

"When you get older and no one comes to love you . . ." Now her voice was softer. "Please understand, Ashel." She closed her eyes. "He came to me. He made me feel like a queen." For a moment she stopped in the road. "Of course, we can't really be together unless we marry. And, of course, I can't marry him unless he finds the truth. But . . . ," and then she paused. "I love him."

Her voice trembled. But Ashel could feel something firm and sure behind the trembling. He was quiet for a long time listening to her talk.

"What are you going to do?" he asked her at last.

"Love him. Convert him to the truth. He's reading the Book of Mormon."

"Mara. He's army through and through."

"He's wonderful, Ashel."

He's wonderful. Ashel sensed the longing in her voice and he felt an overwhelming need to protect her. Always before she had been a woman to him, as his mother was a woman. Now he was taller, and he looked down on her dark hair and suddenly felt himself to be very large, a man.

When they reached the house, the moon had moved behind a cloud. The circle of light behind the cloud looked evil, almost yellow, the color of new wool.

"I won't tell," Ashel said quietly. He wanted to protect her from the soldier, yet he promised he would never tell.

Chapter Four

Phillip Hurst had arranged to come into Provo on Tuesdays and Thursdays to requisition equipment, purchase supplies, or send messages to Washington, D.C. for General Johnston, and then on Saturdays he came with the others to drink for the evening. He told Mara at first that he would meet her at the hotel, but Mara was afraid someone would see and tell Mama and Papa, so they met secretly by James Bean's old cabin at noon on Tuesdays, Thursdays, and Saturdays. Mara brought Phillip some lunch from the bread she had saved from supper the night before and whatever meat or cheese she could find when she was alone in the kitchen. While they ate, they talked. Mara was sometimes afraid of the wild strength of her feelings, for she would watch Phillip as he ate the bread and meat and drank his tankard of beer, and she would realize that she was waiting for him to touch her. When he finished eating, he would reach for her. Sometimes in play, sometimes in earnest. Sometimes she ran from him laughing, and he chased her in the tall grass and the sunflowers.

Once she hid in the cabin inside the silent walls, and laughed to herself that she would surprise him. But he didn't come. He didn't come and he didn't come. Finally she walked out into the sunshine, disappointed, shielding her eyes from the sun with her hand. Suddenly she felt an arm grasp her waist. He had been waiting for her and he laughed with pleasure.

"I've got you!" he whispered in her ear. "I've got you now."

Then she turned toward him, almost painfully pressed against his chest. His face close to her face. And then all the laughter was gone, and he kissed her hard and long, again and again.

"I love you, Mara. I go crazy." He pressed her close. She fell against him with yearning. But she would never let herself go. More and more often now she let him touch her, press her closer and closer. But there would always be that moment when she would stiffen, draw away from him, suddenly becoming afraid, feeling guilty.

"I'm afraid," she would whisper.

"What are you afraid of?"

"I'm afraid of us. I'm afraid I will lose control of myself."

Phillip would draw back then, too, in anguish once again. And she would be sorry for his despair and try to give him all she could.

"I need to be with you," she would whisper. "I need you so desperately."

"Leave them," Phillip would plead, pulling her hands toward him.

But there was too much to leave. Mama and Papa and Sobe and Ashel and Caroline and Rain and the Church. Their cause, their life, the reason they were here in the West. And the love of God. She knew she displeased God. But she knew he loved her still. And if she could just show him that it would turn out well. . . .

"I can't," she would whisper. "I can't," she said so often that it became a ritual for them. And then one day when she found the courage, she said, "But you could stay here, Phillip. When the troops go back, you could stay here."

Phillip did not answer. But he did not laugh as he would have a month ago. She knew he had taken her copy of the Book of Mormon just to please her, and she also knew he had begun to read it. She heard Emery joking about it. And something had made him change. he told her he felt uneasy about the mission of the troops to "quell" the Mormon "threats" to the United States of America.

"It's true," Mara told him one afternoon beside the river. "Phillip, I know it's true. I would be lying to tell you any differently, to tell you I could think of giving up knowing that someday I'll have to answer to God for what he has granted me."

Phillip turned to her. "You have a way of frightening me."

"Then be frightened, Phillip."

He looked away and pounded his fist in the grass. "I don't want to read your book. If it should be true, I'd have to . . ."

"What would you have to do?"

"Something. Become . . ." But he turned his head away, clenched his fist again. He couldn't speak the words. "Damn it all, Mara." He closed his eyes, as though a terrible memory gripped his heart. "You are so much like Lorraine, my lovely little Methodist." He stopped. His words were light, but his voice seemed weakened by tension. "She . . . demanded more of me . . . ," he stopped, licked his lips nervously, "than I could give."

Mara tried to speak with quiet confidence. "It's not hard to commit yourself, Phillip." But she wasn't sure she believed what she said. It *was* hard. Very hard for some people. It was hard for Mama, even for Papa sometimes. Was it only them, their family? It had been hard for Sophia, but she had John, and it wasn't so hard for John. It was hard for Mara because of the bitterness in her heart. Somehow the gospel of Jesus Christ had been tangled up for her in Bret Hunt, in his mission to England, in his cold stupidity after four years of preaching the gospel. If dedicating your life to the Lord for four years couldn't make you better, wiser. . . .

But she couldn't think like this. It would make her weak. She had to think of the strong ones, of those who could help her keep her world together. Who? Bishop Higbee. Sister Allen. Scott Hunt, and his three wives: Ella and Polly and Chloe. Bret's mother and father, how strange. What had happened? Why hadn't their goodness given Bret . . . ? But Scott Hunt himself had married Kate Wright. What would Scott Hunt have said now to Phillip Hurst? What would Sister Ella have said at Phillip Hurst's fear of the truth?

"You have to surrender yourself, Phillip," she found herself saying. "But not to every . . . passion of your body. To goodness, to truth, to the love of . . . Jesus Christ." She said the name softly, suddenly feeling that it did not belong here, in this place, between them. She felt then that she had never really done herself what she was asking Phillip to do, what she had promised so many, many times in the sacrament service. The name of Jesus Christ. Had she ever really taken it upon herself? Forgotten herself for him? Had she ever served him as she should, like Mama did? She realized she never really had. She had been more concerned about herself. She was asking of Phillip more than she had ever asked of herself.

72

It was not a shock to her. She must have known it, always. But now, admitting it, she began to fill with despair.

He sat quietly beside her. She must finish. She must say what she knew how to say, even if she did not know how to feel it. For his sake. "What's hard, Phillip, is fighting against it . . . knowing fear, suffering because you're afraid that if it is true and you don't give yourself to his life, you will have missed everything."

For a long time they sat saying nothing. He bent forward, his head between his knees, his hands clasped behind his neck. She thought of their time together, what he had brought her, and what she had brought him. She was ashamed. He had been rough sometimes, coarse even, when he was with the other men. But his compassion for her astonished her now. She knew he would never force her, and for the first time she marvelled at this.

"Careful, darling," he had said only the day before yesterday. "You don't want as much as you are asking for."

"I think I am asking for everything," Mara laughed. "Body and soul."

"You are. You are that," he said in a faraway voice. "You are." And she was. She would dream that he would force her, overcome her so that it would not be her fault, and she would be glad. But when she let herself out of the dream, when Sully and Nancy came to the hotel and were kind, when Sobe ran to her with a new book, when Ashel put his arm out to help her onto Pawface, when Papa asked how his pretty one was today, when Rain ironed all Mara's things and left them neat in her drawer, when she sat with Mama by Caroline's bed, she would be relieved deep in her heart that it was only a dream.

"It's time to go, Mara," Phillip Hurst said, suddenly rising from the grass. "It's time to go."

Mara often woke at dawn, hearing her mother and Rain in the kitchen below her, preparing hot water for Caroline, or bread for breakfast. She often heard Caroline crying or Sobe talking in his dreams. The smell of autumn came into her window, flowing down from the hills. The mornings grew chill, the days shorter. The leaves changed colors rapidly and began to fall.

The coming of autumn brought the same sadness to Mara as it always had, but now, with the sadness, came the deepest fear she had ever known. Phillip could not stay forever. And he would talk no more of religion. Mara tried to pray for help, for understanding, for Phillip to come to the truth so she could have him. But she began to fear that she would want him even if he did not come to the truth, and she was ashamed in her prayers. She could not remain much longer caught between her religion and her love.

On an almost cold October morning, Ashel came running to her room before he left for the harvest, breathless, his face white.

"They know," he said.

Mara was still in her dressing gown, searching in her wardrobe for her shoes. She turned to him. "What?"

"I just want you to know that I didn't tell them, but they know."

Mara sank to the edge of the bed. Here it was at last. "Mr. Dawes told him. Some boys saw you out by Bean's cabin." Boys. Who? They had been so careful. She thought the trees had shielded them from view. No one lived around there. Mara felt cheap. Someone had seen.

"It was bound to happen, Mara. You must have known it was bound to happen sooner or later."

In the cold kitchen Papa and Mama sat at the big table, their faces clouded with steam from the bowls of hot mush. Mama's wrinkled fingers clutched a wet handkerchief. Papa stirred his mush and blew into the bowl.

"Good morning," Mara said, making her voice as light as she could. She did not look into their faces but stared at the bouquet of asters in the center of the table. Ashel came down the stairs behind Mara, and turned to leave through the kitchen door.

"I will see you in the barn, Ashel," Papa said looking up into Mara's face. "The part to fix the hay loader is in the crib." The door slammed as Ashel left.

Papa kept his eyes on Mara's face. For a few seconds there was only silence. Then Sobe shuffled downstairs, sleep in his eyes.

"Sobe, get dressed," Mama said in a strained voice. He was slow turning, going upstairs. Mara watched him go. She hardly knew him now. He had become Mama's child, though she wouldn't admit it to Mama. She still would have said he was her own. She saw Blueflower in an instant, remembering the dark eyes, and wondered where Rain was.

Then Papa began with strained words. "Mara, we haven't had very much to complain about," Papa said. "You've never caused us . . ."

"Sorrow," Mama said, and the word came out bent, as though anguish broke it before it was said.

"But as much as you've got yourself into now makes up for all the rest. We didn't believe it at first. We couldn't believe what they said about you and any soldier boy. . . ."

Mama did not speak.

"We are ashamed." And Papa looked away from her face at last.

Mara felt uncomfortable, but she had lived through this moment so many thousand times in her mind that its reality seemed almost thin.

"Everyone knows, Mara. I wouldn't be surprised if you were . . ."

"Wait a minute," Papa said, raising his hand to stop the rise in Mama's voice. Mara looked at Mama. She seemed so fragile now, with such transparent skin. She had been crying, her eyes webbed with red veins, the crow's feet pink from the dab of the rough kerchief she held in her hand. Mama was older, Mara thought. She had gone through so much. But she doesn't know what it's like to be me.

"Why. Why, Mara?"

Why? It was simple. I fell in love, Mara thought. But she said, "Why, what?"

"You know what," Papa said. "The soldier. We knew you saw him once. But he didn't come back for a long time. Then suddenly we hear from Dawes you aren't at work at eleven o'clock at all. He finds out you don't do buying for the hotel all the time you say you do. He says that you don't arrive for work until two o'clock!"

"Oh why, Mara, why? You have always been a good girl."

Mara looked steadily at her mother, trying to feel kindly toward her. Mara did not speak. If only her mother would not whine so.

"I suppose you will say you are in love?"

"Yes, Mother. I am in love. But I knew you would not allow me to see Phillip if I told you."

"Phillip. . . ." Mama seemed surprised that he had a name.

"Phillip Hurst. He's a lieutenant. He's a good man."

Papa drew up and placed his elbows on the table. "He may be a . . . good man," he almost choked on the words. "But . . ."

"In love? Love is something you don't even understand. It's . . ." Mama's voice was thin and high.

"Did you love us when you allowed yourself to be made a public laughingstock with a soldier of the U.S. Army?"

Mara was silent.

"Well, did you?" Papa asked again, demanding an answer.

"I'm sorry." She lowered her eyes. "I've never really had anyone . . ."

"Never had anyone!" Mama was wailing now. "You could have had Sully Tuttle. He loved you so much. He's a very good man. You could still have him. You could have had any of these fine Church-going boys. You still could if you would only . . ."

Now the anger began to rise in Mara. "I've never loved anyone. I mean really *loved*. It isn't the Church that makes a man into someone you can love."

"What is it, then?" Papa challenged her, raising his eyes.

Mara did not know how to say it to them. The look in Phillip's eyes when he saw her, the touch of his hand on her cheek, the feel of his arms around her.

"A good man, is he?" Papa spoke into her silence. "Dawes says your 'good man' is one of the worst drunkards in the hotel dining room!"

"He drinks," Mara said softly. "Sometimes he drinks too much. Seldom. But he is still a good man—kind, warm . . . gracious."

"Gracious!" Mama nearly exploded. "Taking a young woman, a lady, off into the weeds. . . ."

"You are an adult, Mara," Papa broke in. "You must know what you are doing."

An adult, yes I am, Mara thought, which is the only way I could talk so collectedly in the face of these accusations and remain calm. "I do know what I'm doing. Phillip Hurst is a gentleman with me. He is more of a real man than a dozen Mormon boys of the caliber you mention. And I love him."

Mama wailed again.

"Mara, just how far has he . . . gone?" Papa demanded.

Mara felt cut, as though her body were sliced by wires. She searched in her mind for an answer. "As far as . . . somewhere in . . . I believe it's Alma he's gone to."

Papa stared.

"That's how far." Mara caught her breath. "He is almost to Third Nephi, for I have been telling him about it, and he is interested."

Papa stared, speechless. "He's . . ."

"Yes, he's reading the Book of Mormon. He believes there's something. . . . He has a staunch Presbyterian background."

Mama stared, unaware that her mouth hung open.

"A staunch Presbyterian background," Papa added. "Except when he drinks too much beer in the hotel dining room and pinches the waitress. . . ."

Mara felt stung by Papa's words. These were her parents. She was twenty-four years old. She was no longer a child, yet she had disgraced them and they meant to punish her for it.

"When I asked you how far it had gone you did not give me the answer I was asking for."

"I know what you were talking about then, and I think you are worried about nothing." The tension made Mara's ears ring.

Her mother's voice was deliberately calm. "I think what Papa means is what your plans are . . . if you . . . are . . ."

"I can't have any plans, Mother, can I, until I know what Phillip is going to do."

Papa leaned back in his chair now, and a look of relief spread across his face. He sighed slowly, the tension going out of him. "You know, Mara Eastman," he said. "I knew you had a head on your shoulders."

But Mama said. "It's no good. It's just no good."

On Sunday, sidelong glances from members of the Church made Mara uncomfortable. She smiled at some, leveled her eyes at others. You don't know what has happened to me or why I do what I do. You could not believe me, for all of you simply leap into marriage, monogamous or plural, at the first opportunity. I have waited a long time to feel what I am feeling now. I would wait forever. It is glorious. You are all beggars, and I feel sorry for you, she said to herself.

Nancy and Sully and Will Jones rode with the Eastmans home for supper, Nancy talkative, inquisitive, Sully almost morose. He didn't say a word. Will Jones bounced his children on the knees of his smooth new creaseless broadcloth suit, the latest style ordered from a Salt Lake tailor. He also stayed quiet, except for once when he turned to make a remark to Sully about the fall weather. At one time he struck up a conversation with Mara about the soldiers who came to the hotel. He seemed to have a sixth sense that she was hurting.

"Some of that military bunch are pretty decent fellows," he said.

Mara thought she had never heard such welcome words. Will was very sensible and kind. She turned fully to him, hoping the others could hear their comments. "Some of them I find really gracious."

"They've been good clients," Will said, continuing to bounce his little girl.

Mara longed to talk more with him, because he was the first who even dared to try to understand. But Mama called them to supper.

The meal seemed forced and silent. No one talked about the soldier who was reading Mara's Book of Mormon. No one dared. Mara quietly excused herself from the table and went to the bedroom. She lay, exhausted, tearless, on the bed. Sensitive about Mara's privacy, Rain stayed away, but Nancy came in behind her.

"I've wondered, Mara, always, if you would ever love anyone again as much as you loved Bret."

"I do," Mara said simply, staring unblinking at the ceiling.

"But he isn't really suitable for marriage," Nancy said with caution in her voice. Then she brightened, or tried to brighten. Mara heard the forced brightness in her voice. "I know someone who has really taken a liking to you, though." Mara heard Nancy's voice . . . a rush, a hailstorm of words on her head.

"You don't pay very much attention to him. As a matter of fact, he's afraid you're a snob. But Mara, he's a wonderful man."

The words beat on Mara's ears. Her head hurt.

"Please, Mara, listen. There's no future for you with Phillip Hurst. He's not one of us." Nancy placed a hand on Mara's hair. But Mara shook it away. "Don't you want to talk?" Nancy said.

"Not now."

Nancy withdrew her hand and sat very still. Mara had known Nancy for almost ten years. And Nancy still didn't know Mara. Part of it had been because of Sully's love for Mara. Though Nancy never showed it, Mara thought it must hurt her to be Sully's second choice. And now, her childlessness. . . . Mara felt sorry for Nancy, but there seemed to be nothing in common between them anymore. Nancy could never understand what it was like to be Mara Eastman.

"I need to be alone for a while."

"Of course," Nancy said. "I guess. . . ."

"I'm sorry, Nancy. Things have never been . . . quite . . . quite right for me."

"I think I understand."

"No one really understands."

"You don't let them. You don't give people a chance to understand."

Mara was quiet.

"You're not the only one who feels lonely. The rest of us understand pain." Then Nancy hesitated as though the words hurt too much. "How do you think it is for me never having had the child I want so much?"

Nancy stopped, turned her back to Mara's bed. "You feel as though no one has been there to care, to understand. But we have always been there to help you if you would only have allowed us to help."

"I don't need to hear it, Nancy," Mara's eyes filled with sudden tears.

"You don't want to hear it, but you have even cut out your mother and father. You've cut out all of us."

Now Mara turned, the hurt becoming anger. Her words were slow, measured. "Because I'm not like you . . . all of you. I don't want to marry just anyone. I want to feel something."

Nancy's brow knit. "Something! Can you feel?" Nancy's lips hardened now. "Feeling love is a way of treating God's children with courtesy. A way of . . . of enfolding everyone. True love doesn't push people away. Love is a way of life. A way of building carefully for the good of everyone." Nancy's voice quickened into a rush of words. "True love isn't playing with fire for the excitement of seeing what will burn. True love would never play with fire."

Mara knew she had played with fire as she had been taught never to do. But she had such a great unfilled need. No one could understand how great was her need. The tears stung in her eyes. "What would it be to anyone if I should satisfy my need, take what I want so much!"

"Mara!" Nancy drew back.

"It can only be good. Our love is so good!" Mara sat up and gripped the edge of the bed.

"Then take it! Have it! Practice your whoredoms! Outside of marriage there is nothing to contain it. You can get into the habit of going from one to the other. Collect them! Keep a record!" Suddenly, Nancy stopped, and the quiet pounded in Mara's head as she turned away from Nancy once more.

"Oh, Mara," Nancy began, her voice soft now. "Of course you are lonely. Don't you understand? There are many who love you. So many of us care so much about what happens to you. We care." Then she stopped again, and Mara heard the tears in Nancy's voice. "Of course you need someone you can respect and love. And there *is* someone—someone of your own faith. Someone of fine character and good promise. Someone who really cares for you. And I want to tell you. Please listen."

Not Sully. Mara turned now, still broken.

As though she read Mara's thoughts, Nancy went on. "Not Sully. I am so eager for you to know," Nancy whispered. She sat on the bed next to Mara and placed both hands on Mara's hands, lying in her lap. Mara did not look at her. Nancy squeezed her hands anxiously. "If you want to know I'll tell you."

But the words rolled past Mara's ears like waves of empty air. She turned her head and looked toward the wall.

"Please turn back to us, Mara," Nancy whispered.

But Mara's heart felt like a great weight: lead, stones, an immovable monument already marked. She ignored Nancy's hands pressing her own. "No, Nancy. No."

For a moment longer Nancy pressed Mara's hand. A dull silence surrounded them. There were waves of darkness that swallowed the hurt in Mara's head, darkness that seemed to cover them up, take them whole, as though it were a dissolution of the world. "But thank you for caring."

For a moment Mara felt herself reaching toward Nancy for warmth, but it was a brief feeling, gone almost as soon as it appeared. She did not turn but kept her eyes toward the wall.

"Mara."

But Mara did not speak. She closed her eyes. Nancy sat still. Breathing was the only sound. Then the bed creaked when Nancy released her weight. There was footfall against the floor as she left, and slowly closed the door.

On Tuesday Phillip wasn't there. She waited in their favorite spot behind a clump of gnarled and broken trees. She took embroidery, as usual. The light skimmed the leaves, playing in the wind like chimes. By the double sound of the town clock far away, she knew it was two o'clock. And he hadn't come.

She felt not panic, but a benign acceptance of the constant threat to luck that dogged her. Of course he wouldn't come today. Someone must have told him that her father knew. Perhaps someone had threatened him somehow. Perhaps he had been needed at Camp Scott. Perhaps he had simply fallen ill.

In the hotel that evening, there were fewer of his old drinking friends. Anderson, the one who had grabbed her that first night, was watching her closely through the dinner hour, his dark eyes staring from beneath the black bushy brows. She did not speak to him while she served the meal. But as time passed, she felt an ache growing inside of her, a reach that would not be still. She found her own eyes meeting his for a moment.

He touched her waist and she turned quickly to him. "Don't you dare," she fumed, gathering the fire of her anger into a tightness around her mouth. "Stop it."

"You waitin' for your lover boy?" The dark eyes narrowed and he grinned knowingly.

Mara turned quickly, without speaking, and left. But on the return to the table, she caught his dark stare again.

"I don't s'pose you're interested in knowing where he is?" The man grunted, seeing clearly into her heart. "Some free coffee does wonders." He held out his cup.

Mara stood for a moment, looking at him, hating herself for knowing him, for trafficking with such scum.

"He's to Camp Scott, lady. Told me to tell you. An emergency call—he didn't know how long. Told me you'd understand."

Mara half understood. He had never breathed a word to her about a new post. He had been with her just Thursday and had said he was almost finished with her book.

"I'll bring it to you on Tuesday," he had told her. "Wait for me at eleven by the tree. I also want to ask you some questions about the Gadianton robbers. And if you know how much it would be to buy some copies to send East . . . Chicago. I don't yet know how many."

Mara had begun to ask him a question but he had been abrupt with her.

"Ask me no questions."

Today he had not come.

She gave Anderson two free cups of coffee. When he asked for the third, she asked him to pay for it. When he refused, she became firm with him and asked him to leave.

"Now, don't get huffy, lady," the man drawled, his drunkenness surviving the coffee.

"Don't try anything," Mara returned, clipping her words.

"Just don't hurry me," the soldier backed up and tipped over his chair. The tablecloth moved and a water glass spilled. His hands scraped the spoons and the knife to the floor. "Come on, Rasmus," he said to his small, dull companion who had never said much but suddenly stuffed his mouth with a few greasy fried potatoes so as not to cheat himself out of any of the meal. The two shuffled to their feet and backed away from Mara, who glared at them. They paid Dawes at the counter and left. Only three other soldiers ate at the hotel that night, and they had come late, tilting their chairs, guffawing, teasing both Mara and Mrs. Dawes as usual, never noticing Phillip's absence.

Mrs. Dawes noticed it. "Your beau ain't present."

"What beau?" Mara said, looking around.

"You are a crazy one, Mara Eastman, a crazy one."

Her heart turned over like pages in an empty book that night. She reviewed the long day at the hotel, the painful absence of Phillip, the empty stares of her parents; but what hurt her most was the unexpected crushing lack of affection from Sobe.

"What did you tell Sobe about me?" she asked Mama.

"I told him nothing! I don't need to. You haven't paid him any mind since you met that soldier. I see it now."

"Somebody's told Sobe something," Mara said, stiffening, watching the faces surrounding the room like white slates in the autumn firelight. "One of you has told him something."

"Not any of us," Ashel said, still white.

"I'm still Mara," she knelt to Sobe, surrounded his shoulders with a trembling arm. He was eight now, tall for his age, with broadening shoulders, a large head. His hair and eyes were the Indian black. But there was nothing Indian about his brows, his nose, his smooth cheeks. His features were the features of a white man, no matter how much she tried to believe his father was Hinte. "Tell me, Sobe. Who has been angry with me?" But the boy's lips were closed.

Mara slept uneasily for a week. Phillip did not write or send messages with Emery or Rasmus or any of his other friends. She waited. The hours at the hotel stretched into long gray afternoons stung by sharp bitter autumn winds in the slanted light. The trees began to lose their color and all of their leaves. The harvest took everyone's time. Rumors came down from Salt Lake City that a U.S. Army judge named Sinclair had nearly sent a bishop to prison for treason against the United States government because he combined church and state by handling a man's water rights dispute in bishop's court.

"They don't want nobody to interfere with U.S. government rights," Papa said. "And it worries me, for the Church is all set up to handle things the way we want them handled."

"Any other government will never do as well as the Church can," Mama said, her voice too high.

"Theocracy," Papa said. He gave a discourse on theocracy from his armchair, warming up to the subject over a couple of bowls of popcorn. Sully and Will Jones were always present on those evenings. Mara came late from work and found them lamenting the presence of the U.S. government in Deseret. "If the south gets slavery, we ought to have our polygamy."

"South may not always have their slavery and belong to the union too," Will Jones said. "Matter of fact, it's getting too uncomfortable for them to give up their slavery and behave like the regular yankee."

"Now how's that?" Mama asked.

"No slaves, no extra wives."

"Just plenty of beer and a few concubines in a whorehouse."

Mama clucked her tongue at Papa for his talk and looked darkly at Mara. But Mara looked away. She was not interested in their talk. It had been two weeks since Phillip's new assignment, and she felt crushed that he had not sent any messages. She told herself that he couldn't or that he was too busy. But the words stuck in her head and never translated themselves into her heart.

It was the day Ashel turned eighteen that Sully and Will drove into the yard with the breathless news that "one hundred troops is on their way with a judge to set up a court in Provo."

So far, no court had convened, but after the example of Sinclair in Salt Lake City, "Some fool soldier wants to court-martial Provo Mormons for treason to the U.S. government."

Will Jones was adamant, his voice strongly against the action of the military. Sully could not keep him still. The men, including George Allen and Ashel, talked late, far after Mara came home and felt she was ready for bed. But tonight she had come home with Ashel by way of the park where the troops were obviously set up for a long stay. Startled, she had searched for Phillip as she crossed the city square, and not finding him, scolded herself for acknowledging the presence of the army at all. She asked Ashel to skirt the block, frightened someone would see them.

Now she watched Will, heated and fuming as he railed against the military action. She had long suspected that he was the man Nancy had meant, the one who cared for her. But she had been so aloof that very little ever occurred between them. He had been her friend. It was not for a lack of courtesy that nothing had happened between them. He was intelligent. He was handsome; she had to admit that. But she saw him as boorish, businesslike and intense. She had heard the women say how many times the bishop had urged him to marry, but he was stubborn, they said, and he didn't have a way with women. Still, Mara knew plenty of women, young and old, who seemed to have their caps set for him all the same. He was the town's most eligible bachelor, Mara couldn't deny that.

"So what will we do?" Mama wailed.

"Nothing we can do but wait."

"Fight it in court," Will said darkly. "Fight it like crazy in court."

"We've got no lawyers."

"But ourselves. Higbee . . . yourself . . . all of us. I'll even take a crack at it." William Jones rubbed his chin, frowning.

"We can do it," Sully agreed.

Papa was silent, shutting his eyes. "Not if they pass a law against plural marriage."

"They wouldn't dare!" George Allen breathed. He now had three wives and would have another one soon.

Sully looked at Mara. There was darkness in his gaze. Nancy had not come down from the house with the children today. Mara thought he stared at her much too openly. Oh, when would she ever be rid of Sully's watching her?

"And if they do? If they do pass a law against plural marriage?"

"They'd have grounds," Will said softly.

"Of course *you* don't need to do no worryin'," Papa said to Will Jones. Everyone laughed. "You might as well be a monk." They all laughed again.

Mara stared ahead into the firelight, unable to concentrate on her sewing. She felt the room pressing in on her from all sides. She felt Sully's eyes.

"There may not be much longer a body can take more than one wife," Sully was saying.

"I never wanted no others. Not me," Papa grunted.

"And I'm glad they didn't call you to it, Hart Eastman, or I would have protested loud and clear," Mama said.

Just that sudden, as Mara watched him, Papa's face clouded. It startled her. Papa looked around at the men in the circle, a look on his face like a plea for help.

"That is something I haven't known quite how to tell you, and so I haven't yet," Papa said cautiously after a moment.

Mara heard Mama's breath draw in sharply. Her face darkened, and she rose in the rocker. Then there was another moment of silence among all of them. Mara knew then what Papa had to tell.

Mama began to speak, slowly and quietly. "And you never told me, Hart Eastman. You been called and you said no, and you never told me!"

There was a breath of anger in Mama's words, but where should she direct it? To Papa for being called? For saying no? For not telling her?

Mara was stunned. How long ago had he received it? She stared at Papa. So, Papa had been called. She had always wondered if that call would ever come and what Papa would do if it did.

"When, Papa? When were you called?" It was a brazen question, and Mara asked it, ignoring the time and place.

It had been almost a week ago. And Papa explained he had been trying to tell Mama and the right moment had never come. Carefully, he steered Mama's anger into security. His voice was soothing, his manner kind. "I knew how Martha felt about plural marriage. And the brethren knew. And one woman has always seemed enough."

The room hung with silence. Firelight flickered on the faces surrounding the hearth. Suddenly Papa looked toward Rain and away again. "The bishop told me that young women in the house outside the family ought to be brought into the covenant. I told him I would have to think about it."

Rain! Mara suspected that someday something would have to be done for Rain. So, as much as the Church had been silent about marriages to Indians, Bishop Higbee had suggested to Papa that if she were going to live in his house, perhaps he ought to marry Rain. Mara looked at her old friend. With all eyes on her, Rain seemed to cower slightly. Her eyes were bright with the reflection of the fire. How must she feel now with Papa nearly rejecting her in front of everyone?

"Rain?" Mama said. "The bishop asked you to marry Rain? Oh . . ." A thousand flickering lights passed through Mama's eyes as she took Rain's hand. There was heavy air in the house. The parlor seemed to darken, the autumn to storm in. "Dear Rain. We would do anything for Rain."

Papa looked at Mama. "Anything?"

Rain drew back at Mama's touch. She looked nervous, frightened, embarrassed. Why was Papa doing this now, in front of everyone? Was he so afraid of Mama that he had to have all these people to protect himself from her?

Sully and Will looked uncomfortable. "We ought to be going," Will said.

Just like him, Mara thought. Give him an inch to get out of a tight situation, and he'll be gone.

But suddenly Rain rose to her feet and began to run for the kitchen door. And from her body came a wrenching sob that she did not stifle successfully. They could hear her cry until the kitchen door slammed behind her.

The first to his feet after her was not Papa, but Sully. He raced toward the door. Mara began after him, but he raised his hand to stop her. "Mara, let me. . . ." Surprised, Mara did as he wished. She stood in the darkness of the kitchen as he left for the yard.

"Rain, Rain," Sully called out to her in the dark. "Please don't go." But as he stopped to look around for her there was a hush in the yard—no sound, not of wind in the leaves or footsteps on the grass.

"Rain. Where are you? Please."

Sully spoke with Rain in a way different from the way he spoke with anyone else. When he felt for her in his heart, she had always been quietly there, like the rain from heaven, which sometimes waited, but had always come at last. He found her behind the barn in the tall hollyhocks, her face streaked with tears.

"Rain. Rain, please. Let me take you home with me." Sully felt no need for thinking on it. He knew it was right when he touched her hand, cool in the autumn air. "Come with me and be a part of my family. Nancy will love you. As I do. As I have for a long time."

Rain's lips trembled, but she moved from the trees toward him, her hand lightly in his. Sully felt a deep satisfaction inside him as he put his arm around Rain's strong shoulders. He felt warm, whole, happy. "Now come in," he said softly. "I should have married you many years ago."

Though it caused a good deal of murmuring in the town, Sully married Rain quietly in December 1858, just before Christmas. Mama insisted on having a small reception in the house when the berry preserves had been put up and the fruit breads baked. She had decorated a small pine tree with candles. Sobe insisted on helping to light them, and he burned himself badly on the wrist. Nancy took the new marriage not only gracefully, but with an air of enthusiasm that Mara somewhat suspected. "He will have the children now, the children he deserves," Nancy said to Mara almost absentmindedly the day of the wedding. Nancy said how much she respected and admired Rain. "It will be pleasant to share the household with Rain,"

Nancy said. Mara knew that Nancy had always steadied her heart for the time when Will Jones would marry and take his children from the Tuttles' house. "It will be good to have Rain's children about," Nancy said. "Will Jones is bound to marry someday." Mara had looked quickly at Nancy, but Nancy was not looking at her.

Mara could not help admiring the way Sully tried to ease Nancy's heart with his careful love. After he brought Rain back into the room that night and announced he would take her as his wife if Nancy would agree, Sully was constantly attentive to Nancy. Rain stood by, quiet, waiting. Mara watched. There was no hurt in Rain's eyes when she saw Sully touch Nancy.

The marriage was performed in the new seminary at ten o'clock in the morning by Bishop Higbee, who admitted before all assembled that Sully's decision was indeed a kindly and generous one. "Not at all," Mara heard Sully whisper to Rain as he laid his hand over hers.

Sully looked happy. He looked at Rain with love in his eyes. Mara had seen enough love from Sully's eyes to know what it was like. Rain looked beautiful, like a dark exotic princess in the lovely dress and cap Mara had helped Mama make from lace curtains and an old ball gown that had been Sophia's. Mara had tied Rain's long dark hair in a bun at her neck and had set up rag curls in the center of it and some above the ears. Rain had gazed shyly at herself in the mirror, a slow smile spreading across her face.

As Rain smiled at her loveliness, the picture of a bent Spirit of Earth, dirty in her reeking leather tatters, had passed through Mara's mind. This is not what your mother would have had for you, Rain, Mara thought. Yet it pleases you completely. How beautiful we have made you.

Mara felt her heart tighten during the ceremony. No one, not even Sully, gave any sign that she should take note of what she was missing—that she was still alone, missing out on her own life. And yet Mara felt she must put walls between herself and Sully and Nancy and even Rain. No one, no one understood her heart.

For, day after day, Phillip had not come. And though she tried outwardly to display an indifference and calm, the turbulence inside her made her weak. If she did not try very hard to hang onto her sanity she would go crazy from the pain that came with the passing days. She drove the anguish deeper and deeper into her heart until it began to fester and drive her at odds with herself, until she felt intense turmoil and a terrible incapacity to believe.

Mayor Bullock finally collected signatures on a petition that demanded Cradlebaugh remove the hundred men from Provo. Cradlebaugh responded on the following day by bringing nine hundred more men from Camp Floyd to Provo.

The citizens of Provo were stunned. The stench of the military filled the crowded streets and surrounded the town. Tents were crowded into every vacant lot and spread north of the city for more than a mile. Bonfires smoked in the corner of every street. Animals snorted, pawed the ground at passersby, and left steaming manure in hot piles that flattened under military boots.

The court continued with arrests and long sessions that tore citizens from their labor in shops and factories. Children began throwing stones into tents, cutting hooves, leaving sharp nails under saddles. They frightened horses and men with captured rats or gophers suddenly let out of burlap bags. The young men began drinking with the rowdies at the Palace Saloon or the brewery, causing general havoc. Some of them actually joined the forces, received uniforms, and began policing their own families. Mara could barely make her way to work through the streets without the crude whistles, catcalls, the ugly remarks of men who shouted, "We're having a good time. Mormon girls don't have a good time!" Mara knew, though, that they found a few who would cooperate in absolute secret. The town shook with laughter—the loud roar of hundreds of men without women.

With nine hundred men in town and camps on the outskirts of the city, and very few women available to the public eye, Mara became a toast. Her sullen anger was taken for a general distress that the military was present. So there were taunts, guffaws, ugly loud names. Finally, her distance was not fun anymore, and when she did not acknowledge the most pressing attentions, they called her stone cold and began to leave her alone.

On her way to the hotel, Mara dared to look around through the tents, shamefully realizing that she searched for Phillip Hurst. She had not seen him for almost five months. She stared at the heads of dark tall men, waiting until they turned, sometimes catching her eye, grinning toward her, often looking straight through her from a distance. Never Phillip. Until one Saturday. She saw him in a circle of men beside a smoking bonfire only a block from the East House Hotel. Phillip! He stood a head taller than anyone else around him, his dark hair shining under his blue cap. Phillip! Her heart pounded. She was afraid.

She stood, waiting, willing him to turn, see her, come to her. But she could not contain her excitement. The power of her feelings for him made her weak. She felt a wave of nausea as she stepped over the tent ropes, around cooking fires, past nervous animals toward the circle of men where he stood. Still he stood with his back to her. Across from him in the circle stood Emery, who gave Phillip a message with his eyes. Emery watched Mara, smirking. Mara's excitement beat down her shame. Emery shook his head at her, grinned at Phillip. Phillip turned.

"Phillip!" Her voice was weak, her heartbeat consuming her.

The men laughed, drew slightly away, moving toward the cooking fire and the open officer's tent.

"Mara." Phillip looked at her, his voice hesitant. He stared at her, his eyes troubled. He opened his arms for her at last. She threw herself against his breast, felt his arms around her, but lightly, as though hesitant to enclose her. Phillip. Phillip. Oh, Phillip, hold me, please, she wanted to say.

He pushed her gently away. His voice was quiet, distant. "Not now. Not now." But then his voice broke. "Mara, I've thought about you." His eyes searched hers. But there was no joy in them. He looked around. The others had gone into the tent. Then he stared at her again. "You haven't changed."

"In five months?" Mara tried to sound cheerful. She threw her words out onto the cold air. Then she dared. "Was it my father?"

"I had orders. I went to Camp Scott." He paused, looking away from her. "I've been to Chicago."

Mara was stunned at his distance. "Chicago?"

Phillip was still looking about. Then he looked at her again, but not intently. "Are you going to the hotel? Can I see you later?"

Mara felt a strange dull terror rising in her. "I'll be there," she whispered.

"I'll try to get in. I don't know when. They've got me on assignment at Floyd."

Mara's head still whirled with the dizzy sickness, an ache that wearied her limbs.

"It's good to see you again." Phillip spoke softly into the air. He looked at her once more, with his blue, distant gaze. "Yes. It's good to see you." He turned, walked away through the tents.

Mara could not think clearly that afternoon. Her throat burned from holding back the tears. Phillip had been so cold. She felt dazed, hurt, aching for talk with him. He was here! And still she would have to wait.

Phillip did not come in that evening, nor the following evening, nor any evening during that week. She looked for him . . . in the tents staked out in the parks, the streets, but she did not find him again. Bitter loneliness surrounded her and fear filled her heart. Why did he not come?

Feeling a strange kind of panic that she must be anywhere she could possibly see Phillip, she went to court with Papa and Will when Cradlebaugh brought Mayor Bullock before him a third time. Will, who had become one of Papa's right-hand business advisors at the investment office these days looked ready to eat Cradlebaugh. He seemed high spirited and fearless in a good looking new black coat and tie. Though he expressed anger toward Cradlebaugh's terrible court and the uncomfortable presence of the military, he again made a somewhat generous speech about them.

"Let's face it. The military's lined our pockets. They've bought my merchandise and stayed at your hotel, Eastman," Will said. As they stepped inside the courtroom, Mara looked up, and Will was grinning at her. Flushing, she was afraid he knew too much about her—that he knew she was thinking about Phillip. And she was. But Phillip was not in the courtroom—he had not come.

"Then who do you listen to if not the people themselves?" Mayor Bullock shouted in the room. "If we can't decide how we're to live, who decides! Who is the United States government!"

"Hierarchy, my dear Bullock," Cradlebaugh said in his oily voice. "Hierarchy."

Mara didn't understand. Mayor Bullock was staring at Cradlebaugh in disbelief. Was there a hierarchy to which Cradlebaugh answered? It seemed he was acting on his own. Mara had never thought to acknowledge any authority beyond the U.S. Army, here in Provo. But it was true that all of them were subject to higher authorities—the supreme court, congress, and the President of the United States. If Cradlebaugh were to acknowledge these authorities, the people of Utah might also go to them.

That evening Papa brought news to the family at home that the council would appeal their case against Cradlebaugh to the new governor of Utah, appointed by the United States government itself.

During the next weeks, the council sent messengers and letters and made personal visits to plead with Cumming to help them solve their problems, to release them from the oppression of Cradlebaugh and the military. Mara waited, not seeing Phillip. If the pleas to the governor were successful, the military would have to go. The waiting would be over. Phillip would be gone.

Finally, on March 14, the new governor came from Salt Lake City to investigate the difficulties in Provo. It was an anxious day. Cumming arrived by coach and four, flanked with foot soldiers. A mild-mannered man with large cheeks, he sat atop the carriage on the way into town. As the four horses stepped through the crowded streets, he waved at staring soldiers and the grave faces of towns-people. A few citizens, out of courtesy, waved back. Mara watched. Would this be the man who would free them? Would he be the one to take Phillip away forever? She thought she would welcome it now. Having him gone for good would be better than having him here, hiding from her. Still, if he were gone, there would be no hope at all, no hope anymore.

"Do you need so many troops in such a small place?" Mara heard Governor Cumming ask General Johnston at the officer's tent. The men from Provo came to the confrontation from the bank, the hotel, their shops. They waited, their faces stern, to hear Cumming order the troops from their city. But the order didn't come.

That evening Cumming spent the night in the luxury suite of the East House Hotel. Mara made up his bed and brought towels. He ordered hot milk at ten o'clock and asked Mara to wait for him just inside the door while he posted a letter to Salt Lake City. A government secretary stayed with him in the room. Two guards stood just outside the door. There were several military officers in the suite across the hall playing poker in the dim light of an oil lamp.

Mara waited nervously, towels still in her arms, while Cumming sealed the envelope with wax and administered his personal seal.

92

He talked to his government aide as he worked, his words almost smothered by the round tones of his voice.

"Johnston tells me he has strict instructions to answer the requests of the judicial branch of the government as well as the executive. It's Cradlebaugh who has ordered these troops to overwhelm such a small, and I might add, seemingly peaceful town."

"It *has* been peaceful, seemingly, your honor."

"But give it time seething under the oppression of a thousand federal soldiers, and it won't be an easy job to convince them or anyone else that the government here should be executed by the United States."

Mara watched Cumming carefully. She was surprised at his kindly disposition toward the people of Deseret. He seemed fair.

"Get this notice to Salt Lake City, and if there is nothing else we can do here, we shall send someone to Washington in behalf of Mayor Bullock, who is certainly much distressed."

Cumming's head was almost round, his hair thin on the crown. His small, green, deep-set eyes sparkled in the light from the lamps. His mouth seemed almost hidden in the large jowls below his mustache. He wore a rich gold chain on the watch fastened to his vest pocket on his stiff waistcoat beneath the ample gray flannel robe he had donned for the evening.

"Your mail, young lady." Cumming handed the sealed letter to Mara who took it in one hand. "Yes, the towels, thank you." Cumming took the towels from her and smiled graciously.

The letter felt heavy in Mara's hands. She slipped it into the postal container, realizing it was Cumming's answer to all of them, the action he had chosen to take to relieve them of their military oppression. The heavy paper slipped into the slot and was gone.

Cumming left for a "friendship" journey southward to visit the people of the territory, the people in his power, Papa said. In the meantime, Johnston did nothing to remove troops. Men were arrested and held for trial without cause. If husbands weren't home for supper, the women flocked to the seminary to see if they had been handcuffed and placed there to be grilled in one-eyed Cradlebaugh's preposterous court.

School, usually held in the seminary, was interrupted, labors were sporadic and undependable. Shops were raided and sometimes robbed, and citizens were frightened and filled with hatred and anger.

"Love your brothers," Mayor Bullock and Bishop Higbee and the others preached from the Sunday pulpits. "This is but another test which God is giving us. If we are to grow into celestial beings we can be prepared only by the most grueling trials of our love. If we can accept the soldiers among us with a smile, with graciousness, if we can turn the other cheek, we shall be an example to them. For Jesus Christ did the same. And we may yet bring them all to the kingdom by our kindness and loving patience."

"Amen," Mara thought, bowing her head, thinking of Phillip.

"Amen, and amen," a chorus of voices followed the prayer.

"Onward Christian soldiers, marching as to war. With the cross of Jesus, going on before."

Mara sang without feeling. She had not seen Phillip again.

Hot weather came in early April this year. Flies crowded the military camps in clouds. The water grew murky and smelled of oil. Men sweltered in the blue uniforms, or began to shed them and unbutton their blue shirts. Mara watched the soldiers in their long mornings of boredom. They slept out their hangovers, did chores with groans of resentment, if they did them at all. As early as four in the afternoon, the men began drinking again and commenced their games. A few ambitious athletes practiced polo in the streets or tossed horseshoes. But the most popular game was poker, and it continued from early afternoon until one, two, sometimes three in the morning. Arguments raged from one tent to another as young men resolved unfair play or resented loss. The voices rang through quiet streets like bells through fog. Mara could hear the bellowing from soldier after soldier as they demanded what they could or fought over what they didn't get. "The Lord only knows what gambling does to people," Papa said.

One day Ashel bounded into the kitchen with the news that although Cumming had still not heard from Washington, Johnston had decided to remove the troops. He was on his way with a contingency from Camp Floyd, and the army would remove itself to the camp today.

"No!" Papa said, pouring the last of the honey into his mush.

"I swear! It's true!" Ashel blurted, the sweat streaming from his forehead. He had run all the way from the post office to tell them.

"It's rumor," Papa said, starting to his feet to look out the window.

"It's true!" Ashel insisted. "Bullock said it. Not me. A message came in the mail to him with the midnight pony express. And he's sent out a boy to check it at Camp Floyd."

"Oh, glory be!" Mama said, wiping her hands on her apron and rushing to the door. From the door, they could see the troops spread out across the park. This morning there seemed to be fewer of them still asleep. Many more men than usual seemed to be stoking breakfast fires, and indeed, a few were pulling the huge tents, like balloons, down to the ground. Fires from the platoons surrounding the city were billowing with clouds of ash. For miles around, there was an unusual waking, a hustle, a hurry to get the work done before the heat of the sun would stifle the day.

"Oh, glorious!" Mama's eyes brightened.

"Can I go see, Mama?" Sobe chanted. "Can I go see?"

Caroline begged Ashel to wheel her chair to the window. "Yes, I believe it's true," Papa said gruffly, wheezing a little. "It's true! I'll be a son of a gun! Looks like they're getting ready for a military ceremony."

The usual seven o'clock bugle was accompanied by a wracking charge from their largest cannon. It sounded from the old fort park, a few blocks up Main.

"With cannon!" Papa added, peering from the window.

Mara felt the excitement invade her, charge her already frayed nerves. She grabbed her sweater and began to leave.

"Stay here, Mara girl," Papa ordered.

"Oh, can't we go?" Sobe pleaded, his black eyes dancing.

Papa stared at the stirring troops. The Allen children were filing from their home in their nightshirts, clapping their hands.

"Let them go," Mama said.

Ashel wheeled Caroline into the front yard. Sobe dragged Mara by the hand into the street. "Come with me!" Mara let him lead her. His joy was so contagious that she suddenly wanted to laugh with him and hold him close.

For two hours tents floated to the ground, fires smoked out, men moved through their packed goods, lifting rolls to carts, stacking equipment, disassembling guns.

Back at the house doing chores, Sobe and Mara spent as much time as they could on the porch watching. Crowds gathered and dispersed periodically until at about eleven an unusual music rang from the north gate.

"They're coming! They're coming!" Sobe shouted. And sure enough, a martial band could be seen marching through the gate southward down Main Street playing "Doo Dah" with as much power as a few trumpets and trombones could muster. Behind them marched the sixteen platoons that had camped in the orchards surrounding the city. The parade of men was more than two blocks long.

Johnston led the entourage, and with him several officers on fancy dressed horses sporting plumes and military brass on bridle and bit. Mara stared. One of the officers was Phillip Hurst. Her heart bolted. She felt the same weakness, the same hurt, but she restrained herself with the same pride that had kept her from searching him out these long weeks since his return.

He was more dashing than she ever remembered, his best brass glittering in the sunlight. His black hair gleamed under the crisp blue cap, his epaulets stood high, starched and sparkling on the heavy wool of his coat.

Phillip Hurst. The name felt strange in her thoughts. She had loved him so much. But he seemed far away, even as she watched him.

The front contingent of officers clipped their horses to the rigorous beat of the drum. The horses danced as though in parade, stepping high, pulling a little at their bits. Phillip's eyes were trained straight ahead as though admitting nothing but duty. None of the officers smiled or acknowledged the cheers or waves of the platoons assembling at the seminary.

The contingent moved south of the seminary until it passed the park and reached the northeast corner of the Eastman lot. Mara, standing in the yard holding tight to Sobe's hand, stared. Philip's horse was perhaps only fifty yards away. She concentrated on his eyes. "Look at me, Phillip," she begged soundlessly. "What went wrong? You could not have forgotten so completely."

For a brief flickering moment she thought Phillip had lowered his eyes to hers. She thought she caught a sidelong glance of recognition. She felt the pressure of the excitement in Sobe's hand. She returned the grip with a warm tightening in her fingers. "Oh, Phillip, I loved you so," she whispered gently, gently. "I wanted to give you everything."

At the Eastman corner, Johnston, astride a huge appaloosa, barked an "About face!" and the martial band stopped playing. For a few moments heavy with silence, the crowds of townspeople now standing up and down Main watched the military platoons, heard an occasional order. Then the platoons turned and began marching through their own rows back to the courthouse where the others had assembled in ragged lines. As Phillip turned his horse, Mara tried to catch his eyes. But he stared ahead. With an unbroken stride, his beautiful mare stepped forward through the infantry and followed Johnston to the seminary lawn.

"Fa . . . ll in!" came the sharp orders as the gathered platoons on both sides of the street began to fall in step at the end of the parade. "Fa . . . ll in!" And the men stumbled and shifted feet and struggled into step as their platoon commanders found a place for each platoon. At the courthouse, a cannon rang out once more with a deafening crack. There was another, and another, and then the band struck up, "The Girl I Left Behind," and every cart and wagon and broken horse followed the march up Main Street past the old fort and the north gate into the road to Camp Floyd.

Mara watched Phillip's back as far as her eyes could see him. He sat tall, not flinching, as the cannon sounded, as the drums rolled, as the band blared "The girl . . . the girl. . . ." He didn't turn. He didn't wave. His eyes never left front and center. Following him, the men marched row upon row, covering with the dust of their footsteps any mark in the road Phillip may have left behind him.

Chapter Five

AFTER PHILLIP'S DEPARTURE, MARA WAS TROUBLED BY DREAMS. She often saw herself walking through a dark valley. At first she felt sheltered from the sharp sun by the shadows of the mist. But as it grew darker, she could not see her way. All she could do was to believe there was light somewhere and that she was following someone, for someone seemed to be moving ahead of her above the mist, just beyond her awareness in soundless air. She felt an urgency to reach whoever it was and soon she was no longer walking, but floating, floating, moving boundlessly into the cool gray hills. The colors of the grass and flowers in the dim light turned swiftly under her feet; the shapes moved and changed and clicked. She recognized the blue of a mirrored lake, patches of willows, goldenrod, sunflowers, and sumac leaves. Then ahead of her in the far distance burned a cool and refreshing light. Her flying feet could not move swiftly enough to reach the light, for it flickered and was suddenly gone. In darkness she woke to an absolute despair, clinging to her dreams. She was alone.

She tried to pray, but when she prayed she thought of Phillip, not God. It was as if she prayed in the name of Phillip Hurst, not the name of Jesus Christ. Where were they, her Heavenly Father and his Son? In heaven? Why not here on earth where she needed them to be? She needed a perfect, understanding Father who would forgive her, love her. A perfect Elder Brother who would suffer all pain for her, strengthen her, heal her. But they seemed so far away.

Then she became angry at herself for her own weakness, her anger at heaven, her bitterness, and she would try again to reach for some kind of peace, struggling with her feelings whenever she knelt to pray. But she had to fight continually against the feeling that she knelt only to an ideal she could not reach, an ideal she didn't even want to reach. She knew she would rather have knelt at the feet of a living breathing man of flesh and rest her head at his knee.

"Where are you, my Lord?" she would say to no one, knowing she could not mean Phillip or Jesus, either one.

For a while she stayed home from the hotel. While she moved about in the kitchen, Sobe tugged on her hands. Since Phillip's departure, she had shown more interest in Sobe. She had felt she should exert as much energy as she could muster—which wasn't a lot—to regain his confidence as her dearest little friend.

"Mara," he begged her. "I found a bee's nest. Come and see the bee's nest." He brought garden snakes to her, mice curled in his hands, sometimes wounded by traps. He pulled her into the barn to watch Targirl foal, the blood pouring onto the straw through the thick, chalky, white water sack. Sobe begged Mara to stay with him in the barn with the colt that night.

"Oh, she doesn't want to stay out, honey," Mama said.

"I'll do it," Mara said, though she still felt numb. She hadn't felt like giving very much of herself and her lonely time to Sobe, or to anyone. But she knew she must try. She knew she was being foolish, knew she had been foolish to hope Phillip would make the sacrifice, give up his life, and accept her on her terms. She knew, too, that she had made the decision herself, that she could have followed him, could have said yes when he had said, "Leave them." But for whatever reason he had left, she had let him go. Their need for each other had not been the greatest force in either of their lives, and she would just have to accept that. Phillip was gone. It was time to get on with things in the life she had chosen to live. Phillip could never have understood this life. And though her longing for him would not subside, Mara knew this was the life to which her soul was bound.

In the barn that night Mara helped Sobe to lay out a pallet of straw just outside the foaling stall. They laid bedding, pillows, and comforters over the straw.

"It's still light outside," Sobe said as he closed the barn door. He ran back to the colt, who stood wobbling with his long slender nose under his mother's belly. "I hope Papa gives me the colt someday."

Mara's mind drifted between reality and dreams—Sobe's face and the memory of Phillip's hands. "Sobe, don't hope for Papa to give you the colt, for then you would have to feed it and groom it. You would have to do everything yourself. Let Papa keep the colt, and then you can just have fun riding it."

"You have Pawface."

"I got her when I was much older than you."

The colt quit its mother and curled up quietly as if it would now sleep. Sobe left the stall and came to Mara on the straw. He wore his oldest overalls and a torn shirt.

"Did my mother have a colt?"

He was asking about his mother, Blueflower, again. "I don't know."

"Was she a good rider?"

"She rode like the wind. All of your people could ride. They rode wild horses over the land flying like the wind. Someday you will ride like them."

"I know I will be a better rider because I am Indian."

For the first time Mara felt uneasy at Sobe's pride in his heritage. She had nourished this pride, but now she worried that she might at the same time have been separating him from the only family he knew.

"Maybe not because you are Indian, but because you want to ride well. Being Indian or white doesn't make any difference. You are able to do something well because you work at it."

"Someday I will be the best rider of anyone because I will work at it. I'll be better than Ashel, I'll be better than Teddy Allen. I'll be the best one and then everyone will know that an Indian can be the best in something. My own people will see me riding, and they will be proud, and they will know that an Indian can be best."

As the sun went down, the shadows deepened in the dusty barn. Mara could see Sobe's eyes, bright with a distant gaze, even in the dimness. As he sat on the straw beside her, she gently touched his rich black hair. She saw the pride rising in him without his being able to recognize it, without having known anything about the pride of his mother, who had turned so violently from her white captors. Though Mara had not been with Sobe as much because of her work at the hotel the last few years, she felt the weight now of her own influence on this child. All of them—Rain, Mama, even Nancy—had influenced Sobe, and now she tried to see the results of their efforts. She saw it in his stance, his bright eyes, the tense limbs, the same energy that bounded in the blood of his people. It was a wild beauty, the rich earthiness she had seen as she dressed Rain for her wedding. She was glad Sobe, her Sobe, was Indian, and she would help him to be the best of what he was.

"Sometimes being better than others doesn't make you happy, Sobe." He looked at her in the dim light. "What's important is being better than yourself . . . better than what you were yesterday."

Sobe was quiet. "I guess I can be better than myself if Papa will give me the colt."

"Maybe you will have to be better in something besides riding."

"Like what, for instance?"

"Oh, maybe like patience, for instance," Mara said.

In autumn when the colt was a few months old, Mara and Sobe rode Targirl to Sully's to see Nancy and Rain. The colt followed and played around Targirl's heels.

For several months now, Rain had been large with child. She hurried toward them from the house, grinning, waving. Mara's emotions at seeing Rain frightened her. It was envy. She held Sobe tightly to her as she pulled on the reins to stop Targirl. "I might have been having that child," she thought to herself, "if I had not been so proud, if I had not separated myself so completely."

"There's always Will," Nancy would tell her almost daily. Will still left his children with Nancy, but stayed at his shop in town, relinquishing his bedroom at Sully's now to Rain. He had made a small fortune selling goods to the troops in Provo, and he dressed smartly in a topcoat and cravat. When the troops returned to Camp Floyd, Will maintained enough contact with them to continue to bring many government dollars into his pocket. He was smooth and friendly, yet shrewd enough to take his share. Now he had bought into a mercantile company with a Jewish merchant, Benjamin Buchman, and the two were borrowing from the Eastman funds to build a mercantile building. They were fast becoming the principal merchants of Provo City, and they finally convinced Sully to join them full time.

Nancy told Mara, "You are missing something not to get to know Will better." But Mara was as silent on the matter as Will was, and nothing happened between them.

Will Jones built a new house on Center Street, and Sully built Nancy one next to it. Rain stayed at the farm, and Mara took Sobe there often. Rain counted her days by dropping beans into a jar.

"Sobe, at last you'll have a playmate who's one of the real People," she told him, a full grin on her broad satisfied face. Mara laughed at Rain's joke and was pleased to see Rain so happy.

Mara and Sobe watched Rain grind corn as her mother did—on stone. They watched her braid leaves and weave with wool.

"All things my mother taught me, Sobe," Rain said. "Most white men believe their ways to be better." She smiled at Mara. "But the Eastmans always let us do things the Indian way."

Sobe loved the corn cakes she made on the griddle heated over the hot stove. He liked the Indian cloth and Rain's clay pottery. Rain told him stories of his mother and his mother's family. Blueflower's mother was a big woman who died of starvation the winter before Blueflower was captured. Her father, a great medicine man, was killed by the white men because he had been with those who stole the white men's cattle. Old Hawk Feather was the medicine man's sister, and Angel Lip, her daughter. Because Mara insisted, Rain told Sobe what little she knew of Hinte, Blueflower's husband, married only two months before he was killed at the same time Blueflower's father was killed. Hinte was the tall young warrior from a neighboring tribe who had seen Blueflower and come to be with her. "Your father, Sobe," Mara said, as Rain looked at her through narrow eyes. "Listen to Rain, and she will tell you of your mother and your father."

Rain shook her head at Mara and turned back to Sobe. "You will forget your people if I don't tell you," she said. "Here," and she tapped his forehead. "Remember, Sobe, if we are swallowed whole by white people you are still part of a proud Indian people."

Sully came every week to see Rain at the farm. If he came while Mara and Sobe were there, and if he was not planning to spend the night, he brought them back to town in the wagon, hauling produce for Nancy in Provo City, tying Targirl to the back and leading her to the Eastman house.

In January of 1861, Rain gave birth to a healthy son. Sully was ecstatic. Mara and Sobe together visited them often to see the baby. Rain stayed broad as a barn, and her undisguised joy filled everyone around her with happiness.

Before their exodus east that spring to fight the Civil War, the troops at Camp Floyd sold a hundred thousand dollars worth of goods to Provo merchants, who in turn resold them at a profit to the citizens of the valley. Will Jones was one of the merchants who prospered most. When Mara was around, he teased her while he talked business with Papa Eastman.

"Even when they leave us, the soldier boys keep making a contribution! Maybe they'll be with us always—even in heaven. Eh, Mara?"

Mara didn't like Will's words. She blushed.

To try to reinstate himself into her good graces, he said "You pout like a Broadway star. Ever think of going on stage, Miss Eastman?"

She looked at him, not sure of what he was trying to tell her, but he actually seemed serious this time.

"One thing we bought from the militia was a stage and we're organizing a drama company. Mrs. Partridge told me she thought you'd be good as Lady Macbeth."

Not sure to what extent he was teasing her, Mara felt nothing but frustration with him at that moment. But reluctantly responding to his invitation, she did meet with the others at the Cluff building to help organize the first professional dramatic company in Utah Valley. Their first production was *Midsummer Night's Dream.*

All she really wanted to do for the production was to help behind the scenes with costumes and makeup, but she was surprised and pleased when they talked her into doing the part of Mustard Seed, although she heard nothing but interminable teasing from Will Jones who wondered if she really had the faith of one. Will himself broke up the audience as Bottom, playing the donkey with exaggerated style. As Mara watched him from the wings, she couldn't help laughing along with the rest of them.

"You're supposed to be working, not enjoying this," Will teased her when he came back stage.

"You're so funny," she said.

"Thanks a lot," and he shook his donkey ears at her.

All of them had so much fun that first summer, that she thought she might yield to the encouragement of the other members of the company to audition for a larger part in the next play.

If it hadn't been for Mama's illness, it would have been a good year for Mara, all things considered. She had begun to find some peace again. She had felt the sweet love of many who were concerned for her. Sometimes when she prayed, she felt she was going to be all right—if it hadn't been for Mama. As autumn faded into gray November, Mama grew weaker. Pneumonia set into her lungs, already weak from consumption. Dr. Bates said she could not last past Christmas. Mama was dying.

"If only I could have seen you safely married," she told Mara, pressing her hand with all the strength left in her. "I wish I could have lived to see my grandchildren play at my feet." Mara sat in silence by her mother's bed. "But it's not like you didn't have somebody of your own to raise and look after. Sobe needs you, darling. He's at such a tender age. Please take good care of him." Sobe was eleven.

Mara pressed her mother's hands, white as tissue paper, shaking and thin. Sobe stood by looking helpless, sad. Ashel wheeled Caroline to Mama's bed every morning. Ashel was twenty now, and his loyalty to Caroline outstripped his mother's wildest hopes. Caroline, pale, beautiful Caroline, was frightened by the illness of the only mother she had ever really known.

"Take care of her, Ashel. I'm trusting you and Papa to take care of Caroline."

"You aren't going anywhere, Mother," Ashel said stubbornly as he wheeled Caroline's chair close to her bed once more.

"I'm afraid I am going, Ashel. My time is over. I feel like God needs me. I want to see Sophia and John, and little Martha, too. I didn't get very much time with her."

Papa never said very much. He didn't eat; he didn't sleep. He paced Mama's room with restless steps, opening the windows to draw away the stifling heat that rose in steam clouds from the stove. He stood at the windows and breathed in and out before he closed them as the cold November wind whipped past the glass. He would stand by the closed windows then and stare out onto the grass in the park. The first snow fell; the birds flocked to the grain which he had scattered in tree wells and on level patches of lawn.

"Hart. Hart," Mama would call in a weak voice. "Will you please change my brick again?" And Papa would reach for the brick inside the comforter at her feet and replace it with the one sitting on the stove. "Thank you, Hart. It feels good," Mama would say quietly. "It feels so good." There were bed pans to empty, garments damp with sweat, and soiled reeking bedding to change and launder. Sometimes Mara felt sick going into her mother's room. But she did not complain as she performed the tasks her father asked of her. He hired more people at the hotel and asked Mara to stay home full time, and Mara worked to make her mother's last hours more comfortable.

Just before Christmas, Mama whispered to Mara. "Bring your father and your brother to see me now." When the family gathered in the room, Mama gazed about, her eyes almost gray.

"I'm about ready to go now. I wanted to tell you that John and Sophia came to see me."

Mara stared unbelieving at her mother's feverish face.

"They stood . . . there. . . ." Mother pointed to the foot of the bed. Mara gazed at Papa. His eyes showed not a hint of disbelief. "And they wanted me to come."

"No." Caroline's voice startled Mara. Caroline threw herself from the wheelchair and wound her arms around Mama's neck. Then she dropped her face to Mama's breast and began to sob.

"Can't you wait until after Christmas, Mama?" Ashel said, almost pleading, lifting Caroline back to her chair.

Mama's eyes brightened. "Would it make so much difference?" Caroline's eyes still filled with tears.

"It would, Mama," Ashel said.

"I thought you'd like Christmas without all the extra work."

"Oh no, Mama," Ashel said. Mara knew he was afraid for Caroline when Mama died.

Christmas was the most difficult one Mara had ever spent. Papa had been building on to his Center Street office to make room for his bank and was encumbered with business problems. Sobe was sulky from being shut up by the bad weather in a house filled with sadness. Caroline was impossible. Frightened of what she knew would soon come, she became irritable and demanding. Ashel had to tend to her needs or Mara could never have dealt with Mama. The bedding had to be washed now almost every day, and Mama was in such pain that she could no longer talk clearly. Mara did not try to converse with her now. For many years—really since she had refused Sully—there had been very little discussion between them anyway. But Mara constantly prayed for her in silence.

Christmas was a quiet exchange of gifts around Mama's bed. Each member of the family had drawn the name of one person to honor. Mara had drawn Papa and she had sewn him a proud cravat. After a confusing midday supper, the Allens came over. Bishop and Sister Higbee brought plum cakes and fruit. Sully and his family made a visit with Will, the two Jones children holding Nancy's hands; big as they were, they still called her "Nana." Rain carried year-old Tom on her hip. Tom looked a lot like Sully. He was lighter than Rain or Sobe, his skin as smooth as cream. Proud Sully could not leave him alone. Rain was expecting again. All of the families filed past Mama Eastman's bed so that she could "have a good look at them."

"Sully and Rain will have lots of very nice children," Mama said in a faint voice to Mara when the day was over and the hot bricks had been placed at her feet. Papa was busy elsewhere in the house for a few moments. Mara did not like to be alone with Mama now when she talked. She kept thinking she heard the death rattle in Mama's throat, and she was afraid her last words would again express her disappointment in Mara, a lamentation for grandchildren not conceived, the familiar complaint. Afraid, Mara chattered about nothing."Can you move your feet, Mama? There. Lift. I'll lift. That's good."

"We have never been able to talk very well to each other."

Startled, Mara heard the words in her vacant head, in a sudden dizziness that emptied her brain. No, that's right. She's right; we have never been able to talk very well. But what could be said now?

"All I've wanted . . . was what was best for you, what I thought would be best. . . ."

Mara was silent, feeling the pressure like a heavy cloud. Mama's head, small and withered, turned on the white pillow in the stifling room. Mara felt conscious of the heat, the November frost on the windows. She felt conscious of death, as though Sophia and John and Martha could have been there in the hot room waiting, and she could have reached out with her hands to touch them; the spiritual essence of their bodies could have been moving with her own limbs.

"We built God's kingdom out here for your children. I . . . I wanted our joyful life to last forever." Mama's words stumbled in thin gasps, spoken with a very grating, choking sound in a faraway throat. "Forever." The last word broke, almost soundless. Mara looked at her mother's frail body, the gray skin, the pallor around her eyes.

"Our lives *will* last forever," Mara tried, feeling like a foolish and helpless child.

"Mara, you've been a lovely girl."

Mara had not heard this for so long. She touched her mother's gray hand. "You . . . might forgive me? For not. . . ." She stumbled on the words now, tried to smile, "giving you grandchildren?"

"I worried about that . . . more . . . than I worried about you . . . giving me yourself."

Mara listened, hearing something she had never heard before in Mama's words. A hope, a strange wild hope rose somewhere inside her.

But Mama turned toward her, her eyes liquid, deep. "Of course, I believe it's possible to have both."

Mara could not answer. She held her mother's hand. She stroked the gray brow. "It's all right, Mama. Everything will be all right." In the final analysis, Mara thought, it would have to be all right if they stayed firm in the faith. "Papa will be here in a moment."

In the morning, Mama was gone.

Mama's death hurt them all. Mara clung to Sobe as though he were the last child on earth. If the Eastmans were to help populate Mama's kingdom, perhaps Sobe would be her only contribution. If not by birth, she could contribute by influence.

Because Sully and Nancy came often to calm her heart, she stayed close to them. They took both her and Sobe with them to go to the market, or to church dinners. Will came with them, and she found herself telling him things she had not told anyone.

"I'm not sure I showed Mother how much I really loved her," she said to him.

Will was quiet. "I felt that way when the children's mother died," he said softly. "And so I keep hoping she overhears my prayers."

Mara looked at him.

He seemed bent. "She knows you love her," he said without moving his head. "She probably heard what you just said."

Mara felt a strange chill as though he were right and as though her mother were in the room. She looked at Will.

Then he turned his head to her. His eyes were bright as he gazed at her and smiled. "If only you could see her you could reach out to touch her, for she is still with us."

Chapter Six

WHEN IVIE RICHARDS HAD LEFT THE NORTH FARM TO RETURN with his only remaining stepson, Clem, to Salt Lake City in 1858 he had made a verbal agreement with Sully that the Tuttles could farm his place. For six years, Sully got good crops from Richards' land as well as his own, plus another share where he had worked up on the bench.

Just before harvest in 1864, Clem decided to bring his wife and young boys to the Provo Canyon farm. Sully had planted wheat.

Rain was the first to see the family drive down from the bench, the wagon heavy with goods, two broken horses straining to keep their footing on the steep grade.

Mrs. Richards was a gaunt woman with stringy dark hair and large, vacant, colorless eyes. The boys were thin, their shoulder blades and hip bones poking out. Mrs. Richards rode on the front of the wagon, her bony knees under the purple flowered cotton shift. Every once in a while she hit the horse with a loose whip and said "Har" with a nasal voice. The boys hung to the pile of furniture in the wagon, their scrawny legs and arms silhouetted against the sinking sun. "Har. Har."

Rain could hear the "har" before she could see them clearly on a stretch of road just at the edge of the bench above a stand of trees. Then they disappeared into the vale where the old Richards house, abandoned for six years, stood near the river in the wash. The oldest boy looked about six years old, the age of Tom. Rain caught sight of him on the side of the wagon nearest the edge, his brow hidden by a shock of unruly black hair. The other two were younger, one small enough to climb into his mother's arms. They were about the same ages as Rain's two small girls, Clarissa and Samantha.

When Sully came on the following day to bring supplies, to visit Rain and their three children, he told Rain she ought to take Mrs. Richards some corn bread.

"The only way we'll survive the Richards family is to be neighborly, to show them how we want to be neighborly."

Rain did not say anything.

"I know Clem Richards' father, Ivie Richards, treated our people unfairly, Rain." Among other things, he had taken a larger portion of land. "But the only way to be neighbors is to show that we care and want to be friends."

Rain remained silent, her eyes cast to the floor, her lips tight. Sully knew her thoughts. "Rain," he said, lifting her face to look into her eyes. "You will be here alone most of the time now that I have to be in town so much with Will." Rain liked being on the farm so much better than being in town that she often told him to let her stay. "If you want to stay here, you'll *have* to make friends. They can help you."

Rain raised her dark eyes to him, black points above the furrows of her broad cheeks. There was more fear in them than anger.

"All right," Sully said softly. "I'll go with you. Let's go now, before I have to go back to Provo. We'll take some beef jerky."

Clem Richards had been the younger of Ivie Richards' two boys, the smallest and the least capable. Sully always thought he was the cowardly one. But Clem seemed a little subdued because he had seen what his brother Tony's rashness had earned him. It was Tony who had killed Old Bishop and started all the trouble so long ago. And the Indians had finally killed Tony—who, sadly, was not missed. At least not missed by anyone Sully knew.

Old pain, old troubles nagged at Sully's memory. He found the man Clem in the yard, trying to put back together the old fence.

"Well, hello, Clem . . ." he said, forcing words, finding them stuck in his throat. Rain followed him close behind with the baby in her arm, Clarissa clinging to her skirt. She stayed behind him.

Clem Richards raised his brown face to them, revealing a three-day beard on a roughly scarred chin. "Sully. Sully Tuttle," he grunted.

His face broke into a broad grin. "My gosh, Sully Tuttle!" He dropped his tools and came toward them. He stared at Rain.

"This is Rain," Sully said after he shook the man's hand.

Clem Richards kept staring. "I thought you was married to Nancy Allen."

"Nancy has a house in town." Sully ignored the meaning in Richards' voice. "And this is my boy, Tom, and my two daughters, Clarissa, Samantha."

For a moment Clem did not say anything. Then he turned and shouted so close to Sully and Rain that he nearly popped their ears, "Susy!"

Susan Richards peered from the broken window of the old cabin and started for the door. The boys, ages six and four, came out and stared at Tom and teased him to play. Rain gave the jerky to Susan, who did not even smile.

"Well, after we spent a few years in Salt Lake Valley, Pa told us we might as well take up the Provo farm again, that there weren't no Indian troubles no more." He stared a moment at Rain. "I hope there ain't any?"

Sully would have to keep calm. "No," he smiled. "As a matter of fact, we're getting along fine."

"I heard about some reservation the government was going to make to keep all the Indians in their own place."

"They have been assigned lands."

Clem's eyes were dark, suspicious. He stared again at Rain. "I thought they was all supposed to be sent to the reservation."

Sully tried not to hear the sneer in the man's voice. "Of course, Rain's my wife. She belongs here, on my place."

"And I thought the government's also trying to work on a law making it illegal to marry more than one wife."

Sully felt the barb deeply now.

"Well, ain't they?"

Rain moved behind Sully and lowered her eyes. Sully felt her like a shadow behind him.

"Rain's the only one up here much now since I've been working for some merchants in town. I do come up once in a while. The mill was abandoned long ago."

"I know," Clem nodded, scanning the countryside. "I know that. But it's still the same country. And you got good crops of wheat!"

Sully smiled. "I've been here alone a long time now." Then he stretched the truth for a purpose. "It'll be good to have neighbors again. Your boys look like strong, hardy boys." The boys seemed thin and scrawny, but they did look tough as wire. Sully was determined he would be neighborly if it killed him. "It'll be good to have you all up here. Our boys can play together. Maybe you can watch out after Rain for me."

"Oh yeah. . . . Sure," Clem said, his dark eyes almost disappearing below his black brows.

Every day Rain watched the Richards' place from the window. The boys came to play, but she never saw Susan. She was very cautious about going to visit. Susan had never said a word to her. The only time she heard her speak was the "har" to the horses and an occasional call to her boys for supper.

The first time she ever saw Susan outside in the fields was a few days before Sully had planned to bring Ashel up for the harvest. Susan and Clem went out into the fields with the horses, and Rain followed them closely with her eyes. She thought they were dragging a harvester and rake. But she couldn't be sure. She stared a long time, unbelieving. At first she thought it couldn't be true, but then she was sure. They were cutting down the wheat!

Rain's first feeling was to mount one of the horses and ride to town to fetch Sully. But she would have had to take the road through the Richards' fields. If they saw her go, the only time she had mounted to ride to Provo since they had been here, they would guess why she was going. Puzzled, she stayed in the house with the children and pondered what she should do, or if she should do anything at all. When dusk fell, she hadn't left their property once that day. Sully didn't come that evening. All of the next morning, Rain watched the harvester behind the horses in the Richards' fields. She watched the wheat come down, the gathering. Tom came in at lunch covered with mud and crying.

"Carl pushed me in the water."

"Stay in now, Tom," Rain said. While she changed his clothes, she asked, "What are they doing with the wheat?"

"They're stacking it behind Mr. Richards' house."

If somebody doesn't go out and stop them they will take all of Sully's wheat, Rain thought to herself in panic and fear. Rain knew

Sully would be terribly unhappy if he were to come up and find his wheat cut. And she must be able to tell him that she had tried to stop them, as terrifying and impossible a task as that seemed to her to be.

She carried Samantha on her hip. She walked slowly toward the fields, stumbling in the weeds, the gopher holes, the knots of grass. She wished for the slender strength of her younger days.

The horses were moving away from her. Now they turned and moved toward her. She saw that Richards spotted her in the distance, but he did not acknowledge that she was there. The August sun beat on her hot hair as she stared at him. When he came closer, she raised her arm. He made no sign in return. She kept walking. Now he was moving away from her again. He would know why she was there.

"Mister Richards," Rain called out. "Mister Richards."

He didn't turn.

Rain walked to the row he was cutting, and when he turned toward her, she stood in his path. Now he waved her aside. But she planted her feet firmly and stayed where she was. He stopped the horses short of her only a few feet.

"Damn you. Move out of the way!" he snarled.

"Mister Richards. This wheat belongs to my husband."

"It's on my land. I'm taking it for rent!" he called out.

"Please don't take it," Rain shouted into the hot sun.

"Get out of here, you dirty Injun! Go to the reservation where you belong. Get out of here, you no good Injun."

Rain's ears stung. She heard the words like hot irons. They seared her, but she did not move. She stood with the baby on her hip in the waving wheat.

Clem Richards' eyes grew dark under the black brows. "Move your carcass!" he shouted now, his voice hard. "Or I'll run you down."

Run me down then, Rain thought. It won't be the first time a Richards has run an Indian down.

Richards screamed then. "I'll trample you to dust, you savage scum!" and he started the horses. "Nobody cares if you live or die, you dirty Injun!" But the animals would not move into Rain. He began to beat them, hard. "Move, you mules! Move, damn it!

Move!" The horses pawed, whinnied, started forward. One tried to move to the side of Rain, but she fell. On the ground she quickly huddled over her child as the horse passed beside her, the baby screaming. The cutter was close behind the animals, and Rain saw she would be cut to pieces. She grabbed the baby and leaped to the side just as the blade tore at her heel. Her ankle was cut and began to bleed. She grabbed the crying child, held her in her arms, and sobbed.

"Sully, I tried to save your wheat," she said softly, watching her blood water the ground, as she held Samantha tight beneath her tears.

On their way to begin harvest on a Monday morning in early September, Sully and Ashel saw Clem Richards, his wife, and their three boys traveling toward Provo in a loaded wagon covered with blankets. There was no reason anything odd should have crossed Sully's mind, unless he had thought about it, but he saw the truth in a moment when he reached the Richards' farm. Not a stalk of wheat was still standing in the field.

Sully found Rain hobbling on a bandaged foot, cut and caked with blood. He was seething with fury when he entered the house, and he could not speak to Rain. He knew she sensed his anger. He wanted to cry when he saw her foot. He guessed without asking what had happened in the field, and he held Samantha a long moment, feeling the soft skin of her cheek, knowing she had been in danger.

Ashel stood about nervously, unable to say anything. He began helping Rain with the cooking and the children, until finally Sully beckoned him to come out into the fields to rake hay.

"I suppose he felt it was rightfully his," Sully said, trying hard to control his fierce anger.

"It makes a fellow angry."

"He could have asked. I would have shared it with him."

"You did all the work."

"And right before harvest, too."

Sully was waiting for Clem when he returned from town with an empty wagon. Tommy, just behind him, ran to the Richards boy, his playmate.

Clem grinned. "Wanted to tell you thank you for planting the wheat. Made near fifty dollars, plus enough for my own use this winter." He grinned furtively from beneath bushy brows. Susan Richards beside him stared from her hollow eyes as though she could not hear a word anyone was saying.

"I would have appreciated if you'd said something." Sully spoke carefully.

Clem started; he must have known, deeply, that he was wrong. "You weren't nowhere around. I took it as rent for the land six years. Was sure you wouldn't mind."

Sully nodded. There was, after all, something to what the man said. "Maybe if you'd just made some arrangements with my wife Rain." Rain's limping nagged at him. He wanted to pound Clem Richards into the ground.

Clem didn't say anything. He half grinned, and the grin curved into contempt. Then he spit on the ground.

"That was a good amount you got for rent, then," Sully said.

"That was a good piece of ground you got use of for six years."

Sully's control of himself thinned. It wouldn't last much longer. His despair deepened. He turned to Tom who was tugging at Carl Richards' foot to beg him to come down from the wagon.

"See my snake," Tom said. "Come on, Carl."

"He can't right now," Clem said. "Get back, boy." He sneered at Tom. Sully remembered how someone had told him that Clem had mouthed off in town about the fact that all his boys had to play with were "half-breeds."

Because Sully was trying so desperately to avoid conflict, nothing more happened over the wheat. He himself did not know whether it was cowardice or bravery to have let Clem Richards take his crop, but he knew he would do almost anything to avoid violence. There had already been too much violence in this place.

He asked, then commanded, Rain to come to live with them in Provo for the winter, which she somewhat reluctantly did. But as soon as spring arrived, she begged him to take her to the north farm again, away from the town. He couldn't understand it. She had lived in town most of her life now. But her preference was to take the children and go out there by herself. She was still at heart a native who loved the vast unaltered land.

The winter had been mild and the early spring months freshened by rain. The grass had grown tall and green, and the trees budded with leaves and fruit. Rain clung to the children as the wagon lumbered toward the farm, gazed at the beauty of her old lands. She had brought corn and squash, and she promised Sully she would make a garden. Sully found much satisfaction now in merchandising with Will Jones, and he decided not to farm much anymore except for their own use. So Nancy raised food in the Center Street yard and Rain would raise as much as she could here.

Clem Richards waved hello from where he was working in the garden. The boy Carl ran to the fence to see Tom. He crawled through the railings and ran with Tom to take him toward the river behind the barn. "Pa built a lake," he said.

Sully and Rain watched the boys go. Tom was taller now. His thick chestnut hair was burnished by the sun, his skin dark like Rain's, his face the image of Sully's. He was a handsome boy. Carl had grown, too, though he was still mostly bones. This year they were larger bones. The smaller boys followed him like ducklings follow their mother.

Susan came out of the house. She gazed out of the same set of hollow eyes. But this year she smiled, briefly, at Sully, though she did not look at Rain.

"Well, now. Will you be here as our neighbor, Mr. Tuttle?" Clem tried to sound friendly.

"My wife will stay here. And I'll be here as much as possible," Sully answered.

"Well, now, fine," Clem said, though Sully knew he lied. He did not look at Rain, either.

Sully hollered for Tom, and he came running, excited about the lake Mr. Richards made in the river. Sully snapped the reins and the wagon started. "It's deep. It's quiet on the top and black as a well," Tom said as he climbed into the wagon.

Sully turned to Rain. He searched her eyes and the quiet in her heart. "He must have dammed the river, or a spring." For a moment they rode in silence. "Are you sure you want to be here alone with the children this summer?" Sully said.

Rain's eyes answered him. They were wide eyes, afraid. But he knew her well. She preferred to be here alone in the open land she loved and to be visited by Sully occasionally. Perhaps one of the strongest reasons was that somehow she was able to be herself here and did not need to try to belong to a people not fully her own. Nancy had always been kind, but it was not the same for Rain in town. No matter how great her fear of Richards, she loved this place and she was not yet ready to surrender.

As he drove into the yard, Sully looked at the small, tight house he had built so long ago, for Mara. He shook his head. Poor Mara. So proud. Such a hard, painful time of it she'd had. Alone, with no one to comfort her, love her. No one but Sobe. However, he had to admit that caring for a child had been good for her. She was becoming a very loving mother; something beautiful seemed to be happening in her heart. It was a shame she would allow no man to enjoy this growing beauty. He pulled up the team by the corral. A good house, but perhaps it was time now to make a new house in town for Rain, on the outskirts somewhere, where he could see her and the children every day.

Tommy climbed down first and ran to the door. "Pa! The lock's broke!"

"Oh, no," Sully said quietly. "Someone has been in the house." Coming to the door, Sully saw that the lock had been pried loose.

Rain entered quickly. Some of the furniture which they had left had been taken. The rocker in the corner was gone. The chest had been forced open and Rain's blankets and pottery were gone. The small black stove had been tipped and ashes spilled over the floor.

"Damn them," Sully said under his breath. As he swiftly moved through the three rooms, Rain and the children stood, numb. "It's empty," he told Rain. "There is no one here." Then he took her arms and looked into her eyes. "I don't want to leave you here."

Rain shook her head slowly. "It's all right, Sully," she said, her voice thick. "The children like it out here. We will be all right."

"You have my gun and know how to use it."

"Yes, Sully."

"I'll stay tonight. I'll come as often as I can. Every day if I can." Rain nodded.

In the morning when Sully left, he saw Carl Richards in the yard. He was wearing a homemade coat. It was made from one of Rain's blankets—one made by her own hands. Sully's heart tore inside him. God bless my wife and children, he prayed.

The summer of 1865 was the year the people in Provo celebrated the final reservation of lands for the Indians. The Utes were now assigned to property entirely their own and would no longer be allowed legally to live where the white man was living. On July 24th some of the Indians who still surrounded the town were invited to a farewell barbecue supper. Rain could not keep the sorrow out of her heart. She knew the whites acted in good will, but she could not help feeling that many of them said inside, "You are now to live elsewhere, our redskin friends. We will give a final dinner for you, and then you must retire to the reservation where you belong."

Rain and the children came with Sully and Nancy to spend the day in the Eastman yard across from the barbecue in the Center Street park. There was a band, a parade, a ton of freshly killed beef, tanks of milk and fresh biscuits and butter supplied by the neighbors surrounding the park. Even Mara had made hundreds of buttermilk biscuits and added several pints of plum preserves made years ago by Martha Eastman and saved for an important occasion.

The men dug pits and fired rocks for hours. In the afternoon, the beef was slung into the pit and turned slowly until crisp on the edges, juicy in the center. The huge shanks were pulled out onto slabs of wood supported by buckets at each corner. The women pulled out their greens and biscuits and butter and everyone ate until they were full.

About a hundred Indians were present, including families Rain vaguely remembered having seen once with Kickingboot, and further back, with Old Elk and Ope Carry and some of the others who had lost their lives fighting the whites.

She thought she recognized an old woman she had seen who once lived with Old Bishop. She was herding some young Indian children and trying to stop the cruel teasing of some older brothers and sisters who were eating crudely, the beef hanging in bloody shreds from their mouths while they laughed.

Cautiously, Rain went to the woman to talk. Her own children came with her, hanging to her skirts. The eight- and ten-year-old boys pointed to Tom. "Bloody half-breed," the ten-year-old taunted. "Bloody apple. Apple, Apple. Red on the outside, white on the inside."

Rain stood back a moment, wounded. What were they saying? How had they learned these English words? What did they mean?

"Get out of here, bloody half-breeds." The Indians laughed. "We got our own land and don't want you on it."

The ten-year-old kicked Tommy and started to run. But Sully caught sight of him and reached out his hand to pull him back.

"Half-breed. Half-breed!" The Indians taunted Tommy. Tommy's fists were tight, his cheeks rivers of tears.

"Bloody apple. No Indian wants you and no white neither."

Rain stood, silent. A sharp sadness welled up inside her blood until she could no longer hold back the tears. She felt the shaking of her body, the fear in her limbs. In an unexplainable darkness she could see a stern look of judgment in the eyes of the Indian women. A strong hand from behind finally took her arm and led her back toward the Eastman yard. It was Sully. Not to embarrass him, she let her tears dry without touching her eyes. She stood beside him without moving, unable to smile at anyone or say hello.

"It's all right, Rain. I'm sorry, my dear wife." She clung to Sully's hand until Nancy came from a corner of the yard and beckoned to Sully to meet someone. Nancy saw the tears then, and moved toward Rain, a question in her eyes, but Rain shook her head. She would not want anyone to know how she felt. Or if she opened her mouth to say hello, tears would come into her voice. But Nancy knew. She moved close to Rain and held her in her arms.

It did not seem possible that one could drown in this desert where there was so little water. There were days when the dew was so vaporous that it was more like breath than water, drying on the grass before the sun rose over the hills. The weather sucked the water from the springs; the hot wind blew an inch from the surface of the ponds almost every day. There were only ribbons of water in the ditches, in the irrigation canals. Rain saw that Clem Richards' decision to build a water hole had been wise.

The tragedy was not because of the depth of the Richards dam or the amount of water in the hole, for it was not much over three feet high on that September afternoon.

It was not the current, for the black water was as smooth as jade, polished like glass; the surface rippled with tiny shadows of insects skimming the cool mirror.

Perhaps it was curiosity, perhaps a long look at a water hummer or dragonfly and an unwise reach for it, a grasp, a slip, a cry, a fear in fighting the rising suck of the pond that closed over him. Or perhaps there had been a playful, or not so playful, push from Carl. Rain would never know.

If Carl had only run to Rain, she would have fought her way into the pond, snatched Tommy's body from the black shade, pumped the water from him, demanded that he breathe. She would not have fished with a pole like Susan who had watched him die.

"Oh God of Heaven, Tommy. You don't want to take Tommy. Not before he had his chance to live."

Sully's son.

On the day of the funeral, Rain wore the black pall of an old winter shift Mama Eastman left for her before she died. It was wool. She felt its weight on her shoulders, the rasp of its sleeves against her arms before it absorbed the heat and stifled the pores of her skin.

She rode on the wagon without speaking, wordlessly, quieting the murmur of the girls. She carried handfuls of leaves. After they took the girls, with Grandma Allen, to be left with a friend at the Allen's house, Sully brought Rain to the tabernacle and helped her down. She took the colored leaves into the chapel. Sully followed her to the coffin lying open on the sacrament table. Tommy's eyes were closed as though he were lost in peaceful sleep.

"Tommy," Sully whispered as he stared at the pale hands. It was hard to believe the fingers would not move.

Rain placed the leaves into a lead bucket the bishop had often used to catch drops from the leak in the roof. She separated the yellow leaves from the rose ones and spread the greener ones across the back into a fan. She heard footsteps on the stone floor behind her. She did not turn her head, but heard Sully cross the floor to the whispering sound. There were soft words. As Rain stood at the coffin, she heard the footsteps close to her. Someone stood directly behind her. Nancy.

"Rain." Nancy's hands were warm on Rain's arms, her voice gentle. "He looks so happy, Rain."

But Rain could not speak.

Behind Nancy the others began: Ashel, wheeling Caroline in her chair, Mara and Sobe, the Allens, the Higbees, members of the Church. Will, looking starched and pressed, expressing his concern and care, held each of his children by the hand. They passed single file in front of Tommy's body, looking in with tears. More than a hundred came, and the chapel filled.

As the bishop crossed to the stand, Sully circled Rain with his arm, led her gently to the front pew, sat down with her. She lowered her head into the protection of Sully's shoulder; she held his hand.

Someone from behind them began speaking in low tones. Sully sat up. Rain felt the tension in his legs. She turned slowly. Susan Richards stood inside the door. She was waiting for a moment, watching the coffin as though the child would at any moment rise from its white silk to cry out to her again. Rain's fingers gripped Sully's knee until she knew it must cause him pain. She was saying in the grip: If I had been there, I would have lost my own life to save him, Sully, your only son for whom you waited so long. You loved him. Now your loss is pressed on your face in furrows of grief. Susan Richards was there, yet Tommy is gone.

All the eyes watched Susan, her face grim as she stepped to the front. Clem Richards followed her a few paces behind. They had always come to church except perhaps once or twice when they had first moved into the hills. Susan's old dark silk dress clung to her hips. She clutched an old lace shawl that looked much like the tablecloth Mama Eastman had given Rain long ago, the one missing from the ravaged chest.

Rain's heart beat loudly. Again she tightened her hands. The shawl was now gray, almost black, well-used. Think this, Rain, she told herself, trying to feel as Sully would wish; perhaps Susan had needed it much more than we ever would. Rain tried to grasp control of the hammering in her heart. Sully squeezed her hand, again and again. Clem and Susan Richards, the last to come, stayed at the coffin a brief moment. Susan turned, her rounded back sloped now, her shoulders bent, her thin arms moving under the dirty shawl.

Rain did not want to see her face, but she made herself lift her eyes. Susan stood beside her, faced the chapel now, as though searching for a place to sit, her wide gaze scanning the congregation, her large hand pushing the dark string of her hair out of her eyes. Her mouth seemed half open as though she wanted to say something to Rain. Clem Richards, like a furtive dwarf, hunched behind her, waited for her, then nudged her nervously.

Sully still held Rain's hand. "You cannot blame her that she was unable to save him. He was not her son," Sully had told her through tears. "When she reached him he was probably gone, or very nearly gone."

"If you will take your seats now," the bishop said, rising to the pulpit, "we will begin."

Still Clem and Susan did not sit down. The only place available seemed to be the front bench beside Rain and the family. The bishop waved his hand toward the small empty space. Clem stood close behind his wife. Susan stared at Rain on the bench. She stood staring, unmoving, as though she wanted to speak, yet she was absolutely still. The bishop waited only a moment.

"Brother and Sister Richards, you might take a seat on the front here. It looks to be the only room left. Or someone can bring some chairs." One or two people were standing in the back. Susan's eyes filled with a strange fear. She might have seen Rain's hands, still clutched tightly into Sully's knee. Or she trembled from some kind of inner turmoil. Rain turned away from her, lowering her eyes and willing that Susan would go away.

Susan did not go away. She stood there. Clem did not move. He stood hiding behind his woman.

Sully still held Rain's hand. She moved close to him. Nancy on his other side moved toward the end of the bench. By moving together, all three of them left enough space for both Clem and Susan. But Susan did not sit down. She did not move. She stood, facing the congregation, her eyes glazed, her face gaunt, folds of loose skin hanging from her jaw.

By now someone from the back was stirring about to find chairs. Finally, across the aisle, Papa Eastman rose. He got up from his crowded bench and came to sit by Rain. A hush fell over the congregation.

Susan sat down suddenly, next to Papa Eastman. Clem sat in Papa Eastman's place. The bishop said the opening prayer. Rain's heart stiffened with unbelievable torment. She felt afraid. She wanted to climb into Sully's hand, to hide, to fade away. Papa Eastman held her in the curve of his arm.

The hush softened to an absolute silence, void of even a breath of sound.

"His Heavenly Father will take him home," Bishop Payne said, sweating beneath his collar, wet hair threaded across his brow. "This little child, one of the first in our area from an ordained marriage of white and Indian, this little Lamanite boy will probably go to Paradise to a work none of the rest of us can do so well as he. Those of his Indian brothers who died misunderstanding the purpose of God's people in this land stand suffering in paradise, waiting for this lad to teach the gospel to them, to tell them we are their brothers, to tell them we love them."

It seemed to Rain she felt the congregation gasp. "Even now," there was a slight break in Bishop Payne's throat, "he may be standing at the prison door and saying to his grandfathers, to Ope Carry or to Old Elk, 'Come into God's kingdom where your old ancestors are and where my mother wants me and her children to live. We are all brothers and sisters. We are all brothers and sisters.'" Rain's heart strained under the repetition. In a wash of terror she felt the presence of her neighbor, Susan Richards. Brothers and Sisters. She wanted to cry out "No!" Susan Richards was not her sister. No sister would have stood by to watch Tommy die.

"We can all live together in God's kingdom. We are all God's children. And Rain . . ." He turned directly to Rain. She heard him and shrank into the shadow of herself. "Your people are our people. Our people are your people. We become one in Jesus Christ our Lord."

Rain's fear loosened into a flood of sweat under the wool. "It's all right," Sully's hand told her, touching her knee. Everyone's eyes must have seen into Rain's heart. She could feel the penetration of each of them.

The bishop closed the coffin after his sermon. Slowly, slipping the lid forward he said, "Good-bye Tommy. All of us wish you well." Only he did not look into the coffin. He looked upward into the kerosene lamps near the windows, the smoothly plastered encasement, the transparent glass. Tommy and Sipapu would be somewhere close by, watching. Rain could feel their presence and hear in her mind's voice their sighs, and there was comfort in their presence—a comfort she knew she would later cling to.

While the people filed out of the room, Rain sat sweating, feeling close to Sully's arm, wanting no one else near her. She could feel behind her the exit of Susan Richards, with Clem following her closely, shuffling in his broken shoes. Papa Eastman rose from beside Rain, patting her heavy arm. She did not look up, or acknowledge him, or smile.

Still frightened, Rain left the chapel, her eyes downcast, her body flushed, shaking. At the door stoop, she pulled back very slightly but forced herself forward. Outside on the lawn stood Susan and Clem.

"Go ahead," Clem said from behind Susan's elbow. "Go ahead if you're going to."

Susan looked out from bleak dark eyes. Rain trembled. Susan began. "I'm. . . ." She could barely speak in a broken voice. "I'm sorry about your boy."

Confused, Rain could only stare. Sully beside her touched her arm.

A weak apology doesn't bring Tommy back, Rain thought. Oh God, it doesn't give Tommy back his life.

"Thank you," Sully said. "Rain. . . ." He would expect her at least to nod her head.

Rain nodded her head.

Susan turned quickly away, also afraid.

Chapter Seven

THOUGH HE HAD TRIED OVER THE YEARS TO BUILD A STRONG FAITH, a patience in pain, Sully's heart could not easily mend from the wounds caused by the death of his son. His grief was somewhat soothed by his knowledge that his son had gone to a happier place, but his heart still ached with loneliness and broken dreams. Only his trust in God kept him from despair and bitterness. He tried to lose himself in his work at the shop with Will Jones and Benjamin Buchman.

Buchman was a tough, squat little man with a wide face who never talked about his German-Jewish background or felt he needed to explain why he had come to the raw West to go into partnership with a Mormon. He talked his way into amazing wealth in a short time, built a fine house on Center Street, even contributed generously to the Mormon Church. Sully liked him.

"Just because we don't believe the same, no reason not to help each other," Buchman always reminded Sully.

But as much as Sully liked Buchman, and as close as he felt to Will Jones, Sully often found himself amazed at the success of the Buchman-Jones deals. When the U.S. forces left Camp Floyd in 1861, Buchman and Jones sold the goods they bought from the army at three hundred percent profit because that was the price they could get. Sully would not have asked so much for used goods, but everything sold at the marked up prices Buchman and Jones asked, and Sully simply watched the money accumulate. Because he worked for wages only, he felt it was not really his place to say anything. He supported the company by making sales and traveling to Salt Lake City for goods. He made purchases from the eastern companies where Benjamin Buchman had made contacts. Goods came by rail as far as they could, then by mule train along the Oregon and Utah trails.

The Jones-Buchman mercantile business began booming in 1868 as the railroad came nearer to running a track completely across the nation. But with rumors that the tracks would join in Utah, instead of a general delight, there was an uneasiness, a fear among the Mormons. They feared the world would have too easy access to them. They had been routed from every other place they had sought refuge. Brigham Young issued a statement that the "railroad would be used as an agency to break into pieces the Mormon Church." Suddenly, he urged the Mormons to tighten their ties by trading only amongst themselves, and as suddenly as he spoke, business fell.

Sully and the Eastmans watched Jones grow morose and uneasy at Brigham Young's announcements. "Just as we were really taking off. . . ." Will complained, and Sully feared Will was edging into criticism of the prophet.

Will told Mara once "We can't isolate ourselves from general commerce," and Mara had said "Why should you complain? You have enough money for your needs."

Will had stopped and grinned at her. "What if I wanted money for somebody else's needs?"

Wondering what he meant, or afraid she knew what he meant, Mara had not answered him.

Though he was disappointed about the policy of isolationism, he never said anything openly against Brigham Young. He understood too well. He stopped complaining after a bit. "He might be right," Will told Sully one day. "If the world comes in, the Church could feel a major impact."

However, there was something besides the general commerce that entered into the picture of the Buchman-Jones cooperative. It was the ugliness that smacked of prejudice. Will drew Sully aside more and more into private meetings outside of Benjamin Buchman's confidence. "Brigham Young wants us to trade among ourselves, and he's encouraging boycotts to outsiders. And look, here *we* are, in business with a Jew!"

At the end of the summer of 1868, Sully watched sales in the Buchman-Jones operation drop to an all-time low. Yet he looked at Ben with confused feelings. He remembered so well how it had been for him as a boy—the only Mormon among the rogues of New York. Could it be that Mormons were as narrow-minded and bigoted now about outsiders as the world was to them when they were outsiders? Sully wondered.

For weeks Sully and Jones fought it. They held auctions, slashed prices, cleared large inventories of merchandise to make way for more homemade goods to appeal to the Mormons anxious to do the will of their prophet. Sully enlisted Nancy's help as a steady seamstress. She produced children's clothing as well as women's dresses and men's shirts. Mara, too, when she was not concentrating on her Academy studies and school teaching, contributed occasional women's garments and hats. She also wanted Sobe to learn to work hard. She was grateful when Sully took him under his wing to run errands, collect merchandise and clean shelves. And Sobe, a bright and loving young man, became a hard worker and a good friend to the men. Even though he was very young, he developed a special feeling for Ben, identifying what it was like to be an outsider.

Finally, in September of 1868, some drunken rioters threw rotten eggs into the windows of Benjamin Buchman's home. He was tough. "I won't give up. Most Mormons aren't like that, sober or drunk."

In private, Will Jones sighed long worried sighs. Sully alone heard them.

"So we ought to buy Ben out good, and he won't be unhappy," Sully said.

"Not Ben," Will said, his face gray from worry as he felt the crunch of the boycott stronger every day. "I don't have the money to buy out Ben for how much he'd want. If anything, I've got to start again."

Many housewives were setting up goods exchange tables in their homes, returning to more primitive ways of bartering and exchange for both food and clothing. They zealously followed the advice of their prophet to "prepare for the advent of the United Order."

After a late autumn Sunday School lesson on the United Order, Will and Sully ran into Provo's haberdasher and general merchandiser, Peter Davidson. "I'm going to get crushed," Will told Peter, his voice intense, almost desperate. "If you would join me—if we could pool our resources together—we might survive, at least until such a time as the United Order does in fact come."

Davidson thought it was not a bad idea at that, and the two went to their new stake president, Abraham Smoot, to discuss the possibility of cooperative merchandising, which was beginning to take root in Salt Lake City as the Zion Cooperative Mercantile, Incorporated, or ZCMI.

"Well, with the railroad coming together next summer and the Church fearing encroachment, God's trying to prepare us to live the United Order. I believe this is a good middle step," Smoot agreed.

On December 4, 1868, Jones and Sully met with Davidson and two others to draft the preliminary organization. Subscriptions from the group amounted to five thousand dollars. By the end of December, the amount rose to seventeen thousand. In February of 1869, one of the other owners, a Mr. Lawrence, offered his entire store for three thousand in stock, and the cooperative was born.

By now Sobe was a strong nineteen-year-old young man, still a willing worker who did a great deal to help the men carry out their plans.

"There is nothing wrong with being a laborer," Sully often told him. "It is steady commitment that makes men great." So in his spare time when he wasn't working for Ashel at the hotel, Sobe continued to haul goods from the wagons and pack them on the shelves. Sully knew that on the side he was studying at night at Dusenberry's school and saving his money to buy books with the idea in mind that he would someday attend the university. He had been inspired by Mara's own studies toward her teaching credentials. He seemed to want her love and admiration as much as Sully remembered wanting it. Over the years he had watched Mara devote more and more of her time to her Indian son. It was a good development, Sully thought, though he felt she would have been a wonderful mother to more children had she married him.

When the last blow fell on the golden spike in the summer of 1869, joining the railroads across the country, Sully was employed by the East Co-op in a building on East Center Street across from the fire station. Benjamin Buchman had struggled to maintain his half of the business under the stress of the boycott for almost a year. On August 4, 1869, another party of drunken rioters forced their way into the tack house on his property and set fire to the premises. The tack house burned to the ground.

Sully, who was spending the night at Nancy's, was roused at two in the morning by a neighborhood cry and the smell of smoke. Buchman and his tiny, pinched-faced German wife came out of the house in their robes, looking amazed at the people in the yard. Buchman began to pump water. The others set the dam up in the irrigation canal and began pulling buckets up, passing them to the house. By the time the tank with the hose arrived, the shed was gone, but sparks that flew to the trees or the house were doused quickly.

Buchman stood in his slippers watching the tack house smolder. "What did I ever do for them to choose me? What did I do?"

Sully felt helpless. He didn't know what to say. He stood with Buchman at the pump while the others fought the flames—Sobe and Ashel among them, hauling buckets, shouting. In the background, the little German woman stood like a gray post.

"What did I do to anyone?"

"I'm sure it's carelessness," Sully said out of breath, relieving Buchman who stood pulling and pulling at the handle.

"No, they don't like me. You know, an outsider has a hard time in this place."

"But we'll fight for your rights, Ben. As we fight for ours," Sully promised.

In the background Sully heard a lot of commotion. As the volunteers fought the flames, a dark figure began leading some horses out of the carriage house barn.

"Somebody's taking my horses!" Buchman shouted. "My horses!"

Before he could turn, one of the firemen heard Buchman's shout. It was Sobe. He ran toward the horses, his long legs making giant strides.

"Get them!" Buchman shouted. "Someone's taking my horses!"

Before the horses reached the gate, Sobe had leaped to the horseman's leg. The big man astride the animal kicked Sobe away. Sobe fell back, but not for long. He was up again. Sully ran with Ben toward Sobe. Another man spun out of the darkness like a wild animal and yelled, "I'll get the Indian. Get out of here!" He raised a club, but Sobe was too fast. He smashed the man's raised arm with a blow and kicked his stomach. Stunned, the man staggered forward while Sully and Benjamin came for him. Sobe again ran for the horse and, barely catching him at the gate, clung to the animal's saddle.

Others were coming to help now. Ashel and Higbee took the second man screaming back toward the house. Sully saw his face—he was a worker from a visiting railroad construction crew.

The horse dragged Sobe about a hundred yards, but Sobe would not let go. The man kicked, but Sobe grabbed his leg and dragged him down. Soon they were off the horse and scrambling in the dust. Sobe was the larger and stronger of the two. There was a scuffle, and then quiet, as Sobe held the man's hands behind his back. Benjamin Buchman ran after his horse which was galloping riderless away from town.

Not long after, Benjamin Buchman's house went up for sale. Sully had watched him thank Sobe that night. He had thanked all of them with a limp handshake and a soft good-bye.

"I'm going back to New York," he told Sully one day in the Eastman investment offices and bank. Sobe was there, working with Ashel and Papa Eastman as he had done off and on part-time for several years. Buchman looked at Sobe. "There ain't enough Indians and Jews to survive all you Mormons. And I considered it, but if I was to be honest . . . I . . . I just couldn't. I tried . . . and I just couldn't join up with you."

Sully saw he meant to reach toward them. He tried to smile. But no one else smiled either. Sully, embarrassed for him, had no words to say.

"We'll be missing you, Mr. Buchman," Papa Eastman managed. "Truly we will."

"I want to thank your Indian for saving my horses."

Sully saw the color deepen in Sobe's face, saw the distant smile in his eyes. He saw Sobe grip Buchman's small white hand in his strong brown one, and he saw Sobe look into Buchman's eyes. It was a private moment between them. Sobe seemed to understand.

"If you decide to come back, Mr. Buchman, please, we would welcome you."

Sully noted Sobe's stature. He was almost twenty years old, Mara's boy.

As Buchman prepared to leave Provo, there was some talk among Ashel and Papa Eastman and Buchman about Ashel's buying Ben's house on Center Street. Then Ben Buchman was gone, and Sully never saw him again.

Feeling some guilt for helping push Ben Buchman away, Sully tried to be kinder to everyone, even Clem Richards. He thought hard about true brotherhood, and he tried to prepare himself for the United Order which was to come. Then he prayed that God would send him another son. And he was not really surprised in November of 1869 when Rain, in her soft-spoken way, announced to him that she was going to give him another child.

Sobe began to keep a journal. Through the long days of his labor, though he seldom spoke with others, he began to record all the feelings of his heart and the great lessons his suffering and the suffering of his friends had taught him. This would be his legacy to his people, to his family. He wrote almost every day.

Few men know who you are, or care. If your father were a chieftain, the last of an ancient line, if you were the greatest runner, bowman, horseman, your skills ten times greater than the skill of a white man, still the white man would look through you as though you were a glass window in a stone wall—stare at you in wonder, or pity, or uneasy gratitude, or wear questions and fear on his face.
Few men can understand who I am.

Sobe had grown old with questions. Some with no answers. Who is my father? Who are my people? Who am I? For what purpose is my life? He had grown old with twenty years of questions. Some of them were answered by the teachings of the Book of Mormon, or by Mara, or by Rain. Some of the answers seemed good, some were only filled with still more questions.

I am on my way through kingdoms. First as an Indian. I have some of the Indian in my body and my mind. I belong to an old people, to the earth. To the ground under my feet where my ancient fathers are buried. And I belong to the people who came here to worship the God who is the ancient God. I belong to them all and to the God who sired us, who chose this land, who created us from

dust, who breathes into us life, who whispers us into dust again—
my fathers are dust in these hills.
I am on my way through kingdoms.

As he grew, nourished by the two women who loved him most, Sobe became restless to know how much he could do. Could he become more aware than any of his people before him, or more aware than any he could see who surrounded him—even more aware than these people who loved him? For he belonged to them all.

The death of Rain's child hurt him deeply. Then when Benjamin Buchman departed, Sobe could not speak for many days. *If there is injustice I must overcome it, if there is pain . . . I shall do all I can to heal the wounds. If there is a place of heaven on this earth, I shall find it.*

Sobe carried his secrets in his heart, working with Sully at the mercantile, or working at the bank and at the hotel, or in the fields. He studied at Dusenberry's school diligently, reading late into the night by candlelight. He searched for the deeper meanings in the words of poets, philosophers, the great minds of all time, which seemed to fill him as though he were a thirsty man on a vast and arid plain searching for water. He studied the Bible and the Book of Mormon. He went to Church and accepted the responsibility of the priesthood of God that was given him. He read the books Mara brought him: Dante, Aristotle, Plato. Mara came to him, understanding as she had always understood, as she had whispered to him of her faith in his greatness when he had been a child. After Papa, Ashel, and Caroline had long been asleep, Sobe would hear Mara's knock on the door of his small back room.

One night she came to him wrapped in a bright shawl, her dark hair flowing about her white face. She glowed like light.

"Papa told me you saved Benjamin Buchman's horses."

Sobe smiled inside. At her words, he filled with warmth. "Yes'm."

"You did us proud."

"I would do it for anyone."

"I know that." Mara was remembering the time he had pulled Pulsipher's drowning cow from the river. He had often rounded up lost cattle, easy for him because he rode so well and knew the animals. But he hoped she would not remind him of these things tonight. She looked wistful sitting at his bedside, the candlelight on her face.

"I am only sorry that Benjamin Buchman is going away," he said, searching Mara's eyes. He knew she would understand how much more Buchman's departure meant. He knew she would know.

"Sometimes we're like frigates or leaves in God's river," Mara had once told him. "Only those who stay in the mainstream will move down the channel. The movers may need to reach out to help the others move."

"We didn't help them." Sobe had spoken of his own people as "others."

"We were too busy for a time, buffeted in our own course, watching for our own safety. The time will come when we are stronger, and then strong enough to reach out and bring them in."

"I want to be that strong," Sobe had told her.

He had not been able to hold Ben Buchman in the stream. Mara knew. She touched the book he was reading. "What is it this time? Emerson. Very good. Emerson."

"Emerson knows . . . what a person needs most to answer to himself."

Sobe waited. Mara smiled. He felt the peace in his room. There was only the bed with its wooden posts, the quilt—one that Mara had made from bright colors. There was a small table under the tiny window, and on the table all of Sobe's books and papers. The candle stood on the edge of the table, almost ready to sputter out.

"Answer this to yourself, then, my friend. Answer Ben Buchman to yourself."

"I know."

She touched his hand. "It's late, Sobe." She leaned toward him and looked deeply into his face. "But it's wonderful that you read. You will be a leader not only among your people, but a leader of many men."

Sobe had heard this from her often. He was quiet. He folded the book and laid it on the pile of the others nearby. "If I know what the white man knows and I know what the Indian knows, I may choose."

Mara took Sobe's hand and looked at him with wet eyes. A light laughter touched her words. "As long as you will always choose me." She leaned to hold him and he smiled as he always did, his cheek against her cheek, his hands on her warm hair.

"I love you so much," she whispered.

Though I am an Indian, I am like her child. All the blood in me says that the answer to every life lies in love. I love her for loving me. But in return, what can I do for her?

Mara had selflessly loved away his hurt, his heartache. She had chosen to give him so much of her life. And Sobe had finally come to see this as a kind of sacrifice she had made which he must somehow bring to bear fruit. As she taught him to love learning, he sought for the answers in the minds of men and the scriptures of God. Often he shared his studies with her, especially when she seemed lonely. He loved Mara with all his heart, and he wanted her to be happy, but he knew he could not give her all that she needed.

No one knew exactly how it had happened, even Mara. She understood only some of it—that she loved Sobe so much that she spent a lot of time thinking about his happiness. And as she worked things out in her mind, she came to the realization that loving Sobe completely meant helping him to move away from her—to move out on his own.

For weeks she pondered how best to help him. She felt she would be able to let go of him if he were situated in good full-time employment and she thought it would be best for his independence if it were employment outside the family. For a long time she had known that Will Jones was the best outside person to help them. He had already hired Sobe part-time and knew his strengths. She had always admired the business ability of their friend Will. She knew he liked her, though she had made it clear to him many times that she was just a friend. Perhaps he could provide a good full-time job for Sobe.

It happened at Christmastime. Will had always come at Christmastime. And this Christmas he had come with Sully and his family as usual. Always eager in his conversation about some wonderful business proposition, this Christmas he reminded them all of his earlier idea of constructing the woolen mill. It was time, he said. Were the cooperatives to pool their resources, such an industry could bring economic security to the area, stimulate independence, add jobs.

Animated in his excitement, Will appeared charming in his new suit of sharply pressed clothes. Although Mara saw him as she had seen him for more than ten years—as a good friend who had always been around—this Christmas she saw him as someone whose help she needed. There was something else she was seeing, too—more energy than she had ever noticed in him, or that he had ever shown. More fervor, more dazzle.

She approached him with a light laugh. "I think you've done it now, Will Jones."

The puzzled expression on his face begged for an explanation.

"The woolen mill is the answer, of course," she smiled. "You knew it all this time . . . keeping it from us . . . a well-hidden secret."

As she took his arm, he smiled and blushed. "Can we talk together . . . about something?"

"Something?" he said.

"Well—someone."

He stopped for a moment. Then he looked at her out of narrow probing eyes. Her heart skipped a beat. He had probably already guessed. She had never been able to keep much from him. "Sobe?" he said.

As well as being a tease, he had always seemed a bit boorish to her. However, he had always been kind. And when—after Phillip's departure—she had made it clear she wanted no one, he had left her alone. It was true that she had made a firm decision never to try love again.

As they had turned to leave the room together, Ashel had wheeled Caroline from the kitchen into the vestibule and stood in the parlor doorway.

"I have an announcement," he had said gravely. He touched Caroline's shoulder with his fingers.

Papa looked puzzled at his son's words. The candlelight on the Christmas tree behind him shone like a halo above his white hair.

"We're going to be married, on St. Valentine's day," Ashel smiled.

There was a sudden response of both joy and reservation. It had not really been a great surprise. For a long time Ashel had struggled with his love for Caroline, their relationship as second cousins, the knowledge that she would never have children.

Caroline's face shone like Papa's eyes. For a moment there was silence. Mara turned back into the room.

"I am pleased, Ashel, Caroline. Blessings to both of you," Mara said, reaching for their hands.

Now, unless Ashel were to participate in plural marriage, which would be highly unlikely, Papa would not have his grandchildren. It was strange how this announcement seemed to press a fervid sense of responsibility upon her.

In the vestibule again, Mara passed the hall mirror. She stared briefly at the figure she saw there. She had not known that time could pass so quickly. She was thirty-seven years old. She looked at her face. So Ashel was going to marry Caroline? She stared at her mouth. There was still strength there in the line of her lips. Only a few wisps of gray brushed her cheeks among the chestnut curls. Her deep-set eyes were still bright, the brows arched. Her cheekbones were high, and her jaw firmly set. She could see more there than she had seen as a child. More of what? Determination? Suffering? Passion to follow a straight course?

Will stood at her shoulder talking briefly with old Bishop Higbee who was on his way into the parlor to pay his Christmas respects to the family. When Mara turned, Will followed her out the door. The sky, icy cold, was filled with stars. Not a cloud sailed in its vast emptiness. Mara was quiet. Will was the first to speak.

"Let me guess, Mara Eastman. The mill and Sobe. Putting two and two together, I would say you want . . . a favor . . . ?"

They reached the carriage drive and turned to cross the street into the park. Mara spoke to him then, keeping her hands tightly on the shawl she had drawn across her shoulders. "I'll admit I am asking you for a favor."

"Sobe is ready now. Ready for something grand. And unless it comes to him quickly, you fear for him."

Mara stared at Will's face. How long had she known him now? Such a friendly man, but often with the businesslike exterior. Sobe had seemed a little restless lately, but she had not dreamed anyone besides herself had noticed. Just how much did Will Jones know about her and about Sobe? She wondered. His perception suddenly made her feel vulnerable. When she saw his eyes in the moonlight, something frightened her. It was not anything about Will himself, it was her own heart that had begun to beat very fast.

There had been that short time after Phillip Hurst's departure when Sully and Nancy had urged her that if she would not join them, she should think about Will Jones. Yet, more than ten years later, Mara's heart had not healed completely. And Will had never done anything about it, anyway. Will's refusal to marry had often become food for town gossip and the burden of bishops and counselors who often told him he was not living the gospel. But Will's business had fully occupied him, and Nancy took good care of his children, who were almost grown.

He folded his arms now and walked toward the center of the park. He looked straight ahead. "He is a good worker. I know that," he said. "He is an Indian."

The words surprised Mara. She did not think it should have mattered to Will that Sobe was an Indian. But there was something different about the way he stood now. He was talking business. It was his world. And he was king in that world, completely professional. As she watched him, her mouth felt dry.

"What do you want for him?" he said.

Mara did not feel like saying much now. She felt overwhelmed by his knowledge of her thoughts. How could she hide from him all that she wanted to hide? "Perhaps not a great deal to begin with," she murmured softly. "The opportunity to work up . . . perhaps manager."

Will was quiet for a moment. Mara's thoughts raced. She remembered she was speaking to the man who had saved his own business by letting his partner go; he had sold the Camp Floyd government merchandise at a profit of three hundred percent. He was very shrewd. In their acquaintance, she had never had a cause to deal with him in his own world. He frightened her. But there was also more than fear. She felt awe. He had a strange way of not looking at her, a way of concentrating on something beyond her comprehension.

He was not looking at her now. For a moment she felt fear that he did not approve of her suggestion and would not hire Sobe—even at her request.

But he did not voice any such fear. Instead he spoke very succinctly, keeping his eyes down on his puzzling businesslike face. He knit his brows and stroked his chin as he searched for the right words to say. He began by clearing his throat. "What you ought to tell me," he cleared his throat again, "is that now that Sobe is grown and Caroline and Ashel are settled, you are ready to marry, and that you and I are the logical choices for each other. That is what you ought to be telling me."

The silence that followed filled Mara with a strange sense that she hadn't heard what he said, and her heart pounded. She stopped walking. She looked up at him as he glimmered with teasing behind the dark eyes. She was stunned. Her first reaction was to deny that she had ever toyed with the same idea.

"Will Jones!" she said, stopping, cocking her head, narrowing her eyes against the bright moonlight. "Who are you to be telling me what I ought to be doing?" She tried to hide something that began to overwhelm her—a powerful feeling of attraction. He seemed very large standing against the moon.

"Who am I? Your future husband!" Will said gruffly, a satisfied grin on his face. "Yes, I think it will do."

Puzzled, Mara searched her heart for what was happening to her. Her mind was suddenly in a race with her feelings—because she knew that for the sake of Sobe's independence, and for her own happiness, this was a very logical plan. If she had wanted to admit it to herself, she knew she had unconsciously buried the same logical solution in her heart—never wanting to look at it for fear it would happen, and she would find it disappointing. But now that it was happening, her head spun.

"It's logical," Will said, as though he read her mind.

Mara waited. She could not believe what was going on in her limbs. They felt weak.

Will stopped. He lifted her chin with his large hand.

"You've dallied far too long, Mara Eastman," he said. "And now may I have the honor of kissing the bride-to-be?"

Hesitant, taken back, Mara felt her knees buckle. "Yes, I think so," she smiled thinly. She had thought about the logic of Will. What she had not prepared for was this powerful feeling that swept through her—this sudden fire.

Will wrapped his arms around her slowly and pulled her close into him. Continuing to warm her, a totally safe feeling she had never felt before welled up inside of her. It was as though she had, at last, come home. She clung to him. And then she noticed how he trembled.

"Oh, Mara," he was whispering. "I've waited for so long."

Mara was completely taken back by his emotion. Knowing so well his usual dry exterior, she never suspected he could feel so much.

"Will?" She pulled away from his face, holding his head between her hands. She looked into his eyes. "Will Jones!"

"Yes, Mara. All this time I've loved you. You don't know." His large hands pulled her to him again, kissing her mouth, warm and long. His whole body was shaking with joy.

Chapter Eight

March 22, 1870. Yesterday Aunt Mara Eastman, the woman who has truly been like a mother to me most of my life, was married to Brother Jones.

I am never going to record the beginning of my life. It has been more than twenty years since I was born. I will tell what I am now. At least half Ute, I do not know. My mother was Blueflower, daughter of a Ute medicine man. I am Sobeshent in Piute, or "green growing" in the white man's translation. As far as I can tell, I am the half-breed sired by a father of the Mormons, but even this I do not know. It is what Rain Tuttle, my mother's friend, believes, though she will not say it. Aunt Mara tells me my father is Hinte, half Snake husband of my mother. She wants to believe it, and wants me to believe it, but she also does not know.

Sobe would not be moving in with Mara and Will Jones for now. Although Will had a house next to Sully and Nancy, he was happy to make plans with Mara for their own new home to be built on the lot just south of the Eastmans, where there would be plenty of room for their new lives together with Will's two grown children. The boy Peter was gone most of the time during the spring and summer with the cattle on the hills. The girl Cynthia was a quiet, plain child with no interest other than keeping house for her father and visiting Nancy Tuttle. Mara still taught school and let the girl do the cooking, although she often made a suggestion or two. During her years in Nancy's house, Cynthia had learned what her father liked to eat. She took great pride in baking whole grain bread and cutting up raw salads for him.

Sobe stayed with Papa Eastman who had been alone since Ashel and Caroline moved into the old Buchman house next to Sully's on Center Street. Ashel and Caroline, however, were also planning to build their own dream house in the lot just south of the new house of Mara and Will. Someday there would be three Eastman houses in a row on the west side of Main.

March 30, 1870. I listen to them talk about their fathers. There is no way people can understand me. I am no one's kin. My ancestors are a simple breed living close to the land, but I am raised by white men. Will I be a white man, or will I bring my people to understand the white man? I wonder.

Sobe won wrestling matches at school meets until he graduated from the Academy that spring of 1870.

He was tall, very straight, with a chiseled bronze face, his body as carefully wrought as a stone statue. He never courted a white girl. Mara stared at him during the commencement ceremony, unable to take her eyes from him. He was beautiful—not ordinary. He looked like a Greek god. She thought he was the finest graduate she had ever seen.

May 24, 1870. Today I received the paper which honors me as an Academy graduate. I am the first Indian or part Indian to receive the award in the new Timpanogos Branch of the Deseret University.

They gave me a citation and made a special mention of Aunt Mara, whose energies have been bent toward my success in these efforts. I know that if it were not for her I would never have achieved what I have achieved. Now I must throw myself into building the mill with good effort so that Will Jones will see I mean to succeed on his behalf as well.

"What you do with your life," Abraham Smoot intoned, "is your own affair. You are the one who must live it. You are the one who sets your own limitations. The lowliest child on the street may hawk newspapers for a penny and later become a success in today's America."

May 26, 1870. How much will this land give to me, I wonder? I who belong to it. I am not a white man. What difference does it

141

make? I can haul and cut and stack as well as anyone. But will the people open their doors to me? How will I feel if they turn me away? If she . . . turns me away?

Since Mara's marriage, Sobe had continued to keep the journal, sometimes sporadically recording the events of the day. Mara learned of it by mistake. She discovered it in Sobe's room one afternoon while she was searching for a book she had loaned him.

Mara wondered who Sobe meant.

June 5. A hot day. We poured foundation. Filled it with aggregate. I saw her with her cousin on the east side of the mill wash. She smiled at me. Sara tells me she will be in town all summer. I am afraid.

The sprawling letters leaned forward in awkward cursive. Mara tried to stop reading, but her eyes, as though they would stumble on something important to her, could not leave the page.

June 6. She is a white girl. I know that love is the force of life. How could I have known I would fall in love with a white girl? How can things be for me, for us? I can only give her pain.

June 7. Mara has told me I should seek one of Rain's daughters. They are still so young. Jane, Jane. Don't come to me. Anymore.

Jane. Jane who? Mara knew of no one near his age by the name of Jane. "*Sara tells me. . . .*" Sara. She knew only of Sara Davidson.

How much of Sobe still belonged to her? If she had ever felt cheated of life—and there were reasons she might have felt cheated—she loved Will. Not as she had once thought love was. But she loved him, knew pleasure in his arms and comfort in his company. She wanted the same comfortable happiness for Sobe, but without the endless indecision and waiting—with more instant joy. She wanted him to have what he really wanted. And yet as she touched the paper on which he wrote, she trembled with a premonition.

June 8. Jane must not know how much I feel.

It was from a light conversation while she was helping to tie a quilt during the Relief Society meeting that Mara learned about Jane. Mara asked few questions so as not to arouse suspicions. Jane Hunt was Sara Davidson's cousin from Salt Lake City. She was seventeen. She would perhaps be attending the Timpanogos Branch of the University of Deseret in September with Sara, if her parents felt it was wise. Who were her parents?

"Why, I believe Scott Hunt's son. What was his name? Bret. And that beautiful younger daughter of Afton Wright—Hannah, yes. Marcia Davidson's niece."

Mara's face grew hot. Were there any in the room who might have remembered? She stiffened. A blank fist of fear pushed up through her and seemed to grip her heart.

Not Bret's child! The very coincidence stunned her. Not Bret. And Hannah! She had not heard of them for years . . . had deliberately lost track of them. She waited for a moment for her vision to clear, for the pounding of her heart to settle. But the skin on the palms of her hands grew clammy.

"Wasn't Bret Hunt the young man . . . who was here in the last war with the Indians?" old Sister Allen questioned, gently.

"Yes. We knew him in Salt Lake City. Scott Hunt's boy."

The flood of Mara's discomfort loosened a profuse sweat along the curve of her neck, under the dark curls. Yes, Bret. The past pushed forward in a strange quiet moment that caused her fear. The damage to her heart had left cherished scars. And unforgettable despair.

She saw Jane in the East Co-op on a Saturday, shopping with Sara for hoops, and she knew she had seen Jane before. The slope of her brow was definitely Bret Hunt's, the dark coloring Hannah's. By all appearances, it was true! Mara caught her breath. Jane was exquisite. Not just pretty, but exquisite, slender waisted with a blush in her cheeks. She looked full of energy, blooming with color Mara remembered well from her own mirror.

Jane! Not Hannah's child! But seventeen years had passed. Mara sank into a murmur of excuses to Will and left without picking up her purchase. Will brought it to her in the evening.

"You left quick when Hunt's girl came in. You guessed . . . it's Hunt's girl." His eyes held the deep knowledge of her which he had always—to her amazement—held.

"Yes, she's Hunt's girl. Did you know it, Will?

"I didn't see that it would do you good to know it, or to know of Sobe's attachment to her."

"Then everyone else knows but me?"

"They have tried to keep it a deep secret."

"But everyone knows?"

Will paused and looked at Mara. "They are in love, Mara, and what can lovers hide?" He smiled.

"Everyone knows," Mara breathed, hoping the shadow in her heart would pass. For she had not been willing to admit what to others had been so obvious. "Everyone else knows."

The summer passed slowly. Mara did not understand where Sobe and Jane had met, but she thought it would have been in much the same circumstances as she had met Phillip Hurst, perhaps during the noon hours.

"Is Sobe gone very long during the lunch hours?" she asked Will one day. "Gone from the construction at the mill?"

Will questioned the foreman Smith.

"Sobe's punctual, an exemplary worker."

"I don't know always when he comes home evenings," Papa told her. "No. He goes his way. I go mine. I'm not like you and your worrywart mother. You two peas in a pod!" He shook his head over her.

But Sobe is part of the family. Your only grandchild! My only child! Mara thought. He was without anyone, and we took him in. But Papa would not understand. He was in the midst of making up his mind to marry a widow lady who lived down the street. He had dismissed responsibility for Sobe years ago.

But Mara could not let go of Sobe. She did not understand all the reasons. She loved him desperately, as though her life lay in his. And she had loved him this way for years.

One evening she intercepted him as construction on the mill drew to a close. She walked home with him toward a hot red sunset. Sweating, he walked with her loosely, his stride separate, his head very high.

"Sobe, is everything well?"

"Yes, Aunt Mara."

"Are you well? Do you feel good?"

"I feel fine."

Construction had been good for him. Through his shirt, Mara could see that his back arched into muscles as tight as knots of twine. He was bronzed, his skin leathery, his brow almost black from the sun.

"Sobe . . . there is something I've wanted to talk to you about. . . ."

His gaze was penetrating. He stood while she stopped him in the park.

"Do you know what I want to say?"

"If it's what I think you would discuss with me—Papa Eastman's marriage—there is nothing to worry about. I'm moving into my own room in July with the widow Kartchner . . . the cellar room."

She trembled.

He took her by the arms. "There is nothing to worry about. I know what I am doing."

She could not say anything more.

"I know what I am doing."

She, like every mother, *must* let him go. He was growing. He smiled at her. She let him go.

It had been a silent elopement, and perhaps illegal. She knew of it only through dark awareness that something had gone wrong. She saw Sobe seldom anymore. She had not seen Sobe's journal again. At the Academy she had seen Jane for the first few days, and then it had been reported that several people believed she had returned to Salt Lake City. But Sara Davidson would never face her and say exactly how or when.

Sobe's room at the widow Kartchner's had been locked every time she came. . . as silent, as dark, as impenetrable as a vault.

The sharp rumors that flew from mouth to mouth blamed the Davidsons for allowing Jane to leave for Salt Lake City with a group of her own finding. They had contacted her parents, who had not heard a word of her whereabouts for a long time. She had never come home at all. Then suddenly, the alarm among the members of the community became a hushed river of deep fear. Sara Davidson's face was worn white. Week after week passed, and Jane had never appeared. Not in classes, not at Davidson's, not in Salt Lake City. But there was an awesome hush in the voices that knew. And never a word at all.

August 1, 1870. You mean everything to me. It is not life without you, and if we should seal it even secretly and enjoy the moments of our love as we have stolen them from time beyond our reach, we shall at least have those moments of happiness to remember. Will you remember me? Every word I drop into your ears is like a carved gem which cannot grow dim by time, but brightens for the heavens of light, in the soul of God who blesses us because we are so happy together. If even for a time, I have been with you.

Jane read Sobe's journal and held it to her. At first it *was* like a dream. A dream she would never have known might come true, for he was the most beautiful man she had ever seen. And the strongest. And his embrace clouded her vision, corroded her will. When she wrote to her parents in Salt Lake City, she wrote firmly, with a strong hand.

His name is Sobeshent. I married him in Springville. You have nothing to say now, for I am with child. My body is full of Indian. And nothing you can say will change that now. Not ever. I love him. I am wildly happy, and no one in the town knows, for I am staying in his room . . . in the home of a widow who is blind. He brings me his love and his books which I read . . . hundreds of pages every day. And I have never known a mind like his . . . he will do great work for his people. He will be a foreman in the new woolen mill. And we are going to move to a small outside town, perhaps Springville. But he fears the disapproval of our marriage, and we do not tell it to the people. He knows that the greater the love, the more terrible is the power to break it. The Davidsons know and protect me. If you come for me or speak of it to discourage me, I will shame you.

At first she believed she was wildly in love, and all she had needed was him. The widow's room in the cellar was dark, but with their love, it became a place of light. She had sewn curtains out of bleached muslin, with ruffles and the braid from an old dress she had brought to Davidsons in her trunk. She wove rugs from the rags they gave to her, small pot holders and table mats woven from old grass.

She read and wove while he toiled at the mill. For almost a month she sat in secrecy, in fear of the footsteps that passed the window wells above her, in fear that Mrs. Kartchner would ask too many questions of her, would discover she was not an Indian, but a white girl whose family was searching for her. But they did not come.

At first the days had been full when she feared their coming. She saw, like the climax of a theatrical drama, the large presence of her mother, floating vulturelike down upon her and snatching her from the claws of her disobedience. And inwardly she smiled. But when they did not come, the hours grew longer, and the drama faded. When no one came, she began to hear Mrs. Kartchner's feet on the kitchen floor. It drove her wild.

"Do you want to go out, then? Do you want people to know?" Sobe would ask.

Jane began to sit in the evenings before the fire and stare at the light. "No. There is nothing I can do now. But wait. I don't want anyone to know." And she began to see Sobe as a furtive guard, a man different from other men, an Indian who kept her as a prisoner in a dark room.

"Maybe I'll die here."

"You won't die."

"If no one comes I'll die."

"I'll come."

Then she would smile and clasp her hands about his head. "You will *always* come back?" But the time wore thin.

And one day she said, "You don't care about me or you would never go."

And he said "I can't stay."

"You don't want to stay. You must hate me dreadfully." And she cried.

And then one day someone did come. And she was terrified.

Someone with large boots and heavy gray stockings that hung wet over the tops of the boots, clumped up the walk. Someone asked for Mrs. Kartchner, and Jane could hear the beat of her heart—and, almost, the beat of the heart deep in her body, though she knew it was still very small. She did not breathe.

"Yes, a young couple, an Indian couple is staying in the basement," old Mrs. Kartchner said. "A little Indian girl. Mr. Eastman, her husband, is working at the woolen mills."

"Thank you." He murmured words Jane could not hear, but she saw his boots. She strained to see the face, but it was too far away.

She told Sobe that evening when he came to her that there had been boots. Who had come? No one had come to the mill. She was afraid. Then who could it have been?

"I have a place for you to go, Jane," he whispered, taking her hand. They boiled chicken soup over a low fire in the hearth. "I will take you tomorrow, and no one will find us. No one will know. You will have to stay in the hard winter, but if it is too cold, I will bring you back into town. Will you mind?"

She was silent and stared into his open eyes. She saw so much in him that was good. She wanted him then, and flung her hands on his neck. "Take me wherever you want to take me," she whispered. "I will go with you, Sobe."

"And I will take you," Sobe whispered, and he lifted her like feathers from the chair. He buried his mouth, his nose, in her neck and carried her to the bed.

In the dusk, in the dusky room, the black beams overhead, inside the dark walls, he found her and buried himself deep into her love. "Jane, Jane, Jane. I can only hurt you," he whispered.

"Then hurt me. Hurt me for a short time, and I will be alive once! I know I will love you even when they take you away from me!" She laughed at him. A silver laugh, and they melted into each other as though they were one.

In the days that followed, Jane watched for people walking above her on the street. She thought she recognized Mrs. Mara Jones' shoes and her clipped walk.

She was silent as she had promised to stay silent if anyone should make a sound on her door. Then she heard the same knock for Mrs. Kartchner. "Are they never home?" came the voice, impatient.

"Oh, I'm sure she was there. You know I don't hear very well, but I am sure she was there, but she is a shy girl. I have never even heard her speak."

A shy girl. She ought to be shy. "I will find them later." The voice thanked the blind woman. Jane's heart froze with fear. It *was* Mara Jones.

That night Sobe quietly prepared their few belongings in a muslin bag, but left the curtains at the windows and the rugs on the floor. "I will still rent this room. There are already curtains where you are going."

Out on the street, Sully Tuttle, a silhouette against the moonlight, sat high in his horse and cart. Sobe carried Jane's bags through the door. They hurried in the darkness to the wagon's bed.

"Hide," Sobe instructed. "Put down your head, or you'll be seen. . . ." He had laid some bedding on the boards in the floor.

Mr. Sully Tuttle said a quiet "Hello, Jane." She had seen him only perhaps once or twice before—a tall thin man with shocks of gray in his curled, sandy hair. The hat he wore nearly covered his eyes.

From the bed on the floor in the wagon, Jane could not see the lights of the street. She could hear only the *clop clop* of the horses as their hooves hit the dusty road. And she heard Mr. Tuttle and Sobe talking, though she could not make out any of the words they said. The moon was high, yet the September darkness seemed to shadow them, follow them, overcome the very black road as the horses moved forward through the choking air.

Jane dozed. She saw her father's face close to her own, his bright eyes penetrating her, questioning her. "And so you have destroyed our faith in you, Jane? How can we allow you to return to our household? Your mother is desperate with grief." Not the words themselves disturbed her so deeply, but the meaning. The meaning crushed her. She looked up; she felt her father's face very near. But it was Sobe. He had come to her. His face hovered above hers, blackened by shadow in the moonlight's glare.

"Jane. I've awakened you. I'm sorry."

"No. It's all right, Sobe. Are we out of town?"

"We're out of town."

He offered his hand to her. She slipped hers into it as though into a warm sleeve. His grip enclosed her wrist and she felt his strength draw her upward.

"We will be there in only a few moments." The air above was lighter, and she could breathe more easily.

"You have met Sully," Sobe said.

"Yes. Hello, Mr. Tuttle."

"He will protect us at this place. Remember I have told you about Rain?"

Sully smiled toward her as he nervously clucked at the horses and urged them to continue forward. In the distance, crowded by trees, were small lights winking in the darkness. They passed the Richards' house, and came to Sully's cabin—the home of Rain.

Jane's hand began to move in Sobe's. She slipped it into his grip more tightly; she pulled his long fingers more closely against her own.

Once the black cabin door opened, a fierce gold light from the hearth filled the road. The front room was steamy with heat.

"And this is Rain."

A large squat Indian woman beamed at her. "Please come in! Hello Sobe, my dear boy." Sobe leaned to her and held her. "Jane, my dear one. Sobe's bride. And we shall care for you as one of our own."

In Rain's arms lay a small child only a few months old.

"Charles," Rain said proudly, her open mouth displaying some decaying teeth. Sully stood by very proudly. He lifted the flannel from the baby's face. "Charles," he said to Jane. "We lost our first boy, Tom. But God has sent us another son."

The light, the faces, the strong odors in the room—a mix of pine pitch, sweat, and a baby's vomit—began to overwhelm Jane's senses. She remembered the sleep of a few moments ago; her eyelids suddenly wanted to close. She felt nausea, and her legs folded under her.

"She's tired," Sobe said, and scooping her into his arms, he carried her into the back room. He laid her gently on the large bed. The logs on the walls inside the room had not been stripped, but still hung close and heavy with thick gray bark. An Indian weaving that hung over the door brightened the place.

"Rain, I am so grateful to you for offering your home." Sobe looked toward her.

Rain smiled. "I shall nurse your lovely one as Mara once nursed me," she whispered. "Don't talk of it. She will be fine."

With the baby still in one arm, she brought in water, towels, and fresh linens folded as thin as tissue paper.

"It is many months away," Sobe said, waiting for Rain to finish.

"She will be fine."

When Rain left, Jane saw the room for the first time, the dark wood, the rough-hewn ceiling, the bright Indian hangings on the walls. She felt Sobe's body near hers; she felt the blanket draped over her thighs. She thought of Sobe's body and touched him. He was smooth and tough, like leather. She smiled to feel the beat of his blood. She felt his hand on her body, on the unborn child. In her dreaming, her mother's eyes fell out of the stars, fell like two saucers toward her—her mother's eyes, swollen, weeping, yet still serene.

"You are never more ours. You are never again ours. I have lost you, Jane. Jane!" Then the voice, hovering on the brink of demand, grew sharply distinct on the air of night. "Jane! Come home to us. Jane!" And the demand vanished into the distance. Softly. More softly, now. Until it was gone.

Not long afterward, Mara instinctively knew what was going on. Waking in the desperate night, feeling the warmth of Will's breath on her arms, she knew deeply from pure knowing, from guessing, from hurting for Sobe, who had done what she had hoped he would never do. She knew from Nancy who had told her that Sully had shared the secret, and she felt that the best for Jane would be silence until May.

Most of the town was quiet or uninterested or believed Sara Davidson's cousin had returned to Salt Lake City. Most of the families in Salt Lake City believed Jane was still in Provo going to school. Most of them—Nancy had discovered from some penetrating unknown silence—most of them did not know.

"Her parents are willing for her to return to her old life," Nancy said. Mara, stunned, stared at Nancy. "But she's married. She has married Sobeshent." Nancy's eyes were faded, gray. Mara looked deeply into them to search for answers. She and Nancy had not seen each other as much recently. But they had both helped raise children not their own. As Will's children grew and as Nancy had become more involved as a seamstress for the store, she had let Will's children go. Mara searched Nancy's face for compassion. "I had to let them go, Mara. I needed them and they needed me, and then they didn't need me anymore, and I had to let them go," Nancy had told her over and over. Why couldn't Mara let Sobe go? She thought she had.

"Has she married him?" Nancy said evenly. "Is it legal? Some civil official from Springville?"

Mara trusted Sobeshent, but it was true she knew nothing about Jane. Only perhaps that such a child under the eye of a Hannah Wright might find herself at some time in her life willing to be reckless, to break willfully away.

"One of the reasons she came to Provo," Nancy said smoothly, "was that she couldn't get along with her parents at home."

Mara did not speak. But she felt in her heart Sobe's distress. Not Sobe. Not Sobeshent. He had loved her enough to want to do things right, if even just for her. From his diary she had sensed that much. She grasped at imagined ways to save him, to save the marriage, to find a release from her own love for him and an unexplainable fear.

"I'll go to see them," she thought. "I'll show them that I can accept the marriage and that others will, also." Yet in those same words, she knew . . . she knew too well. And she breathed it only quietly to Will.

"Please, Mara. Sobe is a grown man. I wish you would let him go. You can't make his way for him."

No, they are not grown until you can feel them whole beneath your heart, silenced in love, accepting of peace. Not until they are happy. Not until they are in God's kingdom. Not until they are right with the drummer whose beat is heard in the neighboring hill. How can I let him go when he needs me now more than ever? When he has turned from me in shame, unable to face the terrible clash of our worlds?

She struggled to make the decision. Should she go to Rain's to see Sobe? She was afraid of knowing Jane.

"Mara, please. At least wait until spring. Don't interfere where you are not asked. Please wait until spring," Will urged.

And so the right time for a visit never came. All winter behind the shell of the mill, the men worked from morning until night. And never did anyone dare to enter into the dark hollow of its vast promises except the men who labored there. Several times Mara attempted to intercept Sobe on his way home from a long day. He would walk in troubled silence, the sunset golden in his bronze face. She found him morose, quiet, on his way to the room at Kartchner's.

"Sobe."

"Aunt Mara." At first she saw the delight in his eyes when he saw her. She felt he wanted to speak to her, to find relief in her comfort.

But then his eyes became stricken, the pupils shrinking, the muscles of his body drawing away from her.

"You need to come out . . . face people . . . make it right," she told him. "What is your plan?"

She had never seen such darkness in his eyes, nor felt so closed from him. He was silent. Silent with his burdens.

"Please, Sobe."

It had been no use. He would not discuss it with her.

"If there is a child . . . ," he finally said once.

She had never seen him so afraid. "If there is a child, then what?"

"My child," Sobe said.

"Your child . . . ," Mara waited, breathlessly.

He had murmured the reasons. Perhaps the parents would not break up a family. If he could show them he was dependable. If he were a foreman at the mill. "It would be best if people let us have the child without interfering." She listened, not hearing sense, but hearing the fearful heaviness, the slow effort of his words, the message clearly spoken without words that her interest was frustrating to him, that if she were to love him truly now, she would leave him alone.

Though she never let herself accept the knowledge that it made any difference, she could see he felt apart now, in an isolation she could not control for him—different and alone.

Though the Joneses spent winter in the new house, it seemed hard, filled with long dark evenings of quiet. Sometimes, while she made half-hearted pencil corrections through essays on Shakespeare and Donne, Mara felt a floating fear. All of it—all of the efforts to make life happen had seemed somehow short of her visions—somehow shorter than the dreams.

From the dining room table, where she often worked while Will and the children read in the parlor or Cynthia tidied up the last things in the kitchen, she could see the garden through French doors that opened onto a patio of stone. The snow collected in drifts there, floating over bushes and flowers like sheets flung at random on the furniture of a closed room. Through winter there seemed to be so much darkness that even the kerosene lamps on the sconces over the doors were inadequate light. The silky darkness was whole, like air or water, turning to stone—the darkness of living in shadows. Occasionally it seemed to be penetrated only by sound: a child's voice, the toll of the town clock, the distant bell.

"All mankind is of one author and is one volume. . . . His hand shall bind up all our scattered leaves."

The darkness seemed proof to her that she had not left Sobe, but was bound up into his affliction, as real as her own.

"Affliction is a treasure, and scarce any man hath enough of it." Donne's words which she saw in the darkness hurt her eyes. "No man is an island, entire of itself. . . . I am involved in mankind. And there-fore never send to know for whom the bell tolls; it tolls for thee."

In February, in March, in April, she clung to rumors of Rain's care for Jane. The Richards had told someone that a mysterious girl lived in Rain's home, a white girl who hated dirty Indians and the squalor they made. Nancy said it was not that bad, but that both Jane and the Richards family were making it miserable for Rain.

Sobe's Jane. Mara thought about the child rising within the daughter of her old friend, Bret. Jane could have been hers! Then she asked questions of herself about her own barrenness, for in February, in March, in April, she had still not found herself with child.

"You've enough worries over Sobe," Will said.

"Who may be my only one. . . ."

"You have done everything you can by him. You have done right by him. Let him go."

Yet the need to cling to him hung over her like a mysterious pall. What was in him that had given her so much to hold? Perhaps most of all, herself.

In the last week of April, Sobe and Jane's baby was born. A girl. Nancy had whispered the news. Unable to bear the isolation any longer, Mara had wrapped presents for the child, prepared bedding, packed pickles and jams.

It was a balmy spring Saturday. The melting snows had drenched the velvet hush of grass over the valley in feathers of rivers and springs. Mara went in a cart now as befitting her age and position, but went alone, hurrying the Tar Babies over the moist ground.

Sully greeted her at the gate. He stared at her as she came in.

"We're honored, Mara Jones," he said, shyly, slightly bent. His body was still tough, still the wiry body of long ago. His limbs did not dance. They were filled out with years of labor; they were slower, more graceful. His eyes glimmered that same shallow blue. The gray in the wiry temples of his hair softened the growing wrinkles around his eyes. "Welcome to our country home."

She had seen him only occasionally of late, at Nancy's, where he kept the delicate balance of life between farmer and merchandiser. At Rain's he seemed more like himself, as she had known him before.

"We haven't seen you much since your marriage."

Mara raised her eyes to his in questions. No, she had not seen Sully much since her marriage. She had been so busy teaching. Except for the times she had gone to the shop or to Church conferences, she had seen Sully little, if at all.

"Is Sobe here?"

"No," Sully said quietly.

"No?"

She remembered it was Saturday, but could hardly believe Sobe would not have been with his own child, whether the crew would have remained in construction or not.

"Some of the mill went into operation today," Sully informed her quietly. "He felt he ought to be there."

Mara searched Sully's eyes. She felt something was wrong.

"Where is the baby?"

Sully nodded toward the bedroom.

"I have waited . . . because Sobe asked me to wait," she began to explain, but Sully was asking nothing from her. There was nothing to explain. Even now she felt awkward and out of place. She wasn't related by blood to this child. Only her love for Sobe gave her the right. . . .

The room's wood seemed to glow with a misted sunlight, or perhaps from the steam or moisture in the room from the kettle boiling over the bedroom fire. The sunlight filtered over the orange and gold Indian blankets on the large bed.

On the bed against the pillows sat Rain, a child nursing at each breast. On the one, a large sandy-haired boy with olive-colored skin and great liquid eyes. On the other breast, Rain held in the shelter of her arm a tiny black-haired girl.

For a moment Mara stared. Then Rain smiled, a broad smile, her eyes very bright. "Mara! I'm so glad to see you! So glad!"

The air hung with silence, then, "Come and see Sobe's little tiny child."

No one else was near. Sully stood behind her—very still, but she could sense his presence, and the silent patient weight of his continuing love for her, a love that would never die, but that had ripened into pure compassion and concern. She felt it now and it warmed her.

For a moment Mara did not want to breathe, and no one said a word. The room was still except for the sound of the rocking kettle.

"Clarissa, please come to get Charles," Rain called to her biggest girl. Quietly, the girl came from behind Mara and took the large rolling boy into her arms. Sully's girls. They were becoming young ladies.

"Come see the beautiful baby!" Rain said, her simplicity pure warmth to Mara, who had found herself hungering for it.

"Oh yes," Mara whispered. "Oh yes. She is beautiful!"

"Yours!"

Mara, wakened, felt the sunlight of the room engulf her like a flood. The child was the size of a corncob doll, her head smaller than Mara's fist. Yet she was a healthy color, a beautiful rose, and she had a shock of healthy black hair.

"Yes. Yes. My baby." For she was beginning to understand.

"We will nurse her," Rain said. The baby rooted toward Mara's breast as she drew the tiny bundle close into her arm.

"You will nurse her," Mara repeated to Rain in whispers. She stared. She felt the life in the body, the tiny life, the possibility for joy.

The baby was beautiful. The mouth a small heart. She felt the warmth in her arm. She rejoiced, believing, knowing, feeling the years crowd into her heart. Then she remembered to ask.

"And Jane?"

Sully was with them suddenly, his voice broken a little. "They came for her this morning. And she wanted to go."

Mara looked at Rain, at Sully. Jane had probably had enough here. She could have seen why: the odors, the earthy food. The children. The closed air. She had not really known Jane. But she could have guessed. And Sobe knew.

When the small child could not find food, she began to cry. The tiny voice wakened Mara's senses. Did Sobe know?

"Sobe knew," Sully said quietly. "They came before he left for the mill. They had quarreled over leaving the child. Mrs. Hunt would not let her take the baby."

Then I must go to Sobe, Mara's heart beat wildly. I must go to him. How would he feel? How could they . . . ? But knowing Hannah Wright, she thought she knew.

"We named her Jennifer."

Jennifer. Jenny. Mara did not see the baby in her arms for a moment, feeling Sobe's anguish. Jenny. The name passed through her consciousness like fog in her dreams. Jenny.

"It's a lovely name," she said quickly. "I promised Sobe that when the child was born, I would come."

She returned the tiny child to Rain, who drew the baby to her breast. "I hope you and Sully will understand. I must leave. I must find Sobe."

Sully moved from the door as she passed. She turned to wave, and he smiled as she sailed away from them.

"Yes," he said awkwardly, watching her move from him. "We understand."

"I'm grateful." She slipped away.

Sobe. The Tar Babies could not move the cart forward rapidly enough. She could not whip them, but her heart ached to be in town. She saw the mill in her mind's eye and saw Sobe's face as though she were instantly with him. Sobe. Sobeshent. You are in pain.

The gate at the mill was always closed. They were still building, but Sully said the carding had gone into operation today. She pounded the gate trying to bring someone to let her in. She shouted. An old man in a faded straw hat lumbered toward her—old Mr. Earl. His large blistered hands swung from front to back, brushing his overalls with a whisper.

"You need something, ma'am? Oh, hello, Mrs. Jones."

"Yes, I need Sobe very much. Did he come today?"

"I wouldn't know."

"I must find him. May I please come in?"

"It's against the rules, ma'am. The plant as dangerous as it is . . . but. . . ."

"I really must know if he is here. . . ."

"Seeing as how you're the wife of the president of the board. . . ."

The main hull, a large factory building, stood newly completed in sparkling brick and stone. Mr. Earl opened the gate slowly, pausing, shading his eyes from the sun. "It's against the rules, so if you'll hurry, ma'am, I won't get into trouble."

"I'll hurry. Thank you so much, Mr. Earl."

Down the corridors of half-built furnaces, the giant stables for various machines, she felt an urgency she feared in the almost magic aura of the new mill. This was her first visit here. The machinery loomed before her. Perhaps I have loved others, she felt, oddly, but it is Sobe I have truly loved. The depth of the huge building swallowed her as she stepped into its darkness. Men stopped working to stare at her. She felt a magic grip her—the same magic that echoed in Milton's lines: "Is this the region, this the soil, the clime . . . this the seat that we must change for heaven, this mournful gloom . . . For that celestial light." She marvelled that men had built this place. Sobe had also built it. A monument, it would loom large, though it was a monument that enclosed men away from the pure light of day.

"Who you be lookin' for, ma'am?" one of the men near the new boiler room asked her.

"Sobe. Sobeshent Eastman."

"The Indian," he turned to other men who stood nearby.

"Hello, Mrs. Jones," the youngest Allen boy came to her, greeted her with a salute and an awkward extension of his hand.

"Sobe?" she questioned him.

"This morning? I don't think he ever came. Did he ever come? Any of you see Sobe come?"

Did they know of his child, she wondered. Did any of them know he was now a father? That he was the proud father of a tiny child? The trouble with concealment was that happy sharing never occurred.

"No, ma'am. I don't think he ever came today. No, ma'am. He never came."

And so he wasn't here. Mara turned away, blinded by the sudden light in the door.

"Have you seen the mill?" Mr. Earl said to her as she turned into him to leave.

"No. No, I haven't. I can't really stay now to see the mill."

"It's going to be the most impressive operation this side of the Mississippi River. This here is the beginnings of the largest boiler room this side of the Mississippi River, no exceptions."

The light in the door made a silhouette of Mr. Earl's hair.

"I really can't, Mr. Earl. I must go. Sobe isn't here."

"You might not get another chance to see the operation until it's dedicated. This here is the fire alarm system. The most complete security of any mill in the east. We spent five thousand dollars on a mill fire security system. If one of the furnaces explodes, there would be alarms set to ringing, the guard alerted at the gate, and a hose system set up to route the water into the mill. We've got twenty-four-hour guard, water security, a five-thousand-dollar hose system." Mr. Earl's dark hair spread like black fire in the halo of light behind his head. The light blinded her so that she could not see his eyes.

"I really must go, Mr. Earl."

"You got one of the best mills this side of the Mississippi going up right here in Provo, Utah, a hot ding-dong of a mill with the most expensive equipment. And thanks to the business expertise of your husband, we have got ordered the best equipment, as bright as pennies. And the security's tied it all up tighter than a drum for a hundred years."

"Thank you," she said. She held out her hand to him and enclosed his blistered fingers tightly in her own. "Thank you for letting me in."

Once again in the bright sand of the lot, Mara forced her eyes to focus on the horses and the cart. She stumbled toward them, feeling weak, nauseated. By now it was past noon.

The horses again traveled too slowly on the busy streets. Second South . . . west . . . she urged them as though she could not breathe until they found Sobe. She knew there was only one place he would feel really at home.

The widow's house, as always, looked drawn and silent, closed. But as she parked the cart in the road, Mara felt a tension as though she had communicated her presence by sound to the blind woman, and by the ache in her heart to Sobe, who must feel that she was now near.

Mara said inwardly, Sobe. You are here. I know you are here. Don't leave before I find you. Lie still. You need to share your grief. And there is not so much grief as all that. You are a father. And in that you will find great joy.

She slipped down the dark stairs, holding her dress above her ankles, the silk feeling hot in her hands. She saw into the windows, the wells into the room. The curtains hid much of the dusk. Nothing beyond the curtains stirred.

Sobe, stay where you are. I'm coming. I've always loved you. You are like my own child.

Now the door rose before her eyes like a black slate. She knocked hesitantly, nervously, still holding the silk of her dress in one hand.

"Sobe." Her voice sounded odd, the whir of butterfly wings above a murky well. "Sobe. Please. You are here, I know you must be here." But there was silence. No sound came to her, not even from the widow's floor.

She tried the door. It opened easily to the slightest touch of her hand. It had not been closed.

"Sobe." The dusk of the room rose to her, absorbed her as the mist of her dreams had absorbed her. It filled her with a cold air. "Sobe, please."

In the corner, in the darkness, he lay face down on the large bed.

But she knew he had heard her voice. "Sobe! Oh, Sobe." She turned to him, closing the door only slightly, as it creaked on its hinge. A slat of light lay across the floor.

"Sobe! Please! Please let me help you. Let me comfort you. You are not alone. Please never stay away from me again."

He turned to her now, the rims of his eyes raw with tears.

"You are my son, Sobe. Please. She was young. Please forgive her."

Turning his body slowly, he raised up on his elbow as she reached for him. She sat with him on the bed, and he leaned forward and fell against her. He fell sobbing into her arms.

Chapter Nine

WHEN MRS. WASHBURN FIRST CAME DOWN FROM SALT LAKE City in the spring of 1870, she purchased the house on the opposite corner of Papa's street, Isaac Preston's small modern Victorian home with a trim porch featuring stone steps and white pillars. And because she had not known where anything was, when she needed directions to the Taylor Brothers Furniture store, the post office, and the pharmacy, she would often stop and question Papa on his way to the hotel or to his office building on Center Street. Soon, in the mornings as she took her morning strolls with Tina—a fine, large, perfectly trimmed poodle with a studded collar and chain—she approached him just to talk.

"I'm here to study music in Provo," she told Papa, and once or twice she took him to her house, played the piano for him, and sang. Papa had been immediately taken by her. He took her to a dramatic company rendition of "All That Glitters Is Not Gold," and he had talked of nothing else to his family for days. He said she was a wonderful musician—she could play the piano and sing. She was highly educated and knew the Academy people. Although she and Mr. Washburn had not been members of the Church, she had recently been converted, and Mr. Washburn had been dead for seven years. She was quite a lady. Or at least, Mara said to herself, a very good imitation of one.

About the time Sobe had left his house, Papa was toying with the idea of asking Mrs. Washburn to marry him. Mara and Will encouraged him. Ashel and Caroline laughed, uncomfortably, a little embarrassed that Papa thought it might do any good to seek their advice.

Papa held a dinner at his house near the 24th of July. Mara held another in her house next door, and the entire family got up a barbecue in Papa's honor not long before his birthday in September just after Caroline and Ashel purchased the lot south of Mara and Will to build the third Eastman house on Main. On each occasion, Mrs. Washburn gave renditions of Wagner's old Norse songs from *The Ring of the Niebelung*, an aria from *Aida*, and a few Negro spirituals. Mara thought she really was not very good, but Papa sat enthralled during the concerts, his eyes riveted, his hands reverently folded.

There was really no economic reason Papa could not have thought about getting married. For a while he was worried because Mrs. Pulsipher's new boardinghouse on the east side of town, built on a lot she bought from Brigham Young, threatened the continuing success of the hotel. That could have been a reason to hesitate, but now his hotel was doing better and bringing in more than it had ever done.

Still, nothing seemed to happen between the two of them. Will joked, "If you wait as long as I did with Mara, you might have to bed down in the graveyard."

Mara playfully hit his arm. "If *you're* anything close to dead, *I'm* not," she said.

Papa laughed, seeming not much concerned. Mara knew he did not want to be hurried into anything. And so there was never an announcement, never a resolution, never an engagement ring.

After Jenny's birth and Jane's departure in April of 1871, Rain finally agreed to move into town. She had suffered sufficiently from Jane's ordeal, and had continued to suffer abuse from the Richards family. After Rain's decision, Sully decided to lease the farm. Mara, juggling things in her own mind, mustered the courage to ask Papa what was going on in his house.

"What?" Papa looked up at her through his clouded spectacles, laying his paper across his very large vest. "Well, the Occidental Boardinghouse hasn't seemed to slow us down yet."

That wasn't it, Mara told him. "I want to know what's going on between you and Mrs. Washburn. You take her everywhere, but you don't ask her to move in with you."

"Hog feathers, girl! You don't go asking a widow lady . . . just like that, to move in with you!" His belly shook as he snapped his fingers.

"I think she'd like to marry you," Mara hesitated, not really understanding Papa, thinking him impossible, and feeling some concern that the dowager Washburn with her very smooth face and the neat peppery gray braid woven tightly about her head would find someone else and break his heart.

Papa glinted at her as he used to do. "I'm the one to make that decision. I don't think I need a lot of help. What's all the hurry, anyway?"

Mara stood impatiently now, trying to keep her silence long enough to let the words come evenly. "I wanted to bring Rain and Sobe's baby to live close to us for a while. And if you're not going to get married . . . you're rattling around in an awfully big house all by yourself!"

"Oh, now, hold on here," Papa Eastman said. "We went through the ledger from one end to the other with Rain." The financier in him seemed to be protesting. He let his spectacles drop on his thick neck and he glared at Mara.

Mara was fortified. "Papa, you know it's not the same. Rain is caring for four children!"

"And she should be living with Nancy and Sully, where she belongs."

"Nancy has agreed to take the two girls and Charles for a while as soon as he is weaned. And then Rain can finish nursing the little baby peacefully . . . near those who love her. Sobe has consented to move in with me and Will, and I just hoped Rain could stay close by. She told me she would."

"Then move her in with you," Papa said.

"With me?" Mara looked at her father, perplexed.

"Because I think now that you mention it, I'm gonna get me married. Real quick." Papa put his paper down almost with a thud. Then he leaned his large frame forward in the chair and pressed hard on the arms to bring his old bones to stand. Mara was stunned. But the effect of her request had not been an ill one.

It was a garden wedding in June. Rain, who with the tiny Jenny had taken the Jones' back porch as a temporary home, borrowed a fine sheer silk from Mama Eastman's closet for the early evening buffet. She sat beneath Papa Eastman's elderberry bushes with Jenny in her arms while Mara and Nancy, Mrs. Eggertson, and a few others prepared the turkey and the breads.

The first time Mara ever really wondered about Mrs. Washburn was in those first few moments at the party when the new bride entered the yard after the ceremony at the endowment house and caught sight of Rain. She looked frustrated in those few seconds, and began to gesture nervously.

"Isn't there some way you could move the Indian out of the yard?" Then she paused as though she had forgotten herself. "Oh well," she finally submitted. "It's all right." And the party seemed to go smoothly after that, except in Mara's heart.

The new Mrs. Eastman wore a bright pink shell silk for the occasion, and had crimped her braids into a long sweeping mass of fastidious curls. No one could deny she was a lovely sight. Refusing to wear her glasses, she looked through some of the guests, unable to focus adequately on their faces. As she looked up at Mara, her painted cheeks slightly sagging, Mara could see a film of gray on her eyes.

"I'm so glad for you, Mrs. Washburn."

"Call me Hilda, and it's Eastman, dear. I'm your new mother, remember!"

The words chilled Mara. She knelt to pet the carefully laundered dog who rolled its tongue toward her and offered its foot for a cleverly executed paw shake.

Except for the few moments she took to sing an unaccompanied "Liebestraum," Hilda followed Papa during the entire buffet, clinging to his sleeve. She talked a little affectedly about studying with the new Academy singing teacher Leitha Grange in the fall, about her connections with the orchestra in Salt Lake City, and her friends at the Timpanogos Branch of Deseret, including the new normal school instructor Dr. Karl G. Maeser, who happened to be a very prominent acquaintance of hers.

Many of the people who came to the buffet were Academy people: the Dusenberries, the Harrises, the Smiths, and the Robertses. Mara observed them all carefully as they watched the new Mrs. Eastman. She hoped it was going to seem all right to them.

"Now your father's all set," Will said to her when the last guests departed from Papa's garden and they were snuffing out the kerosene flames from inside the paper Japanese lanterns that the widow

Washburn had arranged especially for the occasion. "I'm glad he made it while he was still alive!" And he pinched her and laughed. But Mara had seen something else . . . something she had only sensed vaguely before, something she hadn't worried about before. It was the affectedness, the feeling of superiority. And now she was afraid for Papa, much more afraid than she had been before when she thought Mrs. Washburn would break Papa's heart by marrying someone else.

But Papa seemed in such excellent spirits, in more robust health than he had been for years. He had not been merely walking among the guests that night; he had actually strutted, his waistcoat pressed very smoothly over his large middle. He seemed unafraid at last to disclose a little of his success. For the ceremony in the endowment house he had worn the most impressively expensive clothes Mara had ever known him to own.

"So you see, I guess I do believe in plural marriage," he had grinned to the family. "Hilda is my second wife." He placed her hand on his stout arm. "I'll have two wives in eternity!"

"If Mr. Washburn doesn't insist on joining the Church in Paradise," the former widow Washburn remarked, her dark eyebrows rather thick over her eyes.

The two looked the picture of grace, a couple taking the right turn at the right time. Everyone seemed to think about it as something fine. Mara put away any uneasiness—tried to forget about Papa, and she began to concentrate wholly on helping Sobe and Rain to raise Jenny.

Rain stayed in the Jones household long enough to give the baby a good start and then wean her to a cup that Mara held to the tiny mouth as Jenny lay in the curve of her arm. Then Rain consented to stay with Nancy on Center Street in the east part of town. Nancy, who had been lonely, was glad to have her, and Sully was glad to be able to lease the farm. Mara was happy that Rain was closer and that Jenny would be reasonably close to the children. Without a thought she gave up all of her classes at the Academy in order to be with Jenny—except one class she taught twice a week in the evening when Sobe and Will were both home. She found more time to help Will's daughter Cynthia with household chores, and she made it a point to give extra tutoring in English to Will's boy Peter, who was at the Academy studying accounting. She was becoming a friend to Will's children.

And Will needed her. In '74 he fought the rousing religious revival that put the United Order on an elective ballot.

"How are we going to make the transition to the United Order?" Will fumed, puzzling over the economics of a situation idealized but little understood. "They don't know what they're doing!" But the years of emotional preparation for the prophet's promised utopia proved to be enough to swing the ballot to an accepting vote. Distraught, Will had returned from his office after the passage of the order's victory. "They did it! I can't believe they did it!" he boiled. Mara had been rocking the two-year-old Jenny to sleep in her arms. For almost two years she had forgotten the United Order, the completion of Deseret Manufacturing Company's Woolen Mill, and John Donne.

"It will work out, Will. Please don't worry. Do you see how Jenny's hair has grown lighter? I think she won't have dark hair like her father."

Not that Mara didn't believe in Will's work, for she was with him often, poring over figures, checking books, while Sobe and Peter studied their own budget problems in the next room. Although Will might often have felt he and his politics had competed for attention, he was glad for Mara's happiness, and she knew that it did not matter to him that she loved the baby so. Jenny was the light of all their lives.

Peter married in January of 1875, and Cynthia the following year, in May. Both moved to Salt Lake City, and then Peter moved to Pocatello, far away. When Mara took Jenny to the children's school in the fall of 1876 so that she could have time to teach a class in Karl G. Maeser's new Brigham Young Academy, the little girl was five. And she and Sobe and Jenny and Will had been home alone for over a year.

Jenny Eastman was going to be tall. "The Hunts," Mara thought secretly. Her hair was not black, but dark with red highlights like Hannah's and Jane's. She was perfect . . . in almost every way. She had gone through the fours with a nastier temper than Sobe had ever had. To Mara she would stamp her foot and say *"No!"* But she never defied Uncle Will, and from the time she was very small she would run to her father Sobe and throw her tiny arms around his neck and hold his quiet head in her hands.

Sobe had never been so quiet in his life as during the years of Jenny's growing in the Jones household. Mara could not seem to reach into his heart to know what was there; he was not the same Sobe she had known as a child. Except for quiet play in the evening with his little daughter, he was always at work in the mill. And he seldom talked about anything that happened during the day. Not even Rain seemed to know him now. For he visited her rarely, and he would not stay long if he stopped at Nancy's some evenings to pick up Jenny who might have been left to play with the children in the afternoons. When Papa brought his new wife Hilda to see the family, Sobe would wait only until the woman consented to sing for Jenny, who loved the music, squealing and clapping her hands in delight. Then he would usually excuse himself. He did not come back into the room.

Hilda Washburn Eastman had a harder look about her face than she had when she had married Hart, and though there yet seemed to be no appreciable competition from the Pulsipher's east side Occidental Boardinghouse, Papa had begun to look weary and drawn.

"That Indian of yours is awful quiet, Mara. Can't he afford to get out on his own now? You ought to send such a grown man out on his own," Hilda said.

Sobe had been contributing for board and room, but from the tone in Hilda's voice, Mara decided that anything she could say in explanation would only make matters worse instead of better.

"Was he really married? I can hardly believe a mother would leave her child in such a manner! But of course some people don't like Indian blood . . . don't want to have nothing to do with it. Hart, you said yourself you never really got used to the Indians much, but you tolerated them! How in the world did you get such a daughter who raises nothing but Indians!"

Mara held her breath and waited for her father's response. She noticed a bland sorrow around his eyes. "It's all right, Hilda. Mara. Don't talk so. . . ." And he reached out for Hilda's hand and patted it as Mara had never seen him do with her mother . . . as Mara had never seen him do with anyone. Something had changed him. But she could not tell what it might have been. She had seen him several times a week and had always asked him how things were. He would talk about business. That confounded Occidental Boardinghouse was now beginning to give them a run for their money. It seemed there were a lot of merchants moving to "J" Street on the east side of town. "Do you know what that means for us? East House is no longer going to be east. The center of town will be east, and the East House Hotel will be west."

However, Mara wasn't as worried about his financial affairs as much as she was the affairs of his heart—because he wouldn't say anything about how his home life was going. He always said "Fine, fine," and Mara could never draw anything more from him.

Hilda Eastman had not really posed much of a threat as a step-mother, and she had conducted herself in a reasonable manner. Yet, there was something . . . something about Papa that was changing . . . and if it was not in Mara's imagination, there was something that seemed to be causing him distress.

One summer afternoon Mara sat with Hilda and Papa on the front porch drinking lemonade. They heard Sobe's shouts from the yard behind the house, and a wail from Jenny. Mara ran to the back, Hilda close behind her shouting, "Come on, Hart! Come on!"

Mara stopped at the corner of the house. Jenny had let the chickens out of their pen again, and Sobe was leading her into the house by one hand as she kicked and screamed and dragged her feet in the dirt. Mara watched. She herself was angry at Jenny for doing once again what she had been told so many times she must not do. Hilda Eastman, however, was very upset with Sobe rather than Jenny. Jenny was her best, if not only, true admirer in the Eastman family, and Hilda had lately begun taking Jenny aside to teach her a few notes on the piano. Mara could feel Hilda breathing hard as she came up behind her, Papa and the white poodle at her heels.

"Hart!" Hilda cried, her voice indignant as she watched Sobe drag Jenny up the back steps. "Are you going to stand there and let that Indian hurt the little girl like that! Hart!" Papa was puffing at her side, unable to speak.

"Let that child go this minute!" Hilda shouted at Sobe, who was opening the back door. And then lifting her handbag up and letting it fall on Papa's back, she shouted again, "Hart! Do something, you fool! Get over there!"

Mara stared at Hilda, dressed in navy blue today, a crisp white collar at her throat. At her feet stood the immaculate Tina, her pink tongue hanging out, her collar gleaming. Hilda's handbag had fallen open, and two bottles of smelling salts and a pink pillbox had fallen out onto the grass.

The back door slammed, and Sobe and Jenny were gone. "Well, never mind now." Hilda's voice was full of disgust. "You can't ever get yourself going in time, can you?" And she knelt in the grass at Papa's feet to retrieve her salts and pills.

A few days later, Mara was in the office building doing business with the bank, and she found Papa at his desk in the investment division. She wanted to talk to him, to give him a chance to unburden himself. They had already exhausted all the ramifications of the Occidental Boardinghouse, which was threatening to develop into a full-fledged hotel. About the more important topic of his life at home, she didn't know how to begin.

"You know," she said at last, "that the government won't allow plural marriage anymore." She probed lightly, hoping to get something out of him about his own marriage.

"Eh?" He cocked his head to her.

Proud Papa. He would never say anything, never let anyone know he was the least bit unhappy.

"The Congress is going to pass that law after all. The Edmunds Law defining Plural Marriage as a felony."

"Hog biscuits and bee feathers!" Papa said. If he had been a tobacco chewer he would have spit. "They'll never make it work in this territory."

"Don't be too surprised. Anyway, you old goat with your two wives, you best think about it." She expected he would surely have something to say to her joking now, but he said nothing. He lowered his chin and stared over his spectacles for a long moment.

"Hog feathers!" he said, and nothing more.

It was 1882. Sully had been successful in leasing the north farm to an acquaintance of Clem Richards from Salt Lake City. He worked full shifts at the East Co-op and was now helping Will Jones open another co-op on the west side of town.

On a particularly beautiful spring morning, Sully was in the East shop opening the blinds and arranging a new shipment of merchandise when an impressive visitor from out of town entered the store with a piece of news.

He was a short square man with a very gray face. Startled, Sully looked at him twice, for he swore he saw the apparition of Benjamin Buchman. But the man's name was James Harcourt, and he was from the federal government law enforcement office in Salt Lake City. He was here, he said, issuing warnings that the Edmunds law newly passed in Congress would be effective almost immediately, and he was informed that among others, a Mr. Sully Tuttle of the Provo East Co-op was practicing plural marriage. He would give said Mr. Tuttle ten days to release his illegal wife or wives from the practice and establish her or them into single status out of range with the Tuttle residence with the opportunity to seek her (or their) own husband(s) in order to become a wife (or wives) in good standing with the federal government of the United States of America.

Sully fixed his gaze on the rim of the officer's lowered hat as he read the warning decree. Just before the death of Brigham Young several years ago, he had heard rumors that the law might be passed, but that the passage would actually occur he could not believe.

An hour later, when he could finally bring himself to go home, Sully found Rain patiently snapping beans with Clarissa and Samantha at Nancy's table. He looked at Clarissa, a twenty-year-old imitation of Rain, with her large bones, lighter complexion, and amazingly blue eyes, and slender Samantha, now almost nineteen, slapping playfully at thirteen-year-old Charles' hands when he reached into her bowl for a handful of peas.

"Is something wrong, Sully?" Nancy came to his side as he stood watching Rain and her children. He turned and walked out of the kitchen with Nancy, away from the greetings, the broad smiles of his Indian wife and children. He spoke quietly to Nancy.

"They are going to enforce the dissolution of plural marriages."

"Oh, Sully," Nancy breathed softly. "How can they do that? Break up the families? Anyway, how would they know . . . ?"

"They know," Sully said, handing her the paper from Mr. Harcourt's valise. It had already been folded and torn. Nancy read it silently. Then she also folded it and stood with Sully in the quiet hall.

Clarissa stood at his side. "Papa?" She looked at him with her blue eyes. "Is anything wrong, Papa?"

"Would you mind getting the potatoes? I think they are ready," Nancy said to her.

"Yes, Aunt Nancy," Clarissa left quickly, her broad brow knit as if she knew the quiet meant trouble.

"And they will take you to prison for living with your own family?" Nancy said softly, pulling her handkerchief from her apron.

Sully could not speak. His heart ached so much that he could hardly breathe.

"Are you going to tell Rain?"

Sully pushed the heels of his hands into his eyes. Rain. He thought the heaviness in his heart might overwhelm him, kill him. Rain.

He came into the kitchen. Rain looked up at him, sorrow in her dark eyes. "I know, Sully. It's the new law they have been talking about. I know." She spoke so quietly that Sully could hardly hear her. Rain. His wife for almost twenty-five years. The mother of his four children. Children who meant everything to him in this world. Good, kind, patient Rain, who had always taken second best in everything. Rain smiled sadly into Sully's pensive gaze.

"I know I must be the one to go," she said.

Sully sank into a chair in the corner of the kitchen, and for a long time his family sat without moving while Sully's brain raced. He looked away from Rain's good, patient face. He looked away from their two gentle dark-skinned daughters. His gaze rested on his thirteen-year-old son, grown this past winter into a man. He was as tall as Sully himself, and almost as broad. He could wrestle with the best of them, swim more than a mile, and work as hard all day with an ax, a pick, or a shovel as any grown man.

Sully looked away from his son's kinky rust-colored hair, his strong Indian face. For a moment he saw Tommy before his eyes. Tommy, taken from him so soon. Charles had been the gift of heaven, sent to them in their grief for their firstborn son, and Sully had watched over the growth of his second son, his consolation, with particular reverence and care.

And Charles was a good boy, a son a man could be proud of. Though he could tease his sisters unmercifully, he was fierce in defense of them and their mother if anyone made light because they were Indian. He was responsible in his duties, at home and at church. He was a credit both to the people of his father and to the people of his mother. Of course, there had been times when he had needed discipline. He was strong willed. But Rain and his two sisters, Nancy, too, helped guide him. He was becoming the gentle, dedicated man Sully prayed for in a son.

"You see, Charles," Sully told him often. "I never knew my father, and I have always believed that being a father of a son was a particular privilege and responsibility."

Sully stared at the torn folded paper in his hands. He cleared his throat. "It has been a great joy to me these past few years," he began, afraid his voice would fail, afraid he would not be able to speak with strength. "It has been a great joy to have my whole family here together, and I do not want that to change. I can't bear it that any of you should leave." But he knew in his heart that Rain must leave, and that with her, if not all at once, one by one, the children would also go.

Mara immediately offered to take Rain, and whichever of the children wanted to follow her, or trade off staying with father and mother. When the government's ten days of grace had passed, Sully decided he should accept Mara's offer as a temporary effort to obey the law. Other families who did not separate were suffering dreadful consequences. Two of the men in their neighborhood were taken to prison after court cases had proved they were in cohabitation with more than one wife. Soon the community was on the lookout for the "feds." The children created an alarm system by tapping a warning on the door of a household approached by a federal officer. If the man of the family was home, he would have a chance to hide. Abraham Smoot built a special trap door in his mansion on Second South to make himself a hiding place under the floor. The entire community began to feel the weight of a new burden. Men were snatched from work or from the fields, and women watched the dusty roads each morning as their husbands left, wondering if they would return.

The night Rain arrived, Clarissa with her, Mara was deep in preparations for an Academy class, and Sobe was making supper. Rain looked tired, and Sobe led her to a chair in the corner of the kitchen while Clarissa immediately took over the preparation of the meal. Rain said she was fine; she would just sit and "watch the children work." Mara went back to her books on the dining room table. Mara enjoyed knowing they were there in the kitchen, working together.

"It's a good supper you make, Clarissa Tuttle," Will told her, un-tucking the napkin at the end of the meal. "You can just stay with your mother here anytime." He winked. Sobe, eating heartily, stared at Clarissa. She looked at him with her unusual blue-gray eyes. Sobe also nodded in agreement and smiled.

Although Clarissa was planning on staying at the Tuttle home, she would be welcome here with her mother any time. Rain and her chil-dren were going to adapt to the new arrangement just fine. Happy herself with the plan, Mara felt she had gathered more closely those who meant the most to her, except for Papa who still seemed to be reluctant to share what was happening in his personal life.

Not long after the Edmunds law, Papa became very ill. He had done rather poorly ever since his marriage to Hilda, but now he developed a respiratory problem and began to wheeze. Hilda said the interminable wheezing was the last straw. Frustrated by lack of sleep, she finally decided to "regain" her health by staying with her friend Rachel in Salt Lake City for two weeks "more or less." She left in early March, and Papa, coughing and wheezing, stubbornly tried to get along by himself. Using every wile at her disposal, Mara tried to get him to move in with them, but, huffing and puffing and wheezing, he turned the other way.

He found himself often eating over at Ashel and Caroline's or Mara and Will's, however, and serving as an audience to Jenny, who wanted to sing all of her new songs for him every time he arrived. Finally the doctors told him all they could decide was that he had developed a very hearty allergy, something like hay fever, which he had never had before. They began a program of leaving out various items in his diet or protecting him from certain flowers. And sud-denly, though no one knew why, he seemed to be getting better about the time Jenny had her eleventh birthday.

For her and the five little girls who came to her birthday party, Papa performed magic tricks, whistled, and tried to dance. They thought he was marvelous. So did Mara. Ashel and Caroline, who were also present, both laughed in delight. Sobe and Rain and all of the Tuttles clapped at the fun. He seemed to be feeling fine until after everyone was gone, then he had a coughing spell. When Jenny had gone to bed, Mara tried to talk him into staying over just this one night. Rain was on the back porch and Sobe and Jenny had rooms of their own, but there was still room for him upstairs. Mara heated water for him in a tub and made him sit with his feet in it for an hour, while he and Will and Rain waited to see if his cough would die down.

At about nine o'clock, Sobe came into the front room, leading Clarissa.

"Sobe! Clarissa! We thought you had gone back!" Mara said, surprised to see her so late.

"We've been walking," Sobe smiled shyly. Mara had not seen such a happy smile on his face since he was a boy. He reached for Clarissa's hand. "We've been talking about getting married."

Mara's heart leaped up in her throat. She stared at Clarissa and Sobe. Of course! She had told Sobe years ago to marry one of Rain's children. Samantha had already taking a liking to the Eggertson boy. Mara hadn't noticed, but now she could vaguely see that during Rain's stay in the house these past weeks, Clarissa had been there constantly, and not just to see her mother.

She looked over at Rain, who was knitting quietly by the fire. Her eyes sparkled and she smiled.

"If we have your blessings," Sobe said gently.

It had seemed as though the heavens had opened and confounded Mara. It was Will who stood and put out his hand.

"Congratulations, young man. Congratulations. Of course you have our blessing."

"If we can find a place to stay we will take Rain, and. . . ."

Mara knew the next word: "Jenny?"

"Yes," he continued, "if it's all right, we'll take Jenny with us."

The rush of emotion seemed to cover Mara like a great pall. Yet she gathered herself together, feeling both the joy and the loss, and she reached for Sobe's hands.

May 21, 1882

Dear Hart: When I first left to visit my friend Rachel here in Salt Lake City, I had no intentions of staying longer than two weeks. But as you can see by the postal mark of this letter, I have overstayed my visit by five weeks and three days.

You might guess why I am writing this note. It is not because you were ill that I have not come back. It was more what you said about what we were trying to keep together when you were getting tired and old. I thought you would not mind if I wasn't coming back. You never wrote to me to send for me and I left you my address. Miss Rachel's sister died now and she wants me to stay here until such a time as she feels well. I hope you are feeling better. If you want me to come, say so.

Yours, Hilda E.

P.S. Please let Jenny use my piano.

The letter came on a Thursday. It put Papa down with such a cough in bed that he did not come to Mara's for the Thursday supper. Thinking he had perhaps been too busy at the hotel, Mara did not check with him on Thursday. But when he did not come on Friday, she sent Jenny over with a basket of hot rolls. Jenny was back immediately with the news that Papa was not feeling well.

"This is ridiculous," Mara fumed, untying her apron. Papa needs to be here with us, and I'm going to insist on it now. When she arrived at Papa's, he was buried in a mound of bedding. He handed her the letter.

"That does it, Hart Eastman! You'll move to our place right now, or I'll burn this house down!"

Hilda did not come back. Not during May, not during June.

June 18, 1882

Dear Hart: I wonder if you are all right as I did not hear from you? I am still at Rachel's in case you are wondering where I am. And I am taking part in a stake opera on June 22. No, I have not come back, thinking Rachel will be better any day, but when she does not get better I say, was it worth it anyway to try to stay there, we were sometimes so unhappy. Every time I think of coming back to that house I have a bad feeling.

All except for little Jenny. If you could see she gets the proper training to sing. Are you letting her use the piano?

Write if you need me. Otherwise if I don't hear from you I will stay here.

Respectfully, Hilda E.

As Sobe's wedding neared in late June and they had still not found a suitable place to stay, Mara pondered the situation carefully in her own mind before she approached Papa after supper one evening.

"Didn't you write to Hilda?" she asked carefully. Papa looked up at her as though he were almost afraid to face her eyes.

Mara paused. "Papa, did you?"

But she knew the answer; he did not have to tell her. "You didn't, Papa! Are you going to?"

Papa looked very sheepish. He was busy with his newspaper. But he paused to say, heavily, "I don't know. I don't think so."

Finally, on June 20, 1882, Papa consented to lease to Sobe the Eastman place, where three days later Sobe took his new bride, Clarissa, her mother, Rain, and his daughter Jenny, who could now have a piano.

Chapter Ten

T HOUGH SHE NEVER READ ANY OF THE PAGES IN THE BLACK-BOUND books, Jenny had seen her father write at night in them. When she saved enough money to buy paper, she began to keep a journal of her own.

I think it is because I am part Indian that Mrs. Reynolds, a high school teacher, fears me. My father told me that most people are afraid of us because they do not know what we are or what we will do. He wanted to be a champion on horseback and he was. I want to sing better than anyone else in the high school. And I believe I can. When Father told me it was because I am an Indian that my mother's family would not even see me, or claim me, it made me hurt inside for all of us because we are different. And more than life itself, I want to prove I can do the same things that anyone else can do, and more.

Jenny had to sing almost as she had to breathe. She was full of old songs and new songs. She sang "Little Brown Church in the Wildwood," "Oh, Dem Golden Slippers," and "Oh, Suzanna." She sang in the morning when she finished her chores. She sang on the way to school. She sang on horseback. When she borrowed her Papa's old Betsy, she would often ride to the lake with Samantha, or Charles. She would sing there, and Samantha would say "You sound like the lady in old Mr. Eastman's house."

"I *am* the lady in old Mr. Eastman's house now."

She perfected her trills and scales. Her Papa paid for her piano lessons at the Brigham Young Academy. When the building burned down in 1884, Uncle Will Jones offered his office building to hold temporary classes. The music teacher, Leitha Grange, offered to come to the house, where she told Papa Sobe and Clarissa and Rain that she had "never seen a young girl of Indian . . . er . . . Native . . . extraction so talented as Miss Jenny Eastman."

Later, although the Academy had moved to the ZCMI warehouse, Mrs. Grange continued seeing Jenny in her home.

"Only once in a great while is someone born an absolutely natural songbird like Jenny," Mrs. Grange told Papa Sobe. He smiled.

With the birth of her little half brother, Willy, Jenny had another audience for her songs.

Because their little Willy came so soon, Clarissa and Sobe thought they were going to have a big family. But no other children followed. Jenny adored him, sang him to sleep, sang to him as she rocked in the rocking chair, sang him train songs, boat songs, and animal songs until she became too engrossed in her studies. At that time, her teachers, Mrs. Grange and Mr. Partridge, taught her opera and invited her to prepare for the concerts at the opening of Provo's fabulous new opera house to be completed in 1888. And they gave her religious solo music and encouraged her to prepare for the opening of the Provo Tabernacle to be completed at about the same time.

Suddenly, Provo seemed bursting with opportunities for Jenny to sing her way to fame. At the balls or parties where she performed, she was cheered to return for encores, sometimes two, three, or four times.

Jenny knew that her father watched her with fear. When would the white man keep her from doing something she wanted to do because she was an Indian? When would it come to an end?

In the summertime just before Jenny was to go to the Academy, she sang almost every evening with Mr. Wallace's summertime band, which met in the park just across the street from the old Eastman place. Everyone came: the Tuttles, Papa, Sobe and Clarissa, Rain and Charles and Samantha, and Aunt Mara and Uncle Will. Even old Grandpa Eastman came.

Uncle Will and the Woolen Mills, now under the management of Mr. Smoot, provided electric power for the streets; the band held a gala concert to honor the occasion. Along with a group of instrumentalists and a barbershop quartet of Academy boys, Jenny sang in a medley just as the glorious lights went on.

Outside people, men and women from Chicago and the East, seemed to be coming into Provo now. Grandpa Eastman sold a percent of the interest in his bank to an Easterner, Jared Roberts, for ten thousand dollars cash, feeling pleased to have a managing partner. With part of the cash, he bought a piano for Jenny when Grandma Hilda came down to retrieve hers. It was the first time he had seen Grandma Hilda in six years. She did not have much to say to anyone except that she wished they would send Jenny to study with her in Salt Lake City. She had connections with the symphony.

Someday I will sing with the symphony in Salt Lake City. I will see Grandma Hilda again and sing better than anyone has ever sung in this valley before. They have asked me to sing on the opening night of the dance pavilion at the lake resort, and I am going to sing until my voice echoes the voices of all of my ancestors in the dust of these hills.

With the boom in business for the woolen mills and the East and West Co-ops, Uncle Will Jones had money to begin the Sun Foundry, and Grandpa Eastman added the rest of his newly acquired cash resources to Uncle Will's project. There was still an untold amount wrapped up in the East over which he still had some control with Caroline—who had inherited the fortune of her father. Carefully investing his funds, Grandpa Eastman had enough to lend to several projects. One was the dream of a man named Morris who wanted to build a resort on Utah Lake.

When the resort was completed, it included bathhouses, luncheon booths, refreshment stands, and a dance pavilion, as well as a boat harbor. On holidays, Saturdays, Sundays, and even weekdays, people from all over the countryside and out of town came into the city on hayracks and in carriages. The families gathered together at the rail station and rode the streetcar out to the lake, where they swam, boated, picnicked, and basked in the sun.

In March of 1890, between Academy classes and voice lessons, Jenny watched Charles Tuttle tie together a small raft that would pitch and toss on the early spring lake like a cork. When it threw him off, he'd climb it again, haul himself out of the water, stand with his legs spread apart, and ride it astride. Sometimes he would take his friends with him down to fish or simply to ride his raft daredevil on the wind-driven waves.

Jenny and Charles shared something from the beginning. Two children growing together, they offered each other a warm happy love and, more lately, kisses as natural as laughter. The families lived together, picnicked together, packed food together, and stood in the station to wait for the noisy streetcar that took them on warm afternoons to watch Charlie untie his raft on the whipping waters of the lake. Jenny rejoiced for him, crying out with delight when the small craft pitched away from shore. And he would have allowed her to board had it not been for the solemn "No" from Aunt Mara and the stares of disapproval from Jenny's Papa Sobe and Charles' Papa Sully. But Jenny begged all the same.

"I'm going to ride the raft," she told him.

"Shhh," Charles put his fingers to his mouth. They rode in the car pressed together like packed fish, the family around them laughing in the crowd: Aunt Nancy and Uncle Sully, Samantha and her husband Ralph Eggertson and their little boy, Mathew, rocking from side to side, Papa Sobe and Clarissa taking turns holding little Willy, keeping him out of the picnic. On the end of the bench, in smiling quiet, sat Great-grandpa Eastman with his gray hands clasped over a cane, his black bowler set jauntily over the last of his hair growing just over his ears. Next to him sat Aunt Mara with her beautiful gray hair and her black shawl, watching all of the children, her eyes misty with light. Beyond Aunt Mara, Uncle Will, and beyond Uncle Will, the round hunched Rain.

"Well, I am," Jenny told Charles.

"You won't."

"I will."

"I'll tell you what we'll do," he whispered. They sat so close, Jenny could have touched him with her nose. "I'll take it round through the river from the harbor. If you can get away and nobody sees you...."

"Good!" Jenny said, excitement leaping in her.

She excused herself midway through the potato salad and the pickles and breads to go to the outdoor toilets. Nobody would notice if she did not return for a while. She saw Charlie up in a grove of trees, the raft tied to a stump below him on the shore.

"Kiss me first!" he said as she ran to him.

"After!"

"Before and after," Charles said, knowing he had won, taking her waist in his brown hands. Laughing, she pushed him away, but he found her warm neck. For a moment, Jenny resisted him, but she was laughing and he was warming the laugh from her. And she laughed more gently and held him close.

"Funny. Funny Charles. You said I could ride your raft just so you could kiss me!" And then she kissed him, as she always kissed him, giving to him fully, without fear, warmly. As he pulled her into him, she pressed herself toward him for a full wild moment before she laughed and tore away.

It was Uncle Sully who discovered the raft ride down the river under the sun in the splashing dark water. Jenny's skirt was wet. Sully took the raft away from his son Charles for a week, told him he would be done with boating for a while. It was too dangerous. It would come to no good.

Charles also wants to do something to prove to the world that a half-breed can do anything. He wants to race. And I know he can do better than anyone else if only his father would let him join the boat team.

When the Provo Boat Club ordered the thirty-two-foot paper shell crew boats from New York City for racing, Jenny and Charles pleaded for hours with Uncle Sully to allow Charles to take a spot on the Provo Boat Team.

But it was not to be an ordinary boat team. It was the brainchild of Uncle Will's fellow board members of the Provo Manufacturing Company, executors of the woolen mills. So it was an executive, Mr. W. H. King, who came to Uncle Sully and said in a solemn voice, his hat brim shadowing his eyes: "We probably need Charles Tuttle to win the race in May against the Salt Lake City boat team." When Uncle Sully said "All right," Jenny and Charles were wild with joy.

When the boats arrived from New York City, the city fathers and patrons of sport were to host a ball. Charlie and Jenny went with Uncle Will Jones and the others to meet the boats at the station. The paper shell cruisers smelled like new wood—pitch pine.

"My gosh, they're beautiful," Uncle Will said, and he smoothed his hand over the side that rippled and cracked like fire.

"Perfect!" Charlie stood, his eyes black as coal, looking as though his hands were itching with the craze to touch. Jenny stood in awe beside him.

"And there are your winning boats this season!" Mr. W. H. King, president of the boat club murmured, hustling some boys as they took the boats down from the train, hoisted them onto horse-drawn carts, and lifted the thin canvas veil billowing into the air to float down over them like a cloak.

The ball was held in the opera house on May first, and almost everybody that was anybody was there, dressed beautifully in the club colors, gold and black. In addition to the Tuttle and Eastman families, there were families from up and down the Wasatch valleys, press people from Salt Lake City, photographers with large boxy cameras that stood on giant legs like crabs. Outside the opera house the two mounds of boats lay hidden on the street under the black cloth standing like volcanic mountains waiting to explode with light.

Jenny had been asked to sing. William King, the master of ceremonies, took Jenny to the dais on the opera house stairs and shouted through the new electric loudspeaker: "Jenny Eastman, the national anthem."

"Oh say, can you see," her voice penetrated the air with a pure resonance as clear as glass. ". . . through the night, that our flag was still there." Jenny's voice rang until it seemed to echo in the hills.

The dusk cleared to give way to the stars. After Jenny finished, a hush accompanied the flourishing motion of W. H. King and Uncle Will and the others as they peeled away the black cloth to reveal the gleaming crew boats, polished like vessels of silver. After the glorious unveiling amidst the pomp and flourish of instruments, the women of the Provo Manufacturing Company, Inc., and its various arms, had sewn a gilt and satin flag which they now presented to the men. William King received the flag ceremoniously, clearing his throat of tears after Jenny's rendition and the trumpeter's stirring blast.

"And now, may we win the races with the support of you women," he intoned. "You must all be there to see us as we sail to victory!"

Jenny followed Charles to the unveiling; he was skimming the boats with his hands, talking with team members of how they would win. As Jenny moved from the dais toward him, she only half noticed the stranger in the tall hat walking her way. Gray-headed, he was only a blur in her vision as she took Charles' arm. "And we'll win them all with these boats," Charles was saying. "Isn't that right, Jenny?" he continued, looking as though he knew he had already won *her*, taking her hand in his grip. And then he leaned to her and whispered "I love you." Jenny wanted to reach for Charles and hold his face in her hands. Oh, yes, she thought, still aware of the stranger standing at the edge of her vision.

The others from the boat team began cheering and laughing as they prepared the horses and carts to wheel the crew boats to the lake. Jenny sensed that the stranger was examining all of them. Then he walked forward to stand only a short distance from Jenny's arm.

"Miss Eastman, I believe?"

Jenny turned, feeling the presence of the man like a cloud.

"You are, I believe, as they say, the Indian songbird?"

Jenny had not heard the expression before. She stared at the man. She saw only that he was short, a blur. She couldn't speak.

"You don't look Indian."

"Oh." Jenny's head beat. She had let go of Charles' arm, as he began tying the boat to some wheels.

"May I congratulate you! Your singing of the anthem was beautiful."

She wanted to turn away, go to Charles busy with his boats.

"My dear, have you considered serious study?" The words seemed far away, and as though they came to her through a tunnel of darkness. As the words came through the darkness into her head, she seemed to see light at the end of the tunnel. "You are so talented. I wondered if you had ever considered serious study . . . ?" Now Jenny could see the man's craggy face. His hair was light, almost white, hidden under a smart top hat. He wore a draped silk tie.

"Do you know anything at all about the Salt Lake Symphony and its music program?" he murmured. Still she could not answer. "A voice like yours should not be lost in the cultural abyss of a small western town."

Jenny looked at him, stunned, her eyes now open. "Who are you?" she asked, afraid.

"Oh, I'm sorry. I failed to introduce myself. Aburell. Louis Aburell. And I am an emissary from the new Salt Lake City Music

Hall." He presented a smart, white card. "My card, and it would be a pleasure, if you are ever in Salt Lake City, to hear from you."

Now Jenny could see very clearly in the darkness, and she stared. "From the Salt Lake Music Hall?"

"That's right," the man smiled.

"Are you a friend of . . . ?"

"Yes, my dear?"

"Hilda Eastman?"

But he didn't recognize the name Hilda Eastman. "Hilda Eastman . . . I don't believe. . . ."

"Hilda Washburn Eastman?"

"Why, I know a Hilda Washburn." The light flooded into his eyes. "Yes. She was a student of mine."

A student of Louis Aburell. Had she known that name? Vaguely, Jenny tried to remember.

"Mrs. Washburn has urged me to study in Salt Lake City. Are you the one?"

"The one?" The man smiled his question.

"I would love to come."

"Then come."

All of the dreams Jenny had ever had spun in her. "Well . . ." She hesitated.

The man did not say anything. He smiled. A penetrating, welcoming smile.

"My family has said no. They are all here . . ."

Now the man was smiling still, his clear eyes finding the deep places in her heart. "Well, my child, I have seen in you great talent, and I am so certain of your success that I would be willing to wager upon it. I would have come sooner . . . but, uh . . . they told me . . . you were an Indian."

Jenny felt a stab of hurt in her breast.

The man spoke quickly again. "You don't look it, my dear."

The pain spread. She felt Charles draw near. "Are you down here for a very long time?"

"Tonight only, my dear," he said.

By now the band had begun playing a waltz, the lights had dimmed. Suddenly a crowd seemed to sweep around them and drown out the stranger's soft voice. Near her she felt the strength of Charles' arm.

"I see you are ready to waltz, my dear," the gracious musician all but whispered and bowed away.

"Charles, this is Mr. Aburell."

Charles extended a hand.

"Happy to meet you, my dear boy. I'm impressed with the boating team."

"He tells me I should go to Salt Lake City."

By now the sounds of the music drowned Jenny's words. Charles took her hand and backed away with her, moving to the music. The man smiled and nodded, relinquishing her to Charles' hands. But she did not feel the conversation had come to an end.

"Charles . . . that man . . .," she said into his face.

"That man, what, my beautiful Jenny?" Charles hummed the waltz tune.

"He wants me to study with him in Salt Lake City."

Charles grinned now, brought her close to him, held her tightly. "How are you going to go to Salt Lake City if you are going to stay here and marry me?" he said into her ear. Jenny had never heard Charles utter a single word about marriage, although it had always seemed almost understood. She felt a wave of confusion crowd her joy; then her head ached.

"Marry me, marry me, marry me," Charles was singing into her ear as the music drowned out every other sound.

Jenny, alone in her room, Aunt Mara's old room in the old Eastman house, after the ball, still felt the pressure of Charles' lips on her own when she put the white card into her drawer. It had been an impossible evening, a glorious, but frighteningly impossible evening, the forces of the future moving in on her like railroad cars from convergent tracks, bearing down upon her in terrible fury. She sat on the bed and took off her shoes. She felt the pressure of Charles' hand.

"I love you, Jenny," he had said. "There's a job for me better than the mill or the office building. They're promising to begin a pleasure cruise with a transport boat here to make trips across the lake, and I could be first to run it!"

"What about Salt Lake City?" she had dared to say and they had quarreled.

"Well, then, go to your precious opera company to study," Charles had said. "I don't need to talk about marriage. I've got to win the boat races. And when the transport boat is built, I've got to see it across the lake. And I don't need you bullying me about opera in Salt Lake City."

Jenny had cried. She had cried tears into Charles' fingers and then kissed his hands, and he had said he was sorry and they had held each other for a long long time.

"I love you, Jenny," Charles had said then, kissing her over and over again. "And you will see it's our love that matters over anything, over everything. . . ."

"I love you, too," Jenny had sobbed. And now she stood at the drawer and stared at the white card before she carefully tucked it away.

Charles and the team won the boat races. And in the following weeks amidst even greater pomp the team hitched the boats to the side of a railroad car complete with a Chinese cook. Dressed in white sailor blouses and blue pants, the team members waved at the crowd cheering them to victory on their way to the Great Salt Lake. And on the Great Salt Lake, they won the boat races again.

When Charles returned triumphant, there were the garden parties at the Eastman house, the cheers, the songs. However, he spoke less of marriage to Jenny instead of more. Jenny understood he was waiting for the completion of the transport boat, which took most of his spare time. And she was busy with Aunt Mara helping to choose draperies and carpets for the new Academy building to be ready sometime during the next year. There were plans for Academy classes to complete and a trousseau to sew.

Finally, at about the time of her twentieth birthday in 1891, he came to her and took her into the park and held her for a long time. Nothing he had said in the past two years had changed, really. They were going to marry as soon as the transport boat was completed and he knew he had a job steady enough to support her and the children who would come.

And now he whispered in her hair: "It's done, Jenny. The transport boat is done. There are only three other men eligible to run her, and King has told me I'll have a job at least part time. We can marry, soon."

Often, as Jenny pulled a scarf or a handkerchief out of the drawer, she thought about the white card and her dreams to sing with the Salt

Lake City Symphony. But she always put the card back and waited for Charles. Now at home that evening, she took it out of the drawer, tore it up, and threw the pieces into the fire.

April 28, 1891. I am going to marry Charles. I believe it is what I have always wanted. We were meant for each other from the beginning. Aunt Mara has talked to me about love. High adventures in love and life seem to be exciting, she has always said, but real joy comes from building something good and lasting, something eternal. I told her I had thought and thought and thought about going to Salt Lake City to sing, to prove that I could do as well as anyone. "And when you have proven that," she said, "you would still come home to an empty house if you were alone."

I don't intend to be alone, I told her. But then I have thought about it and thought about it. I love Charles more than I have ever loved anyone. And he wants me now to be his wife. He does not care if I have been an opera diva or even if I can sing. If I am there for him to talk to, for him to hold, for him to tell his troubles to, he is the happiest man in the world. Seeing him happy makes me very happy. So it is a love filled with happiness.

And yet, though he may not care, I cannot help caring within myself that I can sing. I love to sing. It also fills me with happiness.

Surely in my life I can both sing and love.

Charles will make a career of boating when the transport boat is built. He will have his job, his lake, the sky, the vast waves. He will also have me. Why is it that a man does not have to choose?

On a warm spring day in May, Charles, W. H. King, and the others finally wheeled the boat out of the shop and fastened its trailer to a four-horse team. As the horses clopped heavily on the gravel roads, hundreds of Provo people came out to follow the *Florence* to the lake. On the following morning, May 7, 1891, they gathered at the dock to hear Abraham O. Smoot offer a christening speech accompanied by music from the Enterprise band playing "Gee Whiz."

Jenny's eyes were always on Charles. He glowed as though behind his eyes was the bright sun. "And we have the good boat team prepared to give us boat rides for the years to come."

Jenny had been asked to sing. She was to begin the national anthem, to sing the first stanza, after which everyone else was to join in.

". . . By the dawn's early light." The sun had just passed over the eastern hills and sat like a fat bright coin on the tops of the mountains. "Oh say, does that star spangled banner yet wave o'er the land of the free and the home of the brave?"

Only fifty could make the maiden voyage across the lake with the new boat. Aunt Mara and Uncle Will and Rain stayed on the shore with Clarissa and Samantha and the children. But Uncle Sully and Aunt Nancy and Papa Sobe came. And Jenny. She watched Charles with breathless delight as he scrambled with the other members of the boat team to cut the ribbons on the causeway, after which the privileged first passengers began to march up the wooden plank and into the beautiful hull. As Jenny walked with the others onto the deck, the people on the shore cheered. Slowly lining up along both the railings and on the main deck and the railing around the small central deck, the passengers waved to the excited crowd that stood on the shore. Jenny waved from her perch near the railing to Aunt Mara, Uncle Will, and Rain, who stood waiting with the others. Uncle Sully and Aunt Nancy were behind her, jostled in the crowd. Her father, Sobe, followed them, looking out across the water as though he had never seen it before.

Jenny watched Charles as he scrambled to the captain's deck and stood pacing, watching Captain King turn the wheel. When the steam engines began to hiss and the paddle turn, Abraham Smoot cut the ribbon, and Charles and the others hauled the ropes onto the deck.

"We're off!" Jenny heard Uncle Sully behind her. "We're off! What a great success! Hats off to King and the boat team, and our Charles!" The morning air was so clear that Jenny could see the farthest hills. As the *Florence* rocked forward into the choppy waves, Jenny flung her head back and happily gazed at the ring of mountains surrounding them, rolling and dipping in unfathomable valleys and crests of stone.

We're here . . . now, at this moment, it seems we have it all. . . . Charles has his job . . . we have the lake, the mountains, the sweet air . . . and our love for each other.

The feeling of joy and excitement overwhelmed Jenny as the boat moved forward into the vast gray water.

"The lake is quite shallow," King was saying through a sound cone. "In the middle of the lake you will see rock shoals close to the surface of the water. The greatest depth is probably not more than thirty feet." The people surged toward the rail, pointing to the landmarks diminishing in the distance, talking in low voices. Jenny felt the breeze in her hair and did not hear any sense in the words around her.

"To the left is Bird Island." Suddenly a cloud of gulls rose like smoke into the clear air. The stone itself seemed to be crawling like a giant land crab lumbering in restless sleep.

"It's alive with birds," someone said behind Jenny.

"Even the land appears to be alive," Sully Tuttle said. "It is the greatest living being among us."

As the boat rounded the island to the other side, new waves rose in the wind, whipping, stirring, churning the water. Nancy suddenly leaned over the side holding her stomach.

"Are you all right, Nancy?" Uncle Sully turned quickly to her.

Jenny held tightly to the rail as the boat lurched, struggled forward toward the gray shore. Her own stomach began to turn, to weigh like a stone inside of her.

Through the cone, King announced, "We were to have a delegation to meet us on the Eureka shore! The new community will blossom with this transport! I can't see them! Can you?"

Charles came to stand beside Jenny just as the wind whipped a froth of cloud over the western edge. He took her elbow in tense fingers and strained his eyes toward the Eureka hills.

"We were to leave some freight. Lumber. Mail. If the *Florence* can take freight, there's the commercial as well as the recreational use."

Jenny nodded. The wind blew her eyes shut, stung her cheeks. She thought she could feel the spray of the icy water on her arms.

"If the boat is a success, I'll have a part-time job for now. Then later there will be other boats, and someday one built only for me. I can carry anything from Provo to Eureka, and the towns will grow like brush fire across on those hills."

For a moment, Jenny saw a forest of buildings rising like ghosts on the Eureka shore. "I can see it, Charles."

"A world of cities, farms," Charles laughed lightly and rubbed Jenny's arm. "And our children will be part of all of it, Jenny."

The wind rushed into their faces again and shut their eyes.

"I don't see the delegation from Eureka," W. H. King announced more softly over the sound cone. "They've been mining there. We'll have communities stretch from Salt Lake City and spread like a fan all across the southwest to California. And more riches than California gold!"

The boat drew near the far shore by now, misty in a haze of smoky gray. The water looked like fabric, a veil hazy and opaque over the velvet brown hills.

"Clouds rising before noon, just as things looked so good. I can't see anybody there," Charles said.

As the boat drew nearer, Jenny could see the dark, treeless land stretch in gravel and sand for miles into vast arroyos of empty stone. Jenny held tightly to Charles' hand. He looked into the emptiness with expectant eyes.

"Stay here, Jenny. Now I've got to help get the freight off the boat to the Eureka people. I'll be back with you soon."

Jenny stared into the blue distance, toward a horse path, toward the hills winding west into the basins and stones. She wanted to say something. She began to speak, but the words stopped in her throat. There was no one from Eureka on the shore. No one had come.

A boat ride around Utah Lake to the Eureka shore cost a passenger twenty-five cents. No more than fifty passengers could ride. The proceeds from the passage of a full boat was twelve fifty. Two rides could be made per day. The cost of the mortgage on the boat amounted to nearly twenty dollars. After the payment of King's mortgage, there was five dollars left to pay King and the boatman. So on the two days Charles could work he made two dollars and fifty cents a day if he was lucky. And during a week, he had to share his post with three other men. Every other week Charles could work twice. So he kept his post at the mill where he made a dollar and thirty cents a day. The economy of Charles' life had not really much changed. But during those first few months of the run on the lake, what had changed was his outlook. He was happier than Jenny had ever seen him.

"Two fifty for a day of sport!" he said, excited. "And they are planning to build another boat now soon!" For two months Charles talked about getting married at Christmastime, but then everyone had been on the lake two or three times and the winds began to chill in the fall.

November 6, 1891. Charles wants to get married at Christmastime, but now that the lake is so cold, the boat rides have not brought in enough to save. Sometimes he takes the boat out with so few passengers he gets nothing at all. Aunt Mara has given me the job of helping to sew more Academy draperies which together we are going to do at home. I believe I want to get married, but Charles does not say very much about it anymore. He is still so wrapped up in boating and boat building. And even though the interest in the boat ride is dropping off, and the freight line to Eureka seems to require less and less, they are planning to build another boat before their races next spring. It is hard to come second to the lake, which has somehow won his heart. I want to do what is right. I have promised him. I will wait to see what he is going to do.

But by Christmastime Charles was in debt. And all he could tell Jenny was that he would marry her in June. But already it was too late. Their June did not come.

At first it was not noticeable. Jenny saw only Charles' dreams failing, and she noticed only his own brooding as the *Florence* sat idle during the winter when the lake was frozen. At first Jenny believed it was only winter that closed the boat runs, the resort. She did not see how business had begun to slow during the year 1892 cold . . . but Uncle Will shook his head, worried that the investors from the East had extended too much credit and that too many land deals had fallen through. And then the Provo City Lumber Company failed. And Uncle Will's West Co-op failed. The General Authorities of the Church in Salt Lake City exhorted people not to make a run on the banks, but it happened anyway—the banks closed shortly after the financial crisis hit. More and more of Papa's bank had been managed and purchased by Jared Roberts, who was devastated. But both partners were hit badly. The depression and the change of the Occidental Boardinghouse to the new Hull House Hotel on the east side of town had taken so much business that the East House Hotel was hard hit. And then Grandpa Eastman fell deathly ill.

Jenny spent the next few months with Aunt Mara at Grandpa's bedside, reading to him, or cooling his brow with cloths, smoothing lotion on his dry feverish skin, helping to change the bedding.

Only Aunt Mara's voice kept all of them calm: "Things will be all right," she said often to everyone.

Ashel had said there was still enough in the other investments to keep them afloat. Mara encouraged Papa cheerfully. "The economy will rebound. You can be grateful you have people who love you to be around. Aren't you glad you have Jenny? If it were not for Sobe and Rain, your adopted children, you would not have a posterity to follow in your footsteps. As it is, you are rich with children who love you. That's being rich."

Grandpa Eastman groaned almost inaudibly as Mara continued. "Your business will come back," she assured him. "The important thing is that we have grown together in this land. You yourself said we would all become a part of this land. We have, Papa. We are this land. You can be proud."

Jenny watched gray-haired Aunt Mara, the woman who had been more of a mother to her than anyone else except for Rain. Aunt Mara ministered to her Grandpa Eastman like a nurse, bringing soup, gruel, the bedpan, the news. Her voice soothed them like music, sounding far away. "And surely now you can see that the adoption of the native children into our family is one of the best steps we took to flourish. You are not alone, Papa. We are with you until the end."

It was true Grandpa Eastman loved Jenny. When she came to him he held her hand for long moments while he waited for pain to subside.

"Is there anything we can do, Grandfather?"

"Sing to me. Just sing to me."

Jenny sang "Songs My Mother Taught Me," "Loch Lomond," and "The Old Oaken Bucket" until Grandpa fell asleep, the summer light fading in the room.

"And when are you and Charles going to get married and bring the next generation?" he asked one morning.

Jenny hesitated, unable to answer him. Aunt Mara had instructed all of them to keep talk of the economic panic from Grandpa. Sometimes Grandpa, in the haze of his fever, forgot about the growing hostility in the competition between the east and west sides of town, about the Hull House Hotel. His mind seemed to move over the past few months uneasily, groping for what seemed wrong. When they asked him, he seemed to believe his finances were still solvent. He could not pinpoint what the problem was—just that there was one.

"It's not good, is it?" he would say.

"We can't marry until Charles has a good job," Jenny finally told him.

"The boat . . . was it the boat? It didn't make a thing, did it? Charles is a good boy. Let him work at the hotel. Get him doing something. Marry him." He did not seem to remember that he had been laying people off at the hotel.

Aunt Mara stood at the door and exchanged glances with Jenny. How could they tell him that there was so little to do? Not much for any of them.

"I know it's tight, but tell Charles we'll get him set up, Jenny," Grandpa said.

"I'll tell him," Jenny answered quietly. She held his gnarled gray hands.

"Sing again to me, Jenny."

And she sang again.

As Jenny wrote in her journal, Sobe also continued to fill his pages with words.

February 11, 1893. It is not like it was. I am unable to make ends meet for the family from the amount coming in from my allowed pay at the mill. The mill is making nothing now, but they are spending far more than what they are able to sell, and the costs of production soar. I am aching in my heart for my Jenny and her Charles. They seem to have no hope, no joyful love anymore. A father should be able to do more for his children than I am able to do. I see my own sadness in the face of good Sully Tuttle as well. We want our children to marry one another as we have always known they would. But Jenny surprises me. The other night she did not return from her voice lessons until dark. She brought a large portfolio of music with her and went straight to her room where I could hear her singing her scales, trying unfamiliar tunes until well past midnight. When I knocked to ask her what was going on, she told me she was practicing a new folder of music which her teacher had told her about long ago but which she had never tried. Now she wants to memorize operas, she told me, although I like her religious tunes best, and the lullabyes that she and Clarissa sing to Willy, our little son.

Mara was not actually surprised when Jenny left. She had suspected it might happen from things Jenny had said, from the way Charles had stopped coming to see her regularly, from the increased practice sessions, from the letters Jenny had been receiving from Salt Lake City, from Hilda Washburn, from Louis Aburell. Letters no one but Jenny ever read.

Then they had argued once about her wanting to go to Salt Lake, but she had not said anything about it for a long time. She had been quiet, morose. Then finally there was the note. *"I am going to sing. Charles doesn't care. You can't stop me now. Good-bye. Jenny."* Sobe had brought Mara the note, heartbroken.

How would she get to Salt Lake? Sobe didn't know, but Mara suspected she would find her way with a train of men who had come through Provo, about three hundred homeless, jobless workers from the industrial marches on their way to the East. A train had been derailed near the Provo yards, a response to a warning that torpedoes lay on the tracks. All three hundred men ended up in Provo, milling about, finding space to lie down in the saloons. Several had been taken to jail. Some found ways to get to Salt Lake City. Though Mara feared for Jenny, she trusted her judgment, felt that the girl was a strong person who would do nothing truly unwise. She talked to Sobe. "She must go," he said, his eyes clouded with grief. "We must let her go."

But Jenny's absence was the last blow for Papa Eastman. When she did not appear for three days, he begged for her.

"She's not here, Papa."

"Of course she's here. Tell her to come in and sing for me. I want some music. It's a dull day without music, without Jenny. Bring her to me."

"I can't, Papa. You don't understand. She's gone."

"It is not possible." Puzzled, Papa lay with his mouth open, his eyes staring at nothing in the dense air. His hands lay gray on the quilt. At Jenny's departure, Papa did not respond to anything for several days.

It was Ashel who finally roused his interest. They were in the thick of the panic of 1893. Though the bank had closed, Ashel had managed to keep the estate intact behind closed doors, draining its resources to keep the family barely going. During Papa's illness he visited as often as he could, although much of his time was spent alone with Caroline, who had been somewhat ill lately. He wheeled her chair to Mara and Will's home for noon suppers, where Rain and Clarissa and Samantha often brought the children, who climbed into

Caroline's lap and begged to hear stories. Caroline seemed more alive in their presence, and her illness seemed to abate on those afternoons.

Papa watched from the settee, his white head propped up on the divan. This was his kingdom, Mara reflected. He surveyed it guardedly, too weak, she knew, to wrestle with the old reservations he held against any of the Utes and their children.

"I . . . I have something to tell Papa," Ashel said breathlessly to Mara on one such day before he had wheeled Caroline to the door. Mara stood to admit him, wiping her hands on her apron, her fingers crusty with flour. Ashel's face looked drawn and very white. It's the estate, Mara thought immediately, though she did not say anything.

"How is he? Can he take something . . . is his heart . . . ?" Ashel sounded more agitated than he usually permitted himself to be.

"He's doing fairly well, Ashel. But if you have something serious . . . Ashel, I think it might be best . . . Does he have to know?" But Ashel was smiling now, already beginning to speak before Mara finished.

"He will want to know." Then Ashel smiled. It was a bright warm smile unlike any smile Mara had seen since the panic had driven them all into this brooding anxiety.

"Is it . . . what is it?" she began as she followed her brother outside to Caroline's chair, wiping her hands on her apron. "We still need to be careful with Papa. . . ."

Together they carried Caroline up the steps, wheeled her into the hall. The hall mirror flashed with light from the sun. As Caroline saw herself in the mirror, Mara noticed a look of absolute joy in her blue eyes. The yellow curls now misting with gray surrounded the softness of her face like a halo of light.

Immediately, Ashel wheeled the chair into the parlor and approached Papa, who still lay asleep on the settee. Mara untied her apron and tossed it into a chair. She stood in the doorway watching, sensing the excitement. Ashel approached Papa slowly.

"We have something to tell you, Papa," he said, gently shaking Papa's shoulder. "Can you wake up?"

Papa's mouth lay open drawing breath in a hissing rush of sound. His eyes looked distant, confused.

"We are going to have a baby, Papa. Listen to me. Caroline is with child."

Mara's head spun with the feeling of dizziness that had lately taken her. The light flooding the room from the windows blinded her eyes.

"Do you hear me, Papa?" Ashel was saying. As he bent over Papa, his light hair fell across his forehead. Ashel was also graying. He was fifty-three years old.

"We are going to have a baby."

"No," Mara whispered. No, it could never be. Not Caroline, who was crippled, who was almost forty-five.

"It's a miracle. It's what her illness has been. And we never suspected, not once have we suspected, yet it's true. The miracle of all miracles is no less true because it is a miracle." Ashel was beside himself now, fairly dancing about in his joy.

Papa raised his head from the white pillow stuffed in the corner of the settee. He raised his head and strained to look into Ashel's eyes. The flesh on his jowls hung limply from heavy bone. He was now thin. All of his weight had vanished into the vapor of the fever that had ravaged him during the months he had clung so desperately to a life he was not sure he could ever live again.

Now the muscles in his neck strained to lift the heavy head. "A child?" he said, the words almost whispered, guttural in his throat. "Caroline is going to have a child?" The bright-haired Caroline looked ageless, alert, in the chair.

"Ashel, give me your hand." Ashel offered his arm. The old man lifted his body with great effort to the edge of the bed.

"Come here, girl," he fought to say to Caroline. "Come here, my girl."

Mara stepped into the room. "Papa . . . take care. . . ." she began, but Ashel hushed her with his hand. The old man's eyes blazed. Mara stood behind the chair and began to wheel it forward into the old man's arms.

Like a giant bear, Papa lifted himself up, out of the bed, his thighs shaking under the quilts, his flesh as loose as old cloth. "Come here, my dear Caroline. I can't tell you . . . it's not easy. . . ." His body shook. He lumbered upward and reached out. "Oh, I am a happy man!" And he fell forward toward her, his arms flailing as he sank to his knees. "I am a happy man!" The bedding fell away from him, he tripped in it, and his body reached the floor with a thud and a ripple of flesh.

"Papa!" Mara cried. "Oh Papa!" He lay sprawled in the sunshine, grasping at Caroline's feet, holding them, softly sobbing, the tears spilling out of his eyes.

"Bee feathers, I'm clumsy," he was saying, but with hardly a sound in his throat. "Forgive me." At that moment, a great wrenching shook his limbs. The white head jerked in the shoulders, rippled through the spine.

Ashel bent over him shaking, his hands grasping at his father's arms. Both Mara and Ashel shook him, patted him, tried to make him breathe.

Mara bent over him, sobbing, hysterical. "Oh Papa! Papa is dead!"

"He is gone," Ashel said quietly and held his old father in his arms.

Chapter Eleven

THE EVENTS THAT HAD LED TO JENNY'S DEPARTURE FROM PROVO had seemed to sweep her along in an inescapable course.

The man's name was Curtis Weintraub. The voice teacher, Mrs. Grange, whispered the name to her when Jenny entered the house on a hot July morning. The little pinched woman opened the screen door slowly into the dark parlor, the music room. She held a finger to her closed mouth. She was housing three men, she said, from the California industrial army that had been derailed on the stolen train. "And one is a gentleman," she whispered softly.

What can she mean? Jenny wondered. What kind of a gentleman? Mrs. Grange answered without Jenny's asking. "He's still asleep on the back porch; he'll probably wake up when he hears your lesson. I've tried to keep quiet this morning. Well, it's almost nine. They came in late last evening. You should hear him! My!"

Jenny followed Mrs. Grange into the dark comfortable music room where a small window let in the morning light through stained glass. Not dust, but mist seemed to fill the air like a cloud hovering about the dark polished furniture, the deep blues and wines of the needlepoint chairs, the plush blue of a stuffed settee across from the piano. Jenny had always loved the room—a haven of quiet and culture away from the rough dusty street. "Hear him?" Jenny said.

"Oh my! Yes!" Mrs. Grange exclaimed. "Sing! You should hear him play the piano and sing!"

Jenny watched the tiny Mrs. Grange explain herself with the same birdlike gestures she had used to teach Jenny the graduated scales.

"He's marvelous! He told me he'd had training in Los Angeles and San Francisco, that economic circumstances forced him into industry, and when the money went down he had to join the march east. He's simply a lovely young man with a treasure of a voice!" Mrs. Grange's whispers had become louder now as she led Jenny to the piano and hunted through the paper music. "He sang this one perfectly! Without so much as a tremor!" She fingered "Die Bildnis Ist" and shook her head gently from side to side. "Oh, I have never heard such a voice in a man." Then she whispered so softly, Jenny could barely hear: "Jenny, I believe it compares with yours."

And they began Jenny's lesson.

"Sing, girl. You can't be worrying about waking anybody up," Mrs. Grange whispered. "Just sing, girl." So Jenny sang, the music filling her head and floating out of her, filling the room with a beautiful ringing sound. And then she began, not to hear him, but to feel the eyes, the penetrating eyes upon her. She saw Mrs. Grange look past her and smile. She nodded at Jenny to repeat the aria.

She was doing Pamina's second-act aria from *The Magic Flute*. It came easily from the well of music inside her. She felt she could rise with the sound and move out of the room with it, soaring to the open sky. She was Pamina. "Ah," she sang, "alles verloren ist."

She finished. She turned and saw him standing in the doorway. His face frightened her at first. He looked dark; a rough dark beard hung on his face. But his eyes were bright with appreciation for what he had heard. He looked at Jenny with rapture and an understanding that she had not seen before from a man.

"You're Jenny," the man said, walking into the room, smiling. "Beautiful," he said, reaching for her hand and bringing it to his lips. The dark beard did not scrape her skin. Jenny stared at him, at her hand where he had kissed her. A smile unfolded inside her, but she did not let it come to her face.

"Mr. Weintraub," Mrs. Grange said, bringing her hand to her heart. "This is the student I told you of, Miss Jenny Eastman. Jenny, this is Curtis Weintraub."

"Very happy to meet you," he said, smiling, bowing slightly from the waist.

"I've been telling her, Mr. Weintraub, about your own voice. Wouldn't you join her . . . in a duet . . . ?" Mrs. Grange shuffled through the music on the piano. "I'll play," she said, settling at the piano bench with a flourish. Jenny smiled shyly.

"My pleasure," Curtis Weintraub said, and moved to stand near Jenny.

He was not dressed like an industrial marcher, but his clean clothes looked much wrinkled by having been packed for a long time in a valise. He smelled of fresh cologne. Jenny thought her hand trembled as she held the music, but his did not.

"E il sol de l'anima" the Italian rolled beautifully from his tongue. At first Jenny held back to hear his voice, but Mrs. Grange would not let her listen. "Feel it, Jenny," she said. "Sing out." And they sang. They sang duets from *Rigoletto, Carmen, The Magic Flute*, the Wagnerian suites. At the end of each duet, Mrs. Grange turned a page and exclaimed breathlessly: "Beautiful!" The other men from the industrial train who were staying with Mrs. Grange looked into the room to listen. Jenny had never felt anything like it in her life. His voice was powerful, a pure tenor filled with resonance and a full strong vibrato. The sound shook her from the tips of her fingers into her head and then deep inside her, setting off sensations she had not known before. When they closed a number, she felt their voices ring together, clasp on harmonies as though reaching through waves to touch and hang suspended in the air.

They had to try some parts over again when one or the other faltered. Laughing, they started over again. Curtis Weintraub was an excellent reader, and Jenny had little trouble even with pieces she did not know. "Wait!" he would laugh gently, stopping Jenny. "I've got to come in sooner, here." When she looked into his eyes she felt fire pouring into her body, but he did not touch her.

They sang. They sang the duet of Wenzel and Maria from *The Bartered Bride*, they sang the duets of Radames and Aida. They sang in Italian and then French and then German. They sang until Jenny was tired and had to stop.

"Are you worn out, girl?" Mrs. Grange asked her.

"I am," Jenny laughed lightly, as she sat on the plush blue settee, and felt her bones sink into the velvet.

"The more practice you get, the better you can last it out," Mrs. Grange said.

Jenny was amazed when she glanced at the mantel clock. They had sung for three hours. She stared at Curtis Weintraub, who wasn't in the least winded, but only seemed to be getting started. They had worked together for three solid hours. She felt she knew him through to the core; she felt she had seen into his soul, had known him a lifetime.

"We'll stop then," he said good-naturedly. "Maybe you'd show me the town!"

Jenny looked at him, felt an uneasiness in her stomach, opened her mouth to answer. But he did not let her speak.

"Come on, Miss Jenny Eastman. Show me what a town looks like if it's between Los Angeles and Chicago and not even on the map!"

"Oh, I think it's a marvelous idea," Mrs. Grange said. "And it's lunchtime already, and I suppose the other boys fended for themselves. But Mr. Weintraub hasn't even had breakfast yet! Will you stay for lunch, Jenny?"

"Lunch would be wonderful, Mrs. Grange," Curtis Weintraub said, hitting his fine leather belt. Who was he? Why had he taken the industrial train east?

During lunch Jenny watched him secretly over the steaming rice, the hot dishes in the white china. Mrs. Grange served the rice with creamed beef, toast, and the last of the green beans from her garden. Jenny met the other men and smiled, trying to lower her eyes. She felt them look at her.

"Now take me," Curtis said to her finally, and stood behind her chair while she folded the napkin and placed it at the side of her plate. "I want to see it all."

Jenny turned. "There isn't that much." She smiled.

"*You* will compensate for what the scenery lacks," he said smoothly.

Then Jenny felt afraid. She could not say why her heart pounded. They walked. He took her hand and put it through his arm. They went north out of town, as far as the broken down Bean cabin, then east to the hills, south to Third Street. They talked.

"I sang in the San Francisco opera. Then there were hard times. My wife didn't want to live the life of an artist. Her family took her, and our child." He paused. "I needed money. I joined the marches. . . ."

"And you came here."

"The train derailed. Our group stole a train at Lehi junction. The rumor was they torpedoed the tracks, so Carter turned the train off the rail. Three hundred of us, or more, fell onto the mercy of the citizens of Provo. They put Carter in jail."

"And now?" Jenny asked him.

"I'm going to Salt Lake City, then east." Without a break in his stride, he turned his head to her and said, "Do you want to come?"

"What?" Jenny could not talk.

"You want to sing. This is no place for a voice like yours. Even Mrs. Grange realizes that. You must have known that yourself for years."

Jenny looked at him, into his black eyes. "Yes," she said honestly, still looking into his eyes. Who was he? A man with his talents did not belong in Provo. She felt awed, amazed, afraid.

"So come with me."

Jenny did not answer. They walked. They found themselves on the outskirts of town, in the scrub oak, by the canals. She felt a power from him as he strode alongside her. She was afraid. Because she knew now she was going to go with him.

She did not let herself admit consciously what she was going to do until they returned that evening tired, having walked an entire circle back to the home of Mrs. Grange. Jenny stood by the wisteria and held to the post of the porch.

"I'll be leaving in the morning. If you decide you want to go with me, be here at six o'clock," he told her.

That night Jenny again went to her room. She closed her door. She reviewed scales. She sang Musetta's aria, sang *Aida* and *Tosca* until her voice broke. Faintly, she could hear the children in the halls getting ready for bed. No one approached her door until ten o'clock. Then her father knocked.

"Jenny," Sobe called through the door.

She stopped singing, but did not answer him.

"It's time to quiet down. The children are trying to sleep."

Jenny was still. "All right," she said.

"I didn't see you much today. Mrs. Grange keep you?" Papa Sobe said, still outside the door.

"Yes."

She could hear his shuffling footsteps leave the door and brush down the hall. Her father. A hard worker, a man cheated of his own people, living his whole life among the only family he had known, a family not his own, a people not his own. Yet they were his own, for although Jenny knew he had in his early years asked what he could do for his own people, he had not been able to help them except to serve as an example of education and hard work. And perhaps that was everything. Yet he was not known by the Indians. He was like a white man. He worked hard at the mill; he came home and quietly presided over the families living in his house.

He was quiet about his past. He never talked about Jenny's mother, or Aunt Mara Jones, or much of anything. He talked about the mill, about some of the workers there who looked down upon hard labor, about his own feelings that hard work was good for anyone—that the important thing was to provide for your family. He sometimes talked to his little boy Willy about his day. But for the most part, he let others talk while he listened. For him to ask the questions he asked tonight meant that he worried. Jenny knew the lanterns were going out, as though a part of the total light of her world were snuffed out at her papa's touch.

She had a big valise and a small case. She folded things neatly. The night seemed liquid in the corners of her room, the moonlight half dim, the cloud shadows ominous as they sailed over the floor. She did not sleep. She heard the chimes at eleven, then at twelve. Then she dozed. She dreamed about Charles. He stood, clouded by mist, in a mire of brackish water and green clay. "Come in!" he called to her. "Jenny!" He waved, beckoned to her. But she could not move her feet. She limped and struggled but could not seem to reach him. Finally he cried out, then called. She screamed—she floated toward him and he pulled her into the water. Down. Down. She woke and heard the chimes: five o'clock. For another half hour she dozed. Then she rose quickly in the moonlight, cleared her head of haziness, made up her room, and wrote a note to her father. She might have written: "As a child, you always wanted to do something for your own people. First, you made a mistake in love, with a white woman. Then finally you have rationalized that you are doing your best to maintain a good family, to remain working at the mill. Was it the example you wanted to leave? I will now go and do something to make you and every Indian on earth proud, my father. To conquer the white man's world. Good-bye." But she wrote: *"I am going to sing. Charles doesn't care. You can't stop me now. Good-bye. Jenny."* And she was gone.

The Grange house was coldly silent. Moonlight cast shadows under the eaves of the porch, darkened the door. Jenny surveyed the silence and climbed to the porch swing, her heart pounding. She held her bags tightly, swung them close to her legs as the wooden bench gently moved back and forth, back and forth. For what seemed like hours, she sat in the silent swing.

Not until the chimes rang at six o'clock did the dark figure of Curtis Weintraub emerge from behind the house. He carried a large bulging valise. At first he did not see Jenny, though he stopped to look around. Surprised by how small he seemed in the darkness, Jenny slowly stopped and got out of the swing. As she began down the stairs, Curtis drew back, startled.

He swore. "Jenny! Is that you?" He let the valise fall. "I . . . I wasn't sure you'd come."

"I came, Curtis," Jenny whispered, using his first name consciously, shyly. "I couldn't keep from coming."

After a moment, Weintraub collected himself and picked up Jenny's valise and his own and began across the front lawn. "I wondered if you'd come. But I hoped for your sake you would." Then he seemed totally preoccupied, unable to think of anything but the business of catching the correct train. The walk to the station was hurried, quiet.

At the station, he instructed Jenny in low tones to stay with the baggage, to keep her back turned, and he would purchase the tickets. Jenny gave him her money, a little she had saved. She stood with the baggage, her back toward Mr. Bailey who would be somewhere about the baggage room or the ticket office as he was from six A.M. until midnight almost every day of the world.

"Jenny, I'm going to stick with the story you are my wife," Curtis whispered in her ear as he passed her. The breath of his whisper made her tingle along her neck and down her back. "Please don't worry. I'll handle everything, except maybe your friend in Salt Lake City." They had already talked about Mrs. Washburn. Jenny had told him that she would probably let them stay. The train ride was in semidarkness, in choking clouds of coal dust and smoke, in quiet. Neither of them spoke except to say "excuse me" and to note after an hour or two that they were coming into the city.

The streets were still empty. It was eight o'clock when the train pulled into the station.

"Your mother lives somewhere. And you don't even know her name."

Jenny looked at him. His head was bent, the shiny dark hair glistening from the morning light outside the train. She noticed his ears, almost transparent.

"I don't know if I could live with that. All my life. And you don't really look Indian. One quarter. Maybe a half. Still, even a full-blooded Indian shouldn't feel ashamed."

Jenny wanted to say *"Especially* a full-blooded Indian shouldn't feel ashamed." But she was silent as the train screeched to a halt. She waited, feeling the motion of the sun outside, the heat of the stone in the walls, the black exhaust. She found herself hoping for clouds to protect them from the sun. Then she heard the whistle in the emptying corridors of the train.

"Does the missus need help with her bags?" the black porter questioned Curtis.

"No, thank you. We'll manage fine," Weintraub said.

They left, lurching through a crowd toward the sunlight. On the cobbled street they found a cabbie in an old carriage behind a sad sway-backed gray.

"To 'I' street," Curtis instructed.

"I'll help the missus." The cabbie leaped down from the step and gave Jenny a hand while Curtis put the bags in the back.

Mrs. Washburn lived in a tall, narrow, brown house with a yellow door. Her friend Rachel had long ago passed away. Hilda was always a nervous sleeper, an early riser. She would be about at this hour, Jenny was certain. On the walkway, Jenny stared at Curtis, searching his eyes as though she must know how they were to present themselves, knowing they must agree.

"Tell her we're married."

Jenny filled with sudden fear. "No!" she said swiftly. "Curtis . . . it wouldn't be right. . . ."

"Then tell her we're intended."

"Curtis . . . I'm not sure."

"Jenny, look, my darling. It would be wiser to tell her we are intended." Then he smiled. "Does it make that much difference, Jenny Bird? I will ask you now if you will marry me. Please say yes. There now, we are intended."

"But . . . but Curtis! You are already married!"

"Aw! Come now! Does it make any difference to a Mormon?"

"But. . . ." Puzzled, Jenny felt herself nearing the yellow door, still afraid. She knew nothing about the talented, enigmatic, distant Curtis Weintraub, or the future that seemed to be pulling her onward. Yet, here at Grandma Hilda's, Mrs. Washburn's, she felt safe.

The woman who met Jenny at the door was a faded remnant of the memory Jenny had of her. She was like old dusty china, very brittle now, her hair in gray wings against a pale face.

"Oh, my darling! I can't believe it! After all these years, you have come!" The woman's eyes were barely slits in the sunlight. "And this is Charles?" she said.

"Uh . . . Curtis," Jenny stammered.

"Oh, I thought you told me Charles?" Jenny held her breath. Mrs. Washburn was the type who never paused. "Well, Curtis, then." She smiled. "Come in, both of you!" As she drew Jenny into the dark hallway, her face changed with the light. "I just can't believe it!" she said effusively for the second time. "It is surely an answer to prayer! Of course! I should have known! A miracle! My darling! I can't wait to explain why it is you have come . . . and now, of all times! You were certainly inspired." The words were like sunlight. They followed the bent woman into the parlor. The furniture, the carpets, the drapes, seemed fragile, worn—a museum of old pieces in delicate ivory and beige. Here the sunlight played against the Persian carpet like old lace. Jenny, her heart beating loud, could hear Mrs. Washburn's voice as though it were the tide on the edge of a faraway sea.

"It is a miracle you have come! I'll explain it, my darling. Sarah! Sarah Gold!" She walked toward a group of pictures on her wall and spread across an oaken buffet. There were faces that looked vacant, haughty, composed—all faces with signatures sprawled beneath their white chins. Jenny saw Mrs. Washburn as a delicate old figurine, one of the shy ones, totally white, which stood glimmering on the surface of the old grand in the corner by the French windows. She was wispy, gray, yet somehow still moving about in a sort of breathless childish way.

"Sarah Gold, our soprano for the *Rigoletto*, became ill this week, and no one to take her place, really . . . no one good . . . just a snip of a girl who knows nothing . . . and for opening night. And now you have come of course!" Mrs. Washburn picked up Sarah Gold's picture from the piano and held it to her frayed lace bosom. "Sarah, I cried for you, but perhaps it is all meant to be!" She turned. She stood facing Curtis and Jenny, looking very white. "Jenny, you can do it! But we must work." She replaced the picture on the piano without looking and wound toward Jenny and Curtis with small peg-skirted steps. "We must work harder than we have ever worked. Oh, my dear God in Heaven, could such a miracle truly be!"

The prayer was lost in Jenny's fear, a rush of fear as though wings were beating beneath her lungs. What was it Mrs. Washburn was telling her? A part for her? Now? The sunlight, the room, seemed to skid across her awareness. Now she could sense Curtis at her elbow, his strong fingers touching her arm. "You told me you had memorized *Rigoletto* years ago, my dear," Mrs. Washburn said. "And Mrs. Grange has written me how very splendidly you are doing. There will be no excuse of course." She sat at the piano and began to play.

Jenny began to sing "Ah misera. . . ." into the vaulted room.

"Beautiful," Mrs. Washburn clapped, turning and squealing with a delight unbecoming to her age. As she continued to play, Jenny moved into the duet. Curtis began in his firm tenor to back Jenny, to support her with rich tones, his breath moving with hers, perfectly smooth. The hands at the piano paused.

"Oh! Oh, my good heavenly days! My goodness! Oh!" Mrs. Washburn breathed. She could not go on. She stared at Curtis as though stricken.

"Who are you?" she asked, gazing at Curtis. "Good Lord. Who are you?"

Curtis smiled his most enigmatic smile, thoroughly enjoying her surprise. "Curtis Weintraub of the San Francisco Opera."

Then Mrs. Washburn began to cry. She cried, holding trembling withered fingers over rouge-rusted cheeks. "No. No! I can't believe it. I really can't believe it," she sobbed. "Thank you, God in Heaven."

"So when do we go on!" Curtis said with bravado, bold as a bull.

"Tonight, my lovelies! Tonight! As guests, as fill-ins until Sarah can sing. And to think," she said to Jenny, "you are just the size of Sarah Gold! The costumes will fit! It's a miracle!"

The morning and the afternoon washed over them like rain. They were not to overdo, but Mr. Aburell gave them a simple staging at three o'clock. They met the cast and walked through it all at four.

Then they returned to the house to wait until they were to meet on stage at seven.

Jenny was dazed. Mrs. Washburn had more energy than she had ever seen in a woman her age, half her age. Her body moved birdlike through the motions of hospitality. "Of course you'll stay here, both of you. Jenny in the attic room. Curtis, you may take the enclosed porch . . . if it . . . if it would not be inconvenient. It is a good cot, and the screen will admit the breeze."

"Fine. Fine," Curtis said.

In the rush of the rehearsals, the day's activities following one after the other without pause, there had been no time to settle, to unpack bags, to breathe.

Mrs. Washburn took Jenny up a small dusty stairway to a room under the roof. The hot and close air stifled her, but she fell to the narrow bed as though she had never slept before. While Mrs. Washburn opened the windows and fanned the breeze with a towel, Jenny fell into a deep slumber. She began to dream. She saw Charles again, reaching for her with shadowy hands, black from the coal dust of the bins at the mill. "No, no," she said, backing away from him. "First I need to sing." The look on his face startled her, and she drew back. At that moment she saw eyes above her, sunken in wrinkled skin.

"Are you all right?" Mrs. Washburn said, concerned. "My darling, I could hear you crying out in your sleep. Are you all right?"

Jenny rolled over, murmured "Yes." In the twilight of her mind, between dream and reality, she searched for something she had wanted to tell Mrs. Washburn.

"You do such a beautiful job, my darling. A beautiful job. You'll be a great diva. And soon."

Jenny's eyes, though heavy with sleep, opened very slightly to admit the light, and Mrs. Washburn's gray face. She needed to talk, then, and tried to find the words. "Please don't tell them I am here. Or they will come for me."

"Yes, my darling. Sleep. Sleep."

In her blurred consciousness, Jenny thought she could see Mrs. Washburn's smile brighten beyond the shadow of her hands whispering together her delight.

Jenny did not wake until it was time to go. Curtis looked fresh and rested when he came to her, ducking his head into the doorway.

"It's time to go."

The tiny room, once undefined, suddenly sprang into color, wall-paper, the dark furniture. A checkered quilt sprawled carelessly over her feet.

"Are you ready?" Curtis smiled. She raised herself on her elbow and looked about. The room seemed tiny, the window opaque.

"Almost," she murmured, unable to make it clear in her mind what it was that was going to happen. She would sing. In an opera. But it was not possible. Yesterday morning before she went to her lesson with Mrs. Grange she was still Jenny Eastman, betrothed to Charles Tuttle, of Provo. As though in sleep, she rose from the bed and steadied herself on Curtis's arm.

"Jenny Eastman—really Jenny Bird," he said. "You and I have had the most incredible luck!"

Jenny shook her head slightly to wake herself.

Curtis, still in mustache, his short beard trimmed carefully, wore a very white shirt with gathered sleeves and a dark green French cravat. His hair looked smooth, almost too greasy, slick.

"Incredible luck. Blink, Jenny, and you will be a prima donna. Blink soon, because they're waiting for you. The carriage is ready."

Still, Jenny could not believe what was happening to her. She stumbled to the mirror on the dresser where her things lay. She struggled to find her hairbrush deep inside the bag. She smoothed her skirt.

"No fussing. Costumes on at seven-thirty. We let you sleep as long as we could."

As soon as the mist of sleep cleared from her eyes, Jenny could see better. She could think better. Slowly, she followed Curtis down the steep stairway, leaning against his strong back. A quickness in her breath seemed to make her light-headed. What was happening to her?

The carriage drew up to the large hall. They had rehearsed there this afternoon. But now there were patrons gathering in the street. Jenny swallowed hard, unable to feel or see clearly, sometimes letting the familiar lines pass through her mind, singing in the top of her head where it buzzed, as Mrs. Grange always told her to do.

"Don't forget, you are better than all of them. All of them put together," Hilda Washburn Eastman whispered, and "we will tell them all who you are, the little Indian girl."

Oh no, Jenny said in her heart, and almost out loud. She drew her breath quickly in to curb her anxiety. "My father doesn't know I'm here. Don't tell them I am an Eastman or someone will tell Papa where I am. He will come to take me home."

"We have already told them you are Jenny Bird," Curtis grinned. Jenny barely heard. Louis Aburell met her now at the carriage door and graciously escorted her to the dressing room.

"Of course no one will take you home! We will see to that!" Mrs. Washburn smiled. "No one will take our bird away from us. Your Papa could only be proud. But we will bill you as an Indian. You are his Indian darling."

Still uncertain that all of this was real, Jenny ducked into the dark dressing room where the other girls were already smoothing costumes, applying bright colors to their faces, curling their hair on hot irons.

A friend of Mrs. Washburn's met her at the door. "Hilda . . . the jester's costume is torn. Will you please help me pin it on?"

The buzzing, the talk, the confusion seemed to Jenny a thousand miles away, a world apart from her. She felt the sickness of fear, almost a hysteria, crowding beneath her lungs. Though she had dealt with her fear during many performances in the past, this time there was a persisting lightness, a sort of euphoria or unreality that sang about her like invisible bees.

"They will all notice you," Mrs. Washburn had said. "It is the beginning of your career. You are a wonderfully fortunate girl."

"And tonight as a special treat, we have a young Indian girl taking the place of Sarah Gold, who was unable to perform this evening. And with her as a guest temporarily replacing Mathew Crane as the duke, we have Curtis Weintraub, formerly of the San Francisco Opera. These two visitors are a fabulous treat for opening night, and we'd like you to give them a special opening applause."

They had not mentioned Jenny's name. But she froze when the symphony finished its overture and the applause died away. The curtains drew open. The audience seemed like a great sea staring at her from behind the brilliant lights. Now it is my time, she whispered to herself. And as in all performances she had ever given, she knew she must sing for herself first, and that like waves of sound, like rainbow light, the music would reach outward in great circles to bring everyone in.

"Non v'e piu al cuno," Jenny began to let the notes whisper, then flow into her throat. Her excitement gave length and breadth to her tone. Suddenly she was alive with sound and became Gilda, more surely than she had ever been in any rehearsal.

"Che qui rispondemi. You will respond to my love?"

At the conductor's podium, Aburell smiled, nodded, an almost divine satisfaction on his face.

"Beautiful," he whispered, closing his eyes at the end of Jenny's first aria. When Curtis Weintraub entered, there was some confusion in staging, but as he began to sing, the sound so overwhelmed the audience that Jenny could hear them gasp.

"Son io coll' anima." Curtis Weintraub's liquid tenor rolled in waves against the pounding bass and the light strings. "Che ti rispondo. My heart answers you."

Like light, like wings, the entire two-and-a-half hours fluttered beyond them—quickly done. Jenny hung to her endings until they whispered away, sustained by a nearly audible breath. She climbed her scales with grace. She did not slur. She did not need to think everything through. It all came.

Jenny had never sung so well. The music was a presence, a flowing spiritual organism with a voice of its own, a power unlike any she had ever dreamed, a force—a magnificent resounding thundering force that penetrated into every part of her body and lifted her upward as though she would fly. And Curtis was flying with her. She felt him move to the rhythm in the sound.

She held to the applause at the close as though it were breath itself. She inhaled, breathing it deeply, feeling its force in her heart as it poured through her. Then there were lights, and crowds, and hands, and people's faces as they shouted "Marvelous! Bravo! A miracle! Beautiful!" She had given them something, and the gratitude poured into her like fire.

"A night like no other in the history of Salt Lake City music!" Aburell shouted to her over the applause.

"We've got to get them away!" The elated Mrs. Washburn led Curtis and Jenny by their hands. "We've got to get out of here, my darlings. Before you're trampled!"

Jenny thought she would never see another face clearly again, that she would find herself always conscious of only blurs of eyes. For there were blurs of eyes about her now that seemed not to belong to individual faces. But in the audience gathering toward her there was one face she became aware of instantly, for it seemed . . . it seemed to be her own. The crowd outside the dressing room cheered as Mrs. Washburn and Curtis led her into the carriage waiting at the bottom of the stairs.

"Oh beautiful," both the smiling men and the women were whispering and shouting. It seemed not so noisy on the street, although groups were gathered to wish her well.

"You are a prima donna without a doubt," a man said. "A wonderful voice. I would like to make connections for you with the Metropolitan Opera."

Jenny nodded, understanding nothing, the tide of the evening sweeping into her like a storm. Then she saw that same striking face, again, as though in a dream. It was the face of a woman at the edge, standing behind the rope that the doorman had fastened tightly from the door to the carriage. The woman was reaching out toward Jenny with both hands. Her fingers caught Jenny's sleeve. Behind the woman stood an older couple, the man's kindly face drawn in a puzzled expression that held Jenny's interest at once . . . for these people stood apart, not wanting to congratulate her but to say something to her. Mrs. Washburn was urging her forward, and there was no time.

The woman suddenly dashed under the rope and held Mrs. Washburn by her arms. "What was her name, madam? What was her name?"

Startled, Mrs. Washburn drew back. Curtis came to them and smiled.

The older lady, staying close behind the woman now in their path, reached forward to pull her in.

"Jane Prince!" she said harshly. "It's no use! It's not her. Come back!"

The old gentleman with her said, "Hannah, they said she was Indian. Let her ask. Let her at least ask."

"It's no use!" the elderly woman insisted. "Even if it were, it would make no difference. You're a married woman now with a son and husband at home!"

212

"What is her name?" the woman pleaded. "You did not tell us her name."

"Jenny Eastman, ah, er, Jenny Bird. Doesn't she sing like a bird?" Curtis stumbled, but smiled genuinely. "Jenny Bird, or Mrs. Weintraub in private life." Jenny was too weak with excitement to notice what he was saying.

"Eastman! No. No," she said, startled. She leaned back as though faint and the older gentleman beside her took her arm.

The older woman reached forward, scrambling across the rope. Mrs. Washburn turned Jenny slowly, firmly into the carriage. Jenny turned to see the older woman grab the faint young woman—the one they called Jane.

"Bret, I'm absolutely livid with embarrassment," the old woman said, appearing nearly to faint, also, her face white as paste. "Oh God, help me! Jane, you should never have tried to see her!" The man called Bret put his arm around the woman Jane's shoulders and led her back into the crowd, whispering into her ear as though to say, "You're embarrassing us, my dear."

"She's beautiful. She's beautiful," the woman said faintly against the man's coat.

Jenny saw it all, like a dream, but clearly. The face. Jane. It was like the face in her own mirror.

It was too much. The night, the singing. Now the woman. She felt Curtis's arms, his hands on her waist. She felt him as though they still sang, the perfect harmony still beating deep within her, tearing her away from the noise, the voices. And the face—so like her own—disappeared into the black night, into the shadows of the crowd, the dark crowd.

Curtis sat close to her in the carriage. She listened to Mrs. Washburn's praises falling on her head. "And if you can repeat the performance until Sarah is well, we shall hold auditions for *Tosca*, or perhaps *Carmen*, which is the last work in our season. "Oh, God bless you! And you are mine!"

Curtis stood beside Jenny as she came down from the carriage. With every step she felt his strong arm. They followed Mr. Washburn into the house, felt the rush of visitors, begged to be allowed to go to their rooms to sleep.

When the visitors left, the house fell suddenly still, and the deep enveloping morning seemed to close over it. Jenny felt liquid in her bones. Too many eyes, too many voices had ravaged her senses. She smiled good night to Curtis and Mrs. Washburn and lifted her feet carefully to the stairs.

"Let me help you," Curtis said.

"No. I'll be all right," Jenny insisted. "Thank you. No. I'll be all right."

She felt strain in each muscle as her legs lifted to mount the steep stairs. The tiny room felt still, closed. She opened the window as wide as she could and breathed the night air. Around her were the pieces of shiny wood furniture, the lace scarves, the quilt on the narrow bed. She had triumphed. But all of a sudden, she felt alone. She had triumphed, but who could she tell?

"And you are alone." She did not think about Aunt Mara's words very long. She shook them from her heart. She was still crowded with the joy, the excitement, the treasure of success.

In a hurry toward sleep she quickly pulled on her nightdress and fell to her knees. "Thank you, God, for this most amazing night." And she crawled into the bed. The bedding smelled fresh, the sheets felt crisp. She dipped into sleep as though it were a draught. She buried herself in her pillow. She fell into her dreams.

Again she saw Charles. He was smiling now. But still he held out his hands. "Are you coming?" he was saying. "Is it enough? Are you coming to me now? This is where you belong." A sound of the door shutting startled her and she awoke suddenly and froze with fear. She dared not open her eyes. But she knew as surely as though seeing it, that a shadow bent near her.

"Jenny darling, don't be frightened. I've come."

Her first thought was to find her robe.

"Curtis?" she whispered, confused. Pulling herself from the depth of her slumber, she sat up and faced him.

"Shh. Don't be frightened, darling. Yes," he whispered.

The shadow moved toward her. She felt his hands touch her shoulders.

"Curtis . . . I . . ."

"Don't be frightened, darling." She froze, with anger at her own fear, the fear that crowded into her now.

"Beautiful, oh, my darling."

He embraced her now. She felt alive; the blood rushed in her, pounded. She wanted to touch him, but she was afraid.

"Oh, my angel. I'm here. Don't be afraid. It's me." His face came close in the darkness, and she felt his dark beard press near her lips.

"My darling, I need you." When he sat down next to her, his heavy body weighted the edge of the bed.

"Curtis, please. . . ."

"Oh, my beautiful Jenny bird . . ."

"It's not . . ."

He kissed the words she spoke. He whispered her away from her protesting. She moved slightly toward him, feeling confusion, anger, yet powerful need.

"Curtis . . . ," she began, but he kissed her.

She held her lips tight. Shut her eyes tight. Held her body stiff. He moved away. There was silence. Then he whispered into her ear. "Jenny, please. Don't be afraid."

"Curtis, I can't kiss you. It's . . ."

He was silent. Then he whispered. "You're pure and untouched. I . . ." Then he withdrew from her only slightly. "I believe I knew that. But oh, Jenny, I need you. Can't you feel how I need you?" He pulled her to him, his beard razing her cheek. "Oh Jenny, I love you so," he murmured. "I need you so."

And Jenny felt her own need rising above all her fears. "I do love you, Curtis," she offered, not understanding all she felt.

Then he turned toward her and searched for her, whispering, groaning. "Then show you love me. Now." He reached for her, but she stiffened in fear once more. The room began to turn. She saw faces turn about her—her papa, Rain, Aunt Mara, Grandpa Eastman, Charles. The face in the crowd—her mother! It was her mother!

"Curtis, please leave me!" she cried out.

"Oh, Jenny! I want to stay with you!"

"No! No, Curtis! It's wrong! The blood spun in her, pounded in her, pounded. "Oh Curtis! Please!"

"Jenny! Jenny!" he whispered, almost in tears.

He brushed his beard against her face.

"Oh Jenny," he cried now. His tears were warm against her cheek. "Oh, Jenny. Jenny! I . . ." But she steadily pushed him away with her hands.

He did not finish his words. He inhaled, gasped, his throat tight. Still shuddering slightly as though he would hide now, he left the room. Jenny felt his anger, and she thought she felt his shame. He left quickly, his footfall pounding the stairs.

In the morning Curtis Weintraub was gone. Jenny never saw him again. That day and for the next three weeks, Jenny fell ill and could not sing.

Mara and Sobe had not really expected to hear much news from Jenny, nor did they, except a brief note that she was living in Salt Lake City, that she was fine, and that under no circumstances did she want them to come for her or to try to find her, but to leave her alone to discover herself. She would not give her address, but preferred to remain unavailable "until I feel like I have done what I wanted to do."

Mara suspected Jenny was with Mrs. Washburn, but they did not know for sure until Papa Eastman's funeral to which Mrs. Washburn came, thoroughly arrayed, shod, gloved in black, and crying proper tears.

No one knew how Mrs. Washburn had learned of Papa's death. And no one asked. All were kind to her, shaking the feeble gray hands, whispering "How have you been? It's been many years."

Mara watched the thin faded woman leaning over the coffin. Jenny had been gone almost three weeks. They had wondered how she would know about Papa and what would happen when she found out. There was no sound as Mrs. Washburn inspected Papa's still face, so white that it looked dusted with flour.

"Did you know he was ill?" Mara said to make conversation.

"Not lately, my dear," Mrs. Washburn said, raising bleak eyes to Mara, eyes swimming in shallow tears. "Jenny told me he had been ill; I had not known before."

"Jenny?" Mara felt her way cautiously. Her answer had come sooner, more easily than she had expected.

Mrs. Washburn looked from the coffin into Mara's eyes again. "Oh my, I have let it go already, but that child . . . why she should put me under such an oath to silence . . . and why she should be so concerned that her loved ones would take her away from a glorious career? Oh, my dear, you should have heard it! Yes . . . Jenny . . . she begged me not to tell, but she has been so ill, and when the news of your father was announced in the newspaper she was stricken with despair. I promised her I would come and tell her about everything, the poor child, though she will be heartbroken that she could not come herself. But ever since that first glorious night, and Mr. Weintraub leaving so suddenly . . . she has been so ill, unable to do anything at all, even sing, the precious darling. But you should have heard the one performance of her life that will mean everything to her forever and make up for all that is missing, should there be anything missing, from her entire life."

What was Mrs. Washburn speaking of? Performance? Who was Mr. Weintraub? Mara was filled with questions. But she was no longer afraid for Jenny now that her whereabouts had been revealed, for she had long ago decided to allow the girl her complete freedom. She was, after all, more than twenty-one years old. But Mara felt a wistful longing to see Jenny again, to understand what Mrs. Washburn meant, to know of her wonderful performance, to make certain her illness was not serious. She looked into the coffin at Papa's white smooth face. Without thinking much about Mrs. Washburn, she said aloud, "He would liked to have known she was doing well. He missed her music. I wish she had told us where she was."

Mrs. Washburn probably did not make the connections that Mara drew between Jenny's disappearance and Papa's death. Perhaps Mara herself had seen too deeply, and not liking what she saw, withdrew herself from believing there had been any connection at all. Papa was old. It was his time. She forgave Jenny completely, understanding how much the girl had needed to get away, to breathe, to find herself completely separate from Charles, and to sing.

Sobe took the news of Jenny with a long stare, and a nod toward Mrs. Washburn that meant "Thank you," or whatever she might have wanted it to mean. He was without words. But words were not necessary.

Mara and Will and Sobe and Clarissa left the services in the chapel behind Caroline, now very large with child. Caroline was wheeled carefully in her chair by a concerned Ashel. Ashel had been inspired by Isaac Higbee's funeral address.

"He said everything about Papa I would have said."

"I would only have had Jenny sing," Caroline offered.

No one said very much more at the site of the grave. There were appropriate flowers, the prayer, the crowds wishing him a peaceful rest. "And we shall always regard this man as a great leader in the community as well as in the Church, and as the beacon light for his family. He has seen the transition of our culture from a struggling settlement to a thriving metropolis. His lifetime is measured by the greatest changes ever made in the history of modern man, from the simplicity of the rural life to the grandeur of the age of the machine, and most important, from the darkness of apostate Christianity to the enlightenment of the restored gospel."

Mara did not hear much of the speech consciously. It was more of what had already been said in the chapel. She *felt* the words rather than heard them. She felt the tremor of the earth as his coffin was lowered into the grave. She felt the weight of all his years, the weight of all her own. Seeing the end of his resistance was like closing one of the greatest chapters in the book of her life. So much had passed since her first memories of him: the stern yet laughing man who often rubbed his unshaven face against her cheek. "Give me a kiss, Mara, baby, you funny girl. Give me a love." Memories could not be buried with his body. Memories of one another were all people had—all they could keep with them, now and after death.

Mara watched the earth falling onto the wood that covered her father. There was a strange relief in her, which caused her to feel some guilt. Could it be that she was actually not afraid now that he was gone? Now she, Mara Eastman Jones, was head of the Eastman family. Oldest at any rate. There was Ashel, who had made a miracle in his wife. But she, Mara—she was the one who held them all together.

She looked at them: Ashel, Caroline leaning close to him with her hand in his as the prayer was said. Caroline could not smother the radiance alive in her even on this solemn occasion. She glowed. Next to her were Sobe and Clarissa, their Willy, and Rain, withdrawn and sad. All of Sully's children and grandchildren, and Sully himself, who had once lived in their small cabin in the fort and begged for Mara with his eyes—they all belonged. They were all part of what had begun with Martha Harding and her secret love, Hart Eastman. Martha. It came to Mara now that it was all because of Mama. It was Mama who encouraged Sully. It was Mama who took in Spirit of Earth and Rain. It was Mama whose family had brought the fortune, and Caroline. Caroline, who carried in her the only remaining earthly hope of sending the blood of Martha and Hart Eastman into the future.

But it was not only the blood that was important. There was more. Martha and Hart Eastman had given something to them all. From Papa, humor, warmth, love, security. From Mama . . . in spite of her fears, it was really Mama. Mama was an angel whose protective shadow fell across all of them. She had kept it going those months when Papa was gone, when John and Sophia and the baby died all together. Those months when it turned from the past into the future. Mama had been without prejudice for the unfortunate. She had cared for Spirit of Earth as no one else would have. She had taught and loved Rain. She had cared for Sobe when Mara herself was sick with passion for Phillip Hurst. Mama . . . if there were anyone she would emulate . . . Mara realized it would be her mother.

Mara tired quickly on the walk from the grave site, and she clung to Will's arm. "I'm tired now," she said simply, holding to him, unable to walk without leaning on his arm. "I'm very tired."

She thought of them all—Jenny, Charles, Sobe, Rain, even Hilda Washburn—with a special grace, a love for them, a promise that anything she could do for them during these last years of her life, she would do.

Almost immediately after Papa's burial, as soon as Charles found out that Jenny was ill at Mrs. Washburn's, he got on the train to Salt Lake City to persuade Jenny to come back with him. Mara knew that in his own heart he was not fully satisfied with his life, that in Jenny's absence he had taken time to think clearly, to make up his mind what mattered most to him, and to prepare to act on those priorities. Mara waited for their return impatiently, imagining the struggle between Jenny and Charles and the anxiety Mrs. Washburn would feel over the termination of Jenny's promising career.

Almost a week passed before Charles brought Jenny to the house. Jenny looked wan in a faded green feather boa and a pink hat.

"Jenny, we wanted you to come, darling," Mara said. "We've missed you so." But there was something missing—or was it added—in Jenny? Something different, at any rate. Mrs. Washburn had assured them she was doing very well. But Mara could not see how that could have been so. Jenny looked very pale, as though the illness had drained her.

Charles and his sisters helped Mara prepare for the wedding. Their church friends also helped them prepare a feast more sumptuous than Mara remembered from any of the other weddings in the family. The tables groaned with sweetbreads, pickles, relishes, meats, desserts, persimmons, and bananas—and even a rare pineapple in a centerpiece fit for a heavenly kingdom.

In spite of its sumptuousness and its modern style, the wedding of Charles and Jenny was reminiscent of other weddings in the family because it was so right. It was the union all of them hoped for. It would continue Sully's name.

No one was surprised in the following year when Charles announced they would have a child. At almost the same time, a beautiful healthy son was born to Caroline and Ashel. They named him Hanson Hart Eastman after Papa and another grandfather Hanson Harding. Caroline surprised them all by her vigor and her health after the birth of the child.

Jenny's child, born in 1895, was a girl they called Grace. The baby was fair and very beautiful. The entire family rejoiced, and no one seemed happier about it than Jenny. Jenny *was* happy. Mara saw it. Jenny looked at Charles with deep love, and she basked in his adoration of her. But Mara noticed a sort of peaceful sadness in Jenny's eyes sometimes when she softly sang the baby to sleep.

It was in March of 1895 when their little Grace was two months old that Charles received word that the *Florence*, the boat Charles had taken many times across the lake without financial success, was to be shipped to Los Angeles after the summer was over. Jenny was worried for Charles when he heard the finality of it. The transport route to Eureka had never been opened; roads had become more important for shipping than the waterway. The city of Charles' prophecy never materialized on the other side of the lake in the bleak brown hills. The dream of his boating for a living had dissipated with his continuing years at the mill.

But it had not mattered to him as much since their marriage. He took the news as cheerfully as he took everything these days. Jenny understood why for old times' sake he wanted to take the *Florence* for one last glorious fling before it was loaded on a railroad transport and forever taken away. And she was excited to go with him, to watch him live his dream, for the last time.

The Florence had not been run in almost two years. All that summer Charles could hardly bear to see it sit idly for the season. But it was early October before Mr. King agreed to one last afternoon outing for Charles and those of his family and friends who had wanted to go. The baby Grace had been cross, so Jenny left her with Aunt Mara and Rain in the wagon. Aunt Nancy and Uncle Sully did not go either. Papa Sobe had to stay at the mill. But Clarissa took Willy. And Samantha and her husband, Ralph Eggertson, brought their two children, Mathew and their new baby Eliza. Charles' friend Russell Teague and his two children all climbed into the boat. "To better days," Charles said, launching the old boat with a grand wave of triumph.

Jenny waved to Aunt Mara, who was holding the tiny, two-month-old Grace in her arms. Aunt Mara nodded as the families drew away from the dock, cheering. Charles came to Jenny's side a moment, and together they waved. Then he was gone to tend the boat.

"Good-bye! Good-bye!" Jenny shouted, waving to Aunt Mara, blowing kisses for little Grace.

"Good-bye, dears!" Aunt Mara called, nodding, taking the baby's tiny hand and waving her fingers to Jenny.

The boat moved out on the water with good speed. An unexpected wind came up, and Charlie, exultant, sped to the center of the lake. Jenny felt the motion of the waves, watched Charles, the breeze blowing his hair, the spray in his face. He stood at the wheel while his little nephews and their friends crowded around him and begged to be allowed to help him steer.

At first it seemed to be only a stiff wind. But in a few moments, the waves began crashing against the side of the boat. The children gathered around Charles, and he began to motion them away with his hand.

"Let me do it," Jenny's eight-year-old half brother Willy cried out, moving his cousins aside.

"No, it's too dangerous," Jenny said. She helped Samantha move the children back so Charles could steer.

"Let her go," Russell Teague said. "She'll be swift in this wind without steerage."

"Not yet," Charlie said.

"It's a storm coming up," Ralph Eggertson said, pointing to the southwest. Huge black clouds were sweeping over the far horizon. The sun was suddenly gone. The air around them darkened.

Jenny looked out over the bleak hills. It was so cold all of a sudden. And then it happened. In the wind, in the clouds, in the fine rain that had begun to fall, the speed of the boat and the direction of its speed drove the hull against something large and sharp in the water's depth. The ripping cut into the ship's hull; the vessel shook, shuddered, and began to turn over.

"Oh, dear God." Charles wound the wheel away from the thrust of land. "That shoal! I forgot it was there!" Jenny saw him push the wheel with all his might. But it was too late. "Man the lifeboats, the lifeboats," Charles screamed. Eggertson and Teague hurried to the lower deck to rip the lifeboats from their chains. Jenny ran to Charles, clutched his arm as he ran after Teague. And then he stopped as though unable to move further. "Oh, God in Heaven! No." In their excitement to ready the *Florence* for its last cruise, King had not made sure the lifeboats had been fastened to the side. And they were not there.

"Charles!" Jenny screamed.

"Watch the children!" he shouted to her through the rain. The floors shook, the wind flew up. The vessel cracked against the stone, ripped, and then flew upward, tipping the deck to a fearful angle. Three of the children slipped from the deck into the choppy waves below. Willy, who was standing on the edge, was thrown off and tossed like a leaf toward the hills.

"My babies!" Samantha screamed, and she and Ralph Eggertson leaped into the water. As they swam toward the children, the wind beat them. Jenny clutched Charles, screaming. The boat turned and twisted, and the railing struck Samantha in the head. Charles and Russell dived after them. The sound of children rent the squall: crying, calling, gasping, struggling for air.

"Charles!" Jenny cried again. The boat twisted and groaned under her. The wind, the waves climbed into the hull and sucked at her skirts. "No, heaven. No!" The others were swimming in the dark water, clinging to the children who cried and sobbed for life.

Then it began to snow. Not light wispy snow, but wet, frozen, icy snow folding across the deck like white wings. None of them had imagined. . . . How were they to know? They hadn't prepared for what was happening to them. None of them could have known.

"Charles!" But Charles was in the dark water gathering the children to the rail. Samantha, her face bleeding, climbed the jutting hull of the boat that was sinking fast into the dark water. With her arms outstretched, she gathered Mathew and Eliza from Charles and laid them like wet laundry over the sharp edge of the hull that had not yet sunk into the waves. Clarissa was screaming, "I can't find Willy." She was bobbing and choking. She could not swim well. Sarah Teague stood against the boathouse, in the water to her waist. She held her two children above the water with every ounce of strength she could muster.

"Charles!" Jenny's voice died in the crushing air. She stood aside on the steep floor, trying to avoid the water, but it sucked at her skirts.

"If we could just get the ship aright!" Charles shouted, gasping for air. "Shift it over . . . right."

But the boat was wedged against the rocks, which gnawed and tore the wood until the boat was almost in pieces. The snow kept falling. Jenny thought she heard cries of other children in the water. She thought she could hear Willy!

"I'm going to swim for help," Charles cried out.

Still clinging to the rail, Jenny screamed. "No, Charles!" she cried. Samantha's Mathew was slipping down off the rail. When she heard his cry, Jenny reached out to fetch him, but she lost her footing and landed in the water. Once in the water, she knew she could hear someone far away—it was little Willy, and he seemed to be at quite a distance on the other side of the boat.

"I'll get him," Jenny cried to Clarissa, who was doing all she could do with Ralph and the Teagues to hold the children on to the slippery hull. "I'm coming, Willy!" She cried out to him.

"I'll get him," Charles yelled. "Get back to the ship, Jenny! You'll exhaust yourself! I'll bring him back before I swim for help!"

"No, Charles! Don't go! They'll come back to find us!"

But Charles had cut through the dark snow and water toward Willy, who sobbed and then choked as he bobbed in and out of the deep waves.

Jenny followed Charles. "I'll bring him back!" she cried out. It was four or five minutes before she caught up to them. Willy was gasping and clinging to Charles' neck as Charles struggled to make his way back.

"Go, Charles, if you must. It's too far to be swimming back and forth. Go! Hurry! I'll take him back," Jenny screamed. She struggled against the water. She felt the boy's fingernails in her neck. She fought the water.

"Can you take him all the way back?" Charles cried out.

"Yes. Go, go if you must!" Jenny was screaming now, and she thought she could feel hot tears streaming down her cheeks.

"We'll be waiting on the boat for you!"

Charles hesitated for a moment, and stayed for an unnecessary instant to look at her.

"Go!" Jenny cried out. "I'll be all right with Willy."

Jenny saw his last look. His eyes were large with a look of compassion, and . . . fear. He cut out across the water, and the swirling snow swallowed him up in the dark.

Jenny struggled with the boy on her neck. When she turned around, she could not see Charles anymore. Then when she turned back, she could not see the boat or the mountains. She did not know where she was. Though she knew the boat was somewhere out there standing on its edge, half out of the water, she could not see it beyond the veil of snow.

They waited on the shore for an hour, and when the boat did not come in, they went out quickly into the storm. For eight hours, King and Will and Sully and Sobe and fourteen others in the long boats and two canoes fought the snow to find the *Florence* on the dark waters in the squall.

Mara sat waiting in the carriage in the drifts of snow at the dock. She held Grace close to her under the blankets in the warm protection of her arm. Rain and Nancy sat with her, huddled under a tarpaulin. The women stared into the blur of night.

One after another the rescue boat and the canoes came in. They carried the shuddering parents and their small freezing children into a circle where they built a fire, warmed them, rubbed their freezing limbs back to the color of flesh again. They waited and they waited. Jenny and Charles and Willy never came in.

Mara would not believe it. Her eyes felt a sting of terrible pain, as though she had been struck in the head. The snow whirled, folded, spun around them and hid the lake from their view. Rain began to sob, at first with her shoulders moving and no sound, and then in long cries from deep inside her lungs. "Oh. Oh. Oh." Nancy did not make a sound, but clutched the tarpaulin over her hair.

Ralph Eggertson groaned. Samantha was seated on a log holding the blankets over her children. She was still bleeding and moaning over her baby Eliza. The Teagues huddled beside her, holding their children in their arms. "Charles and Jenny were rescuing the children," Sarah Teague cried and would not stop crying. "Clarissa could not swim very well."

Clarissa was in Sobe's arms, unconscious. Mara watched Sobe hold a torch to her face. The flame of the torch smoked, brightened the flakes of snow, licked the wet sky with orange. Sobe stood holding the torch over Clarissa's eyes. He leaned down against her ragged breathing.

"Clarissa," he sobbed. "Where are the others?"

But she did not answer him.

"Clarissa," he whispered. But she was cold, her white hands limp in his. "Clarissa!" he screamed. "Oh dear Father, no!" he cried. "It is not possible." He sank his face against her cheek. There was no breath there.

Mara held the blanket over the child in her arms. She must hold the baby tight and not cry. Not go to Sobe. Or else her heart inside would break and she would die. Rain ran to Clarissa, lay over her, sobbing, and would not be removed. Gently, Sully pulled her away, and by torchlight brought her to Mara and Nancy. "Take her with you," Sully said, his teeth clenched to keep the tears from his voice. "Take her away."

He looked at Samantha with the blood running down her face. She was not making a sound. Her eyes were half closed in shock.

In the deepening darkness, Sobe walked to the edge of the water and stood against the lapping waves, holding the torch high in the whirling snow. The sound of grief in his breathing echoed the terror that tore at Mara's heart.

The others walked to the carriages that came for them, and they began to move to their homes. The lights from the lamps flickered in the dust of the snow. Sobe stood holding the torch against the lake for a long time. He did not speak. He looked up, and out into the water. He stood without moving. He would not come away.

Mara drew Rain close beside her in the carriage. Someone came to drive them away in the dark snow. She did not even know who it was. She was numb. Charles and Jenny, and little Willy—and Clarissa. Oh, Sobe. Was this all there was to be for you and your people? Families who dissolved—evaporated—into a smaller and smaller drop of the birth-giving waters of this earth, who became only shadows of what they were? It was as if they belonged to the earth, and the earth would not let them go. She held the baby tight to gather her strength. She did not cry. Not yet. Someday she would let her tears go. She would feel it all flood through her and clean out the pain. Their dear Father in Heaven would need to stay close for this one. She knew.

Chapter Twelve

FOR MANY NIGHTS AFTER THAT DAY ON THE LAKE, IF MARA CAME to the Eastman house in the evening, she could hear Samantha singing to her baby Eliza in the middle of the night. It was a short lullabye that she repeated over and over. Occasionally, Mara could hear little Mathew trying to sing along.

Hush, my baby, lullabye.
Oh, lullabye, oh lullabye.
Hush, my baby, lullabye,
Lullabye.

God is good and he is nigh,
He is nigh, he is nigh.
God is good and he is nigh.
He is nigh.

Sobe asked the Eggertsons to stay with him and with Grandma Rain until the new Eggertson house was completed near Ralph's parents in Salem. Sully and Nancy and Mara and Will came to be with them in the evenings. They sat beside the fire, rocking Grace and Eliza and looking into the flames while Uncle Will read to them out of the scriptures. "And when the Lord saw her, he had compassion on her, and said unto her, Weep not."

"Is little Will in heaven?" Four-year-old Mathew Eggertson interrupted him.

"Yes, Mathew. He is in heaven with Clarissa and his parents," Mara whispered to him. She took him on her lap, or let him cut the ginger cookies out of the dough with Uncle Will's shaving mug.

"Will he ever come to see us again?"

"We'll see him again," Mara whispered in his hair.

Samantha leaned over Eliza's little head inside her elbow and crooned her to sleep while Sobe held Jenny's baby Grace in his arms.

"He that was dead, yet shall he live."

The new house was ready that spring for the Eggertson family. After they moved to Salem, the houses on Main Street seemed very quiet. For a long time, Sully and Nancy came often from their side of town. Sobe and Rain, caring for their little granddaughter Grace, stayed in the house together alone. Mara and Will from next door stayed close, often bringing food for their meals. Ashel and Caroline, who continued building on to their new house just south of Mara and Will's house, brought their little boy Hanson, who slept like a tiny doll all curled up on his mother's lap and over her shoulder while the families talked far into the night about many things. Quietly about their sorrows. Quietly about the blessings they could still share.

For several weeks Sobe moved automatically to the mill and back. He rarely spoke. He wrote to ease his pain, and when Mara asked after him, he gave her his written words. The loss of his wife and both of his children was for him a part of life's betrayal that he felt would never let him free.

It was a while before the others began to feel the sweet peace that follows devastating loss, yet the peace came. It came in little ways: while they watched the sunset together from the lake, when Ashel and Caroline planned the details of their new home, when the Eggertsons came and brought their children, when they began to concentrate on helping each other. While the others healed, Sobe, alone with Mara, still sobbed to her, knelt at her feet, and leaned his head in her lap. He cried out that he knew he must let the love of the Father heal him so he could go on with his life, and he asked her to help him to let go.

Not until Sobe walked home one evening and found Rain lying on the couch with the letter in her hand did he begin to let hope back into his heart. The letter from Salem broke the news that Samantha's little Mathew had disappeared from the fields. Sobe tried to take the letter from her hand, but Rain wouldn't let go. Finally he read that Mathew and his little friend Bud Kunz—

Mathew called him Butter—went off into the hills and Butter's little body was found later at the bottom of a cliff. They thought that Mathew had been kidnapped, perhaps by Indians. They were looking for him, but he was nowhere to be found. Sobe knelt down by Rain and sobbed on her hands. But he sobbed for her pain, and he began from that time to be grateful for the life of his own grandchild Grace, and for the blessings that still abounded in his life.

Grace, Grace. How appropriately she was named. It was for her that Sobe began to put his life back together. It was because of Grace that Rain finally returned from Salem once she knew the Eggertsons—Samantha and little Eliza—were doing fine. There were so many Eggertson aunts, uncles, and grandparents that Samantha's family was in good hands. Rain came back to be with Grace. It was for her—and for their own peace—they now lived. Grace, who must grow.

In the evenings when Will and Sobe worked late at the mill, Mara sat with Rain, watching her rock the child to sleep in her arms. As she rocked, Rain's head would fall back against the painted chair, and her black eyes sunken in the heavy cheeks would close. Mara would hear the uneven sound of her breathing as she whispered herself to sleep.

"Come to bed, Rain," Mara would urge. It was often ten o'clock before Sobe would come in. Mara knew, when he came, that Will would be waiting at home for her, but she took the time to settle Rain in the upstairs room and to cover the baby before she left them both to sleep.

Whenever she could, Mara took Grace to stay with her and Will. "Let Rain and Sobe rear the baby," Will told Mara often. "She is their grandchild."

"But I need her," Mara always replied. She also needed little Hanson Eastman. Often, after Ashel's house was built, Mara made her way south to their place to fetch him every chance she got. Hanson was a charming, fair-haired angel with a broad smile, as fair as Grace was dark, and every bit as beautiful as she. He was in very truth the miracle Ashel and Caroline had prayed for. Ashel hired a woman, Mrs. Corey, to help care for the child and to do the work Caroline could not do. But Ashel and Caroline saw to every moment of Hanson's upbringing. As he was "prayed here," Ashel so often said, Hanson must be prepared in all ways for whatever God should see fit to call upon him to do. And so Hanson was instructed and disciplined and above all loved, as befitting a gift from God. It was, in fact, impossible for anyone seeing little Hanson not to love him, as it was impossible not to imagine for him a great future. Mara saw it, imagined it as she kissed his smooth face, watched his young body grow, remembered at night how she had held him tight, laughing with him at his struggles to break free, remembered how he wiggled in her arms and leaned his head backwards laughing, "Nana, Nana, Nana!"

At the turn of the century, Mara was well over sixty years old. She had grown completely gray. She walked past mirrors and watched her brown eyes. The color itself seemed to grow dim, but the light she saw in them seemed to grow brighter with the passing time. She had settled into a peaceful life of giving to others and accepting the profound miracle of simply being alive. On Saturday afternoons, when both Grace and Hanson were out of school, she walked with them to the Center Street park where in the spring the children took off their shoes and stockings and dangled their feet in the ditch. Sometimes Samantha brought little Eliza to be with them. Then Mara would tell them all the stories Sobe had no time to tell, stories she knew Ashel and Caroline or the Eggertson and Tuttle families did not know.

During the controversy over the placement of the railroad station, Mara walked the children to the site of the new depot to watch the steam engines roll in on the wide black tracks. She read to the children. She helped them with their mathematics. She relieved both Caroline and Rain of their responsibilities for the children whenever it was possible for her to do so.

In 1906 the Provo Library suddenly sprang up on a corner east of Main Street. Then Mara took the children to the library where they could find books they could bring home to read. There were marvelous discoveries, then. Hanson discovered whales, and Grace discovered Betsy Ross and Pocahontas.

Grace was a quiet child, like her Grandfather Sobe. She knew of the tragedy in her grandfather's life, and she soberly watched him for signals to approach him for the attention she needed.

"Grandpa, if you were an Indian, did you wear paint?"

Sobe liked to talk to the children, but he never seemed to talk for very long. And Sunday was his only day. When he did spend time with them it was with full concentration. "I was not a fancy Indian," he told Grace. He loved her and needed her, and he watched her swiftly grow into a woman. And as she grew so like her mother, Mara knew his heart remembered Jenny, and that he had learned to accept where she lived with the Father in joy far from this earth life where they were subject to so much pain.

But Grace was more beautiful even than Jenny. She was musical, although she did not really like to perform in front of others. Often one could hear her humming or singing a little tune when she did not think anyone else was around. Her greatest love was literature; she loved to read. Mara told Sobe that Grace looked like Blueflower, and he smiled, for that was what he wanted to believe more than anything else. And it was true. With Charles' darkness in her skin, and Sobe's own patrician features, Grace was very much like Blueflower indeed. But there was something more, a delicate refinement of face that might have been the contribution of Scott and Ella Hunt and their handsome son Bret. There was even an arch to the brows that put Mara in mind of Hannah Wright. . . . It was all there: the best of so many of them in Grace. Oh, Grace, Mara said so often in her heart. You belong to everyone but me. Yet, you belong to me most of all.

In her childhood, Grace did not visit her Grandpa Tuttle and Grandma Nancy as often as she visited Mara and Will, for the Tuttles lived farther away. But Mara knew how much Grace loved to be taken there, and Sully came often to see her, to praise, to offer financial help, to give Grace his own kind of steady, happy love. Mara was glad to see it, for since the tragedy at the lake, Sully had withdrawn into quiet meditation. He had become arthritic, uncomfortable with pain. As Grace grew up, and as it got harder for him to come to her, Grace made her way more often to Grandpa and Grandma Tuttle's—on her way to or from the library.

"I think Grandma Nancy makes cookies just for me," Grace told Mara once.

"How do you know that?"

"Grandpa never eats them."

"Are you sure?"

"I never see him eat them."

"Grace, do you ask for cookies?" Mara was almost ready to scold.

"No. I never ask. I always wait and pretty soon Grandpa says 'Don't you want some cookies?' and he smiles and laughs and I just can't say no. Grandma bakes such good things!"

Mara smiled.

Grandma Nancy was a good seamstress as well. Mara was pleased when Grace began asking for sewing instruction along with her cookies and milk. Nancy taught her to stitch and embroider, and before many years had passed, Grace was making her own clothing. Grace especially loved to create women's hats and pinafores for children. She began to make clothing for the East Co-op and she brought in enough money to set aside for her own books and her college education.

Grace was learning so much from so many teachers—mostly family members who loved her. Mara was pleased.

In 1911 when Grace was sixteen, she helped Mara, Nancy, and Rain with the commission to produce more new draperies—this time for the Brigham Young Academy's new Maeser Building, which had been built on the northeast hill. That year, the Academy felt a growing concern over academic freedom in the school when some professors brought Darwin's writings into the classroom. There was so much publicity over the conflict that the entire community got involved. It seemed that all of Provo attended the dedication, at which Senator Abraham O. Smoot spoke honoring the deceased Maeser, who had been commissioned by Brigham Young to teach even the "multiplication tables with the spirit and power of the Holy Ghost."

Impressed by the dedication, and excited about the course of study for which Mara had prepared her, Grace was ready to enter the Academy in the fall, to study English literature. Hanson was already there, interested in scientific studies, and active in varsity sports and debating. Debates were exciting and often heated, as the group of teachers who wanted the university to take its place in the world as a reputable university had begun discussing "the philosophies of men." The Church leaders wanted the school to remain a training school for teachers, and they frowned upon too much worldly knowledge. There were rumors that some of the teachers would leave, and that there would be a new president soon. It was an exciting time, and Hanson loved being a part of it all.

Just as Charles and Jenny before them, Hanson and Grace spent their childhood knowing they would love each other always.

"I already know who I am going to marry," Grace told Mara one day.

Mara smiled. "I'm sure you do, my dear." She held Grace's hand. "And it is most wonderful, because already he loves you. But there are things you must do, both of you, before you are ready to begin your lives together."

"Hanson's mission for the Church," Grace said, looking down into her lap.

Mara nodded, proud, smiling upon Grace, who did not look up at her. "That is one thing, yes."

"It is so hard, Aunt Mara, to think of Hanson leaving. We have not been apart even one whole day for as long as I can remember. I don't know if I can live without him near." There were tears in Grace's voice now, and Mara was ashamed of herself, of them all, for not giving one minute's thought to the anxiety all their preparations for Hanson's future might be causing Grace.

Mara laid her hand on Grace's bowed head. "I understand, my dear."

Grace looked up now, tears filling her eyes that had not yet fallen onto her cheeks. "*Can* you understand, Aunt Mara?"

I waited for a missionary once, Mara wanted to tell her. She had thought of it often as she had watched the growth of Bret Hunt's great-granddaughter. Now she searched the girl's eyes. Should she tell her? She had heard that Bret had passed away, last year, in Salt Lake City, only a few months after the aged Scott Hunt himself. Ella had been gone for many years. "I understand." But she had never wanted to confuse Grace with her old memories. Now those memories seemed to jar loose from the deepest hiding places of her heart.

"How can you understand, Aunt Mara?"

Mara struggled with her memories for a moment. How much should she tell? "Did you know that I almost married a missionary once? He finally married someone else and became your mother Jenny's grandfather and your great-grandfather."

"Before you married Uncle Will?"

"Yes, before I married Uncle Will. I thought I was very much in love. And it was hard to wait for him. And when at last I saw him I found out he had already promised to love someone else."

"Oh, that's so sad, Aunt Mara."

"Yes, Grace," Mara looked far away. I do know how it is to want to hold on to someone you love. But I also know that Heavenly Father takes care of you after all."

The tears spilled onto Grace's cheeks now, and Grace pulled a handkerchief from her apron. "You mean I might not marry Hanson! Oh, it's so hard, Aunt Mara," she said. "It's so hard. I'm sorry."

"No, my dear. Don't you be sorry. You go ahead and cry when you feel like it. Cry when something really needs a good cry." Grace looked at her, the tears stopping.

Mara continued. "I want to tell you something, my dear. And what I tell you will save you much foolishness and much heartache in your life, if you will heed it. Now, you listen."

"Yes, Aunt Mara," said Grace, drying her eyes.

Mara drew a long breath that hurt her old lungs. "What I want to tell you, Grace, is to live always the best you know how, and not let your heart go after foolish dreams." Mara paused, wanting to say just the right thing. Grace waited for her to speak.

Mara looked hard into Grace's eyes now. "Grace Tuttle, you know you love Hanson Eastman with all your heart, don't you?"

"Yes, Aunt Mara."

"And you know he loves you."

"Yes."

"And it is a good love, too. You are fine young people and you admire each other, with good reason. And you share your love of family and of books and learning." Mara paused again, feeling the tears come now into her own throat, looking away from Grace into the room.

"But most important, you are good faithful Latter-day Saints, the best this family has yet produced, I dare say. You have been taught to love the Lord above all, and to seek to know his will and serve him." She looked at Grace again, and Grace's eyes were bright. "And I believe, my dear, that you truly do love the Lord."

"Yes," Grace said.

"Well, then," Mara said, smoothing her skirt with her hands. "You remember that. You have faith. You trust what you know is right and true. You trust Hanson. You trust the Lord. And all will be well with you."

"I will try, Aunt Mara. But . . ."

"Mara raised her hand to Grace's protest. "I know it is difficult. But will you do it?"

"I will try, Aunt Mara. Even when my heart wants Hanson here now, now and forever."

"If you want him forever, my dear, you must let him go now."

When the time for Hanson's mission came, he was called to England, with the possible assignment of helping the work move into some new areas, perhaps Belgium. The family rejoiced. Grace did not speak openly about her feelings for many days, although she tried to appear glad.

In the summer evenings she came from Grandpa and Grandma Tuttle's, passed the fire station, the Co-op, and met Hanson at the investment office. They walked together down Center Street toward home.

"You won't have very much time to write."

"I'll have as much time as every other missionary."

"So write me now."

"Write you now?"

Grace smiled into his eyes. "Yes. Just tell me a letter. Then I can be with you when you write to me. Dear Grace. . . ."

Hanson drew back a little and grinned at her. He was tall now and very straight. He was light, like Caroline, his hair light red, a strawberry-colored blond. His skin was fair under the thick red-gold beard that colored his jaw like a shadow when the day was done.

"Dear Grace. . . ."

Grace laughed, her feet feeling light on the grass. "Come on. Dear Grace. Then what?"

"Dear Grace," he began. "I am doing fine. How are you?"

"Go on." She took his arm and squeezed it with her hands. They walked together without missing a step. "I want to be a missionary all of my life. The Lord is with you at every moment. If you call on him he is there."

Grace felt his words with pride. He was so very good. But his letter made her very sad in spite of her pride in him.

"Now . . . how are you?" he asked.

"Sad," she said.

"Sad?" Hanson looked at her.

"I don't want you there . . . off . . ." she pointed, "far away. Can't you be a missionary here? I want you here . . . where you really belong."

"Where I really belong?" Hanson mused. Then he looked at her again. "You need a missionary here," he grinned. "Is this where I really belong?"

"Yes," Grace laughed. Then her laugh stopped at his solemn face.

"Do you mean it, Grace?"

She looked at her feet, ashamed of her longing, her selfishness.

"If I promised you I would come back? I need to . . . I have to do a few things first." He smiled at her now. "And then, if I promised you I'd come back . . ."

Grace smiled again now. She nodded, shaking her curls. "Oh yes, Hanson. Promise me that."

He stopped, then, searching her eyes. For a long time he looked at her as if waiting for the right words to say. "I'm coming back," he said finally. "I'm coming back, Grace. I promise you that. But the question is, will you still be here?"

For a moment Grace was silent herself.

"Yes, I've thought about that," Hanson said. "I don't know, you see, that you'll still be here. . . ."

Grace felt the afternoon sun as they neared the park. She felt the warmth, the heat. She felt the people of Provo hurrying from their work to their homes. She saw the horses and carriages, the streetcar, the lights, and felt the gravel and then the grass beneath her feet.

"I know I'll be back, but I can't make any promises about where you'll be by then."

Grace was happy, as though filled with light. "Well, I'm the one who makes the promises about me," she said, smiling, both inside and on her face.

Hanson covered the hands she had entwined about his arm. They reached the grass in the parkway. He turned to look into her eyes. "I do love you, Grace, and if you're still here when I return we'll talk about what you and I will do together. We'll talk about it then."

Grace heard his words in the sun. She felt his hands on hers. She loved him so much. Aunt Mara was right. Their love was good. It made them happy. It was the kind of love she knew could last them forever. She also knew that in so many words, Hanson was telling her it was all up to her.

"I'll be here," she whispered softly.

"I hope so." Hanson looked at her, then took her in his arms, held her, kissed her forehead. "I hope so."

For Hanson's farewell to the mission field, Caroline and Ashel held a huge party. Almost everyone from the city came. The Kings, the Paxmans, even the Smoots, wished Hanson good-bye. They told Ashel and Caroline, radiant in her wheelchair, that their boy was as fine a boy as ever had been raised in this town. He was a credit to the community, a blessing, and he would make a marvelous missionary.

Will, Mara, Sobe, and Grace stood with the Eastmans and the Tuttles to receive the visitors. Even the Eggertsons came from Salem. Ashel had hired a string quartet, and at one time in the evening, Hanson asked his Aunt Mara to dance. And on the brightly lighted lawn, Mara had accepted, moving out with him into the crowd, feeling the strength in his young body, looking into his eyes.

"Hanson, we're so proud of you," she smiled.

"Aunt Mara, you can still dance."

"Of course I can still dance." She was in her mid-seventies. "I'm not in my grave yet, boy."

Mara stepped out, a little unsure of herself, but bravely moving the limbs that still worked for her, that carried her over the grass still lightly as she made her body work with the feeling and the concentration of her mind.

"You are one we came here to this valley to create," she said softly, realizing Hanson would not hear her.

"What, Aunt Mara?" he said, drawing back.

"Nothing, Hanson."

"You're a good dancer!" he smiled, and he held her with a strong arm at the close of the round dance.

"Come back to us," she whispered again.

His eyes were warm with light. She saw him as a perfect answer to the meaning of everything Papa and Mama Eastman would ever have wanted.

"Oh," he said smiling, "oh, I will," and with a graceful, courteous bow, he was gone.

At first Mara tried not to think of him as gone. She and Will spent more time with Ashel and Caroline. They also entertained the

Tuttles, and Sobe and Rain and Grace. At supper in the Jones' house, Sobe and Rain would sit close to each other at the table, Grace near them. The Eggertsons sometimes came up from Salem on special holidays to join them. They spent Sunday afternoons together, and often evenings during the week until Sully became so crippled with arthritis he found it difficult to make his way over with Nancy, even in the carriage. He retired from the Co-op, and he and Nancy lived a very quiet life, happy whenever Grace came to visit them. And often Grace took her friends to see them too.

Whenever there was a letter from Hanson, enjoyment of it was a family affair. The Joneses, the Eastmans, and Grace and her friends shared it, rejoiced, and Grace brought it to Sully and Nancy who read it and nodded, and read it and laughed, and read it over and over again with Grace.

At first the letters came often, expressing love, concern for family members at home, a desire to do the work in the mission field the way the Lord would have it done.

I am working hard. We rise in the mornings at five-thirty for study and for prayer. My first companion is a man from Salt Lake City who has left his wife and four children to preach the gospel for a few years. We are having some success. The people rejoice to receive the news that God has returned to earth to speak to us once again.

By the end of the first year, letters came only once every month or so, letters which assured the family members at home that Hanson Eastman's thoughts were so much with the work God had requested him to do that there was little time for much else. Most of his mission Hanson had spent in England, but by April of 1914, he and several others had begun working in Belgium and were trying to learn French.

We have had to set aside two or three hours each day to translate from the dictionary, decipher newspapers, memorize idioms, in general try to learn to speak a language that seems impossibly difficult to pronounce and to conjugate, at least for English-speaking elders from Utah. But 'C'est la vie!' as they say.

Then he wrote: *If I can master French well, I may stay longer to help further establish the mission in this area. People here are not receptive, but they are impoverished for something that will put meaning into their lives. And there are humble people here someone needs to care for. I have grown to love them, and I will do all I can do.*

Ashel stood tall when the letters from his son were read, and Caroline seemed to shine with an even brighter light than in the previous twenty years, if that were possible.

Grace waited well, and Mara was pleased to see it. Grace became engrossed in her studies at the Academy, she cared for the adults in her family, she enjoyed her friends. There was one very fine young man, a Robert Cloward, who pursued her, courted her, tried to win her heart, but Grace was certain that Hanson and she had been meant for each other. Though she saw other young men in town and enjoyed their company, they soon learned of her determination and left her relatively free of romantic attachments during Hanson's absence. She waited; she worked at her studies. She began working part-time at the mill, and she taught Sunday School classes and Primary.

She showed Mara her letters to Hanson on occasion, and Mara was warmed by the depth of character and the quiet spirituality they revealed. She remembered her own lack of wisdom at that age. She felt proud of the contribution she had made to Grace's upbringing and to the upbringing of others who had raised Grace.

I remember you, Grace wrote to Hanson. *There are times I cannot remember how you look. But there are memories more powerful—memories of what life makes real for a person at a moment of truth. I know you are doing the Lord's work, and so at this time he owns you. You are his, and he is the master of your heart. The message you must bring to the people of the world is that if they will make Christ and his love the center of their lives, they may have the happiness you and I can share even at this distance—knowing we are both serving him together and will reap the blessings of his tender love. May God bless you there to overcome the reluctance of the people to accept the gospel with all their hearts.*

On Sunday, June 28, 1914, the Archduke Francis Ferdinand and his wife Sophie, heirs to the throne of Austria-Hungary, were assassinated by a young Bosnian student who lived in Serbia. Austria declared war on Serbia, and the smoldering hostilities of Europe burst with the fury of fire.

Trouble has broken out between Austria and Serbia, Hanson wrote. *Troubles that have brewed in Europe for years. People in the streets are frightened. Some are more ready to hear the gospel.* The hasty note was received by Ashel and Caroline several weeks after the news that the Germans had begun to march through Belgium and that Great Britain had declared war.

"They are still quarreling in Europe," Will said to Mara over an early evening newspaper. "Russians and Belgians crushed by Germans. Peter told me over the telephone today that Liege and Brussels have fallen."

"Hanson," Mara breathed, a cold throb in her heart.

Will, though still extremely influential in the business community, had not been an active participant for several years. Yet still he made his way to the office to pore over documents and reports. Peter had come back from Idaho and transferred the stock brokerage to Salt Lake City. Cynthia's husband worked with him there. Both of Will's children had families, grandchildren of their own, and they all came to visit occasionally. Mara and Will were glad to see them, happy for their visits. But the distance prevented their visiting often, and business had to be conducted by correspondence and telegraph. Now the marvelous new telephone swept the country just as indoor plumbing and the horseless carriage had done.

"They'll take Hanson out of Belgium," Will said slowly, reading, thinking.

Mara took the newspaper in her own hands and read everything, every word.

"They won't let him stay now that there are foreign troops there, I'm sure," Will said.

Mara was not sure, but she folded the newspaper, placed it in a drawer, wrapped herself in her shawl. The September sun was still warm, but a light breeze blew in from the lake.

"Where are you going?" Will questioned her.

"To see if Ashel is home from the office."

Will checked his pocket watch. "It's not even five."

"I just have a feeling," Mara whispered, hurrying from the door. As she walked toward Ashel's home, she saw Grace rushing toward her. Grace was crying, her hands outstretched toward Mara. "Hanson wrote . . . Oh!" she covered her face with her hands. "He will not leave. There is war in Belgium and he will not leave! And now Aunt Caroline is very ill."

Mara saw the sidewalk as though it were a gray ribbon stretching before her eyes for blocks ahead. It seemed to spin as though on moving earth beneath the softness of her shoes.

"Aunt Mara, come quickly!" Grace cried. "Please hurry!"

The house seemed solemn, silent, when Mara entered. Both Ashel and the maid, Mrs. Corey, stood beside the bed. There was darkness in the room, and a strange dark odor. Only small shafts of sunlight flickered between the heavy velvet draperies through the lace curtains.

"I don't want to give up," Caroline said when Mara knelt beside the bed. "I don't want to give up yet. But I'm so afraid for him."

Ashel handed Mara the letter.

Dear Mother, Father, Grace, all who will read these words:

As you no doubt read in the news at home, there is war in Europe. Oh, if you could have seen what I have seen when the Germans marched upon Brussels. A few small groups of soldiers struggled to close the roads, but to no avail. Some were killed. The pitiful handful of Saints here have lost three of their stalwart members . . . all men with families counting on them for sustenance. Mme. Dubois, the concierge of the house where we stay, begged her husband to let the Germans come rather than lose his life, but one of the soldiers entered their bedroom and began to assault her. As the soldier forced himself upon her, he held his gun to her head and cursed her. She cried to her husband to be still so that the soldiers would spare their children. "I hurt for our children and for you so that they will go away," she cried, and we heard her in our room and ran to see as the man, in the last moments of his violence, hit her face to stop her cries. M. Dubois leaped for the soldier with great fury. The soldier cried out, and three others entered the bedroom, throwing my companion and myself against the wall. They shot M. Dubois through the head. Seven more soldiers entered the house, all carrying guns and shouting. They have gone now at last, moving on in their march of death and horror in this gentle land. Mme. Dubois is a good woman, a fine Latter-day Saint woman. She has three young children, and now their father is dead.

I cannot leave these families now. Though the brethren are preparing to send all of the missionaries home, my companion and I have pleaded with them to allow us to stay here. The Lord will help us to do his work if we are faithful. He will watch over us. Pray for us.

Your own, Hanson Harding Eastman

Ashel, Caroline, Grace, all—even Mrs. Corey—were silent as Mara folded the blue paper in her lap. Mara closed her eyes and saw Hanson's face in her imagination, and she wanted to block out the terrible agony of his words: "Oh, if you would have seen what I have seen."

"They need him. They need the gospel," Ashel said simply.

Yes, I am sure his message is needed among all the people of Europe, all of the people of the world, Mara thought without saying anything. But . . . silent, she did not open her eyes. She felt a hand on her shoulder, then a touch on her hair, soothing fingers on her cheek.

"He will be all right," Grace whispered. "God will be with him. Hanson would want us to be brave. He will come back."

Mara felt Grace's hand as she would have imagined a bird's wing on her face. She looked upward, then, and opened her eyes.

"You have great faith, Grace," Mara said, holding out the letter to Ashel.

Caroline reached for the letter, held it a long moment; she drew in a sigh and tucked the letter under her pillow. "Hanson would want us to be brave," Caroline repeated. Almost immediately, as though she had received a priesthood blessing, Caroline brightened. Her color improved; she lifted her head and stretched her hand to Ashel.

"Are you going to be all right?" Grace asked her.

"Yes."

"Then we should let you sleep."

Caroline's eyes began to close.

"It would be a good idea," Ashel said slowly. He pressed her hand back under the cover, went to the window to shut the drapes. Mrs. Corey shut the second window, and in the darkness Mara clung to Grace's hand, let the girl lift her, and using her slender body as support, made her way down the steep stairs.

Chapter Thirteen

HANSON DID NOT COME HOME, EVEN AS THE WAR PROGRESSED. AT his pleading with the brethren, he received an unprecedented special promise that he would be released in the field and be allowed to stay to aid his Belgian families through continuing months of fear. And there were greater causes to fear. The fighting increased. Although the Allies stopped the Germans at the Battle of the Marne that September, there was an offensive blockade of Britain in February of the following year, and by May even the Italians had joined the war.

Grace could remember Hanson's face only with great difficulty. She prayed for him and for the poor desperate people he wrote of, every night and every morning and all through the day in her heart. But she could not remember his face.

During the battle of Verdun of the following year, some in the United States began to talk about joining the Allies. But there were no supporters of the idea in Provo. With the exception of the Tuttles, the Joneses and the Eastmans, and some others with relatives in England, no one even bothered to follow very closely the progress of the hostilities on the other side of the world.

If the people in Utah could only see what it is like for their own brothers and sisters in the grip of war, they would not ignore it. They would soon have very strong feelings about helping their brothers from destruction. I do not want to leave our converts in their suffering at this time. I have not wanted to mention to you any future plans for the impending close of my mission. Mother, you knew I was dedicated to the Lord. What you don't know is how I feel about these people who have accepted the gospel and how I have dedicated myself to them. If this dedication should extend to military action on my part, though it may be of great concern to my loved ones at home, it must be a decision I will have to face alone.

With the letters of the following months, the family watched Caroline grow thin, drawn. At times her faith did not hold, and she returned to the dark bedroom to wait. Often Grace waited with her, bringing flowers, sewing in her room.

The following February, 1917, with the news of German submarine warfare on trade vessels, Hanson wrote that he had offered to join the British forces. But there was talk of the Americans joining the war, so he would wait until the American forces reached France, and then he must "join them to do all I can do."

Though Christ has taught us to love all of our brothers and ourselves, there are times when we must stand for what we know is right, to be prepared to take lives to preserve freedom and righteousness, to give our lives, if necessary, for the cause of freedom. Giving my life does not seem as difficult to me as taking the life of another. I pray that I will not have to. Pray for me. The Americans will stop the war. And then I will come home.

On June 26, 1917, American troops began landing in France.

"The war is ours now," Grandpa Sully Tuttle told Grace over an evening supper she spent with them after a long day sewing at the mill. Under the new management of Jesse C. Knight, the corporation had built a new cutting and sewing department and was producing mackinaws, flannel shirts, and heavy blankets for markets in the northern states. There was much work to do.

Grandpa Sully was reading the newspaper at the table, something Grandma Nancy had never liked. "The war is ours now, and no one knows how far the fighting is going to go." He put the newspaper down and raised his cloudy, gray-blue eyes. He looked at Grace as he had looked at her often these last few years. She was conscious of his love for her and of his praise for her beauty, though she herself wondered if her beauty would last as she waited for Hanson to come home—Hanson, an almost imaginary figure to her now. She was twenty-three.

Grandpa gazed through the thick spectacles, his head bent, the sparse, kinky hair at his temples snow white. The wrinkles around his eyes gave away his weariness. Ever since the tragedy on the lake, Aunt Mara said, he had grown sometimes almost eager to leave this life so that he might visit with Clarissa, his sons, and his little grandson Will.

"My dear," he said slowly, "if they should come to fight here we don't have much we could do to stop them."

"Don't worry, Grandpa," Grace placed her warm hand on his arm. "The Americans will stop them before they reach Provo."

"Well, you might be the only one who will be here to see." He laughed then. "Could you save us all, Gracie?" he asked, patting her arm. Then he chuckled, quietly, as though he had thought of something. "Maybe we could get the Indians to help this time."

It was a big world now. Grace felt the arm beneath his wrinkled cotton shirt. The flesh was thin, the bone almost brittle. He was crippled with arthritis. At the ends of his arms, his hands were deformed, like claws.

"Grandpa, you did your share of saving us," Grace whispered. "There's nothing to do now. You just relax. Let us worry about the big war. It's our turn to worry."

The old man smiled.

On the following day, however, he insisted that Grace take him to the rally at the courthouse held prior to the departure of the Provo men who were to join the U.S. troops drilling and preparing for war. Grandma Nancy came too, walking more steadily than her husband, but leaning on Grace's other arm. Mayor James R. Daniels gave a fiery speech in honor of the twenty-eight solemn soldiers seated on the built-up outdoor stand. Each man wore a ribbon on the lapel of his coat. Each stared out toward the crowd seated on the benches of the courthouse lawn. Some of them would never see their families again. They knew that. Their drawn faces held frightened eyes; their mouths seemed tense, revealing their fears.

"Provo is no longer a small town isolated in the West. It is now as much a part of the United States of America as any town in this country ever was. And what is more, as a part of the United States of America, it is part of the world we live in just as much as any town or country in this world ever was."

A prominent figure on the stand was ninety-one-year-old Uncle Will Jones, who, as a City Father, said a few rousing words at the invitation of one of the honorable commissioners, LeRoy Dixon. "We have worked long and hard to build a city of God, invulnerable to hardship, hatred, and pain. But nowhere on earth is there a way to escape the difficulties of this world. That's how we grow. May we all grow by giving our support to the war effort, to these valiant men, to our sons and daughters who must carry on when we are gone."

Uncle Will tottered like a broken toy from the stand when Aunt Mara went to fetch him down, but it was not Uncle Will who was to stumble. At the close of the meeting, Grandpa Tuttle rose to reach for Grace's hand, and he fell. Grandma Nancy rushed to him, followed slowly by Grandma Rain.

"Oh, he is hurt!" Grace gasped, afraid.

Aunt Mara and Uncle Will came to them, and Aunt Mara knelt to the ground. "Call a doctor," she said. "Is there a doctor on the grounds?"

A doctor came forward, settling his spectacles on his nose. Grandpa Sully's face had turned blue. Grandma Rain fell to the grass at his feet.

For a few moments everyone was as quiet as prayer. Grandma Nancy held her breath. Grandma Rain sat bowing her head, her hands touching Grandpa's ankles, holding his feet. The doctor stood, shaking his head. "He's gone," he said. "A stroke. I'm sorry."

Grandma Nancy leaned forward onto Grandpa's chest, her face in her hands. Aunt Mara gently smoothed the white gray hair away from Grandpa Sully's eyes. Rain held his feet and rocked back and forth, tears running down her wrinkled face. She was so wrinkled, so old, so good. Of all those in grief for her grandfather, Grace wanted most to comfort Rain. She had been a mother to her father Charles.

"He was a good man," someone said.

Grace took his head in her arms. "Grandpa," she whispered. "Now you won't have to worry anymore."

As the war continued, Provo made a community effort to rally to its cause. President George H. Brimhall of the Brigham Young Academy gave hours of school credit for war effort to free up young people to labor in the fields. "Food will win the war" became a popular slogan decorating posters, ribbons, and athletic events programs.

The basketball and football team promised so many hours of work in agricultural pursuits. No one went back to school that fall until all of the crops had been harvested.

Even after school began, war and related activities dominated school programs. Instead of going into intercollegiate athletics this year, the student body initiated group contests, including military training, as part of their everyday regime. Three times a week students would get out and take long marches around the countryside to build up their stamina.

Though Grace no longer participated in Academy activities, she joined the effort to train the young girls in nursing and first aid. Every day she and several other single women taught classes in College Hall that centered around dressing wounds and treating shock. From the center she also helped distribute materials to the young girls who wanted to help by sewing and knitting for the overseas troops and Belgian families. The girls produced 174 sweaters, 50 pairs of socks, 23 shawls, 19 scarves, and 3 helmets. They also made clothing for Belgian infants and children—dresses, jackets, and other items. The wives of the Academy faculty members participated in money-raising luncheons and other activities to purchase bonds. Students also used savings from their own labors to buy bonds. They worked part time on Saturdays, after school, and during many other hours of the week to accumulate donations toward the war effort.

When the federal government decided to set up student army training corps in the universities, the Academy wanted to help, but it had to scramble to produce facilities for the military training units. There were no dormitories or barracks available, but the City Fathers in support of the training movement asked the women if they thought they could get supplies together for housing in the Maeser Building. Without hesitation, Aunt Mara and Rain and their Relief Society gathered three hundred mattresses and nine hundred quilts—in only five days. With the students' help, they placed the beds side by side in the vast marble halls, creating a giant barracks.

Just as the unit underwent its most gruelling training, the 1918 influenza epidemic hit. The Eastmans were stunned when they heard from Ralph Eggertson in Salem that little Eliza had gone from them. Not long after that, Samantha, who had cared so devotedly for the girl, contacted it and also passed away. Though Rain and Mara escaped the epidemic by refusing to leave the house, Grandma Nancy threw herself devotedly into nursing the young boys of the military units back to health. All of the women of the Relief Societies baked bread, biscuits, cakes, and cookies for the units and took care of the soldiers' needs while they were ill. Grace did her part, and as a result contracted a slight case of the illness, but recovered quickly. However, Grandma Nancy became gravely ill, and in May, about the time Germany was launching its last great offensives in its efforts against the strength of American and Allied troops, Nancy rejoined her beloved Sully.

During the last few months of the war, Hanson's letters had not been arriving home regularly. Once in December Ashel and Caroline had received a packet of three letters all at once. But from January through April, May, June, nothing came.

Grace began to feel time pressing on her. All of the young men and women she had known were now married and having families. She spent most of her time sewing at the mill and then sewing again in the evenings by the fire, alone with Rain. Grandpa Sobe was gone more often than he was present. During the increased production demands for the war, he had begun working at the mill both days and nights.

"You need to believe in him," Grandma Rain said, her smile still warm, but weary now. Grandpa Tuttle's death had caused her to feel a loss that was greater than grief. It was hard for Grace to imagine that Grandma Rain had been Grandpa Tuttle's wife. He had always lived just with Grandma Nancy. But they, Sully and Rain Tuttle, were the parents of her own father—"Handsome Charlie" she heard the townspeople call him—a father she had never known. A good man who had married Jenny, the child of silent Sobe and an unknown white girl. Jenny, the beautiful Indian songbird—her mother, another someone she had never known.

"We need to believe in the Lord and his way for us," Grandma Rain told her by the fire. "You belong to a people that came out of this earth. Believe in this earth and its powers. Believe in heaven and earth and the powers they give to one another."

Grace heard her grandmother's disconnected talk, sounding still as Indian as it must have in the days she had learned to speak English more than sixty years ago. Grace marvelled that through all these years living among a people who were not her own, Rain had given so much to so many. Grace watched her hands. Often Rain would sew with her now, knit with her, or sometimes weave mats out of grass the way she once did with her mother, the legendary Spirit of Earth. "Never forget who your people are. We send you into the white man's world to learn the true gospel of Jesus Christ, to become his and to teach your children and all the children of our people who will listen to who they are."

Only occasionally was Grandpa Sobe there to join with them in their talking, his hands always soot-blackened, his shirt collar gray from the sweat of his daily labors. When he was home, he always sat in the same chair by the hearth, an old Morris that had belonged to Great-grandpa Eastman. He read the newspaper and a magazine or two. Then he would pick up the Book of Mormon and read far into the night, the electric lamp glaring dead white on the page. Sometimes Grace would find him asleep over the passages from Alma, Third Nephi, or Mormon, his favorites. She would wake him and lead him to the stairs.

"I'll be all right," he said gruffly, trying to mark his page before the book closed. "Don't worry about me, Grace. I'll be all right."

Sometimes Aunt Mara came to visit him on the evenings he was home. She always sat in a straight-backed chair beside him and sometimes placed her gloved hand on his knee. "You know, we are always saying how we are teaching the Indians—making people out of them. But I think *you* made a person out of *me*, Sobe." Mara smiled at him. "That might be the bond we had with each other before we came. You promised to teach me to love."

"*You* taught *me* to love," he said simply, and held her hand.

He often said nothing, but seemed bent now, quiet—an Indian man in deep thought about the changes that had happened so rapidly around him. Yet he never complained about anything. He buried himself in his work at the mill, supported Rain and Grace without complaint. He faithfully went to church and did all that was asked of him.

Grandpa Sobe did not talk much about the war. Grace knew his greatest concern was for her and her determination to wait for Hanson. Quietly he watched her, as she clung to her fading hope. She tried to be cheerful, hopeful. At times she saw in his face more sorrow for her than he could bear. For him, she tried to be brave. It had been so long.

When the months of January through July produced no mail, and no reports of Hanson's location, no government lists suggesting the whereabouts of his regiment—there had been reports of prisoners and the dead, but Hanson's name had not appeared on any of them—Grace could not help herself. She grew distraught with grief. She sat with Aunt Caroline, who lay waiting in the shadows of her dark room for news of her son.

Nothing but war appeared in the newspapers: the Germans marched on the Somme, Ypres. The hearts of the American people froze with fear. Finally one hopeful note sounded when the American marines captured Belleau Wood. But Germany simply retaliated on July 15 with a powerful offensive on the Marne.

Chapter Fourteen

T HE FURNACES AT THE MILL WERE FULLY STOKED NOW FOR TWENTY-four hours a day to keep up with the demands of war. Mara knew that Sobe was spending even more of his time at the boiler room during the month of July because he could not bear Grace's growing despair. With a heavy heart he had thrown himself into his work, feeling that if he could not fight in the battles, find Hanson, or relieve Grace, he could at least make a contribution by keeping the production at the mill at an unprecedented high. Which he did.

During those last days in July while the news of the war returned lists of hundreds of thousands of men killed, confirming reports that raging hell scoured the battlefields, even Rain became ill.

On the afternoon of July 29, Mara brought a stew for supper. Grace was not in the house, but Mara was surprised to find Sobe in the kitchen.

"You're off work this afternoon!"

Sobe was standing at the pump bringing up water for Rain. "Problem with one of the furnaces. They will fix it today, and I will work it this evening."

"Oh," Mara smiled, moving slowly to the oven, bringing the dish to the stove and setting it down carefully. "It's nice to see you home, Sobe. You work too much lately. What do you get out of all that work? You're long over sixty years old. Are you going to retire one of these days?"

Sobe raised his eyes to Mara. "Matter of fact, I was thinking . . ."

"You were thinking of it?" Mara said. "Finally? It's about time. I'm glad you were thinking of it," she said, smiling.

"Soon as this war's over."

Mara cocked her head, gazed at her Indian child, now dark, not with sun, but with shadows of soot. "You've given most of your life to that mill, Sobe. You ought to have some years to sit on the porch and nod."

Sobe quietly shook his head. "Don't know what I'd do with myself just sitting."

"Read. Read like we used to . . . the old books . . . your Book of Mormon. Remember John Donne—for whom the bell tolls? Or write, Sobe. Remember, you used to write such beautiful things?"

Sobe looked at Mara, really looked at her for the first time in many months. He half closed his eyes, and looked at her. "Do you believe Hanson is still alive?" The question seemed sudden and out of place, but Mara understood. It was an agonizing question for all of them—a question they kept from asking themselves for fear the answer might be no.

Mara stopped, steadied herself on the cold oven, looked at Sobe. "Sobe," she said, looking intensely at him. "You've always been my only son." Sobe smiled slightly, nodded. "After all these years . . . after all that you and I have seen, Grace is really all we have, isn't she?" Sobe stared at her now. The loss that had almost destroyed them years ago was but a quiet singing in their blood. "For Grace, yes, I have to believe Hanson is still alive."

Sobe lowered his eyes, nodded. "I just wondered," he said. "I also believe he is still alive."

Mara took Sobe's arm. She felt the strength in it, the substance of his flesh, the bone. "For all the time that we believe, we may have peace. When we know, the peace we have had cannot be taken from us."

Sobe was still quiet, nodding. Mara stood beside him for a long moment. He overshadowed her. "The darkest shadows loom behind the brightest light," she whispered. Then she added, "If we are standing in any shadows, I pray they are the shadows of angels."

The tightened muscles around Sobe's mouth seemed to relax somehow. "I've got to go now," he said.

Mara nodded. "Do you want supper?"

"No," Sobe said. "I just had something."

"Shall I leave the stew here on the stove? Or do you have ice to keep it?"

"There's ice on the porch. But Rain will be up and around in a few moments. She's feeling some better. Just leave it on the stove." Sobe stopped, shook his head. "She's done so much for me. I feel helpless to repay her even when she is ill."

"You've done your share," Mara said.

He stood looking at her as though he did not believe her.

"You are my spiritual giant," she smiled. "Remember . . ." For some strange reason—she was not able to put her finger on it—she wished to keep him, with philosophy, with something shared—with anything. She did not want him to go.

So he waited. He waited as though he also did not want to go. But he shifted his feet, put his hands in his pockets.

"Remember Milton?" Mara said.

He nodded and smiled.

"'Who best bears his mild yoke . . .' You teach us all by example to bear it, my dear Sobe."

He was hesitant, but he began to speak. When he began, Mara knew he wanted to tell her something he had never told anyone before. "Maybe . . . ," he hesitated. "Maybe if I taught anybody anything it might be in my books I wrote. They're in that box under my bed."

"Your books?" Mara put the bowl of stew she had picked up to put away back down on the stove. "Sobe," she said gently. "You've been keeping journals all these years!"

He smiled and nodded.

She put the pot holder in her hand on the table and walked around to him. "Oh, Sobe. I would love to read them. Everyone would love to read them. They are wonderful books, I know! If they are filled with you, they are filled with good things."

He glanced shyly and began to back away. "Thank you, Mara. I've got to go, now."

"Sobe," she whispered. "You know I love you. I love you so much." She reached out to him. She gathered him close to her and held him for a long time in her arms, still not wanting to let him go. "I love you, my teacher who taught me how to work and to love."

"You, too. I love you too, Mara. Good-bye," he said.

"I'll go to see Rain now. I will tell her you love her."

"Yes, Mara. Good-bye."

"Take care. Please don't work too hard."

Mara did not see Sobe go. She heard the screen door shut. She went upstairs to see Rain. Rain was now in her eighties, almost as old as Mara.

Rain lay very pale on the sheets in the small front room.

"I brought a stew," she told Rain when their eyes met. "I don't want you up and around cooking when you don't feel like it. You work too hard, and that is why you get down."

It was at that moment that Mara noticed Rain's eyes were full of fear. She shook her head slowly as if to dispute Mara's invented reason for her suffering.

Rain's voice was a mere smothered sound. "Have you heard from Hanson yet?" It was the question she had asked a hundred times in the past few months, the question all of them had asked as the newspapers came burdened with the lists of the missing and the killed.

Mara braced herself for the second time. "No," she whispered. "No, Rain. But don't you worry, he'll be all right. And your Grace will be all right."

Rain's eyes still flashed with concern. "Little Grace . . ." she began. "Beautiful little Grace." Then she paused. "I nursed her mother. Remember?"

"Yes," Mara whispered, her voice choked. "I remember."

"And her father."

"Yes, I know," she whispered. "Now you just be peaceful here and put the worry out of your mind."

But Rain wanted to talk. "Grace cries in the night."

Mara hadn't known this.

"I hear her in the quiet when her father is at the mill. I've been praying."

"Rain, for your own sake, you cannot worry. You cannot bear Grace's sorrows."

"It's about Hanson. I know it's about Hanson."

"Yes, Rain, but there is nothing you can do."

"I know something no one knows."

Mara had never heard Rain so eager to talk. "What do you know, Rain?"

Rain leaned back against the pillow and closed her eyes. "I prayed for Hanson to be born. If it hadn't been for me, Caroline wouldn't have been hurt. . . ."

"Rain," Mara whispered. "You can't think of it as your fault . . . it was an accident! You know that! Rain . . . please . . . all these years. . . ."

"I told God I would give anything if she could have a child . . . and . . . and . . ." Rain paused, her heavy lips moving only slightly. "And now Mathew, Eliza, and Samantha." Her voice began cracking. "He has taken almost all of mine. All of mine."

Mara stared dumbly at the gray wrinkled face on the pillow. The skin was scarred with age now and almost in folds along the temples, along the ears. Rain's quiet now invaded the room, hurt with silence.

"I prayed to God I would give anything if Hanson would come home, marry our baby. All I have left is my life. I want God to take it . . . to save Hanson."

Anything. Mara stared at the woman who lay quiet now, still with broad bones, the mouth resigned, the lips pursed as though done with pain. Mara felt numb. She spoke now. "Rain, that is nonsense. I've never heard such nonsense. In the first place you're not responsible for Caroline's accident or Hanson's birth, or the tragedy on the lake! All that you say is only as true as old Indian tales . . . You've still got your old Spirit of Earth in your head." But Rain did not answer.

Anything. All I have, she had said. Perhaps it was true. But no, Mara shook away her uneasiness. Was there some reason Rain should talk this way, or was it simply delusion? Mara reached her shaking hand and steadied it on Rain's arm. Then she knew. Of course. In every other crisis Rain had always stepped in and given of herself completely. But now there was nothing Rain could do, except pray and offer herself.

"Never you mind," Mara whispered. "You feel as though all you have is your life to give . . . well yes, but your life *alive*, not gone. You still haven't done all you could do. It's all nonsense, Rain. Sobe still needs you. Grace still needs you. You've got to snap out of it and get up. Rain, I've put a stew on the stove downstairs and it needs warming for your supper. You'd better get up and after it." The words Mara spoke seemed to tug at the spirit of death in the room. "Hurry now. Can you do it?" She held her hand out to Rain who grasped it lightly. Suddenly, Mara grew uncertain. She began talking for herself more than for Rain. "Hanson will come home.

You are going to live. There will be children who will bless the name of their pure Indian great-grandmother. I promise you all of this." But in the corners of her heart there began to be dread.

I have given a promise to Grace that her life would be safe from all the suffering our people made for ourselves and the heartache the white man made for us. Now I promised her life here in this valley, and the whole world is suddenly unsafe for her.

The whole world. Sobe created words in his mind; he talked to himself at the gate, moving the great steel bars back as he pushed it open into the mill. At this late hour, almost everyone else had gone to their homes.

The vast boiler room was dark, admitting only gray light through the high factory windows two stories up in the cavernous hall. Only the watchman tinkered at the door. Tonight it was Ralph Eggertson, who had remarried after the death of Samantha and the loss of his children. Though he had gone about a new life, he maintained a respectful friendship with his first father-in-law. He still loved the family and considered them his.

"You have the night shift in the boiler room tonight, Father Eastman?"

"Yes," Sobe said simply. He smiled and waved. The hall seemed darker tonight than usual, the fire brighter, and the fuel more generously consumed.

Sobe stoked the furnace when he first came in. As he often did, he added some trash that had accumulated during the day, some scraps of wool, paper, some parcels of waste materials. As usual he checked the boilers, waited for the fire to die.

Tonight it did not seem to die. He looked into the flames several times to determine what had been burning so well. At one point he rummaged into the flames with the poker and tried to turn over some heavy pieces of material that lay hot white amongst the lumps of coal. They seemed to be heavy cans. He jabbed one with the iron rod.

Suddenly an explosion thundered into his eyes and metal cut into his face.

He screamed. "Fire! Get the water! Get the fire under control!"

Blinded, his eyes stinging with the hot heat of pain, he dashed for the controls to the water system. But the water did not go on.

"Eggertson!" Sobe screamed. There was another explosion and another, and the flames began to lick the wood on the floor, burn along the wood planes in the machinery, devour the benches, the tools, the doors.

Flames leaped along Sobe's clothes. Screaming, he flung himself on the ground and beat, beat at his body. He heard Eggertson's hollow cry. "The water system! The water system! The idiots that just repaired the furnace left off the damn water system! Roll, Eastman, roll!"

Eggertson fairly danced over the flames toward Sobe, reaching out to beat at the fire. But there was another explosion and the flames reached Sobe's hair, and then Eggertson's hands.

"Run!" Sobe screamed.

Eggertson beat at his own clothes. Screaming, he pulled and dragged Sobe toward the inside door. But the fire raced. A beam at the door began to fall. Like a spear it pierced the floor and hit Eggertson's hands as he gripped Sobe's arms. Eggertson screamed and let go. The beam fell on Sobe and pinned him, burning, to the floor.

"Fire! Fire! Fire!" Eggertson pounded from the mill, screaming at the top of his lungs, crying, choking with smoke and the stifling air. "Fire! Oh God! A man is killed!"

Mara had gone to bed thinking about what Rain had told her. Hanson. Where was Hanson? For the sake of all of heaven there would not have been any reason for God to take Hanson.

It was about eleven-thirty when she heard the cries and realized people were out on the streets talking, running, moving about. From her window she could see men on horseback, unsettled, waiting for others who were hitching wagons. There were two neighbors with drays dragging milk buckets into the street to load behind them.

"What is it?" Will said from the bed, turning, raising his shoulders, wiping the sleep from his eyes.

"Men in the street," Mara replied. "Something's wrong." And then she saw the light. From her bedroom window looking eastward she could see far enough to outline the black silhouette of the mill chimney against a bright spot in the sky.

"There's a fire!" she whispered, frightened. "There's a fire."

Instantly, with a speed not ordinary to her years, she dressed, gathered a shawl about her shoulders, and sped to the lawn. Will followed her, but he moved more slowly, his ninety-two years heavy on him.

"Where is the fire? What's burning?" Mara asked the neighbor loading his cart.

"It's the mill."

"No. No!" Mara gasped silently to herself. "Sobe." Then she turned to the neighbor once more. "Was anyone hurt?

"They say one man was killed."

"He is not done. He is not done with his work." All Mara could do was murmur softly as she rode the neighbor's cart to the scene of the fire. She did not even wait for Will. Her heart lay pounding like a drum in the fragile old flesh of her breast. "Oh dear God! What shall we do? We love him and need him. Grace, Rain, Sobe! Sobe, it is not you who have gone. Not you who have been killed."

As the neighbor's cart tracked down Center Street, hundreds of people ran forward to the dazzling holocaust. Sprawled like a hot orange coal on Second North and Second West was a giant fire, licking into the sky. The waves of fire beat, beat upward into the black sky. The heat flowed out toward the street, drying the throats of the firefighters, burning their eyes and singeing their hair.

The thread of water from the fire hose dried up in the hot flames like water on a griddle over a black stove. The flames roared, deafening onlookers. Beat beat beat, the sound of waves of fire fell like huge cymbals into the street. The inside walls collapsed, the machinery curled and vanished. The air filled with the rancid odor of burned wool.

"I could not get him out! He's dead," Ralph Eggertson sobbed, his face black with soot, his eyes dead white.

Sobe was gone. His body consumed by the fire.

Mara sat on the bench of the cart and felt the men moving about her, wielding buckets, attempting to form a fire-fighting line. That is his monument. The bright living fire. At least, that is a monument that will never be forgotten, though he and his seed seem to evaporate in the curl of the flames. Mara's heart broke in two.

"It's no use," someone said. "Watch it burn."

"Maybe we can get it in the morning."

"Now whatever we do is nothing. It is not enough. It is nothing at all."

Mara saw the flames lick the windows, sear the roof, burn from the shingles. She saw the walls open, crumble, the flames crowding through the doors. Against the sky was the most spectacular light she had ever seen. The firelight filled the entire city with a radiant golden glow. Glittering, flashing, it brightened the rings on Mara's hands.

Numb, Mara watched the flames consume Sobe—the mill, his monument. . . . She saw the old mill begin to disappear like a wisp of paper off the face of the earth. When the heat glazed her eyes, she lowered them to her old hands.

Will came later in another wagon rigged up by Ashel and Grace as they drove by the house.

"It's Sobe, isn't it?" Will said as he climbed slowly down out of Ashel's carriage to come to Mara's seat in the neighbor's cart. He stood beside her and watched the flooding flames. "Yes. It's Sobe. Mara. I'm so sorry. Bless you, my dear. Please come home now. You need to sleep. Please come home. We can't stay. They say the fire may burn for days."

In silence, Mara watched the fire. Will spoke again. "We had that mill for forty-four years! And Sobe was its mainstay for forty-four years."

Now Mara felt her tears come. She felt the stinging pain. Sobe would not be coming home.

"Please come home now. Sobe meant so much to you. It is a great loss. But we must go on."

Mara felt Will's hand on her arm. There was a soft pressure in his fingers that startled her, as though his presence were waking her from a terrible dream.

"It's time to come home now."

As though she understood his words consciously for the first time, she looked into Will's anxious eyes. The mill. Will's own mill. His work, hard work for so many years. Will's monument, too.

"It's time to come home now," he repeated, the old head nodding, urging, the gray hair bright from the flames as though in a shower of sun.

Then Mara saw Will's eyes. They were filled with smoky tears.

"Oh, I am so sorry, Will," she exclaimed suddenly. "Your mill— oh, I am so sorry."

"We are all sorry," Will said softly as she bent toward him and climbed from the cart into his arms. She felt his words on her ear. Will was still beside her. He had stayed beside her all these years. She knew that she loved him with a love that was sure and deep. "We are all sorry. We shall have to go on living just the best we can. We shall all have to go on living the best we can." His throat seemed choked from smoke. . . or tears. His hands shook as he helped her up and led her to Ashel's dray. "We have each other. We are very fortunate in that. Sobe lived a good life. We will all be together in God's kingdom. One day soon, my dear. One day soon."

We have each other. On the way home in Ashel's cart, Mara held tight to her old friend Will Jones' gnarled hands.

Mara had not seen much of Grace since she had been working full days in the sewing department at the mill. As soon as the fire was out and the smoke had cleared away, Mara went to Grace who was bent over the wrinkled Rain in the front bedroom. She held Sobe's precious books in her hands.

"Look at these, Gracie. Look at these."

They read some of the words on the pages: *Some men look down on lifelong labor. There is dignity in work. Work is a prayer.*

Grace's eyes filled with tears. "Can I have them?" she whispered.

"Sobe," Rain said softly. "Sobe said what all of his people wanted to say before they were gone."

"These are wonderful," Grace rifled through the pages.

"Yes, darling," Mara said. "But why don't you bring them back to my house with all your things? Why don't you come and live with me? Please come and live with me," she said. "Please, both of you come and live with Will and me."

"No," Rain whispered. "This is Grace's home." The old Eastman house. It now belonged to Rain and Grace Tuttle. Mara surveyed the bedroom, once hers and Rain's, now Rain's alone. She saw the park from the window. She remembered suddenly that Rain once walked across that lawn to fetch her to school.

"I'll take care of Grandma," Grace said softly. "She wants to be here where everything is familiar. I'll take care of her."

Chapter Fifteen

THE HEAT OF AUGUST BROUGHT NEWS OF BRITISH SUCCESS AT Amiens. In September even more favorable reports of Allied success began to sing on the wires. As autumn drew into the canyon with its fresh cool breezes, the newspapers reported the successive crumbling of the central powers. One armistice after another was signed in the European arena. Russia at Brest-Litovsk, Bulgaria at Salonika. On November 3, Emperor Charles signed the last armistice, leaving Germany by itself, floundering in the conflict. When the German soldiers began to mutiny in the wake of dwindling supplies, Hindenburg urged Kaiser Wilhelm II that Germany must also seek an armistice immediately or be destroyed. In a drizzling rain on November 11, 1918, the German delegates entered a railway car near the Compiégne Forest and at five o'clock A.M. signed the treaty that ended the great World War.

ARMISTICE SIGNED! END OF THE WAR!
BERLIN SEIZED BY REVOLUTIONISTS!
NEW CHANCELLOR BEGS FOR ORDER!
OUSTED KAISER FLEES TO HOLLAND!

The headline of the *New York Times* reached Provo newspapers a day later. On November 12, Will read the evening news on the front steps and brought the newspaper into the house with a spring in his step, his spectacles dangling.

"It's over, Mara!" he called into the kitchen. Mara was slowly preparing warm milk for their evening meal. "The war is over! An armistice has been signed!" Will said. "Says here they will give us lists of all the missing and all the prisoners as soon as they are able." The clatter of cups on the table almost drowned his words. "They'll be sending the troops back on the train."

The war was over. Mara paused over the kettle, feeling tears crowding into her eyes, feeling the heat of the steaming milk like a warm breath of life on her skin.

The war was over.

"Don't be counting on too much," Will said, to protect Mara's heart, she knew. "There's lots of men missing, prisoners. There's lots of casualties." But her heart would not be protected. It pounded with hope.

Slowly, Mara and Will ate their bread and drank the warm milk.

"I'm going to see Grace now," Mara whispered when she had eaten only half her portion. "Can you get along all right if I take the paper?"

Will set the paper down, looked over it with his spectacles. He looked for a long moment at Mara. "Sure, take the paper. But don't you go getting Grace's hopes up. Bless her heart. Don't you go getting Grace ready to expect something that may never happen."

Grace looked drained, pale, thin, when she opened the door to Mara. "It's Rain," she whispered. "Aunt Mara, I don't think she's going to last!"

"Grace, the men are coming home on the trains! The war is over!"

Suddenly Grace's eyes were alive with fire. For a moment she did not speak. "Hanson!" she whispered.

Mara nodded. Then she raised a quiet hand. "Grace, Uncle Will tells me I should not expect . . . we should not hope. . . . Please, Grace, please don't hurt until all of the trains have come in. You have Rain to care for! You must not lose hope!"

During the next several weeks, Grace met almost every train that came into the station. The walk to the station on Sixth South and Third West was just enough for a brisk stretch of exercise in the cold weather. Grace had promised Aunt Mara she would not hope too much, that she would let her heart down easily. Rain continued to fail, and Aunt Mara came in to sit with her in the mornings while Grace fairly ran to the station to see if any veterans would disembark at Provo. Often she found Uncle Ashel coming from his house down the street making the same trek, warming his hands in his pockets, nodding hello. Together they waited in the growing cold for the train to screech to a halt and for the passengers to exit. November brought several carloads of men, a few coffins filled with remains of loved ones, and many sad tales. No, no one had heard of Hanson Eastman. Had he been in the American forces? Or with the Belgians?

Grace began to find, then, that she became afraid when the doors to the train would open. The darkness of the morning station seemed filled with black smoke, the noise stifling. When the train stopped, there was an endless pause until the porter stepped down from one of the front cars and slipped the bars that let the metal doors open to release the moving figures out into the gray dawn: businessmen, women, sometimes a few soldiers.

Weeks passed, but Grace did not relinquish the vigil, now almost a sacred ritual, which she had begun to keep regularly.

On the morning of December 18, 1918, a Tuesday, when she awoke, her bedroom was shadowed. The sounds of the street seemed stifled, muffled as though they moved through layers of air. She turned over, raised her head and listened, believing she heard the music of snow.

A skiff of snow, the first of the season, lay like scattered white crumbs around them. It had been falling only a short time, but now it came with fury.

"It's snowing!" Grace breathed softly. She opened the shutter outside her window, felt the flakes melt on her fingers.

"Grandma," she cried bouncing into the front bedroom. "It's snowing. Come to the window and see. The first snow of the season."

But Rain did not answer.

"Grandma!"

But as she went to the bed, Rain's face seemed white, frozen.

"Water," Rain said. "Water," and the words seemed to climb from somewhere deep in her throat until there was no breath left to push them any longer.

"Grandma! What's wrong with your breathing!" Grace placed her hand on Rain's forehead. "You have a fever! Grandma! Maybe I should call the doctor."

"No. No," Rain gasped, getting air with difficulty. "Please don't call the doctor."

"You are not well."

"Please, Grace, I want only you to be with me."

Grace saw that the clock said ten minutes to seven. Only a half an hour and she should be down at the station to meet the train.

Rain turned in the bed and stared into the room, her breathing uneven now and raspy, grating, a rattle deep in the center of her lungs, where no cough could have dislodged it.

"I'm cold," Rain said dimly, still staring. "Cold as ice."

Grace fetched the blankets and a shawl which she wrapped carefully around the old woman's thick body.

"Oh, thank you, child," the old woman whispered. "Now please bring me some water."

As Rain drank, Grace watched her anxiously. She sat on the bed and tucked Rain's blankets around her. "Do you think you could sleep while I go to the station?"

"Oh yes! The station! Yes, dear, you need to get Hanson!"

"Do you want some breakfast?"

"Maybe a little."

In the few minutes she had left, Grace brought up a tray with some bread, a little milk, and some crab apple butter. She watched Rain's eyes as she took a bit of bread, a sip of milk. Then Rain began to cough. As she coughed, the bread and milk rose up and sprayed into the sheets and over her hands, light and oily."

"Oh, I'm sorry!" Rain said helplessly. "I'm so sorry."

Grace saw that the clock now said seven-fifteen. Weary with anxiety, Grace wiped away the food, held Rain's hand, and kept placing her hand to Rain's forehead.

"I shouldn't eat." Rain's voice sounded far away.

"What?" Grace asked, her mind anxiously scanning in her imagination the doors of the train.

"I shouldn't eat," Rain rasped. "It makes me cough."

"Oh Grandma, dear, Grandma. It's all right." Grace felt the impatience make her body ache.

"You have to clean up the mess," Rain said almost inaudibly.

Grace watched the hands of the clock move past seven-thirty.

"Now your train," Rain said. "You've missed your train. Please dear. You go on. I'll be all right."

"No, no," Grace said softly, feeling an overwhelming frustration. "Not at all, Grandma. I need to stay with you. You're not well."

"I'm all right. I'm fine," Rain tried to whisper. Grace smoothed her hands over Rain's face.

"Please don't talk. Just rest. You are very ill." Grace smoothed the rough skin. "Just rest. Dear Grandma, you have taken care of so many. Someone needs to take care of you."

There were only a few minutes of quiet until Rain fell asleep. Her breathing seemed more even as Grace rose from the bed and slipped through the doorway into her own bedroom. As she wrapped herself in shawls and bonnet, she tried not to be heard. On the stairwell in the empty house she tiptoed. Sound did not seem to move anywhere, but failed to echo as usual, as though it were muffled by snow.

Out on the street, Grace stepped in a froth of dry powdery snow. It had fallen more than two inches by now. And it continued falling, layering the grass with white, gently lacing the fences and bushes and trees. Though a few people were in the street, there was an unusual hush for morning as though everyone were whispering under the giant shroud as light as a feather in the wind.

Grace did not know why she felt so light in the beautiful snow, but her feet fairly flew along the walk. Soon she could not help it and she ran. At Third South she ran past the old Eggertson house and turned the corner on the next street along the road toward Ashel and Caroline's place. Her feet continued to fly. And then she saw the figure coming toward her in the blinding snow.

At first it was a very dark, small shape with no definition, but its size grew as the swirling snow grew more transparent like a thinning veil.

At first Grace would not believe it. Then, yes, she would believe. She must believe. Hanson. It was Hanson . . . in his blue, the uniform like a heavy mark of paint smeared on the white of the wind. It was Hanson coming up the walk.

Grace's heart leaped into a thousand drums. "Hanson!" she shouted. Her voice rose on the cold air. "Hanson!" She raced toward him with her arms flying under the shawls. Like wings, her feet carried her over the grass and the gravel.

"Hanson! It's me! Grace!"

Hanson stopped in the middle of the block. He dropped his satchel by the side. She saw him clearly as he drew nearer. His thin face, scarred and beaten by the sun, fairly shone under the shock of bright unruly red-blond hair, pushing from his cap, and his lips parted into a smile behind the heavy red beard.

"Hanson! You're home!"

As Grace ran to him, she felt a rush of power speed her feet to the walkway. She felt the power lift her, rush her into the large waiting arms.

"Grace. My darling! Yes, I'm home."

Aunt Caroline wept uncontrolled tears at Hanson's return. Ashel held his boy until Grace thought he would never let him go. There was so much to say. There was all that had passed while he was gone, and there was the future in which they would have to rely upon Hanson's help to restore business to the West side of town and the East House Hotel. But there would be time later for all of these things.

"You weren't hurt!"

"I was in a trench at Verdun. Got shrapnel in my leg. But there were others. . . ."

"Are you well?"

"I feel stronger than I've ever felt."

"You're so thin."

"And I'm as hungry as a dog."

"I . . . I really shouldn't stay," Grace finally said, hesitantly, quietly, behind more of Ashel's questions. "It's . . . I really must go. It's Rain. She's very ill."

Without saying more, she turned away from the family in the drawing room, from the joy, the tears. Not until she reached the foyer did Hanson back away from his father. "Just a moment Papa. Grace, where are you going? You must stay."

"I'll come back. But right now I should really check on Grandma Rain. I . . . she is so ill. I really mustn't leave her for very long."

Hanson looked at her. He was so tall and thin, this stranger in his red beard. But it was Hanson, just the same.

"Would you . . . do you mind if I come along?" Hanson asked.

Grace breathed in quickly. Above the pounding of her heart she heard her own voice, "Oh yes, Hanson. Please come with me."

Reluctantly, Aunt Caroline let Hanson go. "If you come back as soon as you can, we'll have a big breakfast. We'll talk about . . ."

she hesitated. "We'll talk about everything we have to tell you when you return." Then she begged Ashel to take her upstairs. "Tell Rain, Mara, and Will hello," she said, waving weakly, happily, at Hanson.

Grace sparkled with gratitude. In the cold air the two raced each other on the walkway, Hanson holding Grace's elbow with his steady hand. "And here's Aunt Mara's and Uncle Will's place, just like I remember it," Hanson said.

"Rain," Grace said urgently running toward the house. "Rain. . . ." She felt a darkness in the hall, glad for Hanson beside her.

"Front bedroom upstairs," she said quietly. Rain was asleep. They walked slowly into the room.

"Grandma! Hanson is home!" Grace whispered gently. "He is home." Then she said to Hanson, "For a while she might not hear."

But there was no movement from beneath the covers. There was no sound of breathing, nothing at all.

"Grandma Rain! Grandma!" Grace whispered again, this time a little stronger. Her voice seemed close in the small dark room.

"She's sleeping very soundly." Grace, puzzled, went to the woman's face and touched her cheek. But there was no breathing on her hand.

"Hanson! Something's wrong!" Grace said suddenly. She slipped her hands under the Indian woman's large head and turned it, rocked it back and forth, patted the cheeks. She called to her: "Grandma Rain! Grandma! Wake up. Oh please! Hanson's here! And you waited so long for him."

But the large head was cold and motionless, the color in the cheeks like clay.

"She's . . . she's dead! Oh Hanson! Rain is dead! Oh Grandma!"

Grace felt a great shudder move through her heart, and she reached out in anguished pain, for what, she could not know, until she suddenly felt Hanson's arm beneath her elbow as he held her steadily. His grip tightened on her arm as she held herself from falling.

"Rain," Hanson finally said, peering into the frozen face. "Rain." Then he circled Grace's waist. "She was a good woman. And she lived a good, long life. I wish I could have spoken to her again—the great-grandmother of our children," he whispered. Slowly, he released Grace from his grasp, stood near the bed, took the edge of the sheet and lifted it over the dark face until its shadow sealed her to the earth and to the angels where she belonged.

"Knock, knock." They heard a voice through the open door, and footsteps in the hall. "I saw you! You can't escape my eagle vision! The idea of you creeping past my window on your way home, Hanson!" Aunt Mara said as she stood at the bottom of the stairs.

"Rain has gone!" Grace said, the words fogged in her throat. "Aunt Mara, Grandma is gone!"

"Rain!" Aunt Mara said, and Grace was afraid the old woman would fall. "Rain!"

Grace could see that Aunt Mara had been almost running to the Eastman house—at a speed dangerous for her age, demanding more of herself than she should have demanded, as she always did.

"Rain has gone?" Aunt Mara said, in half a question. She leaned heavily on the stair railings as Hanson rushed down the stairs toward her. She put up her hand to stop him.

"Rain is gone," Aunt Mara repeated again. "Rain is gone."

Aunt Mara steadied herself on the railing at the bottom of the stairs. Then she climbed one step slowly. Her legs had been moving so fast they seemed to be shaking. But she climbed another step. Hanson stepped down to meet her. She seemed determined, as though she said by the language of her body, "We all must go on. We must all go on."

As Hanson met her on the landing, she reached upward and folded herself into his arms.

"Oh Hanson, our dear one," she cried. "You are home!"

There was a light in the room Mara had not remembered seeing before. Struggling forward, she came to the bed and sat on the edge. The light filtered through the lace curtains and the snow from outside the window.

"Oh, Rain, Rain," Mara held her hand. She brought the hand to her lips and patted it. There was no life there.

All of them were quiet for a long time. Mara did not really want to call the funeral director, Mr. Hull, who was also the owner of the new Hull House Hotel—though she knew someone would have to get him soon. For now she wanted to allow this moment to last as long as she could. Finally, she noticed the book lying face down on the table beside her dear friend. She picked it up and turned it in her hands. It was one of Sobe's journals.

"Rain used to read it," Grace explained. "I often read it to her."

Mara read the words softly, trying to make sense of everything, loving every stroke of the pen her own Sobe had put on the page. The words he wrote, like music, always sang to her and would sing to his family for generations to come.

Measured by the white man's progress, where are my people? Not far. Perhaps, as Milton says: "Wisest fate says no."

Yet it is my people who can teach the white man of another kind of progress—a spiritual progress. It is Rain who could teach about sacrifice and of the spirit of the earth.

How long will God's kingdom struggle until it includes the gifts of everyone? When will the faces in the shadows turn to the embrace of our angels who stand waiting to reveal the light?

As she read from the book, a shadow crept across the pages. When she raised her eyes she saw that Grace was eagerly leaning forward. Mara smiled at the two young people as Hanson took Grace's hand. He pulled her close until the shadows left the pages and the light illuminated every word.

This is the end of Shadows of Angels, *sequel to* Thorns of the Sun. *A third volume, entitled* Royal House Hotel, *will continue the story of the Eastman family.*